STILL
LIFELESS

STILL LIFELESS

RUSSA JARI

Still Lifeless
Copyright © 2021
Russa Jari

Interior Design and Formatting by:
E. M. Tippetts Book Designs

cover painting by stacy a. e. smith

SUBSTANCES

Care,
Cry,
Heal.

Thanks.

CHAPTER ONE

THE KEY in the corner hadn't always been lost. Three trips around the interior of the house, checking the usual crevices over and again, turned up nothing. The man of the house offered no help and Cade had started to worry as his ride would be there any moment. But the place he hadn't looked was where the key was hiding.

He had peered into the master bedroom and even approached his sleeping mother where he desired to curl beside and hold her. Instead, he stood and calmed, watching her breathe silently. He pondered waking her and telling her how much he cared. He wanted to express his sorrow for avoiding communication as the world had been turning fast in tune with family dissonance.

This night, L had him visualizing his maternal ascendant childlike and, as she had put it last he heard her voice, *weak.* She lay before him, grey from the light upon her face shining out of the television as a dash of moonlight struggled to come in from behind still drapery. He wouldn't wake her, not in this moment of healing. The sound and flicker of a mundane commercial emitted behind him. Malnourished tree bark developed into her skin while his mind played a little with that deception.

Then the vision before his eyes became his reflection. *Team, Cadey.*

Talk was cheap, especially in the Caybul house, and no one had been selling for a while. Looking over the nightstand, his sight took hold of a book of matches next to the phone and the ashtray. There was a lighter too which he pocketed as he turned and headed back toward the hallway while the floor creaked beneath his steps that echoed in the barren living room below. A nearly peaceful heartbeat triggered remembrance of where the lost house key waited for him and he grabbed it on the way down.

No promises were left to be made while Cade felt the presence of his trusted friend waiting patiently in the driveway.

In this life, there is an overflow of semiconscious belief that the only wrong answer is no.

LIFESWITCH

Everyone at the party several miles across the border of Eggertsville, New York had a reason to indulge. The treacherous moniker "safest town in the United States" wasn't appealing to those of juvenescence seeking to escape its unseen walls. Word of a gathering outside the suburb and well within the confines of the "City of Neighbors" offered an opportunity to get drunk without the potential intrusion of police. The "safe" suburbs were dangerous in this sense. Even teenagers who weren't out to vandalize or hurt anyone were still under a microscope in their striving to find a safe place to party.

The transformation of Main Street from wider, cleaner Eggertsville to the more narrow, colorful, compacted Buffalo, University Heights brought a realm of consolation to humans too young to drink. Despite the crime on the other side, it was just far enough from home and offered a world of difference.

They set out for Lisbon Avenue to the party that they heard would be there. It was common to whimsically drive to that area of Main Street but tonight would be an act of premeditation as word had gotten around.

"This looks like the spot," said Jake as he drove past the house on the other side of the median. He whipped his car around in order to be directly in front. Jake liked to be seen. It was just after 11 pm and everyone in the car, including him, was already drunk and on LSD.

Jake looked in his rearview mirror and arranged his Figaro chain so the clasp lay properly on the back of his neck. Kelly and Berk exited their respective doors from the rear of the car, taking their last swigs of forties before tossing them on the lawn by the curb. It was Halloween weekend and no one emerging from the vehicle was wearing a costume. The four boys approached the front door of the house. Upon entering, the music and chatter coming from the basement resonated with the foursome, but they stayed on ground level, bypassing the dark blue light below. Synchronized, the hallucinatory effect increased.

"Hey, what's up?" Jake said to someone. "Can we pay somebody to get down on the keg?"

"I don't know, I'm just hittin' this Jack," the stranger said as he raised his bottle. The three, following Jake's lead, continued through the living room.

"Hey, what's up?" said Jake to another male human who was older and dressed like a Care Bear. "You know who we should pay to get down on the keg?"

"There's no keg, bro!" he shouted over the noise.

"Well, shit," said Jake.

"Jungle juice!" said the Care Bear. "Five bucks." All four newcomers apprehensively paid as none were expecting the second person they encountered at the party to be in charge. And nobody knew what jungle juice was. The Care Bear pointed to the kitchen with a sympathetic grin.

"Hi, boys, love your costumes!" said a lady football player with painted stripes under her eyes and a lingerie bottom. "Cups are over there!"

Jake grabbed four and handed them to his friends who were still confused. They looked about the kitchen, discovering a large plastic tub with four rope handles atop a table, then cautiously approached and looked in. The liquid inside reflected the dark blue color of the tub, making it almost black.

"Do we just…?" said Jake.

"Here!" the football lady said and handed them a big metal ladle. "Although some people are just scooping their cups in there. You guys paid Justin?"

"Uh, we paid the Care Bear," said Kelly, stirring the batch.

"What is this?" said Berk.

"It's jungle juice!" said two more lady football players, entering the kitchen. Their smiles went unanswered by the boys, still regaining comfort upon the intense change of environment.

"What's in it?" said Jake.

"Rum, gin, tequila, um…vodka…" said one of the girls.

"Is there voka?!" said another.

"Yes, Becca, there is vodka in the jungle juice!" said another. "And there's a D in vodka!"

"And whiskey, I think," continued the first girl. "And a shit load of juice and pieces of fruit. It's sooo good! Did you pay Justin?"

"The Care Bear," said Jake.

"What?" she said.

"The Care Bear is Justin?" said Jake.

"The carnivore is Justin?!" she said. "No. Justin is dressed as a colorful Bear."

"Yeah," said Jake. "The Care Bear."

"Right. Pay him and you can have jungle juice!"

"Except Justin doesn't care about anyone," said the girl who hadn't spoken yet. She had the calmest voice of the three football ladies. And she was the tallest of the three by half a foot and the only one who wasn't smiling. Berk and Kelly had filled, taken sips, and were deciding if they liked it.

"Whoa!" said Jake. "This is delicious!"

"IT'S JUNGLE JUICE!" said the two short girls simultaneously.

"Cade, try this shit, bro!" said Jake.

"Yeah, Cade, try that shit," said the tall girl, copycatting. Jake scooped his friend a cupful.

"God *damn*," said Cade. "It doesn't taste like anything. There's liquor in here?!"

"Yeah, like, every liquor there is," she said. "I'm Jane. You must be Cade. That short for Cadence or what?"

"Um, yeah, Cade," he said. It was clear that she was having the least amount of fun of anyone nearby. And she kept looking at her cup, scanning for unwanted debris.

"Is it clean?" said Cade.

"Is *what* clean?" said Jane.

"The cup."

"Is the *cup clean?*"

"Yeah, you keep—"

"I don't know," said Jane. "Probably not." Cade went to fill his again. "Wow!" she continued. "Are you done with your first already?!"

"Yeah," said Cade.

"Dude, be careful," said Jane. "That shit is creeper."

"Word?" said Cade.

"Yeah, *word*," said Jane. "There's like twenty bottles of liquor in there."

"Twenty?!" said Cade. "Like, full ones?"

"Yes!" she smiled, watching as Cade nervously became acquainted with his second beverage.

Jane had long dark hair, tan skin, and dark eyes with dark eyeliner, making her sclerae appear extra white in the dark room with its orange and white lights strewn about the ceiling. She continued to stare, waiting for him to say or do something while he, with his chin close to his chest, fixed his gaze downward as the pattern on the tiled floor took control of his mind. Her intrusive eyes drank him in while her anxiety diminished, making way for intrigue. Cade's three friends noticed all of this though he remained unconscious of her interest.

"Keg is here!" said a male voice from the other room.

"Ugh, I don't even *like* beer," said Jane. Her words were steamrolled by an entourage of raucous newcomers. A clown and Duff Man were dragging a keg into the dining room as a cocky Hunter S. Thompson entered the kitchen swiftly.

"'Sup, football ladies," he said. "Or football sluts is more like it."

"Jesus Christ," said Jane to the direction of Cade.

"Gentleman. I bid you hello on this finest of nights. And I welcome you to the party."

"Thanks," said Jake.

"Five bucks for the keg and the juice," said Hunter.

"They already paid, Brett," said Jane.

From the living space came the sound of glass shattering and shouting. People gravitated into the room to see what was happening. It was a fight. "BLOCK THE WINDOW! BLOCK THE WINDOW!" shouted a male voice. A big guy without a costume made himself a cushion between the fight and the vulnerable window in the corner of the room to keep it from shattering. No one was attempting to stop the ruckus as someone shouted to turn the music down.

Everybody watched while the two pounded on each other—one dressed as a cop, the other dressed as a ballerina. He had been wearing an afro wig but that was nowhere to be seen, just a pink tutu, white tights, and a stocking cap to conceal his true shaggy hair. People gathered, smoking cigarettes and drinking from red cups. One man brought a full drink casually to his friend who had run empty. The women in the room had quit yelling for them to stop and spectated like it was a performance. Some had their heads tilted to one side but peered at the brawl through squinty eyes and the gaps between their fingers as their hands ambivalently covered their faces.

The cop's Maglite fell to the ground with an unexpectedly loud thud which made some wonder whether or not the gun was fake. The ballerina was more physically fit and had gained control by straddling the waist of the cop and grabbing his shirt for leverage. He cocked his right hand back and got in a few blows to the head. Girls screamed, triggering more of an effect than the actual fighting. Four men ran over to stop it.

As the more victimized of the two grimaced, reeling from his disposition, and the ballerina was pulled off, the cop rolled over casually as if changing a sleep position from supine to side. Then those who had pulled the ballerina off and up to his feet let go. The ballerina walked, uninhibited, to the cop on the ground and hit him on the side of his head.

"JAMES, JESUS! THAT'S FUCKED UP!" a man shouted.

The cop got up surprisingly quickly and headed off to the porch as some stayed in between the two, coaxing James the ballerina to chill.

Cade, like his friends and most at the party, remained a neutral onlooker but had wondered how the cop was not crying. His audacity both impressed and intimidated Cade, more so than the impression left from the fight's victor. And his breath became more hurried, a characteristic he didn't notice taking over. He wondered how the two fighters would remain under the same roof after what had just happened.

The girls sought consolation from each other. The ballerina grinned as his friend turned the music up. Someone brought a drink out to the cop on the porch and the party began to regain its natural essence.

"I hate fights," Jane said.

"Yeah." He barely stopped himself from adding *me too*.

"WHOA HO HO HOAA!" shouted Berk, making everyone smile and chuckle.

"I didn't think I'd see a beef this early," said Kelly, adjusting his waistline. Their eyes found assurance and safety in each other and it was unanimous: they were safe now.

"This jungle juice is fantastic," said Jake after they moved back into the kitchen.

"Yeah, I never thought I'd be ignoring a keg of beer ever in my life," said Berk.

Some people from their neighborhood funneled in and everyone was happy to see each other. And although no one at the party posed any particular threat to the four, they felt stronger among their friends.

After camaraderie and hugging, Larry, one of the newcomers, asked if they wanted to smoke opium which had recently become common in the Amherst suburb. Nearly everyone had their hands on it at one time or another of late, either from buying or being friends with someone who had bought. However, it was not opium, but rather incense mixed with glue and sold as opium.

They mixed the "opium" with weed and rolled it in a green Antonio y Cleopatra cigar after gutting and removing the tobacco and dumping it in the big outdoor trash can in the kitchen.

"Should we just puff here?" said Larry.

"I would feel more comfortable near the jungle juice," said Jake.

"I think it would be better for all of us, both as a group and as individuals, to be close to the jungle juice," said Berk.

"What is that?" said Larry. He was now the largest of the group and biracial. Both qualities were calming for all the boys who felt stronger near him.

"Jungle juice," they all said except for Cade whose eyes had rediscovered the hypnotic floor.

"Did you pay the Care Bear?" said Jake.

"I paid somebody," said Larry. "I'm not sure if he was a Care Bear."

They puffed the cigar which burned slowly. Larry turned the stog around with his thumb and forefinger and made eye contact with Cade who accepted the task with a raise of his brows. Larry made the fiery tip as small as he could by blowing grey ash off. Then he bit down gently on the leaf paper with the hot ember in his mouth, sealing off any entering air with his lips as Cade moved his face to Larry's where smoke shot out of the end of the cigar into his mouth and lungs. Larry pulled it out of his mouth, careening from heat as Cade exhaled and choked.

His eyes watered. The women in the room watched.

"What's the matter?" said Larry. "You've never seen two men kiss before?"

The Care Bear came in. "Smoke it downstairs, please, boys."

"Damn, you can barely see in here," said Jane, moving about the plume with her hand.

They made their way, the five of them, through the party, their steps almost in unison. Larry, holding the cigar, slapped people's hands and smiled, disguising his trepidation best.

Descending the stairs, the music became louder. The light darkened and transformed to purple and blue. The basement was huge and open and there were tons more people here.

They drifted toward the light, music, and people. A song was ending. A new one began. There were nearly fifty humans who all began to dance. The boys stopped when Larry did. Confused, his eyes moved swiftly from left to right and back again. He herded his friends toward a placid corner, hit the cigar once, and passed it to Jake.

The movement of the mass of people was captivating for the four boys on acid. It was a colossal uniform of movement and joy. They corralled each other, forming a circle, and smoked the blunt together. Cade took a sip of his juice. He had planned improperly. The cup was almost empty. Jake started moving a little to the rhythm of the music.

"You want a gun, Kelly?" he said.

"Yeah, don't kiss me," Kelly said.

"There's no guarantees, hot stuff," Jake said as he moved the cherry in between his teeth and bit down.

"Cause if you touch your lips to mine then I'm gonna—"

"ALL RIGHT! JESUS! LET'S GO!" Jake said just after expelling the hot cigar from his mouth to his palm where he picked it up safely. "We gonna do this thing or we gonna have a conversation about your suppressed gayness?!" Unaware to what extent he was being insulted, Kelly puckered up. Cade looked at Jake who was preoccupied and then at Larry.

"I'm empty," he said.

"Better go re-up," said Larry.

"Oh, yeah," said Cade who headed upstairs.

"Yo, Cade!" Jake said. "Bring me one." With the sound of Kelly's coughing turning to laughter, Cade wondered how much of it was directed to him.

Upstairs, the new environment hit him harder than the basement had despite its quieter inhabitants and spacy atmosphere. He saw the ballerina and cop talking to each other calmly. A man dressed as Jesus came over to the group and handed the cop a frozen bag of fries for his head.

"My savior," said the cop.

Cade made eye contact with Jane who was noticeably more intoxicated than she was before. She smiled at him as one of her girlfriends observed. Cade barely smiled back before Jane whispered to her friend. Then they both grinned at him.

He entered the kitchen, finding plenty of jungle juice. He filled his cup, took a look around, and downed the entire thing. He did it again. Then he filled his cup plus another for Jake and headed downstairs. Moving his shoulders to the music a little, he tapped Jake on the back with his elbow. Jake took the drink.

"Aw, Cade, what is up?!" said Berk as if his friend had been gone a long time.

"Chillin'," said Cade. "The juice is good."

Berk laughed harder than expected.

"They still playin' Snoop?" Larry and Kelly looked at each other.

"I don't know, Cade, does it sound like Snoop?" said Kelly, still peering at Larry and sharing a devious grin.

"Oh, I—"

"Thanks for the juice, homie," said Jake.

"No doubt," said Cade. "There's still a lot left."

"No doubt," said Jake sternly. "Blunt's out."

"Word," said Cade. "I'm really high." And with that, the boys were together again. They laughed and drank for hours while the vibe became less edgy and more fun.

The house on the side street of the perilous neighborhood seemed a safe haven this night as admission payers uncoiled. The weather was unseasonably warm for Buffalo in late October 2001. There were people outside laughing, stumbling, and hugging one another. Cade shared a hug with a stranger his age as a delightful consequence of bumping into him without purpose. And there was no fear.

The moon and streetlamps shone upon the humans and their connectivity and appreciation of each other. And in the night's wake, like the leaves shed from their trees, laid the disconnection of each individual human with themselves.

The cups strewn about the lawn made odd props amidst the cars in the road as even more unusual manmade commotion. The fog was thick and it cradled those playing inside of it, soothing and protecting them.

Cade gathered with some people, including Jane on the porch. They came toward each other, devoid of effort, and hugged like friends. Jane, with her eyes, altered the mood and they kissed. As they kissed harder, Cade's friends watched and smiled at each other as their comrade's clumsiness grew apparent.

"I've been watching you," she said. He opened his lips to speak but no sound came out. She smiled. "I knew something would happen with us when I saw you."

"Oh yeah?" he said as they kissed again. Her smile and eyes engaged Cade. It was nice, but he also felt trapped as his friends watching made him uncomfortable.

As they kissed harder, Cade felt as if her tongue was too aggressive. He opened his eyes while they kissed deeply to see that hers were shut. They were out of sync and Jane didn't care. They stopped kissing. She opened her eyes, smiled, took him by the hand, and led him inside.

They passed a group of stumbling folks playing beer pong. The ballerina man was kissing a girl dressed as an angel, squeezing her nearly naked bottom. Jane intentionally bumped hips with a chick saying hi.

"What do you want from me?!" a man yelled from beside the beer pong table.

"Drink it, bitch," Jane's friend said.

"You gotta sink it to drink it!" he said.

"Ah!" Cheating at the game in plain sight, she shimmied to the cup of beer at the end of the table and dunked the ball in. "I always get what I want in!" A happy concession, the chap downed the beer. This while Jane, still holding Cade's hand, whispered to her girlfriend who whispered back. Cade liked the way Jane's hand felt in his. He liked that a woman that pretty had chosen him.

"How ya doin' there, Cadesie?" said Jane's friend.

"Chillin'," he said, barely keeping his cool.

"You gonna give my friend what she wants?" she said. Jane pretended not to listen but grinned as she put down her drink after a big sip.

"Uh…" said Cade. The ladies around the table laughed as Jane led him to the rear of the home.

"We can get more accomplished in my room," she said as it became quiet.

"You have a room here?" said Cade, his response delayed.

"Yes, silly! I *live* here!" she said as they entered the bedroom.

The LSD effect rejuvenated as she closed the door behind them. She put her arms around him and kissed him aggressively and repeatedly.

He began to sweat so hard that he thought they were standing under a cascade of water. He dismissed the hallucination, keeping his composure in allure of the embrace. She kissed fast and hard. They made out for so long without him making any advances that it puzzled and irritated her.

Cade was attracted to Jane. And he fantasized about sex and masturbated routinely. This night, however, he was caught off guard. Unlike most of his friends, he had never been as far as he was seemingly headed. He had never experienced fellatio. A woman had never touched his penis. He had only seen, felt, and kissed a woman's naked breasts.

To sex, he was a stranger.

His unanticipated paramour, on the other hand, had had plenty.

"You have the most amazing eyes." She thrust her tongue into his mouth.

"Thanks," said Cade, hurried.

Jane pushed a brief laugh through her nose via a loud puff that sounded like a snort upon his mouth.

"I'm gonna get us a couple drinks," she said. Music to his ears. "Check out my bed!" she said as she exited the room, barely closing the door behind her. ...The door opened, exposing a healthy sliver of light while Cade sat on the bed by himself, listening to the sounds of the party he had abandoned.

Drying his hands on the blanket, he waited. And waited. And waited. He took off his hat and wondered where to toss it. He put it on Jane's pillow. He stared at it. Then put it back on his head. Then back on the pillow. He grabbed and frisbeed it across the room where it landed on the corner of the floor next to the door.

He looked at it there. He stood, walked over, picked it up, put it on his head, and sat back on the bed. A moment passed, then he frisbeed the hat back to the corner of the floor.

Jane entered noisily, laughing. She sat next to Cade, handing him a cup. He took a sip.

"Beer?" he said.

"Um...ya, there's no more jungle juice," she said.

The unexpectedly low alcohol content of the beverage he had anticipated had him disillusioned while his spoiled taste buds withdrew from the lack of flavor they'd been enjoying all night.

They sat and sipped their beers. Jane giggled, touching Cade's hair with her fingers.

"Where's your hat?" she said, smiling.

"I threw it across the room," he said.

"Cool," she giggled. He kissed her out of obligation and illness from silence. He thought he'd better get cooking, but still had a beer in his hand. He stopped kissing for a moment and downed most of it, heavy handed, then put the cup on the floor and kissed her again. He was the dominant one now.

They made out hard until he took hold of the bottom of her shirt and pulled up. She raised her arms. He went for the clasp of her lime green bra. She waited. He took too long. She smiled softly and took it off herself. They kissed more and he felt a breast with one hand and started to become hard. She sensed his heart beating faster and stopped kissing to speak, maintaining a soft comfortable tone.

"You're wearing so many *clothes.*"

"Crid po cro," he said.

"What?" she said, bearing a smile.

She puffed a laugh again then piddled with the buttons on his shirt. He unbuttoned all the way down and discarded it, leaving an undershirt that he hoped to keep on.

Lustless, he ran his hand between her thighs atop the denim. She leaned back and scooched her head to the pillow. He felt pleased about his current hat placement.

Jane assumed a relaxed supine position while he shimmied to his side and laid next to her. They kissed as he felt her breasts. He ran his hand, this time more comfortably between her legs. She unbuttoned and unzipped his shorts and began massaging. She squeezed harder and faster causing discomfort and pain. He slid off his shorts and boxers completely then unbuttoned hers as she raised her butt from the mattress to help him. Tossing the clothes to the floor, he heard his beer spill. Now Jane was only in stockings.

Cade waited for her to make a move. He kissed her redundantly as his mouth became drier. But she just laid there, kissing back. He yearned for her assertiveness that had once made him afraid. He softly caressed her vulva through the thin stockings, triggering her hand to squeeze his penis harder, causing it to soften and sting. He stopped fumbling between her thighs and moved his hand to her hip, hoping for a reprieve. She didn't let up. He knew it was time.

He unrolled her stockings, consequently moving his body steadily down the bed to her feet, yanking and pulling, but could not get them off entirely. She giggled politely, breaking the tormenting silence, and tried helping pull her feet out as they were snared. Cade got off the bed and stood on the floor, painstakingly rolling each stocking off and down. Now, at the thought of being seen naked, he became flaccid.

He crawled back to her side. They massaged each other's genitalia as he felt himself become smaller. He wanted to enter with his finger but her labia weren't so eager which confused him. He didn't know where to put his fingers. He looked at her face. Unexpectedly, she was calm and entranced. Her eyes softly closed and her mouth opened, pushing hot air in and out. His visage furrowed as if this were a test with only seconds until *pencils down.*

There was nowhere to go. Nothing to do. He heard noise from the party. People were shouting and having fun. His friends were probably outside smoking cigarettes and checking out chicks. He wanted to be outside with his friends, smoking cigarettes and checking out chicks. What was Jake up to? Did that cheating girl win beer pong?

She took up his bumbling hand and wet the tops of all four fingers, moving it back down. She began masturbating with his fingers, which he let her control. He felt wetness as she opened for him. He became calmer yet his penis still felt like a second belly button. Her legs opened wide as she massaged her clit with his fingers. He was beginning to understand.

She placed the tip of his index finger atop her vaginal opening and moved it circularly and then in. She breathed heavier and let go of his hand. Her eyes remained closed as her fingers moseyed to her clit while Cade's index finger moved in and out of a real live vagina. She spread her legs further and raised her knees up some. His breathing slowed. He got harder. He became calmer. He enjoyed the texture of her vagina. He looked at her face. Her eyes were still closed. Her breath smelled like beer. He kissed her and became harder. Her stomach went up and down. He examined his wet, shiny finger going in and out. He slipped it just out of her vagina moving left to right upon her anus, glazing it with wetness. She didn't mind. He pushed the tip of his finger in and out and then back into her vagina. She didn't mind. He became almost hard enough.

She re-embraced her grip on him and massaged. Feeling him soften, she redeployed, gathering him in her mouth. Harder now as she had at it, his arm fell asleep. From his side, he flopped onto his back, allowing her to give him proper head. He watched her bob up and down and moved her hair away from her face behind her ears. He put his hand on the back of her head and guided her further down and up. Now he was hard.

"Do you have a condom?" she said.

"Yeah, in my wallet," he said.

"Get it," she said. He hurried to his pants and got out the wallet and the condom. He unwrapped it and confusingly put it on. As she watched and waited, he softened. He was out of ideas.

In surrendering, he flopped and did nothing. She gripped the rubber atop his penis and began tugging. Frustrated, she grunted, pulled the condom off, and began sucking. She sucked and got results. He watched her silently. She worked and worked and had him fully erect again.

She swiftly laid on her back and opened her legs. He got between them. He moved the tip to her vulva and tried sticking it in. She moaned in half-pleasure, half-frustration. He poked and poked.

"Lower," she said. "Yeah, yeah." She watched as he fumbled. They both watched. He softened.

"Put it in," she said.

"I—"

"Put it *in*," she said. He couldn't find in. "Just shove it in me as hard as you can!" He softened more. "Just *fuck* me! Come on!" He was sweating too much. His mouth turned to cotton. He pined for tenderness. He pined for a reprieve. He wanted out. He wanted to be gone. He wanted jungle juice. She looked up at his face.

"Oh my God!" she said. "You're not a *virgin*, are you?!"

"No, I fucked two times before." He squeezed the bottom of his penis, putting pressure on the base, pinching and drawing inward toward his body in desperation while she watched. He became just hard enough, squeezed and moved all the way in as she moaned loudly with pleasure.

"Can I cum in you?"

"WHAT?!"

He ejaculated.

"WHAT THE FUCK?!"

"Um…shit, I…"

"GET THE FUCK OFF OF ME!" she said. He stood. "I CAN'T BELIEVE YOU JUST *CAME IN ME*, YOU FUCKING ASSHOLE VIRGIN SCUMBAG!"

"I…I…"

"Yeah fucking *I…I*—FUCK YOU!" she yelled.

Just then they heard a thud from the party. Then another. Then lots. They heard yelling. It was a fight. Women screamed. Then more and more screaming. They heard screams as if someone had been killed. From on the bed, they looked at each other, wide-eyed and naked. No answers. Jane's eyes were childlike as her animosity turned to vulnerability and dependence.

"Put on your clothes," said Cade. They got dressed and opened the door. Cade peeked out while Jane hid behind him.

"FUCKING STOP HIM!" they heard. Cade walked out to where the party used to be. A girl paced on the phone with police.

"SOMEBODY HELP HIM!" said a weeping angel on her knees.

It was the ballerina. The cop had beat him in the face and head with his Maglite before running off. He was unconscious and bloodied on the floor.

Cade slowly approached. His brain processed the motionless body of the ballerina man as a prop on a set. He looked about the room and at the people's faces which all projected the same shocked expressions besides some women who were crying, some sobbing.

His vision found Jake then he turned to find Jane. Her eyes had regained coldness but she was still afraid. Cade passed the unconscious ballerina and the surrounding humans on their knees who had no idea how to help. A girl had placed her hand under his head like a pillow as two men were shouting at him and slapping his face trying to wake him.

"Dude. Bounce," said Jake. Cade barely nodded. As Jake turned to head toward the wide-open door, Cade had another thought. He turned and walked toward the crowd and the victim and Jane. Moving slowly, he grabbed a cup from the table on his way to Jane who was next to the keg. She held her sobbing friend whose face leaned on her chest. He picked up the spout and pressed down. Jane, in disbelief, watched him as beer struggled to come out, causing Cade to shake the spout in confusion. Then, softly, he heard Jane's voice, "Ya gotta pump it." Their faces were a foot apart. He stood motionless with his finger on the button, looking into her eyes. She could hear the sound of the keg struggling as she processed Cade's blank face and still hands. "My bad," he said. She reached for the keg and pumped and as beer poured, he turned from her and watched it flow. Jane pumped until the cup was full then stopped.

Cade turned around and walked toward the door where Jake was waiting anxiously for him. They got into Jake's car and he drove.

"Where's—"

"Berk and Kelly bounced with Larry," said Jake, speeding toward Main Street. "One more for the road, huh, Cadey?" he asked with an almost-smile.

"What?" said Cade, looking forward.

"Nothing."

Cade's parents and his obligation to them had crossed his mind. He detested keeping them informed. They cruised past the intersection that would lead them to their neighborhood but went onward to meet at Berk's where they'd convene in the basement to hang.

Just before the border between Buffalo and Eggertsville, Cade tossed his empty cup. Acclimating to the suburb and its quieter energy was as easy as the transition from the party to the car. There weren't many vehicles on the road where the shadows, like lungs, performed for the journeymen. The ironic return to the village had them appreciating the calm.

Knowing they were on the same tab of acid, Cade felt the urge to ask Jake if he was mindful enough to drive but dismissed the thought as absurd, considering they were already halfway through. He could easily sense his friend's self-trust and road awareness despite his own hallucinations.

Jake's mellow mood carried with it the thought that Cade would soon be in search of more beer, as was typically the case when he had run out or any time for that matter.

They passed a Town of Amherst squad car waiting at the light. The speed limit was forty. Jake was doing a confident 46 with one hand on the wheel when the light behind them turned red. The cop went straight and the two friends shared a silent sense of comfort.

They talked about the party with Jake understanding that his friend's mind was elsewhere.

"So how did it go?" said Jake.

"What?" said Cade. Jake looked at him. "Ah. I wish I…I wish…"

Jake turned away and looked ahead. "Did you get her clothes off before that shit happened?" said Jake.

"Yeah," said Cade.

"And?" said Jake. Cade heard his friend's voice, "Was it over mad quick?"

"What?" said Cade.

"*And?*" said Jake. "You fucked?"

"Yeah, kinda," said Cade.

Jake sensed discomfort and eased back. "They're gonna wanna talk about it," said Jake.

"Talk about the beef or the chick?" said Cade.

"Well, probably both," said Jake. "But the chick for sure. Everybody was sayin', 'Oh shit, Cade is fucking,' and shit. We were like...cheering for you." There was silence.

"Dude," said Cade. "I'm *so* glad that she doesn't live around here." Jake laughed then they laughed together. They stopped laughing then laughed more. They stopped laughing again and then they laughed the hardest. There was no call for detail.

Arriving at Berk's, the street was surprisingly desolate.

"There's nobody here," said Jake.

"Dude, I'm kinda glad," said Cade.

"Dude, I feel like—" Just then, a car pulled by. It was Larry, driving his parents' Volvo. Berk was sitting shotgun and he and Kelly were flashing different signs from non-existent gangs at Jake's car.

"Whup, here we go," said Jake.

"Yo, let's make it kinda quick if we can," said Cade.

"I gotchoo," said Jake.

The group recollected themselves as one and headed for the door, unconscious of how loud they were. Berk hushed them before opening. His step-father resounded from the sofa in the dark.

"No, David."

"It's Jon, D-Nelly," said Berk.

"I don't care who it is," said his stepdad. "Your mother's drunk. Everybody out."

"Sweet," said Berk in suppression. He closed the door, remaining outside with his friends and said:

"You guys wanna—"

"It's 2 o'clock in the morning, Scott," they heard muffled by the door.

"Wrong step-son, Mister Nelson," said Berk, grinning somewhat angrily. His bloodshot eyes found Cade's who was, at this moment, relieved. "You boys drive safe."

They parted. And once again, Cade and Jake headed away together.

"Your 'rents will be home?" said Jake.

"My 'rents are always home," said Cade.

"You got smokes?" said Jake.

"I don't think so," said Cade.

"Look in the glove," said Jake. "Is there a box of reds in there?"

Cade opened the compartment in front of him. "Yeah," he said.

"Then here, take these," said Jake, giving him his current pack that was half-empty.

"Thanks," said Cade. "You still tripping?"

"Yeah," said Jake. "You?"

"I think I'll know when I get inside and my dad starts interrogating me," said Cade, opening the car door and stepping out.

"Don't sweat that shit," said Jake. "That shit always happens the first time. This is just the beginning."

"Word," said Cade. "I'm gonna go have a drink."

"Peace," said Jake.

Cade walked up his driveway while the motion light did not detect his presence. He keyed into all three locks to the door and stepped inside before recalling his father's words *Hell Again* which he stated almost every time he came back from work.

He went quietly to the liquor cabinet which had an unlocked padlock dangling off of it. He grabbed Seagram's 7 and poured some into a glass. There was no noise from upstairs. So far, so good. He put on music at soft volume and sought out the window blinds. *Still tripping.*

He went and got a beer. After sitting in the corner on an ottoman next to the sofa with beer and whiskey, he turned the music up delicately. An hour went by. He talked to himself.

Before him came a vision of a dark brown owl that flew to the bookcase without perching but rather hovering. It looked through not at him, making the encounter a bit easier to swallow.

The airborne owl hovered circularly before its head and body blended together and coalesced as if it were atop the standing silhouette of a human.

Books fell from the shelves, but rather, the same book from the same place on the shelf fell repeatedly. The book came out from the case as if it were chosen and pulled by someone who let it fall to the floor.

Like dripping water, the vision repeated over and over again as if something had broken and the scene could not play out like it was rehearsed.

The glitch did not torment its seer. The shadow beneath the owl darkened, filling in, gathering attention while the eyes of the strix stopped blinking as its face became as if it was dying. The body darkened while the eyes became still and lifeless, turning from white to yellow. Its feathers fell to the floor.

In the room with the boy was now more of a human form and face than a bird's. Its mouth opened slowly. Then closed. Then opened. The mouth opened and closed to the cadence of the falling book. It hovered there, patrolling the fearless watcher who could both speak and move but his open mouth only leaked thick salivation. The shadowy body turned from dark matter into skin where wounds congealed like slits running from above to below. The face redefined itself to birdlike and fairer sexed. The fear of the beholder made itself known. He drank from the cup.

The book continued to fall as the owl reappeared and the body vanished, its scorned yellow eyes now deciding to size-up its perceiver. Cade's gaze redirected to the kitchen. He saw his father with his back to the liquor cabinet.

"Dad?" Cade smiled. Motionless, his patriarch. Cade giggled and turned toward the owl which now blended into its background. Each of its parts retreated in opposing directions to mingle with the furnishing of the home then slowly disappear.

Looking ahead, Cade fashioned his eyes upon wilted flowers in the vase on the table. He stood and fell to the ground. The fall surprised him, as if it were an attack. More aware, he crawled to his cup and can and drank the rest in each. Again, he stood and headed toward upstairs, stopping at the liquor cabinet for some more.

He walked through the dining room to the stairs and fell forward onto them. He stood and ascended three stairs before losing balance and fell backward, landing on his back and hitting his head on the floor.

Standing again, he ascended four stairs then leaned against the wall and dragged his shoulder against it for balance.

He made it to the top. As he ran out of wall at the second floor, he fell forward to the ground. He stood and lost his balance once more, gravitating backward. In a moment of grasping reality, where he was, and the consequence of falling from this high, he swiftly grabbed for the door jamb of his parents' bedroom atop the stairs, smacking it noisily and desperately taking hold, preventing the plummet.

The door was ajar, which was strange. The sound of a television commercial traveled to his ears. He peered inside and saw no one on the bed. Intrigued and concerned, he stumbled in.

Don't be ashamed of your yellow teeth anymore. Have the confidence you've always wanted. You'll love your brand new smile. Call the number on your screen and be on your way to…you'll love your smile…healthier…just… payments…order now. Call 1-800…9…3 thousand….9… thousand…

"Mom?"
Order….today….smile………healthy…..white….say   no……smile… easy…….

He tripped on her foot beside the king bed and fell onto her body, smacking his skull on hers. He pushed up from the floor with his hands and looked at his mother who lay there on her side, eyes closed, making no sound, her face in a pool of blood and vomit. He shook her shoulders.

"Mom?! Dad? Dad?!" He pulled himself up by the mattress, looking about the room before falling backward on his mother's lifeless body. He shook her again. As he stopped, her head moved and settled, chin up, eyes barely open. He thought he saw her in there.

"Mom!" Mom!" Liquid from her mouth seeped out onto the carpet. "MOM!" he yelled. He cried, reaching for the phone, knocking it off the nightstand. The sound of the dial tone rang out.

Aloha! Now you can trim and slim your body without ever going to the gym! Take the WORK out of your work-out! Say goodbye to embarrassing flab. Say goodbye to horrendous thighs and your embarrassing…

Cade stood, grabbed the television, and pulled it to the floor, silencing it. He sat on the mattress, crying and wailing.

Stopping to wipe his eyes, he moved to the side of the bed and slapped her face so hard, his hand stung. "FUCKING BITCH!" he screamed. He cried and walked out of his parents' bedroom, through the hall, into his room, shutting the door.

Waking to daylight, Cade's tongue was thick and dry. Through hazy vision, he got up, walked to the bathroom, and urinated. The excretion was almost brown.

The skylight revealed a menacing sun shining brightly upon white tiles, typically dingy and dull. The faucet dripped. He turned it on and placed his hand underneath. Pooling the water to his mouth where he fed his ailment, he stopped, letting the water overflow to catch his breath. His body, victimized by desiccation, feasted. Breathing became easier while his sight strengthened too.

The expulsion of phlegm to the toilet strained his throat, nearly triggering vomit. He breathed deeply through his nose and mouth, moving his head and tilting his chin toward the sun's light. He returned to the water.

He perspired as he redirected the hand pool to his face while he bathed slowly. He groaned and spat, rinsing his mouth, swishing and gargling, then swallowed more before finally killing the life switch.

Returning to his room and bed brought no consolation except for providing a venue to stretch his now nearly hydrated muscles and joints, which quivered in thanks. He took the pillow from underneath his head and laid it over his eyes. Silence then, and darkness.

The world outside was cold and calm. The flow of traffic was typical on Olney Drive which catered almost exclusively to local vehicles. Birds talked. A dog barked. It was morning for tethered humans abiding within their quiet shameless hearths. And none of the ovine white-collars could hear or see in through the boundaries and barriers to the fear and mutton. A typical day had begun.

Palpitations. He packed a bong of grass and knelt by the window. Using a dryer sheet tied around an empty toilet paper cylinder to exhale through the window, he disguised the scent of unlawful flowers. As the LSD reconnected to his brain, he coughed, muffling the sound. Looking at the door, making sure it was closed, he finished the bud and swatted his hand around in the air, vainly eradicating the lingering smoke before returning the bong to its hiding space. *Too early to call Jake,* he thought.

He showered, becoming higher from the cannabis under the water's cascade. He appeased the call of his mouth for wetness with ease, swishing, spitting, and drinking the hot water. Upon washing his penis, embarrassment returned. He stretched his hands up on the shower wall while his head sunk.

This was the ideal place for self-reproach. He recollected the sound of

Jane's furious voice. In defense of her, he understood the outcry. He was almost 18 and girls thought he was handsome. How was she to imagine that, to sex stuff, he was a stranger. Regret for his treachery set in.

But the sensation of hot water running over his head and body kept remorse at bay. He stepped out, toweled off, and drank more from the faucet with his hand.

Fresh clothes now and a part down the center of his hair with a comb, he went to the backyard to enjoy a stick of Jake's donation. Shading his eyes, he smoked.

The sound of a woodpecker rang from somewhere as he gazed at black birds on a wire. He remembered the owl. There were no neighbors with whom to wave as he returned to the house and picked up the phone to call Jake. Rapid beeping had replaced the dial tone. He hung up, then picked up, hearing the same sound. He moved through the kitchen to the garage. No car. He walked about the living room to the bottom of the stairs.

"Mom?!"

The loud sound of his own voice sped his heart. He ascended the stairs and tested the phone in his room. There was one more phone in the house. He peered into his parents' bedroom and saw no one on the bed.

GUILT IS NOT a fickle demon. Cade sat on the couch in the living room after paramedics confirmed his mother's death. It didn't take an autopsy to call it pills and booze with intent while his father in absentia seemed the catalyst. The paramedics were nice but no one held him while he cried.

Some neighbors who couldn't miss the flashing emergency vehicles came into the home without knocking. His aunt who lived an hour away was notified.

It was difficult for Cade to hear or focus. His childhood friend's mother, Rose, hustled to him on the sofa and pulled him up from underneath his armpits like a child. She stood and held him tight, affecting his breathing. He cried harder and she cried with him.

"It's ok," she said over and over. He hyperventilated and cried. She hushed him like an infant sensing his breaths after she calmed herself. She did it right.

"I'm sorry," he whimpered, noticing her clothes becoming wet with mucus and tears.

"It's ok," she shushed him tenderly. "I'm your towel. I'm your towel," she said. "It's ok." Her embrace didn't falter. "Breathe with me. It's ok. Breathe with me."

People came and gathered. Maureen Helton and her husband Ray, who had lived across the street since he could remember, came inside. Maureen reprieved Rose like they were on an assembly line and held Cade. Her vocal tempo was slower and, unlike Rose, she wasn't sobbing. Cade felt the change. Her body was thicker. She smelled differently. Her volume was lower as she almost whispered. "It's ok," she said and shushed him. He cried but held back.

They sat him down. Ray located his cigarettes and brought over some whiskey. Cade tried lighting a smoke but was disoriented and shook. "Here," said Maureen. She put the cig to her lips and in her naivety said, "It's been a while." She smiled and pulled from the stick, setting it on fire. "Ok, I think I did it," she said, offering the day's first attempt at humor. This comforted everyone, including Cade, who was the only one who did not visibly or vocally react to her bumbling.

"You looked good with that cigarette, Mo," said Ray.

"It didn't feel good," she said.

"C'mon, you didn't even inhale!" said Ray.

"I think I did a little!" said Maureen, still smiling. Cade smoked and drank and became quieter as Ray rubbed his knee while Rose cradled him from his side. Maureen stood in order to tend him from the other side.

That's when Carla walked in.

"Oh my God! What happened?! Is Margaret ok?! What's going on here?!" Her tone was labored and nosy. Maureen, Margaret's most trusted and loyal friend, sensed this immediately and became defensive. Maureen had never trusted Carla and suspected her of stealing from Margaret and taking advantage of her kind spirit and problem with alcohol.

"Hello everybody. Cade, are you ok?" Carla sounded like a substitute teacher who didn't give a damn.

Maureen informed her that Margaret had died from an apparent suicide and that Cade had found her that way and that Margaret's husband, Cade's father, was gone.

"Well, gee whiz, is Cade a suspect?! Not you, Cade, of course I mean Cade Senior. Geezum crow, I mean, so, wow, so is her body still upstairs? Where did she die? In her bedroom? Was it on the toilet? I mean, where, where did she, ya know, I mean, where did she, ya know, take her last breath? Was it? You said it's upstairs? I better, you know, I better, I'm gonna, because she was my friend too," said Carla, who exhibited no signs of grief or sadness. And while Rose and Ray tended to Cade and his battered mind, Maureen dealt with Carla who was displaying a desire for entertainment rather than caring. From the kitchen, Maureen planted her feet, obstructing the path between Carla and the stairs in the living room.

"Listen to me," said Maureen with spite. "If you think you're gonna go up there to gawk at my friend's body for kicks, you've got another thing coming."

Carla's eyes went blank, penetrated by Maureen's adversarial tone and stare. "But I—" said Carla.

"You're what," said Maureen without blinking.

"I?"

"The only people who have any business going up there are Cade, his aunt when she gets here, myself, the paramedics, and the fucking coroner, do you understand me?"

Carla left, stunned and disenchanted, mouth wide open. Maureen returned to her maternal endeavor while Cade remained oblivious to what had just occurred. She kissed him and spoke softly: "Ray, please pour some whiskey for me, ok?" She kissed Cade again, "I'm Irish too ya know." She kissed him softly for a third time. "You're gonna be ok, ya know. We're gonna take care of you."

Cade's Aunt Jackie arrived and they cried together. His body became sore from being squeezed so much. After everyone settled, they spoke together. Cade, unlike any other time in his life, sensed his mother's energy powerfully within his aunt. And although he had an understanding for the truth as to what had happened between his parents, the answers for now remained unrevealed.

He'd spend weeks that spilled into months, nebulous and tired, shell-shocked in between nightmares. He moved to the Heltons' house, and shared a bedroom with his oldest friend Miles.

Ray opposed the move, concerned with the stresses of life as it was with three children. And his clandestine affair with Margaret years ago also skewed his conviction. Nevertheless, he was overruled by his wife Maureen, whose outbidding put away any probability of Cade opening this chapter of his life elsewhere.

He'd be in and out of the home where his mother died while his aunt prepared it for sale. Formally, he'd reside with the Helton family, antithetical to the withdrawn nature of his upbringing. And when he finally finished crying himself to sleep every night and could see his way around, Miles returned to the bedroom that he had partially relinquished for his friend and they lived in it together.

What remained the same for Cade after the initial shedding of woe was the vice for disconnection and hunger for solitude. It was for this that he'd have to adapt, to continue dwelling chained between walls of self-destruction that had been his purpose and lifeform for as long as he could remember.

3

———————————

GUARDING OF THE RAIN

It smelled like a family. It definitely smelled like a family in here. His feet embraced the softness underneath them with each step down the stairway, the wood making the slightest sound, barely giving in to his weight below the carpet. He felt as if each turn could lead him staring directly into the eyes of another human—another human who might want some answers. His toes hit the ground floor and he turned into the kitchen.

"Dude," said Miles, just craning his head up after poking around in the fridge. Miles was shirtless with a red bandana on his head plus lazy corduroy shorts and brown Birkenstocks on his feet.

"What's up, man," said Cade.

"Nada much, bra, nada much. How's it going?!" Miles liked to enunciate, taking confident steps along the big kitchen floor to prepare his food. To Cade, he appeared like a happy, centered Jim Morrison had a head-on collision with a truckload of freckles.

"Um, pretty good," said Cade.

"Dude, me and Sammie are gonna hit Dairy Queen later if you want to join us," said Miles. "Maybe see a movie."

Sammie was Miles' girlfriend. She and Cade had been classmates since kindergarten. They had been romantic in elementary school and were each other's first kiss. Throughout high school, they remained friends and developed common interests like marijuana and drinking where at 16, she had given him his first ecstasy pill. Their relationship after grammar school was strictly platonic.

"Yeah, maybe, man," said Cade. "Thanks."

Cade opened the fridge and looked around out of obligation. There was so much food in here. The freezer was beneath the refrigerator unlike the set-up at his home, which was smaller and side-by-side.

He crouched down and looked inside. The anti-social positioning of his head and body provided relief from interacting with Miles who now could only be heard from behind and no longer seen. Steam rose from the bags, boxes, and plasticware in the freezer. He knew that it might be a good idea to eat but wasn't sure where to start. Then he thought the time he took in front of the cold food had overrun as Miles hadn't spoken in a while. No doubt, he was being judged. He heard dishware connecting with other dishware. The microwave beeped. The silverware drawer opened and closed. Miles cleared his throat. Cade closed the freezer and opened the refrigerator. He started to sweat. His hands began to shake. He drove his toes painfully into the kitchen floor beneath him.

"Hungry, bro?" asked Miles, his gentle hand on Cade's shoulder.

Cade turned to his friend's welcoming eyes. He had prepared two sandwiches and couscous and had a plate in his hand for alms.

"Uh, yeah," said Cade. "Thanks, bro."

The two young men sat at the kitchen table where Cade was relieved, knowing that he would be eating by the side of his friend rather than face to face. They ate most of their sandwiches without talking.

"What is this?" asked Cade.

"Couscous," said Miles. "I fuckin' love this shit."

Cade nearly spat as his laughter unexpectedly spouted. They laughed loudly together. When they came down, still laughing, Cade asked, "Well, what the hell is it?!"

"I don't know," said Miles. "It's couscous!"

With his fork, Cade toyed with it. "I've never seen anything like it."

Injecting a big mouthful, "Me neither, bra," said Miles and they laughed again.

Sammie had high cheekbones, black hair, green eyes, and long legs. She had a tongue stud and, like Miles, smoked Camels and wore Birkenstocks. Gorgeous, but at the same time, she had a one-of-the-guys vibe. What Sammie lacked in the mammary realm was made up for in posterior. She wore silver jewelry around her neck and on her fingers and rocked a patchwork bag. Her voice carried when she spoke and she was as verbally assertive as her legs were long. It was easy to be close to Sammie.

"Hey, Cade!"

"Oh, hey, Sam. How, how are you?"

"Goooood." Her voice escalated in pitch. "Whadayou up to?"

"Jus' chillin."

"We're gonna blaze and then get ice cream if you're down, dude," said Miles.

"Yeah, might just crash," said Cade. "I haven't really been sleeping too—"

"Oh *fuck*, who made fuckin' brownies, man?!"

"My mom," said Miles, approaching Sammie and putting his arm around her. His hand slid past her hip and below her waist. "They're good, right?" He kissed her while her mouth was full. They held each other. She pushed away, swallowed, and said, "Your mom makes the dankest fuckin' brownies."

Cade was on his way to the bedroom that he shared with Miles. He ascended the stairs and started to breathe a little better. It was quiet and he was alone.

The attic bedroom was big. It had clean white wall-to-wall carpet, multiple ceiling fans, a big TV, and a pool table in the center with red fabric. Miles' posters were strewn about: mainly Beatles and Grateful Dead. There was an old Bob Dylan tapestry that was his dad's. Cade approached the couch by the windows facing the front of the yard. And there in the big quiet room, he sat alone.

He realized that a few drinks might do him right. He hustled down the three flights of stairs, got into his car, and drove to the hood store just outside of town. It was there where an 18-year-old guy would most likely slip in and out without being asked for ID.

It began to rain as he drove away from the house. This was a peaceful, hopeful moment. The CD, *Colma*, by a masked, enigmatic artist played as he drove.

He had been going to this gas station to buy beer for about two years now. Cade was six feet tall, had chinstrap facial hair, and wore baggy clothes. Although the Buffalo, New York Eastside bodega had black clientele, he didn't care. That is where he typically purchased beer and it worked every time. Today's task would be easy, given that it was daylight and there was a light drizzle.

He parked in the tiny lot near the old gas pumps that didn't work as other customers were loitering near the entrance. The loud sound of bass hitting metal resounded from a Cadillac nearby. Passing cars presented glimpses of different rap songs. He thought he heard, *I put the pistol to my head and say a prayer.*

Moving casually through the lot, he heard two humans laughing loudly then made eye contact with a kid wearing a long white tee shirt.

"'Sup," said Cade, unrequited while he entered the small store looking back as he held the door open. There was no one coming in behind him so he let the door close. The Middle Eastern man from behind the dirty counter said, "Hello, my friend."

"Hello," said Cade.

It smelled of stale air and unclean diapers. There were tube socks, Nyquil, scissors, and other miscellaneous items here and there down the aisle on the way to the corner where the beer was kept. He saw the six-pack of tall Red Dogs and grabbed them out of the fridge. They were nice and cold. A short line of humans had formed so Cade got behind them while no one had anything in their hands besides him. The clerk looked at the first person in line.

"Yeah, Swisher Sweet," the teenager said. The clerk grabbed a five-pack of skinny cigars.

"Nah, one, nigga!"

The clerk reciprocated his high volume, "One! One Swisher Sweet!"

"Stupid nigga, man. One *only*. Jus' one!" The clerk frustratedly located a single Swisher cigar and put it on the counter.

"Newport."

The clerk collected a soft pack of Newport cigarettes and put them by the cigar.

"Box!"

He replaced the soft one with a hard pack of the same brand then the kid paid and left.

Next was a middle-aged man wearing alligator shoes and a slick hat. The bass hitting metal rumbled from the lot. A couple with a crying baby came in. While they crossed in front of Cade, the baby and he made eye contact for a few seconds. The crying diminished and then stopped.

After the man with alligator shoes had his fill of lottery tickets, Cade approached the counter.

"Yes, my friend," said the clerk.

Cade put the beer on the counter. "Camel filters box, please."

The clerk retrieved the smokes. The art on the pack spoke to Cade. He glanced at the phallocentric message hidden amidst the drawing of the colorful camel as the vessel laid upon the counter. The clerk had placed them face up after a swift fluid motion as if to show them the respect they deserved. And this time, the proponent revealed the cigs without a blemish in the deed. As he delivered the Camel Filters, he did not becloud the desire of the patron to have filters upon his cigarettes. For it was not rare that an employee would hear the word *filter* and, in haste, go for a pack of Camel *Non*-Filters, presenting the much shorter pack that delivered unwanted strength. Not today, though. This man knew the difference. This man knew his Camels. And Cade, the gracious heir, felt as if they needed a home. They were up there with the other bland variations in unstimulating lifeless packaging and finally, they were coming home.

He paid cash.

"Thank you, my friend," said the clerk.

"Thank you," said Cade. He walked through the lot feeling like the winner of a small contest.

On the ride back to town, he was able to enjoy the fruit. He pulled over to the side of the road right at the border of the city and the suburb. He opened one of the Red Dogs and relaxed. Looking out for cops, he perceived each passing car without making eye contact with any of the humans within. Draining the beer and lighting a smoke with matches, he pulled away from the curb and heaved the empty tall boy to the side of the road, equating the crime to tossing a poor man a nickel.

The CD still spun the instrumental melancholic sound as the late May precipitation gave way to no celebration. He drove his car through the streets of the familiar town. After the sharp curve that was well known to him, the intersection ahead was tricky. If not anticipated, it could catch a driver off guard. Flowing comfortably with the music, Cade merged from left to right and went through the green light straight-on.

AT THE HOUSE, MILES and Sammie had arrived. They were stoned in the attic bedroom. Sammie lay spread across the bed on her stomach playing with their cat, Lucy.

After lighting a stick of Nag-Champa, Miles perused music. He flipped through the huge sleeve-book of CDs, pulled one, and approached the stereo atop the dresser by the window.

"Dude, is that *Blues for Allah*?" said Sammie, keeping her smiling eyes on the cat.

"Uh, yeah," Miles giggled. "How did you know?"

"Because you always play it," said Sammie.

"No, I don't," said Miles.

"'K, whatever," said Sammie.

He put on the CD, took off his shirt, and, sitting on the bed and handing Sammie the small greasy tube, said, "Lube me up, baby." The cat scattered away toward the stairs and disappeared.

"Again?" she said.

"Yeah, it needs it," said Miles. "I can feel it."

Sammie squeezed some out onto her hand and sat up. She applied a generous amount to Miles' new tattoo on his upper back which was a Celtic knot done in green and bronze ink.

"Not too much," said Miles.

"I know, I know," said Sammie. She gently rubbed in the lotion with her finger as music played.

"How is it living with Cade?" she said.

"It's cool," said Miles. "He really needs us."

"Yeah, where else would he go?" said Sammie.

"I don't know," said Miles. "I think his aunt or uncle's but they're old and shit."

"It's so cool of your parents to let him live here," said Sammie.

"Yeah, my dad took some convincing," said Miles.

"Really?" said Sammie.

"Yeah, man," said Miles. "Mary started high school last year. She's about to get her driver's permit. And you know how troublesome Major is. Dad said that we shouldn't take him in cause it would be too much."

"Oh my God," said Sammie. "I cannot picture Mary driving a car."

"I know," said Miles.

"What's gonna happen to his house?" said Sammie.

"I don't know," said Miles. "Sell it eventually."

"We should have a party there," said Sammie.

"Yeah, right," Miles chuckled.

"Dude, I bet he'd be down," said Sammie.

"It's still full of his parents' shit," said Miles.

The CD skipped. Sammie put the cap onto the lotion, walked over to the stereo, and pressed pause. She approached the white couch and knelt on it as its back rested against the wall and windowsill. She looked out from the third-story view at the house that sat at the very end of the street that ran perpendicular to it. She focused down the road toward the residence where Cade's mother died which could be seen if it weren't for the slightest of curves. The vision of the houses and land now freshly christened with rain blurred with her reflection.

She dreamed of the past and being pulled out of her fifth grade class to be brought to the office. There, her neighbor waited to take her to her home where she was told that her mother had died in a car wreck. She remembered the long trek after the vaguest of explanations as to the unexpected predicament. And her neighbor's unrefined mannerisms in the car, an attempt at making the task appear casual and as if nothing was wrong.

She remembered the rain. She recollected how the passenger's side windshield wiper needed replacing and the noise that it made as it barely cleared the water from her view. And after entering her home to find her teary-eyed father and wailing sister, her socks were saturated from the storm outside.

She remembered the restless night in her room and the sun coming up through the window when she realized that she still had her wet socks on underneath the covers.

And two weeks later, her nervous return to school and to her peers on a sunny day an hour late. And making her way past her teacher's pitying eyes and the hard stares from the classmates to her desk in the middle of the room. And seeing the dry umbrella that her mom had handed her the last morning she was alive exactly where she had left it: in the back corner of her once pleasantly familiar classroom.

"It's raining," she said.

"Good thing we're inside," said Miles.

He was closer to her than Sammie expected as he put his hand on her back and sat with her on the couch to join her in the guarding of the rain. They kissed and kissed some more.

Then they heard the sound of the door opening at the level below and silently questioned whether or not they heard feet ascending. Miles' mom's head appeared as she climbed the stairs.

Sammie whispered, "Shit, we gotta be more careful." They smiled together.

"Aup! I'm not interrupting anything, am I?!" Maureen's voice was loud and jaunty.

"No, Mom," said Miles.

"'Sup, Mo!" said Sammie.

"What's going on?" said Maureen. "How come there's no music in here?"

"There was but the CD was skipping so we decided to make out instead," said Miles.

"Hey, Mo, you wanna do some bong hits?" said Sammie.

"Aup! There is no bong in this house, is there, My?!" she said.

"No, mom, just my bowl," said Miles.

"There better not be!" said Maureen jokingly. "Have you guys seen Cade?"

"Earlier," said Miles. "Not sure where he is now."

"You better not be gettin' pregnant, Sam!" said Maureen.

Sammie gasped and looked at Miles.

"No, Mom, I always pull out."

"Pull out?! What is that?!" said Maureen. "You two better use condoms! I'm not interested in grandchildren."

"We're good, Mom," said Miles.

"Ok," said Maureen. "Sammie, honey, are you staying the night?"

"I don't think so," said Sammie. "Miles is gonna take me home later."

"Ok, tell your dad we said hi," said Maureen as she made her way back toward the stairs and down.

"Sure thing, Mo," said Sammie.

She had to get back if her dad was at home rather than at his girlfriend's just out of town which is where he spent most of his time. When the mother of his children had died, he had picked up the slack along with his oldest daughter, but when Sammie was old enough to survive on her own, his fathering became feeble. He developed several relationships, and the third time seemed a charm. While that love line meant he lived like a ghost at the house he owned, some rules stood strong: he didn't like her crashing elsewhere, nor did he like boys to sleep with her at his place.

Evening turned to night and they piled in Miles' dad's jeep and took off.

4

____

ONLY FIRE

Down the road, Cade was in and out of sleep within the quiet walls of the place where he used to live.

Just before sundown, he had parked his car around the corner to be inconspicuous to his neighbors. He drank half the beer in the car in order to lighten his load when on his feet. With a few full cans in his pockets, he walked from his parking place, minding the particularly nosy neighbors directly across the street then darted for the side door and entered. Amid his solitude and sadness, he locked the door behind him.

The rooms were still completely furnished as if nothing had changed. And in silence, he sat on the couch and drank.

With each beer, he breathed slower and deeper. He looked at the illuminated drapes in front of him. They were still. The noise that used to be heard when his mother would walk in her bedroom above where he sat was gone, yet he listened for it anyway. Soon enough, he fell asleep, only to wake a few hours later. He returned to slumber.

Cade dreamed as if he was a cigarette. He laid upon his back and comprehended that he could not move any part of him except for his eyes, as if he was rolled tightly. He looked down toward his chest to see himself lying upon the couch in the living room, his body a roll of tobacco. Each time he inhaled, his chest hurt some and the rising of where his lungs used to be diminished a little. The pain of it all increased with each breath.

Every inhale, his upper-mid section disappeared more. In a moment of acceptance, he closed his mouth and exhaled through his nose, altering the attack to taste. But the more he smoked, the more billowed and the more afraid he became.

Still unable to move, he tried to yell, but the sound wouldn't come. The fear and silence gave way to the unmistakable sound of someone walking above. Despite his immobility, he tried to urinate. Maybe that would wake him. The familiar sound moved from end to end of the ceiling. The smoke came faster and thicker until it was coming from his entire body. It would slow for a moment just to accelerate twice as fast. He was almost completely ablaze as the flames and smoke breathed in and out.

Sensing a presence no longer on the floor above but much closer, the sound of his motionless body burning sounded like a human inhaling and exhaling. He was the powerless watcher of his own self transmuted into the rapid ebb and flow of the fiery breath of a beast. And then there was only fire. Behind him, he heard a foot taking the solitary step down between the kitchen and the living room. The mania gave way to the dedicated fear of wondering who was there.

"Cade."

As his head jerked him up and into consciousness, he looked about the room. With racing heart, he wanted to run down the street to the house on Hendricks Boulevard and crawl into bed with Maureen. He wanted someone to hold him. He thought about Miles in bed with Sammie. He thought about his neighbors and whomever else he had seen that day, comfortably asleep in their beds. Lighting a smoke, his hands shook. The clock on the wall said 4:29 am. He wished that his feet were warmer. With no reason to move, he'd stay in that position until night turned to day.

THE SATURDAY SUN SHONE brightly. Cade knew he had an obligation to get back to Heltons' home at some point. He thought that if he got there early enough, he'd be able to get in without seeing the entire family at once. That way, he could gradually become accustomed to normality again.

He exited the house, got into his car, drove around the block, and parked in the street close to family manor. Damaged from sleeplessness, and jittery, he made his way up the driveway. No sound. So far so good.

Cade liked their attic room. It was usually uninhabited and inviting. He slowed his stride as he approached the door. Looking up at a bird on a wire, he stopped. Hearing a car pass slowly from behind, he turned to see that it was gone. The bird had vanished too. His eyes stung in defeat of the sun's light and out of obligation, he continued toward the rear door and opened it.

Immediately, the sound of chatter and dishes connecting with dishes met him there in the small mudroom, shoes scattered about the floor. And the smell. He closed the door behind him. It was family feeding time. Who knows what kind of conversational refuse was being transmitted? He dreamed of escape.

"Is that Cade?!" he heard Ray inquire. Ray was twice as confident as his son Miles and ten times as loud.

"Probably," said Mary indifferently.

"It must be," said Ray. "Major Helton, who is at the door?" Cade heard Major's hurried steps, proudly answering the command of his father. Cade took off his shoes and stood to face the challenge as Major identified him.

"'Sup, Major," said Cade.

"You smell like beer!" the seven-year-old exclaimed loudly. He was deaf in one ear and sure as hell sounded like it. Mary gasped.

"Shut up, Major!" said Miles, coming to defense of his friend. He walked over to his little brother and shooed him from the door where Cade was creeping in. Their eyes met in a moment of tranquility. Miles was a compassionate friend that Cade could count on.

"How's it hangin', bro?" added Miles calmly.

"Um, pretty good," said Cade.

"There's grub if you want to sit with us," said Miles. "If not, I think I might head out with Sammie soon and you can relax in our room if you want."

"Uh, yeah," said Cade. "Cool, thanks."

"Cade, why don't you sit down with us?! There's eggs, sausage, potatoes," said Ray. "And HAL-AP-EENO-POP-EARZ!" he added in a bad accent.

"Yeah, ok, thanks," said Cade as he entered the room and fixed himself a plate. There was a place and chair reserved for him at the head of the table opposite Ray. Noticing that his friend did not pour himself a beverage, Miles stood and brought him water.

"Honey?" said Maureen tenderly. "Are you feeling ok?"

"Good, how are you?" said Cade.

"I'm fine, thank you," said Maureen. "I was hoping you would be joining us."

"So, Cade, where'd you sleep?" said Ray, mouth half full of food.

"He smells like beer!" said Major.

"Shut up, Major," said Miles. "Or I am going to drag you outdoors where you belong and beat you until you can't even wipe your own ass anymore."

Maureen smiled as Mary laughed.

"Well?" asked Ray.

"Ray?! Please, let's just eat breakfast," interrupted Maureen, processing Cade's sweating while he quickly ate.

"Guess what, Mom?" said Major.

"What, honey?" said Maureen.

Major had a tendency of forming multiple words per sentence with a pitch that turned up as if every few notes was its own question. It was either that or he was plain shouting or screaming. When he spoke in a slow calm manner, it was like a vacation for the people around him, especially Cade. And depending on one's mood, his manner of speaking might be considered cute. Major felt very comfortable around his mother and chose to be as close to her as he could. He turned to her and said:

"*One time*, I was walking down the stairs to the base*ment*, and *Miles was in the basement*, but there was no *TV on*, and also *Sammie was in the basement*, and I heard them, rolling *around on each other*, and Sammie was making such strange *noises*, and I think, you know what *they were doing*? They were—"

"Shut up!" laughed Miles.

"You don't say?" said Ray. The ladies at the table laughed too.

"Yes, I say!" said Major.

"Well, maybe you shouldn't say so much, Major!" said Mary.

"Miles has sex and Cade drinks more beer than Dad!" shouted Major.

"Quiet, Major, finish your eggs," said Maureen.

"And your HAL-AP-EENO-POP-EARZ!"

Cade was embarrassed, but he suddenly felt a sense of belonging as he and Miles were unexpectedly called-out publicly by Major *together*. They finished eating and dispersed. Maureen beckoned Cade with her finger just before he had the chance to escape to the attic. They spoke quietly away from the rest of the family.

"Cade, I'm responsible for you, ya know?"

"Yes."

"And I want you to be honest with me."

"Ok."

"Look! Are you honest with me?!" She drew her friendly yet assertive eyes closer to him. Maureen liked to narrow the range of vision of the person with whom she was talking via unwavering eye contact. When you were talking with Maureen, it was as if she was the only one in the universe.

"Yes," he said. Communication was foreign to Cade especially with people living in the same house as him.

"It's ok that you go to your old house from time to time, but one of the stipulations to you living here is that you live *here*."

"I know."

"*Do* you?"

"Yes, Maureen."

"Ok. I love you, ya know. You're my third son."

"I love you too, Maureen. Th-thank you."

She smiled, tickled by his flawed conciseness and respectful responses.

And she believed he did mean what he said and probably much more.

As they drifted ways, Major came by, dragging a blanket, a thumb in his mouth, making a suckling sound. Cade headed to the attic for solitude.

As fear dissipated, torture took over. Mentally, Cade treated himself like a remorseful killer. The silence and alone time that he was desperate for served as ammunition for transgression. He sat on the bed with his back to the stairs, feeling the need to be treated like an insect by ornery adolescents with a magnifying glass and scissors.

The life that he lived before the worst discovery was isolated and agonizingly frustrating. And now, it was abundant with human connection but just as lonely. Fear, torment, and spiritual apathy had existed inside him for years, but now, they had taken control and were breeding.

The nighttime brought no repose as Cade was without Miles to share the large bedroom. He reached under the loveseat to where he had stashed his bottles, only to find they weren't there. After 1 am, he headed out to the hood to get some beer.

Going to the store in the black neighborhood was a different ballgame at night. He hoped for a desolate parking lot but arrived to see what looked like a party.

He parked the car at the only spot that would make for an easy out. There were people sitting on the trunks of cars, drinking from bottles inside paper bags. He looked all around before getting out of the car: no cops and no white people. There were multiple systems playing music with lots of bass simultaneously. He walked toward the door of the illuminated convenience store that he was used to entering but it was locked. He heard a banging at the glass to his left. Looking over, he saw the clerk point to the window in front of him where people were waiting, so he got in line.

In the front of the line, a patron was being served beer through a large slot. The human directly in front of Cade turned to him, looked him up and down, grinned with a toothpick between gold teeth, and, making eye contact, said, "Ice." Cade, deducing that it was an offer of sorts, replied, "Nah." The man with the gold teeth held Cade's vision for a moment. He had never seen irises like that. On the other side, Cade had never seen sclerae so yellow.

Having a more difficult time disguising his fear, Cade counted on the idea that it would be in the other guy's better interest to break gaze first as he would have to turn round to buy whichever poison suited him. The contest ended as others gathered behind Cade and the man with gold teeth turned to face the front.

It became raucous with chatter as folks in line had seemed to know each other. Cade hoped the loud humans behind him did two things: respect his place in line and initiate zero conversation. The man with gold teeth collected his goods and very slowly got out of the way. Cade approached the window.

"12 pack," said Cade. "Blue bottles."

"Can't fit," said the clerk.

"What?" asked Cade.

"CAN'T FIT!" said the frustrated clerk, pointing to the drawer, acknowledging its less than ample size. "You want cans?!"

"Oh," said Cade. "Um, yeah."

Looking as if Cade was doing him a great disservice, he got up and walked to the refrigerated section and got the beer.

Outside, it had become louder and smokier. The clerk pushed open the drawer and his customer put in the money. He made change and slotted it forward. Cade grabbed the change and the beer by its cardboard handle and walked toward his car. Fidgeting with the dough and the box of beer with both hands, the handle broke, the box fell to the ground, and Cade tripped over it and fell.

Amid laughter, Cade identified the sound of at least one can fizzing open and embarrassment gave way to the task of collecting all the beers. He scrambled for them with his back to the majority of the audience. The laughter was tumultuous. They yelled and cheered and did ridiculous imitations. He collected all the cans and most of the eleven dollars change that had hit the ground. Feeling beer leak onto his shirt from the box, he got into his car and could still hear them laughing as he pulled away.

His body was stiff as he drove out of the city and back to the foot of the burb. He parked while locating the fizzing beer then sucked on the tiny puncture wound. He finished that one and said aloud, "Fuck this," and cracked open another, chugging until it was dry.

Cade turned up the music, smiled, then headed back to the house.

THE NEXT MORNING, HE awoke in his bed to the loud sound of Maureen calling his name.

"Cade! It's almost noon! Are you up?! Are you naked?! I'm comin' in!" She sat on his bed. Her demeanor was forgiving but forthright. "Look, Cade, you're drinkin' too much. I saw beer cans in your car and Ray found your little stash of empties under the loveseat!"

"They weren't all empty."

"Aup! Don't you get wise with me! Jesus, your shirt reeks like fuckin' beer, Cade!"

"Yeah, a....thing happened."

"A *thing* happened?! What *thing* happened?!"

"Um…"

"*Um*, you got drunk and drove all over town and spilled beer on yourself!" Her smile was comforting as he smiled back. "Oh, this is funny?! You think this is funny," she said.

"Yes!" said Cade.

"What, drivin' all over town and gittin' drunk is funny?!" said Maureen.

"No, that…I.."

"No-that-I-what," Maureen said as she poked him with her finger.

"I didn't do that! YOU are funny! THIS is funny! Stop poking me, Maureen! I've got a hard-on!" said Cade.

"No you don't!" said Maureen as they enjoyed the moment.

"Listen," she said. "You take care a' that hard-on and come down and talk with me."

"Well, it's gone now! You took care of that *for* me!"

Maureen's unique hootish laugh echoed from down the stairs. Cade stood and turned on the music that Miles had left in the CD player. He decided he didn't like it and went down to the bathroom to shower.

The morning merriment made him feel better. He entered the fresh-smelling bathroom. The tub was loaded with stuff for the family of five: multiple conditioners, women's hair products, strange puff balls, wooden things for he-didn't-know-what, lady razors, hair ties hanging from the shower caddy, ah, there, a bar of soap. It was new and had to have been moisturizing soap. What a world. In his home where he had grown, all there had been was a cheap hunka soap next to a bottle of bland shampoo. In this kingdom, he had to look around for the shampoo in a small pond of bottles.

After a long shower, he descended the soft stairs and entered the kitchen to see Ray standing by the window.

"Hi, Ray." Cade opened the refrigerator door and looked inside.

"Cade," said Ray. "Some guy came over from next door and said you were yelling and cursing at his mother, the old lady who lives there."

"That's...weird," replied Cade. He continued browsing the family food. That's when Ray approached him slowly and stopped. "Did you do it?"

Cade turned to Ray. He took in Ray's demeanor, meeting his stern, persistent eye contact. "Uh, *no, Ray*. I have no idea what you're talking about."

"He says that you used obscenities from the window in Miles' room. That you called her a bitch and other things." Cade's jaw dropped. "Look, Cade, we care about you. And we miss your mom and dad. And what happened was terrible, but you can't be doing this kind of crap in this house."

"Ray, I'm telling you, I don't know what you're talking about. I never called anybody anything. Why the hell would I—"

"Look, Cade, when you're in this house, you need to behave. I already had to throw out all those empty beer bottles from up there. This isn't a frat house. And swearing at our neighbor, do you know how this makes us look? I can't believe I had to hear that today. This isn't what I need."

Ray walked away. Stunned, Cade peered out the window, hoping to see the red van that Maureen usually drove. The driveway, unlike usual, had a vacancy. He thought himself in circles as to how this fiction could've come about. He wished that Maureen was there with him. He imagined her setting things straight.

The world of confusion became darker and boggier for Cade. He went out that night and partied with friends and spent the next few days in a haze. Finding comfort in being in his car wedged between loud speakers, he drove the streets aimlessly, incumbent upon mingling with the people of the town.

He'd run into friends and friends of friends and couples at the taco joint by his old elementary school whose sight projected sympathetically. He'd see people who, in childhood, used to treat him viciously. Now they pretended as if he wasn't there. He'd run into girls, some younger, who, unbeknown to him, looked at him with eyes curious and endearing.

He'd get high with his friends and by himself, always keeping the threat of cops in mind. Although he had little obligation, this world was one that contained Cade rather than allowing him to be free.

KILLERS

Morning came at Sammie's home across from the park with the basketball courts and gazebos. She exited the bathroom that she shared with her father only as her sisters, all older, had moved out.

Sammie was the youngest of four girls. And although life had been hard for the family of five since her mother died, she and her sisters always had a nice place to live and plenty of money. Her father was an engineer and her mother was killed by a seventeen-year-old driver who had been inhaling lighter fluid before the wreck. Her dad had sued the store, a corporation, for selling it to the underage girl and won a worthy settlement when Sammie was a child. The suburban home was furnished nicely.

Sammie stepped out of the shower onto the heated floor while Miles was still asleep in her bed. She dried herself and entered the bedroom where they had slept together the night before.

"Duder. My dad could be home soon. We should get out of here." She had meant the bedroom. Miles, just waking, was groggy and comfortable. He reached for her body which he pulled closer.

"Isn't your dad at work?" he said.

"No, it's Saturday," said Sammie. "He's in Fredonia at Liz's. He could come back any time."

"It's only like 10 am!" He smiled.

"Yeah, I know, but I don't want him to catch you in here."

"It's like a 2-hour drive!" said Miles. He kissed her neck. "Oooh, you're clean."

"Yeah, I showered." She smiled. They had had sex the night before like they were accustomed. They kissed harder and Miles began kissing her breasts.

"My dad might come home soon," she said again.

"It's too early for him," said Miles.

Sammie disguised her nervousness with a seemingly comfortable tone. But she also knew that it was unlikely that her father would be returning soon. Her anxiety was of another kind.

Sammie had been having sex since she was sixteen and now, two years later, she was used to it with Miles. And although she enjoyed kissing and intercourse, foreplay and receiving fellatio was distressing. Miles, who was comfortable in this realm, was oblivious. Whenever he initiated such intimacy, Sammie became afraid and tense. She would make it her objective to hide her trepidation from Miles which, due to his amorousness, was easy. He went down on her like he usually did and she became wet, but mentally, she was upset. She did not know how to explain this to her boyfriend of five months, so the stone laid unturned.

This morning, as she expected and desired, they'd copulate like they did the night before. But her most cherished part of the physical union with Miles was the ending of foreplay which was, naturally, immediately followed by sex. Miles, upon the first stroke of penetration, would process

Sammie's visage as one of excitement and pleasure. But the look on her face that he was so endearingly and confidently staring into was in fact one that reflected a swift sense of relief from fear.

Post-coital togetherness left Miles feeling invigorated. They kissed and he exited the bedroom, went into the bathroom, and turned on the shower. Sammie could hear him singing.

She sat up on her bed and looked at herself from the reflection of the tall mirror next to the bed with Grateful Dead bears adorned. The clock in the room read 10:22. She was in a sexual relationship with a fellow whom she felt she could trust, unlike the three partners from her past that she now could see as having had devious agendas in relation to her innocence. She reflected on moments with those boys, with whom she never had an orgasm. This was a tradition that proved consistent with Miles and even despite countless efforts when she was alone.

THE NIGHT HAD BLED into day differently for Cade. He and his friend Jake had taken LSD and headed to the familiar secluded spot near the power lines. They were with three other friends who were only drinking and puffing herb.

Jon Berkeley, called "Berk," was short with scruffy facial hair and wore nothing but tie-dyed shirts. His mother had died a year previous as he was the first one to lose someone close to him in this circle of friends. He lived with his stepfather named Dave Nelson whom all the kids referred to as D-Nelly.

D-Nelly was the most relatable and tolerant guardian of all of the boys, so Berk's home was often the hang-out spot both before and after his mother's demise. His stepfather was admired by his friends due to his lackadaisical and friendly parenting which could partially be attributed to his alcoholism of which Berk was somewhat ashamed.

There was Kelly Hannon, an athletic stoner who prided himself on getting into fights, arm wrestling, and things of that nature. His voice and speech were low and monotone. He wore tank-top shirts, which showed his muscles. Often, to his friends and those around him, Kelly seemed to have something to prove.

Tyler Jai was a shorter skinnier Indian boy whose parents were born in Mumbai. Upon coming to the United States to live, they had chosen American names to call their four children in order to allow them to better blend with American culture. Tyler's birth name was Aditya. But unlike Tyler's two sisters and one brother, his pseudonym took on a charming characteristic that his loving parents did not intend: when it was cut short, his first name rhymed with his last. And Tyler was almost never referred to as Tyler or simply Ty. It was nearly always "Ty Jai."

Besides Miles, Jake Armao was Cade's best friend. They were like brothers, having many sleepovers and sharing lots. Jake was tall and slender, had shaggy black hair he'd toss, and was the first one in the crew to drive a car. He grew up the poorest of his friends, his mother a nurse and his father a cook at a pizza joint. He had two brothers, one older and one younger. His home had three bedrooms and he slept in the basement with communal laundry machines.

Cade had discovered marijuana with Jake and they spent their adolescence and teen years smoking together. It was their livelihood for years until Cade turned toward alcohol, a vice for which Jake did not share the same stomach.

All of the boys smoked cigarettes.

"Yo, you got a smoke, Cade?" said Jake.

"Yeah." The two communicated via sly eye contact as to their secretive adventure into the spirit realm. They had begun to trip in the car ride to "the spot" which was a place that had proven to be an environment free of humans who might bother them with their underage drinking.

Jake drove as Cade sat shotgun. They had parked near a pine tree in the Buffalo suburb where they all lived. As long as they and their beer were undetected by the neighbors as they ran from the car to the land obscured from the street, they'd be home free for the night.

They moved swiftly to the abandoned train tracks and walked the grassy way to seclusion. After stashing the beer behind nearby bushes, they waited for police for twenty minutes. No cops had shown, so they cracked open the brew. Ambient with moonlight, stars, and isolation, "the spot" offered comfort to the five eighteen-year-old chums.

"Ty Jai, you tryna split this 12 with me, right?" said Kelly.

"Uh, yeah," said Ty. After pooling their money at the hood store, there were two twelve-packs of Labatt Blue bottles. And Cade had chosen two forty-ounce bottles of Olde English. They kept close tabs on who was drinking what.

"Berk, you got my lighter, yo?" said Jake.

"Yeah, I think so," said Berk as he finished urinating. "The spot is so awesome."

"Fuck yeah, it is," said Kelly.

Pretty soon they were all smoking and standing in a kind of circle.

The power lines at the spot ran across the night sky. There were gravel paths on either sign of the train tracks that met with grass that sparkled silver and white for Cade and Jake during their unusual journey.

The wind gave birth to the movements of the trees and grass that lingered for their eyes intertwining with the glow on the ground in symphonic cause and effect. It was in this holy place, away from cars and people and clocks, where a young man could really connect to something beautiful. And their fickle conversation was just shifting gears.

"...I don't think he was an actual retard. I think he just looked that way."

"I haven't had Old E in a short," said Kelly.

"How's it taste, Cade?" said Jake.

"Really great," he said, smiling.

"I had an Irish Car Bomb the other day," said Kelly.

"I have two questions," said Jake. "What is that and give it to me."

"It's Bailey's, Jameson, and Guinness. I was at McHeenan's downtown and Steve from the pizzeria got me one. You pour half a shot each and drop the shot glass in the Guinness and drink it real fast. First one to drink it wins. I won," said Kelly, taking a big swig of beer.

Jake's eyes met Cade's and the two laughed, triggering unanimity of high spirit. But when the other three stopped laughing, moving onto something else, Jake and Cade's eyes returned to each other reflecting the happy notion that their trip together was becoming more intense.

"Why is it called an Irish Car Bomb?" said Jake.

"Because there are car bombs in Irish-I mean Ireland," said Berk. "It's like, typical and shit."

"That's kinda fucked," said Jake. "I'd be pissed if I was Irish."

"Aren't you Irish?" said Ty.

"Yeah, but like real Irish," said Jake.

"What the hell is *real* Irish?" said Berk.

Jake remarked, "Like from Ireland. Imagine you live in Ireland where there's bombs that go off in cars and kill people and shit. Then you come to the USA and people are ordering Irish Car Bombs, laughing it up, trying to drink them the fastest. It would be like if people in Ireland had a World Trade Center shot."

"I never thought of it like that," said Kelly.

"Neither did I," said Jake, sipping his beer. "Oh wait, I just did."

Cade had ventured over to a more secluded area to urinate. As he strolled through the night air, what he envisioned shone as if he had a small lantern above his eyes, illuminating the ground before him.

He approached an area that separated low grass from tall and it looked as if the other side was a rushing river of green. It flowed to where he and his friends were that now seemed like an island. At first, he found himself fighting the hallucination, but stepped through the border of small bushes onto the river, half-thinking he'd wash away.

It felt as if he had walked into a different room. He stood and looked among the taller grass as it swayed with wind. Then, he peered into the sky. There were endless stars that were sparkling and shooting. He wondered if they were only moving so dramatically for him...and maybe Jake.

He found comfort in his temporary solitude but realized he ought to be getting back while his urinating took twice as long as usual. Plus, beer tasted differently than when he wasn't tripping and strangely unnecessary. He zipped his jeans and inhaled deeply to power his venture back to the fellowship when he heard Jake's voice, so close that he gasped and jumped.

"Dude! Whoa, this is nice in here! Like another world and shit!" Jake angled his back ever so slightly and began to urinate with no delay or hesitation at all.

"Dude, are you seeing this shit?!" said Cade.

"Aw, hell yeah, this is awesome!" said Jake. "Do you see all this fuckin' grass and shit?! Wow!" They rejoiced and laughed together in their shared trip before moving back to the others.

Ty walked toward Cade to get himself another beer and stopped to chat as Jake continued away. He twisted open a fresh one. "So how's it going at the Heltons? They treating you ok?"

"Yeah, it's cool," said Cade.

"Yeah? That's good," said Ty.

"It's a trip living with a family," said Cade.

"I'll bet," said Ty. "Not what you're used to."

"They like...have dinner together and stuff," said Cade.

"For now, you see the dark side," said Ty. "Are you sleeping ok?"

"Um, that's another thing for another time. I don't know what the hell is going on. I uh…"

Ty then noticed the odd size of Cade's pupils.

"Holy shit, are you tripping?!" said Ty.

"Ha, uh, yeah, me and Jake are," said Cade.

"Holy shit!" Ty began to whisper courteously to his friend, "How is it? Mushrooms or acid?"

"Really great, man," said Cade. "Acid. Green gels. Dude, it's so nice. Best tabs I've ever been on."

"Nice, nice," said Ty.

"I really wish you were tripping too, man," said Cade.

"Do you...have any more?" said Ty with his patented sinister smile.

"I wish, dude," said Cade, smiling. Their secretive conversation was interrupted by the uproar twenty feet away.

"Dude, are you tripping too, Cade?!" said Kelly.

"Uh, yeah," said Cade.

"Fuck!" said Kelly.

"They saw my eyes, bro. They know *everything*," said Jake.

"You guys...wouldn't...happen to...have...anymore, would you?" said Berk.

"All we had was two, man!" said Jake. "You two have been riding us since we got here! 'When are you gonna get us some acid, Jake?! How come you didn't bring us enough acid, Jake?! How come you aren't getting us more acid now, Jake?!'" he continued, inciting laughter.

As the energy of the group shifted, Cade realized that as the number of beers had dwindled, he still had almost half a forty in his hand and his second remained untouched. For reasons of practicality, he downed the one in his hand quickly. It was warm, but that didn't stop him. He opened his last and took a nice pull.

The trip took a turn now that the primary focus was on him and Jake. During the adjustment, Jake seemed to have no trouble. With Cade reeling, Jake took the liberty of doing a handstand to entertain his followers. He rolled around in the grass and as it nearly came off, he removed his shirt.

With that, he ran toward the power towers and did a cartwheel. Captivating his audience and reaching the tower that was about three hundred feet away, he jumped on it and began to climb. As the others seemed to be tickled by their squirrelly friend, Cade did not share the same enjoyment. Although he was somewhat confident that his friend would probably not be electrocuted, there was a healthy sliver of doubt.

They watched Jake climb for a moment and hang by his legs as if he were a kid on a jungle gym. In an instant, he ceased movement. Hanging nearly motionless with his back to his friends, entranced by something that could only be seen by him, he plopped down upon his feet. Transfixed, he kept staring.

"What is it?!" shouted Berk from a distance. Jake remained fascinated and silent with his back to the crew. The four began walking toward him to see what he could see. Berk swung on the tower mimicking his friend.

Upon gaining, they noticed that they were on higher ground which led to a kind of valley. And beneath them was a playground near a school. Suddenly, they didn't feel as isolated as they thought they were.

"Oh, shit, we must be behind Winston School," said Berk. "Whadaya know." He spoke of a private school in town. It was now easy to see what had captivated Jake so intently.

The fog was thicker around the playground which was next to a basketball court. Berk and Kelly noisily accelerated toward the discovery and the other three followed cautiously.

"Should I get the rest of the beer?" said Ty.

"Um, I don't—I'm not—I don't care," said Cade.

"Sure, Ty Jai," said Jake. "I'll go with you." Ty and Jake headed back and Cade moved forward out of obligation. He watched as Berk and Kelly hopped onto swings. Walking without purpose, Cade's discomfort increased with each step. He looked up at the sky and tried focusing on the stars again but couldn't find any.

"There's only one beer left!" said Ty, smiling. "Do you want it, Cade?"

"Um, no thanks," said Cade as he swigged hard from his warm forty.

"I'll give her a home," said Jake as he launched his empty, grabbed the last one, and twisted the cap.

"What are they up to?" said Ty, referring to Berk and Kelly who seemed to have lost interest in the swings. Kelly tried to pull a child's riding seahorse out of the ground with his might and eventually succeeded. Berk, noticing that the destruction had given Kelly pleasure, grabbed a rock from nearby and threw it at the windows of the school, missing the glass and hitting brick. "Berk!" shouted Ty. "Shit, man! What the fuck!" Berk and Kelly laughed as they romped amidst the playground.

There was a canvas structure there that they started to dismantle and destroy. Kelly took out a knife and started slashing. They laughed with glee as they vandalized the park, throwing stones at the school, connecting with glass which didn't shatter from the distant throws.

Frustrated, Berk ran up to the school after selecting a particularly large rock and threw it from point blank range, shattering the window. They both cackled with delight as the destruction gained momentum. The other three stood and watched.

"Oh my God," said Ty, who laughed fearfully as the third window shattered. "What. Oh my God. What are they doing?!" Cade wasn't so talkative. He stood mesmerized by his two companions whose only noticeable crime thus far was drinking illicitly. His mind refused to process what shone before him as it remained engulfed by worry.

As the grass glowed bright green like the tabs he and Jake had taken, the light projecting from the fixtures outside the school was breathing in and out, harmonious with the shadows.

The building, to Cade, transformed into a living being with a pulse that pumped before his eyes at which his friends, the determined killers, chipped away, stone by stone. The more glass they broke, the harder the building seemed to breathe and struggle.

"Dude, this is...cops could be here any second," said Ty.

The three stood watching as Berk and Kelly destroyed as many windows as they could. Ty took off running. Cade and Jake together processed the swiftness of their friend's body cutting through the night then turned back to the carnage. They both took up their beers and drank simultaneously then watched in silence.

Cade, with difficulty, pondered why a human would be so destructive. And he was perplexed as to how Berk and Kelly had gotten so drunk so fast. Having no desire to join, he found comfort that his trusted friend was standing next to him.

"I have to help them," said Jake who ran after the others, throwing stones and wreaking detriment.

Cade stood and watched with bitterness on his tongue and the crickets' sad song around him. He watched the building sigh and wither like an old dog who couldn't take any more of the beating while the moon illuminated the slaughter.

For relief, he finished the warm beer and tossed it gracefully to the side. Reaching into his pockets for his Camels, he pulled out a thick piece of paper that once served as the medium for the two green hits prepared by the man with the acid.

Forgetting what it was, he unfolded it and saw words, words that before, in haste, he hadn't noticed: *Romans 12:10: Love one another with brotherly affection. Outdo one another in showing honor.*

Lighting his second last smoke, he burned the paper to ashes, engulfed in deep, promiscuous thought.

At Heltons', Maureen was tidying the kitchen as Ray had left for work just after dawn. While her glance made it through the window to Cade's car, there was a sense of relief that he was home. She finished some cleaning and eating and walked upstairs to check on things, only to find the bedroom devoid of human presence.

Cade, Jake, Kelly, and Berk had spent the night in Berk's basement living space. D-Nelly had given the boys some purple weed and had a hit with them before going up to his bedroom. Kelly and Berk had fallen asleep as Cade and Jake stayed awake, fascinated by the large tapestry draped along the basement wall. They were out of cigarettes and were bumming from Berk's pack of Marb Reds as he slept. Smoking one at a time and sharing, the night offered pure comfort for the first time between the two as their friends slept silently.

Sharing a meager amount of cigarettes was something that Cade and Jake had been doing for years. They smoked without talking, passing cigs back and forth patiently and in fairness with each other while some music still played. Cade's hands were familiar to Jake and vice versa.

Their voices had been dormant for a while now, and after the second cigarette was smoked down to the butt, Jake spoke, "That tapestry is so fucking awesome." They both laughed, trying to contain the sound so as to not wake their friends. One can really become entranced within the designs of simple decor while tripping, while the requirement for a television or banal chatter will vanish.

"Are there any beers here?" said Cade.

"I don't think so," said Jake.

"Am I here?" said Cade.

"You tryin' to get more smokes and bounce?" said Jake.

"Yeah," said Cade. "You drivin'?"

"Yeah," said Jake.

The two cautiously stood amidst the smoke in the air without looking at their sleeping friends. They had left two cigarettes in the pack on the table.

Moving through the dangling beads that separated the furnished colorful section of the basement, they ascended the stairs just past the laundry machines.

The kitchen brought a dose of reality as the sun shone through the windows of the two-story home. Heading toward the front of the house, the two noticed Berk's stepdad laying on his back on the couch, shirt off and eyes closed. This unexpected vision paired with the sudden susceptibility to daylight disoriented Cade.

"You boys be careful," said the man abruptly from the couch with his eyes still closed.

"You too, D-Nelly," said Jake smoothly. "Thanks for the herb."

"They won't remember you," Cade heard.

"Dude, I wish my dad were half as cool as that guy," said Jake just after the swinging door closed behind them.

"Uh, hell yea," said Cade in a delayed response.

The two entered the old green Sentra with too many air fresheners. The more intimate environment brought relief and a sense of safety.

"You straight to drive?" said Cade.

"Straight as I'm gonna be," said Jake, lighting an old cig butt with about a half-inch of tobacco left.

"Is that clock right?" said Cade, looking at the radio which read 10:51.

"I don't know, and I don't care," said Jake, offering his friend some of his smoke with his hand.

"No, thanks," said Cade.

They cruised to the corner store which was open 24/7. Cade went in and got two packs of smokes: Camels for him, Marb Reds for Jake, and some water.

The store was a typical hub for Amherst police with time in abundance, but as a plus, there were no cops inside. The clerk barely made eye contact with Cade, still hallucinating, providing a relatively smooth in and out.

"Water! Nice," said Jake.

"Yeah," said Cade, twisting the cap of the solitary one-liter bottle and handing it to his friend who chugged a third and handed it back. Jake started the trek toward Helton's, a mere four-minute drive from his own pad.

The sun-kissed morning offered a pleasant cruise as not many cars were on the road. The streets were lined with garbage cans ready for emptying.

"Dude," said Jake. "I keep seeing manatees when I look at the trash cans and bags lined up."

"Manatees?" said Cade.

"Yeah, I'm not sure why," said Jake. "I saw them once and now I keep seeing them. The trash piles look like manatees!"

Cade readied his mind for a moment before looking to his right to see if he could identify with the unique hallucination of his friend.

When his sight met the dark objects positioned near the driveways, he recognized them as bludgeoned sea creatures stranded on land, desperate and in pain. The more houses that passed, the more intense the hallucinations became. His brain conceived the appearance of adult manatees made up of larger garbage masses surrounded by smaller sacks of trash that took the form of smaller, baby manatees. All writhed captive to the waterless air and bled as if there were a recent massacre by men with sharp weapons. Cade's mouth dried and his heart gained momentum as he took in the emotions of the babies. They squirmed and wiggled in confusion and mourning by the side of their procreators, becoming motionless in death. Cade looked away from the horror and chugged some water.

"Drop me at the park, yo," he said.

"All right," said Jake.

The park at the top of the hill was about a four-minute walk from Helton's house and it was a three-minute walk to Cade's previous home. This was the place where Jake and Cade used to sled in winter and where they smoked their first cigarette by the dumpsters. Both their collective along with Cade and Miles had seen the evolution of the playground from old rusty swings and slides to the newer, safer plastic equipment in the middle of soft mulch for padding.

Jake drove the car through the alley near the familiar dumpsters of the office buildings in front of the park. He stopped the car and they each lit a smoke. Cade was still suffering from the slaughter of the manatees.

"I don't want to go back yet," said Cade.

"That's cool, that's cool," said Jake. "You think Miles is home?"

"I don't even know what day it is," said Cade.

"Fuck days," said Jake.

"Yeah, days are stupid," said Cade.

"Does Sammie kick it over there a lot?" said Jake. Cade inhaled his smoke. "Yeah," he exhaled. "She does."

The boys were calm, speaking softly and slowly to each other. In sync, their deep voices and tempos were almost identical like usual. And being amidst a trip together, what had been a heavy trip together, considering the intense act of vandalism that had taken place, can make trust between friends thicker.

Both of the front windows all the way down, Jake blew smoke rings out of his window, saving the last two rings to show his friend as he turned to the right and shot them modestly across Cade's view. Cade followed the circles out of the car with his eyes until the morning air devoured them. There was no call for a congratulatory effort or acknowledgment of the impressive presentation as such a display of smoldering matter was commonplace to Cade's sight when accompanied by Jake.

"She's got such a hot ass," he said.

Although Sammie's body had been a redundant thought for years to Cade, he wondered how his friend could be thinking of sex at a time like this. "Yeah, she does," he said.

Sitting together mostly in silence, the two finished their smokes plus two more. Cade said goodbye to Jake and borrowed his sunglasses just before he exited the car. He walked from the alley into the park as Jake drove off. Weakened by social anxiety in anticipation of returning to Heltons', he decided to stay in the park and smoke for a while.

The sun shone brighter as a washed-out Cade sat on a bench overlooking the park with its mosaic of colorful monkey bars, swings, and slides. He watched crows fly and land and walk near him as if he weren't there. He wondered if he, himself, was there.

The sky, blue and white, seemed closer than it had ever been as his eyes hid behind his friend's cheap shades. A couple holding hands made their way from one side of the park to the next, avoiding looking in Cade's direction. He attributed this absence of acknowledgement to fear, which further prohibited his being comforted. He watched them for a moment, sensing that their walking together was labored, as if the deed were a caveat of one of the partners in order to breathe life into an otherwise dying relationship. And their steps were too much in unison.

"It's over," he said aloud to no one but himself and the blackbirds.

Waiting until the two were out of sight, he walked toward his childhood home and Heltons' place.

"Aup! Well, if it isn't Zombie Cade back from the dead!" Although he knew he'd get an earful, her presence alone in the big kitchen was comforting. "Where ya been?" she said with a grin, getting closer for what the teen predicted to be a kind of interrogation. Maureen fixed her eyes on Cade, who began to reflect her smile.

"Where have I been?" said Cade, still hallucinating and adjusting to the environment change. "Where *haven't* I been?" She initiated a hug which made him feel the need to cry almost instantly, a sensation that he tried to hide.

They held each other there in the big quiet kitchen. Wearing blue plaid pajamas, Maureen spoke softly to him as they continued to hold each other with her providing the pleasant physical dominance.

"Yeah? You been around town, sweetie?" Her gentle, sympathetic voice close to his ear was consoling. His body abandoned its hypertension, giving in to her embrace as was Maureen's intention.

"Yeah." His voice quivered. "Here and there." She brought her body closer and tightened her grip and he followed suit. The smell of her hair and clothes, and the closeness of her breath made Cade feel even more calm and emotionally vulnerable. The state that overcame him then was of nearly total relaxation. Quietly and softly, he cried as they held one another.

"You're gonna be all right, you know. You're my third son, ok? The son I never had. I loved your mom...*and* your dad, ok? Despite his faults," she paused. "And her faults too." Cade adjusted his head to submerge his eyes within Maureen's hair and neck. "Your mama was my favorite person." He cried harder and louder as Maureen tightened her grip.

Without regard to tears and mucus in abundance, neither mortal faltered in performing their respective cathartic duty. Alone and as one, the mother of three held the 18-year-old as if he had from her own womb descended.

Amidst the rare expression of Cade's lament, he felt the urge to say so much but most of his words failed as he sobbed them out in one incessant tumultuous utterance. In the thick of the noise, the only coherent phrase that Maureen could decipher while the boy moaned and wept was, *I don't know.* As she gently shushed and caressed his back and head, she tried to understand more of what Cade was saying. But all that she could undo from the blustering unveiling were the words, over and again, *I don't know.*

He settled some as he heard a faint creek on the kitchen floor in front of him. It was Major dragging his blanket slung over one shoulder. He went for the fridge and opened it without acknowledging his mother's and Cade's embrace which weakened a bit by his presence in the room. As Cade spooled from the breakdown, Maureen kissed him on the cheek and looked into his eyes.

With that, the back door opened and they heard Miles and Sammie, talking comfortably. With Cade's back to the entering couple, Maureen withdrew, doubling the space between their noses, holding his gaze with hers as they remained in physical union. She knew he'd be uncomfortable crying with his friends unexpectedly there.

Cade, at the mercy of her face like a guide, looked back into her soft dutiful eyes then downward to the freckles on her cheeks and across her nose. With his visionary path returning to hers, he admired her like a painting. His greyish blue surveillance then traveled along her short messy hair, almost consummately matching the dots above and below her unkempt brows then down along her cheeks to her subtle chin cleft. And finally back to her now shining and smiling caramel eyes.

Sammie entered before her boyfriend. "Hey, Mo!" she said. "'Sup Cade!"

"Hi, Sammie," said Maureen, still looking at her third son. The embrace weakened as Maureen moved her head to the right to share the same smile with Sammie who noticed that Cade was distraught and she, herself, became uncomfortable. Miles moseyed in and greeted his mom and friend. He too, processed that they had stumbled upon a heavy exchange of emotion but smoothly pretended not to notice.

"Hey," said Cade as Miles gently placed his hand on his friend's back as a half-greeting half-condolence. With Maureen intentionally drawing Miles' and Sammie's energy closer, her unspoken words signaled them to remain in the kitchen and the three formed a merger, giving Cade the opportunity to leave the room unaccompanied.

He exited the kitchen where his feet met the area rug in the hall and headed for the stairs. He put his fingers on the banister. Its contrast of shade and texture to his eye, seemed to be energized like drugged electricity running slowly up and down the wood, dark and light. His trip had made a comeback while his feet hit the runner carpet on the stairs and ascended past the cat walking in the opposite direction after a nap. Cade drank in the essence of the dispassionate feline making her way down the stairs and out of view. In that moment, the pleasant beast was a kind of idol to him.

He rounded the main flight and onto the shorter deck with three more stairs to go. It was quiet. He breathed slower while he opened the attic bedroom door and closed it almost entirely.

In need of solitude, he crept up the final stairwell with the knowledge that the vision of his own reflection would be emerging ahead of him in the window. The sight of which, like the cat had done, he avoided any head-on observation. He took off his shirt, pants, and socks and got acquainted with his mattress only fifteen feet from Miles' fancier bed.

The alarm clock that the boys shared said 11:55 am.

Cade started to relax. He remembered some Brandy he had stashed under his bed a few days ago and was comforted by the thought of it being there as daylight compounded playfully with the shadows of the room.

To his left, the shades that hung before the windows seemed to stir as if someone was twisting them open and closed ever so faintly. He thought he heard the door at the bottom of the stairs creak as if being opened, so he quickly went from side to supine and fixed his eyes on the ceiling fan spinning at its slowest setting.

He felt something getting closer. It was Miles who approached him directly.

"Dude," said Miles.

"Yeah, 'sup," said Cade.

"Telephone," said Miles as he handed over the portable device and left the room.

"Hello," said Cade.

"Yo," said Jake.

"What's up," said Cade.

"Yo, did the cops show up at Helton's place today?" said Jake.

"What?" said Cade. "No. Why."

"They hit up Berk's place this morning. Apparently, he dropped his ID last night and they found it. Kelly just called me and said cops might be on the way to my place. 'Cause apparently, what? ...hold on!" Jake shouted at someone in his household. "'Cause apparently cops found his ID by the towers, went to his house, and he and Kelly squealed on me or some shit, I don't know. And they got busted for breakin' all those windows and shit. And apparently they mentioned my name to cops." Cade heard Jake inhale from a smoke. "And I don't know if they mentioned your name too."

"Fuck," said Cade.

"Yeah, apparently those pussies got scared when 5-0 showed up, I don't know," said Jake.

"Ok," said Cade. And there was a long silent pause. "Are you still tripping?"

"Yup," said Jake. "You?"

"Yeah," said Cade.

"Fucking sucks," said Jake with his comforting laugh that Cade knew well.

"Yeah," said Cade.

"Oh, sweet, I think the cops are here," said Jake. "Awesome. Ok, I gotta go. I won't mention your name. If I was you, I would be on the lookout. Peace." With that, Jake hung up.

Cade maneuvered from laying on the bed to sitting. He reached under his mattress for the eight-dollar bottle of Brandy. Finishing what was left, he moved the container up and away from his lips and held it there for almost ten seconds, allowing the very last drops to fall into his mouth. He replaced the cap then put the bottle back in its hiding place.

6

———————

PREY

Miles and Sammie had taken a drive in Ray's black Cherokee as it started to rain. She had her feet up on the dashboard as reggae music played. Sammie was intent on telling Miles that she loved him on this ride.

She packed Miles' pipe that he typically placed under the tape deck, hardly disguising it each time that he got into the SUV and they got high. She liked to adoringly watch him while he drove and he didn't mind.

"You have dimples," she said, smiling.

"Uh, huh," Miles responded.

"You're pretty," said Sammie.

"So are you," said Miles, trying to contain the ego boost.

"We should eat," said Sammie. "Do you have money?"

"Uuuuuuuh, yeah, I think so," said Miles.

Digging through her bag, Sammie found the pack. She lit her last two Camel Lights, handing one to her partner. Before discarding the empty pack in her bag, she removed the *Camel Cash*, a blue note that was

80

placed in every pack of Camels between the cardboard and cellophane. Like always, she placed it in her wallet with the others, strengthening her long term objective.

"Where do you want to eat?" said Miles.

"Uuuuum, I don't know," said Sammie, concentrating on smoking.

Both kids wore sunglasses. With Sammie's feet on the dashboard, her inner-upper thighs were exposed and peeked through her light blue shorts. Her toenails were painted blue, including the one with a ring on it. She wore a white tank top with a Grateful Dead bear necklace that nearly matched her patchwork bag and the bears on *it*.

She ashed her cigarette and pulled down the visor to look at her face in the mirror. Her tinted blue half-lensed shades drooped down the bridge of her nose. She scanned her teeth and lips, up her nose, and eyes...her eyes that she underappreciated unlike everyone she met.

Miles peered slyly out of his periphery from behind his Ray Bans at her legs and thighs which were difficult to neglect. He wore faded jean shorts and a tie-dyed shirt.

"My dear, I exclaim, you have the nicest legs I've ever seen," he said.

"My...*dear*?" said Sammie, questioning the endearment.

"Yes!" he smiled.

"*Exclaim*?" said Sammie.

"I can exclaim!" said Miles.

"Sure ya can, buddy," said Sammie. She shorted her cigarette by meticulously flicking the cherry off so it landed safely out the window and grabbed the herb from the black and grey film canister. Miles sensing her movements, knew it'd be a good idea for him to short his cig as well and gracelessly introduced the new task to his agenda, along with maneuvering the steering wheel. Sammie, packing the pretty glass pipe, noticed him fumbling.

"I'll take that, chief," she said as she placed the goods on her thigh. In one fluid motion, she brought his cigarette with one hand to the open window and, catapulting her middle finger from her thumb, flicked the cherry off and outside. She put their two shorted smokes in the pack, lit the bud, and inhaled deeply. Then she passed both lighter and pipe to Miles who, making use of both hands, steered with his knee. Sammie looked away from her boyfriend and exhaled into her reflection on the side-view mirror. She liked the way she looked exhaling smoke.

Miles hit it and coughed, swiftly handing it to Sammie, freeing his palms and fingers. He hacked so hard that saliva shot out onto his knuckles and the glass concealing the speedometer.

"Fuck," he said when he could.

"That's the stuff, boy-o," said Sammie, carelessly taking a second hit while peering at Miles who was still coughing. He saw through his hindered vision that they were about to be passed by a Town of Amherst squad car.

"Dude 5-0!" said Miles. The cop passed and he watched intently from his rearview mirror.

"Dude?" said Sammie. "What?"

"That was a cop that just passed us!" he said as he gained confidence that the officer was almost out of sight behind him. "Hold the bowl a little more downward." Displaying the smoldering pipe while lowering the pitch of her voice and emulating a proud rapper, Sammie said, inducing relaxation within Miles, "Dude, fuck cops. These cops can't see me! I'm rollin' round, smokin' weed! I own this fuckin' city!"

The two continued driving until they stopped at a diner boasting a *99 cent breakfast* sign. Just after finishing the bowl, the last of their weed, they eagerly lit their shorted cigarettes and relaxed in the smoky car.

"I am *so* high," said Miles.

"Really?" said Sammie. She turned to face him. He grinned and fixated at something outside of his window then superfluously flicked his cigarette over and over as she watched him from a cozy sideways position in the passenger seat. She circled her index finger about his knee slowly while he ignored the touch and sang to the reggae music. He turned and faced Sammie, meeting her eyes with his then tapped on her finger still stroking his leg and sang loudly. Her body abandoned its position akin to amorously watching him and took on a more traditional one.

"I'm starving," she said.

"I'm high," said Miles.

"Yeah, I got that," said Sammie as she opened her car door bound for the front of the diner. Miles followed to her side.

"You got money?" Sammie said.

"Yeah, I think so," said Miles.

They ate and left a meager tip before running into some friends who informed them that they had heard Kelly Hannon and Jon Berkeley had been arrested for vandalizing property at Winston school.

In the room with curtains drawn to defend the sun's prey from the assault, the noise from the ceiling fan had bored a hole into Cade's mind. Its repetitive motion created a maddening sound that resembled an odd intrusive presence. It was a multiple-hearted union of voices bearing a message of conspiracy with its focus on the only human in the room laying on his back with eyes wide open. The room kept the source of the attack secret.

Cade, who had fallen in and out of sleep for two hours, now lay victim to the fan, oblivious to its sole responsibility for the imperceptible presence of beings trespassing upon him through whispers. He looked about the room with eyes darting to the window blinds as a trusty informant of whether or not he was still tripping. The blinds were motionless. As he stood from the bed and walked downstairs, the noise faded, providing relief yet fear of the potential return.

He entered the bathroom and sat on the toilet lid. After closing the blind, he turned on the cold water and let it run. He disassembled a skin razor and held the blade in front of his eyes before stroking the skin on his hand with it, cutting into his palm. He made an X while he watched the skin open turning white then pink then red with blood.

He made a vertical line through the X before closing his fist, frustrated, and squeezing the blade into his palm. Before using the toilet for its intrinsic purpose, he discarded the blade and squeezed some toilet paper to help stop the bleeding.

Wandering back up the stairs and being met with the return of the meddlesome sound, he lay on his bed confused and afraid.

The blades of the fan spun round the sturdy center. The watcher's vision blurred completely, an alteration that at first diminished the fear, then left him feeling more vulnerable. He refocused his eyes and listened hard for what the voices were saying.

Although he was sure of the auditory presence sounding like humans whispering rapidly, the words were indiscernible as multiple entities seemed to emit their own conversation in dissonance simultaneously with the others. This realization changed his mind. He no longer thought that the voices were conversing with each other about him, but rather, they were all speaking *to* him at the same time. Staring at the fan, he listened, attempting ineffectively to decipher a message in the haze.

He tried latching onto one voice and following it like he would select and follow the bassline of a song, but failed to perceive a clear message other than the abstract malevolence.

A paragon, he tried with all that he had. Cade believed that if he could understand what one of the invisible apparitions were trying to convey, the voices would stop as if maybe they were on his side despite the evil air all around him. But the harder he tried, the louder it became and the stronger the confusion ate at him.

Conceding, he put pillows, one in each hand, over each ear, his eyes still on the guilty fan. As the voices faded, he felt a physical presence coming closer. His body hair shot up along with his pulse.

Repositioning from his back to his left side, he turned away from the staircase still holding the pillows to his head. This childlike act of blinding himself to what could be entering accelerated his fear but he wanted to hide.

His eyes now fixed on the windows on the far side of the room and as the thing got closer, he was able to confirm that it *was* coming from behind. He cringed. His hands took on a form like talons and shook. Similarly, his toes separated from each other and buckled and vibrated. His mind convinced itself of its helplessness. And to a voluntary paralysis, he gave in.

"Yo, Cade."

"Yo," said Cade.

It was Tyler. Cade turned to greet him. Still hearing the voices, his body began to decompress.

"Can I turn on a light?"

"Yeah, sure," said Cade. Unaware of which switch worked the light, Ty fiddled with one of the four knobs on the wall. By ill purpose, he turned off the fan and the voices Cade heard slowed and stopped. Without either human knowing that the fan had stopped circling, Ty located the knob for the light and turned it up and dimly on. Sensing that his friend was uncomfortable, he approached Cade slowly.

"'Sup yo," said Ty.

"Ty Jai, my brother, why don't you have a seat." Cade calmly beckoned him to a space on his bed. "Tell me about your day."

Ty smiled, sat, and exhaled. "My day?" he said.

"Yes, Ty Jai, your day."

"Well, thought I'd see what you were up to. Maybe you wanna get some grub."

"Do you know what day it is?" said Cade.

"Um, is it your birthday?" said Ty.

"What? I don't think so," said Cade. "Shit, maybe it is." Ty was amused by Cade's typical embracing of the high life. Although he admired the heart and mind of his friend, he viewed Cade as a guy who could handle his drinking and drugging well, a characteristic he envied yet found humorous.

"Well, when is your birthday?" said Ty.

"It's in October. I remember because that's about when I found my mother in a pool of blood and shit," said Cade, meeting his friend's eyes with a grin which was reflected with compassionate laughter.

"Then it's not your birthday," said Ty. "If it were, I'd get you something nice."

"Who's here?" said Cade.

"Maureen let me in," said Ty. "I didn't see anyone else. Have you slept?"

"I, uh, I'm not sure," said Cade.

"You're not sure?" said Ty. "How are you not sure?!"

"It's strange," said Cade. "You ever feel like there's somebody here?"

"Like, you're not alone?" said Ty.

"Yeah," said Cade. "Like if there…were…people who you didn't know were there?"

"Sounds like paranoia," said Ty. "I get like that when I smoke too much. Or just smoke at all. Like at school and shit."

"Yeah," said Cade. "Do you ever get paranoid by yourself? Like when no one's around?"

"Nah, I don't think so," said Ty. "How can somebody be paranoid while alone?"

"Yeah," said Cade. "Me too. Guess I'm just having some trouble sleeping."

"Yeah, dude," said Ty. "You're in a new place. You're living with a family now. I bet that shit's kinda weird."

"Yeah," said Cade.

"This room is dope, though," said Ty. "You wanna play pool?"

Reeling from the strange attack, he knew his own hands would shake, so he didn't want to play. Cade was comfortable with telling Ty *no* which was a strength he lacked around many others.

"No, thanks," he said.

"WHASSUP, NIGGAZ," said Sammie, entering. "Damn, I'm not interrupting anything, am I?" She passed Tyler and playfully roughed up his hair. Cade eyed her backside as she swiftly walked past the pool table and leapt on Miles' bed.

"'Sup, Sam," said Cade.

"Yo, you wanna play pool?" said Ty.

"Sure, Ty Jai. I'm stoned!" she said. "Sooo, Berk and Kelly." She stood and comfortably strode around the pool table from one end to the other, taking the cue from Ty's hands. "I wanna break," she said as Ty went to the other side to rack. "UM, HELLOOO!! What the hell happened?!" said Sammie with her eyes on Cade. Did you guys get busted?"

"Um, well, um—"

"*We* didn't get busted...yet," interrupted Ty.

"Yet?!" said Sammie. "Holy shit. Are you guys wanted or something?! And why isn't there any music playing? What's in the CD player, Ty Jai?"

"Um, Bob Dylan," said Ty.

"Take it out and put in something else, would ya?" said Sammie. She turned on the ceiling fan. A moment later, Ty had switched discs and music began to play.

"So what happened?" she said eagerly, connecting with Cade. Amidst the beam of eye contact, both felt their spirits weaken.

"We fucked—we were all hangin' at Winston school last night—was it last night? ...and they fucked up the building and shit by throwing rocks," said Cade. "It was pretty...intense. Jake said cops found Berk's ID at the scene 'cause he dropped it or something."

"How come you two aren't arrested?" said Sammie.

"They have no idea we were there unless someone tells them," said Cade. "Ty Jai bounced mad early, and I was tripping so I didn't do—"

"You were tripping?!" said Sammie.

"Yeah, me and Jake were," said Cade.

"Acid or mushrooms?" she said.

"Acid. Green gels," said Cade. "Holeeee shit." They heard the door open at the bottom of the stairs.

"Why did they vandalize shit?" said Sammie.

"Cade." Maureen's voice was stern and fatigued.

"Yeah, Maureen," said Cade.

"Come down here, please." At that moment, Miles entered from the staircase. The two old friends passed each other.

"'Sup, dude," said Miles. "Cops were here but my mom sent 'em packin'."

Having a troublesome time processing that, Cade descended the stairs to the waiting eyes of Maureen.

THAT HOT AND BREEZY night, Miles and Sammie went out for a drive. Passing common Maple and Red Oak trees, they cruised up Eggert Road past Saint Benedict's School where Sammie had attended during her elementary years.

"There it is," said Miles from behind the wheel. "Your alma mater."

"*Fuck* that place," said Sammie, abandoning her pipe-packing task to her lap so she could extend both her middle fingers at the building.

"That'll show 'em," said Miles.

"Fuckin' nuns," said Sammie.

"What was Catholic school like?" said Miles.

"Fucked up and lame," said Sammie.

"Is that so?" said Miles.

"It *is*," said Sammie, increasing her pitch before lighting the bowl and inhaling.

"What was Cade like at Saint Ben's?" said Miles.

"Cade? I don't know." She passed the pipe. "He got into trouble." Miles, steering with his knee, lit and inhaled intermittently then veered toward the curb before regaining control.

"Easy, chief," said Sammie without any real discomfort. He passed back.

"You guys were classmates?" said Miles.

"Yup. Since kindergarten," said Sammie who then turned, gazed at Miles, and smiled. "First kiss, ya know."

"What?" said Miles. She kept looking at him as her smile grew until it was bright white.

"Cade. He was my first kiss," she said. She let the silent moment pass. "And I his," she added, still smiling with laughter imminent.

"Really?" Miles said, as his partner laughed loudly.

"Yeah, man!" said Sammie. "We dated in grade school."

"Whoa!" said Miles. "What was that like?"

"I don't know," said Sammie. "He was hot. I was hot. It was a match made in heaven." They laughed and smoked. "He kissed me right over…. there!" she said, pointing at her friend Katie's house as they drove by it on Main Street.

"At Katie's?" said Miles.

"Yeah, on the hammock," said Sammie. "It was traumatizing."

"What?!" said Miles.

She inhaled and spoke with lowered pitch. "It was one of the weirdest experiences of my life," she exhaled.

"Why?" said Miles.

"He shoved his tongue down my throat like he was trying to suffocate me. I couldn't wait for it to be over. It was brutal. It was difficult to look him in the eyes the next day."

"Oh my God!"

"Yes. I could feel his hard-on poking through his pants. I think they were Nylon. Nylon basketball pants. He humped me a little while he was doing it. But I think it was a hump that he didn't have control over, ya know?"

"Like a dog?" said Miles.

"Yeah. Like a dog," said Sammie. "Where ya headed, kielbasa?"

"I don't know," Miles said as he steered the car past the homes of wealth on Lebrun Road. "Damn, I had no idea."

"He was scared," said Sammie pensively. "I never knew that until right now."

"How long were you together for?" said Miles.

"I dunno. Four months," said Sammie. "Those were the days. Those were the wacked out days."

Miles was still processing the unexpected info as the bowl pack reduced itself to white ash that Sammie tapped onto her palm and blew out through the window. She unbuckled her seatbelt and put her head on Miles' shoulder. "We were kids," she said, closing her eyes and placing her hand on Miles' lap. "We were stupid kids."

They drove aimlessly down side streets lined with American Foursquare houses, becoming silent and restful. Sammie's eyes converted to half-open, hardly blinking. Her lips moved to the music faintly. She was comfortable and stoned, remembering her kiss with Cade as children in adolescence.

She thought of the way the hammock felt against her body. It had been a summer night not unlike this one. She could see the stars. The setting was perfect. A huge fenced-in yard where they felt alone. She was excited to be kissed. And while their mouths engaged each other and she struggled to keep pace with her bumbling lover, the aspect that kept her from feeling victimized was his lack of devious intention. And the kiss goodbye, also without subtlety, blended with the making out in a way which left her confused and disappointed. And when she returned to her eager friend awaiting news of the first kiss, the cumbersome moment was bandaged with honesty and laughter.

Miles saw, in his rearview mirror, a police squad car turn onto the same road as them. It accelerated.

"I've been meaning to tell you something," said Sammie softly. Their heart beats quickened, Miles' faster than hers.

"There's a cop behind us," said Miles.

"Fuck him," said Sammie.

"He's pretty close," said Miles.

"I'm pretty high," said Sammie.

"Shit," said Miles. The darkness of their cozy vehicle was at once devoured by light.

"Shit, dude, what the fuck," said Sammie.

"I don't fuckin' know." Miles quivered while he spoke, steering the car to the side of the road. The cop car was so close that Miles was surprised there hadn't been a collision yet. Sammie reached for the seatbelt slowly and inconspicuously. She put down the visor to see herself.

"Fuck, I look so stoned!" she whispered loudly. Miles shushed her, barely getting the sound out from his lips. He did not have a dry mouth until this moment.

To his left, the approaching officer's presence was felt, not heard or seen, by Miles. He adjusted his neck to greet him. Making eye contact, Miles' neck and vision strained. Sensing fear, the cop said nothing.

Before a word was spoken, a flashlight illuminated the ground around Sammie's legs and feet. Then came the flashlight from the left, invading Miles' lap. Miles abandoned the task of making eye contact and looked forward.

"Hands."

"What?" said Miles.

"Hands." Miles extended both hands out through his open window.

The light from the right perused the back seat then up through the middle console and onto Miles' face stealing his vision.

"Put your hands on the wheel." The officer to the right of Sammie moved his flashlight up Sammie's body to her cheek and chest. He spat on the ground. She turned to look at him. Her face illuminated. Her eyes closed.

"License."

The rudimentary demand was not anticipated by Miles as he took out his wallet and, trembling, displayed it for the officer who let the teenager's hand quiver visibly before taking it.

"Where are you coming from tonight?"

"My house," said Miles.

"Where's your house?"

"It's on my ID," said Miles.

"Did I ask you about your ID?! I said where's your house."

"Hendricks. 342," said Miles.

"Had anything to drink tonight?"

"No, not at all," said Miles.

"Where ya headed this evening?"

"Just...nowhere," said Miles.

"Just *nowhere?* You don't say."

"Just out for a drive," said Miles.

"Just out for a drive?"

"Yes," said Miles.

"What about your little girlfriend. Has she had anything to drink?"

"No," they said.

"Ok, Miles, tell ya what I'm gonna do, if you give me the pot, I won't arrest you, but when I search the car, and I find it, I'll arrest you. Do you understand?"

"Yes," said Miles as he turned toward Sammie and asked her for the rest. She reached into her purse and handed him just over a gram of cannabis in a sandwich bag. The officer to her right who had positioned his flashlight to shine on her hands turned and headed back to the squad car providing a sense of relief for Sammie. Miles handed over the bag.

"Anything else?"

"That's it," said Miles.

"What about that?" said the cop as he pointed his flashlight under the radio to the glass pipe.

"Oh, just the bowl," said Miles, handing it over.

The cop shone his light, inspecting it. "Sit tight," he said and walked to the rear of the jeep and placed the weed and the glass on the hood of his vehicle.

More cops showed up. There were two more squad cars convening behind the original one. Finally, a third. They communicated with each other as Miles and Sammie had a moment to themselves.

"Dude," said Sammie. "What's gonna happen?"

"I don't know," said Miles.

"There was a cop to my right," said Sammie. "I think he had his hand on his gun, but I couldn't look."

"Yeah," said Miles. "It's ok."

"Dude, I'm fucked if I get arrested," said Sammie. "My dad will kill me."

"I think you'll be fine," said Miles, regaining his composure. "I'll take the blame."

Sammie took ahold of his forearm and looked at her partner's face. He peered straight ahead of him.

"My cop's pants are too tight," said Sammie.

Miles' focus redirected to her and they smiled with each other. Police approached the vehicle with their flashlights again.

"Step out of the car, Miles." He guided him to the rear of the jeep where the others were waiting. "Keep your hands at your sides." They searched him vaguely, found nothing incriminating besides rolling papers, and put him in the rear squad car.

"Let's see your ID," said another cop to Sammie. Unprepared and afraid, she reached into her bag and fumbled for her wallet. "What else you got in there, little lady?"

"Just my wallet and shit," said Sammie.

"*Whoa*. You wanna not swear when you're in the presence of an officer?!" Two more came toward the car, one on the right and one on the left.

"You should hear the mouth on this girl," he said to his approaching coworker. The cop on the right opened the driver's side door and began searching.

"Step on out, little lady." They watched her exit, shining their flashlights on her legs and hips. The dominant one's lower jaw protruded and he salivated. Another confidently strolled to greet Sammie and took her ID from his coworker.

"Where's the rest of the pot, Samantha?" he said.

"What?" she said.

"Turn out your pockets," he said as he fiddled with her shorts that were quite visibly, due to their size and binding tension, containing nothing.

"There is no more," said Sammie. "We gave it to you."

"Come on. Where's the rest?"

"Miles says you have the rest of the pot."

"What?" said Sammie.

"You're shakin' like a leaf. Is the pot in the car? What are you so afraid of? You gettin' anything, Bill?"

"No, not yet," said the cop, searching the car.

"Go help him," he said as another joined in the quest inside the jeep. The dominant cop stroked Sammie's hair, an action she attributed to looking for a joint hidden behind her ear.

"Ya been drinkin'?"

"No," said Sammie.

"What about Miles?"

"No," said Sammie.

"Where are you headed?"

"Just out for a drive?" she said.

"Just out for a drive. Whereja get the pot?"

"I don't know," she said. "A friend?"

"A friend. This friend got a name?"

"I don't know," said Sammie.

"You don't know. You don't know your friend's name?" The speaking officer bent down and unbuckled her sandals. "What kind of friend doesn't know her friend's names? What do you call him when you buy your pot, Samantha? Michael?" He stood. He stared at her, chewing his gum rapidly, his voice escalating in volume and tempo. "Jermaine? Tito?" He broke gaze and looked upward, nearly stuttering, "Janet?" He returned to squatting and removed her sandals. She heard a car drive slowly behind as her sight took in the darkened green field ahead and to each side. "You go to high school?"

"I graduated last year," Sammie said.

"So where did you get the weed?"

"I don't fucking know!" she said in honesty as her eyes began to well.

"You swear one more time, little lady, and we're takin' you in just like yer little boy toy. Now turn around. Where's the pot." He felt inside her back pockets, becoming lustful. "Bill, you find anything in the car?"

"No."

"You sure?!"

"Yep!"

The strongest adversary lowered his volume, "I just gotta check you out to make sure you're bein' honest with me, little lady. Turn around. Hands on the car." He unbuttoned her shorts, unzipped the fly, and shimmied them to the ground. "Open your legs." He ran his hand up and between her thighs and over her underwear while his coworker shined the light. Her ears processed his breath and the casual clicking of his tongue to the roof of his mouth while he sang a little tune with *doo*s and *da*s.

He pulled her underwear down to her ankles.

"Spread 'em," he said. "Little more. C'mon, little lady, little more." He pushed the middle of her back toward the jeep as her feet moved consequentially. "Keep your feet still." He eased her back toward the jeep again. "I said, keep your feet planted." He held her hips with each hand and slid his right to the middle of her back and pushed forward. "Keep those hands on the car, little lady. Now...spread your feet." He ran his hand along her vulva, searching for her vaginal opening, and put his index finger all the way in as she restrained. After withdrawing, in one motion, he put the same finger in past her anus and into her rectum. "Easy there. As soon as you ease up, this will all be over. I gotta feel inside here, little lady." She relaxed her posterior and he slid his finger as high as it could go. He withdrew, turned round, took several steps to his coworker with the flashlight, placed his finger under his nose, and smiled.

"You better have a look," he said as he took the flashlight. His companion repeated the process although this time, the perpetrator used his hands to hold and spread each of her buttocks before penetrating both cavities simultaneously with his thumb and forefinger.

"Get dressed. You think you can get this car home?"

"I said you think you can get this car home?"

"Yes," she said like the living dead as she buttoned her shorts.

They all returned to their respective cars except for Miles, whom they hauled away.

Sammie drove to Helton's and parked the jeep up the long driveway. She walked in through the mudroom and saw Major with his blanket over one shoulder looking into the refrigerator.

"Hi, Sammie," said Major.

"Hi, Major," she smiled. Before ascending the stairs, she acknowledged the noise from the television and poked her head around the wall jamb, seeing Mary.

"'Sup Mair," she said.

"Hi, Sammie," said Mary.

Moving up the stairs, she felt and heard the presence of Ray and Maureen in their bedroom, almost asleep.

She informed them that Miles was taken to jail for possession of marijuana after the traffic stop, omitting the lascivious details. After speaking for a spell, the police were called via the non-emergency number in the phonebook. Ray did the talking as Maureen was in tears.

They drove to the station where the information was passed along: Miles Helton, 18 years old, detained and arrested for possession of black tar heroin.

Sammie, after the morose conversation with Ray and Mo, opened the attic bedroom door to Miles' and Cade's shared room. Her feet moved gracefully, meeting the top of the stairs, and she traveled forward within the familiar place underneath the ceiling fans and dim lights. Cade laid atop his mattress awake, seeing Sammie appear strangely. Ghostlike, she sat on his bed and lay down on her side.

Not a word was spoken as she maneuvered her back to Cade's chest, took his arm, and placed it over her body. He held her there. It wasn't until Cade became the least bit comfortable inside this enigma that she took notice of music playing.

"What's this?" she said.

Cade responded with delay, "Floyd."

"I like it," she said softly.

"Me too," he said.

7

NO LUCK WITH FROGS

"You should be treatin' me like a your highness!" said Sammie, strutting along the middle of the street with the ends of her scarf in each hand, hammocking the back of her head.

"A *your highness?*" said Miles.

"Yes!" she said.

"You'll always be a your highness to me, Sammie," said Cade.

"I know! Good!" she said, altering the scarf's position to her lower back and bottom, tugging left to right. The intoxicated posse of three meandered through the suburb streets. Miles and Cade watched Sammie lead taking long, at times provocative, strides. Cade lit a bowl and tried passing it to Miles.

"Drug court, bra," he said.

"Oh shit, I forgot," said Cade.

"I ain't in drug court, pass that shit ova here, nigga!" said Sammie.

Ray and Maureen had afforded an excellent lawyer for their son who had the false possession charge reduced to a misdemeanor. *Drug*

Court was an alternative to real jail time with the caveat of him going to meetings and having his urine tested regularly. However, the truth was made clear as the rapport between Miles and his parents was no match for the lies of the police.

But the charge still stood. And the minutiae of the physical atrocity remained unknown as Sammie uttered not a word against her unscathed assailants to anyone.

She exhaled a plume of smoke unabashedly from her path in the middle of the street. Her feet stopped short noisily with a *clip CLAP* of her sandals stomping the pavement as she waited for the boys to catch up to her.

She passed it to Cade who underwent a more careful ritual of looking around before he struck the lighter and burned the flower. Sammie sped and did a cartwheel right there on the street without concern for her pantless attire.

"Whoa, darlin! You'll show that perfect body to the whole neighborhood!" said Miles.

"I'm wearin' underpants!" she said.

"We know," laughed Miles. "They're green and sexy."

"It's not like it's anything that everybody hasn't already seen," she said.

"What?!" said Miles.

"Just kidding, baby," she said as she stopped and turned, waiting for Miles to reach her. They kissed for a good moment as Cade kept forward. Catching up to him, the three walked together laterally.

"Has Cade seen?" said Miles smiling.

"No, he didn't get that far," said Sammie, grinning as she extended her head forward from the right and observed Cade blushing.

"No, indeed I didn't," said Cade. Sammie laughed a loud one-syllable sound feeling, in a way, esteemed.

"Yeah, I didn't know you guys dated in grade school, bro," said Miles.

"Yeah, we did," said Cade.

"First kiss," said Sammie.

"Wasn't *my* first kiss," said Cade, feeling pressured to speak again.

"WHAT?!" said Sammie. "What the *hell* are you talking about?!

"I don't know," said Cade.

"Bullshit, ass face!" she said as she hustled over to his side, her demeanor happy and engaged.

"I'm just sayin'," said Cade. "How would *you* know who I kissed?" As they proceeded up the road, she got in front of Cade and walked backward. Her accusing eyes set in on him, caught between a place of fun and betrayal.

"Who could've you kissed?!" said Sammie.

"No one," said Cade. "I mean…"

"Who?" said Sammie. "Jake?! Did you two experiment before we dated?"

"No!" said Cade.

"I bet yes!" said Sammie.

"You'd bet wrong," said Cade.

"I'd bet gay!" said Sammie. Cade's eyes wandered with anxiety, his high turned around some. "Yeah, that's what I thought!" she added. Sensing the discomfort of her friend, Sammie relocated his eyes with hers, smiling.

"I—"

"Yeah, you were my first kiss or yer gay," she said.

"I'd just go with it, bro," said Miles.

"Seriously, was I your first?" said Sammie, without smiling.

"Yes," said Cade.

"I knew it," she said. "You're gay."

They happened across some folks in a parking lot.

"Microphone check, one, two, what is this?!" said Sammie.

"Who is that...Sammie?" a voice said.

"Uh, yeallo," she said.

"Wanna sign my hat, Sammie?" said another.

"Rolondo. 'Sup, man," she said. "Sure. What are you guys doin'?"

"Here. Don't put a marijuana leaf on there. That's what everybody does." Sammie, murmuring to herself, wrote on his brim with his pen and put it on his head, covering his eyes. He took it off and read: "*Stay high. Sammie 2002....* Stay high?"

"What, you said no weed leaves," said Sammie. "I did words instead. Word leaf."

"*Stay high?*"

"Yeah," said Sammie. "That's good advice."

"'Sup, Miles, I heard you got popped by 5-0."

"Yeah, it was some bullshit," said Miles.

"They didn't just take your stash and let you go?"

"No, they said they would," said Miles.

"Damn, that's fucked up, man. You just got possession? Was it less than an ounce?"

"Something like that," said Miles.

"My brother's house got raided. Over fifty plants. They even killed his dog. Smacked his girlfriend around."

"They *killed* his *dog,*" said Sammie. "Where? When?"

"Last month. Ashland Avenue. Behind Elmwood."

"They get his weed?" said Sammie.

"Over fifty plants." Sammie's face turned ill.

"'Sup Cade."

"'Sup," said Cade.

"You wanna hit this dust?" Cade reached for it instinctively.

"You don't wanna hit that, dude," said Sammie lowly.

"Uh...nah," said Cade.

"Ok, mommy," said Rolondo.

"No one wants your stupid dust, Edgar," said Sammie.

"It's weed too!" said Edgar.

"Cool," said Sammie. "Great work." Her demeanor changed again. "What kind of dog did your brother have?"

"Pit," he spat on the ground. "Pompeii."

"What?" said Sammie.

"Her name was Pompeii. She was a sweetie."

"Did she attack the cops?" said Sammie.

"Nah. They didn't have to kill her. They broke down the door and came in. My brother said she barked and growled and shit. They shot 'er twice. A bullet went through the floor and into the basement."

"Did it hit anybody?" said Sammie, wide-eyed.

"Nah. Fuckin' pigs."

"What happened to your brother?" said Sammie.

"I don't know."

"You don't *know?*" said Sammie. "What do you mean, you don't know?"

"Busted, bitch!" Sammie stared back at him blankly, taken aback while her jaw dropped a little.

"Life is pain," said Cade.

The group went silent as everyone looked at Cade looking at Edgar.

"Yeah it is," said Edgar, spitting. "Damn, Cade, anybody ever tell you you're intense as fuck?"

"Uh…" he uttered, worried. Sammie positioned herself next to Cade and put her arm around him. Her full lips smacked his cheek then she smiled at Rolondo and Edgar, "He was my first kiss."

The trio moved onward after Sammie assertively ended the conversation and hugged the two older boys without them standing to meet her embrace.

They stopped at another friend's. Sammie, as gregarious as the breeze, made entering the party easy.

They ate mushrooms and continued drinking throughout the night. There, Sammie was more tactile and intimate with her partner Miles, but the two never diverted socially from their friend, Cade.

A cocktail of confusion and admiration, Cade witnessed Miles' smooth calm demeanor especially while Sammie was getting attention from other men. Cade's mind exemplified men, even women, checking out Sammie's body and the drunker they were, the more obvious and blunt the visual intrusions. And Miles didn't seem to care or even notice.

Cade, the same age as Sammie *and* Miles, had never had a true relationship with a girl throughout high school. And although he was well-liked by many, he did not visualize himself as anyone worthy of a relationship, a lifestyle that he both desired and feared. And Miles, who seemingly succeeded in everything he did both socially and academically, intimidated Cade. And this night, through hallucinating and blurred eyes, both friends and strangers acknowledging Sammie's form was taken as invasive and angered Cade. And his jealousy, amplified by Miles' indifference, reared its head more powerfully than it had in the past. Cade struggled to keep these emotions hidden, unaware that Miles was suffering just as much as he was, tormented by the same demons, only better at pretending.

The threesome set out to Sammie's house after the shindig as she told the crew her father would be gone. The three walked, now stumbling, through the suburban streets, engaged in the lull of alcohol garnished by the caress of psilocybin. The new outdoor environment free from pressured conversation with their peers offered a new, refreshing path. And this one was alive and guided by the moon's awesome light and essence.

"OH MY!" said Sammie. "IT FEELS SO GOOD OUT HERE!"

"Dude," said Miles. "I wanted to get out of there so bad towards the end."

"Why did we go there in the first place?!" said Sammie.

"I don't know," said Miles, smiling. "I thought *you* did."

"Reed had fungus!" said Sammie.

"Meeb had mungus!" said Cade. They no longer hungered for the privacy they now reveled in and laughed into each other's trustworthy eyes. Sammie spun swiftly, arms extended high, as if dancing, and stopped short, letting her scarf graze the street behind her. Then she pulled it upward upon her butt, raising her skirt up to her lower back before allowing it to fall again. She wrapped it around her shoulders tightly as if it were a cold night and felt, for a pleasant moment, cocooned within its confinement.

"I don't know if I've ever told you this, but you in that scarf is awesome," said Cade. She strutted, grinning.

"Her *and* the scarf or her *in* the scarf?" said Miles.

"Um shit…her and…I don't know. She looks awesome," said Cade.

"He said 'me *in* the scarf,'" added Sammie, happily biting her lip then going ear-to-ear.

"Your smile is amazing," said Miles, kissing her.

"I know," she said neutrally.

"The air feels…like…water," said Cade.

"The air *is* water!" said Sammie.

"Isn't that humidity?" said Miles.

"What?" said Cade.

"Check out schoolboy over here," said Sammie.

The sight of the busier Eggert Road ahead infiltrated their minds, tweaking the illusion of solitude. Headlights shown from a person starting their car several driveways ahead.

"Whoa," said Cade. "Human."

"Indeed," said Sammie. The group consolidated as fun diminished and they became quieter.

"What do you think he's doing?" said Cade. The man's eyes acknowledged the three. Then he pulled out of the driveway and took off.

"I have no idea," said Sammie. "Being a human?"

"I don't like the idea that other people are in the world," said Cade.

"Me neither," said Sammie. "They have no idea how beautiful it is." The two boys walked in hushed awe of that statement as they approached the busy street.

"I'm thirsty," said Sammie.

"Dude, that's a good call," said Miles. "Is Red Apple open?"

"Dude, I don't even know what open means right now," said Sammie.

They approached the huge intersection known informally as "six corners."

"Wilson Farms is closed. Red Apple is...closed," said Sammie. Strolling through the vacant gas station silently, they approached the third of the convenience stores. "And Robo is…...not."

"Ok, here we are," said Miles. "Who is...gonna...go…"

"I will. What do we need?" said Sammie. "I need smokes."

"Smokes and water," said Miles who handed her money.

"Just smokes and water?" said Sammie, looking about. The sound of bass from nearby cars and distant police sirens trickled over their skin.

"You guys gonna wait here?" she said.

"Yeah," said Miles. "We'll be here."

"Wait," said Sammie. "Do you guys wanna come in with me?"

"If you want us to," said Miles.

"No," said Sammie. "I'll go in."

"I think it'll be easier if we all go in together," said Cade.

"You think?" said Sammie.

"Yeah, cause then we'd all be together," said Cade.

"Yeah, we can all go in," said Miles.

"Ok. Well, wait," said Sammie. "Why would all three of us go in if we're just getting smokes and water? Isn't that, like, too many of us? For like, not that many things?"

"Well, how many packs of smokes are you gonna get?" said Miles.

"I don't know," said Sammie. "One?"

"Just one?" said Miles.

"I don't know," said Sammie, becoming nervous. "Should we get two? I can get two of the same brand. If it's two brands, that might look suspicious."

"That's right," said Miles.

"Ok, so, two packs of Camel Lights, *God this is making me want to smoke*, and water," said Sammie.

"What kind of water should we get?" said Cade.

"What?!" said Sammie.

"I mean, like, what size?" said Cade.

"Oh, like three sizes?" said Sammie. "I mean, should I get three bottles? Like three different ones?"

"You could do that," said Miles. "Or just one big one."

"You mean like a jug?" said Sammie.

"Yeah, like a jug," said Miles.

"I'm not getting a *jug* of water," said Sammie.

"I'll carry it," said Cade.

"Ok, I'll just go in and get some fucking water, and then I'll get two packs of smokes," said Sammie, frustrated.

She headed toward the front of the store. Cade and Miles stood looking at each other. They eventually turned their backs to the store and looked out over the intersection and the intense glow of streetlamps and traffic lights. The shadows before their eyes breathed in and out while the—

"They're fucking closed," said Sammie.

"What?" said Miles and Cade.

"Closed," said Sammie. She fiddled about in her bag, exhuming cigarettes and a lighter. She lit one and inhaled. "The door was locked and I knocked and the guy looked at me and said 'closed.'" She exhaled.

"Do you have smokes?!" said Miles.

"What?!" She extended her arms after a quick rummage, "Yeah, I've got two packs in my bag."

"Well, what the hell do we need smokes for?" said Miles.

"I thought you needed smokes," said Sammie.

"What?!" said Miles.

"Fuck it," said Sammie. "Let's just go to my house and get water." And all three of them shared a pit of odd laughter.

Walking to Sammie's home down the aptly titled Longmeadow Road provided relief and comfort. Avoiding the generous sidewalks on both sides, they were back on track along the darker street away from noisy intersections as there were hardly any cars driving by. They smoked their cigarettes and chilled.

"We should get some ecstasy someday soon," said Sammie.

"Would that—" said Cade.

"That could be cool," said Miles, glaring at Sammie.

"My sister can probably get it," she said, smiling back.

"Whaddaya think, Cade?" said Sammie.

"Sure," said Cade.

They walked without speaking for a while. The silence among friends, often dreadful and ominous, was no match for the visual splendor they were taking in from all around them.

Cade saw, leaping in the grass, a frog. A fun task, his eyes stayed with it while camouflaged between hops to see it reappear. He knew the effect of the mushrooms was the catalyst to his success of following the amphibian in the dark. At times, the question of whether or not it was real or just hallucination reared only to be brushed away.

He followed the frog until he no longer could as it traveled through the blades of darkened green toward the rear of a house and out of sight.

Rather than announcing the anomaly to his journeymen, the experience was kept concealed.

He continued thinking about the frog.

Sammie had let go of the gas station faux pas and was having her own kind of fun. Her feet were following cracks in the road that were illuminated and pulsating for her eyes. Almost like a child playing hopscotch, she sprang and meandered left to right suddenly and nearly involuntarily to catch up with the erratic stylings of lines in the pavement. Coddling the straighter schisms, she moved mimicking a tightrope walker while humming a shamelessly fickle song in tune with her jostling lungs, mind, legs, and feet upon the road.

And Miles was breathing slowly and deeply lost in the warm inviting tie-dyed dress before him.

Then, ahead, the presence of an SUV, noisy from the motor and laughter moving fast, came to a stop sign at the road from a perpendicular avenue. Its inhabitants were the same age of the three. The tires screeched upon braking and everyone in the car peering left stared at Sammie and her companions. They became quiet. The car rolled backwards several feet then forward. It rolled back and forth again before turning right and proceeded eerily slowly.

"What was that?" said Sammie.

"Didn't—did you know them?" said Miles.

"No," said Sammie. "Looks like a bunch of pussies to me." She altered her walking to long, typical strides. Their eyes followed the vehicle until it turned right two blocks ahead.

"I saw a frog earlier," said Cade.

"What?!" said Sammie.

"Yeah," said Cade. "Super cool."

"Where?!" said Sammie. "You didn't see a frog! Where?!"

"It was in the grass," said Cade. "Back there."

"Where was it?!" said Sammie. "Did it hop?!"

"Yeah, it hopped a whole bunch a' times," said Cade.

"When, *when* did you see a frog?!" said Sammie.

"It was in the grass," said Cade. "I didn't want to tell anyone."

"Why not?!" said Sammie. "I wanted to see a frog."

"Me too," said Miles.

"I thought it….I thought it would…I don't know. I just saw it," said Cade.

"That's cool, bro," said Miles. "It was your moment under the moon."

"Well, next time either of you see a frog, I want to see it too, got that, pot-nuh?!" said Sammie. They continued walking.

"I'm really thirsty," said Miles.

"Yeah, we gotta make sure we don't die by drinking too much water," said Sammie. "That happens, you know."

"What?!" said Miles.

"Yeah," said Sammie. "People get too fucked up on drugs and it makes them really thirsty and then they drink more than their stomach can handle and poof. Dead."

"That's hard to believe," said Miles.

"Believe it," said Sammie. "Somebody told me it was true."

"Water is gonna be *so* clutch," said Cade. They walked in silence for a few minutes as several cars passed them peacefully.

"Can you light me a smoke, babe," said Miles.

"You want *another*?" said Sammie.

"Yes," said Miles. Sammie reached into her bag, pulled out a pack, and handed him a cigarette and lighter.

Cade busied himself by looking at the homes they passed. More specifically, the ones with flags in the front. He questioned the purpose of each as he hadn't before. His eyes happened upon a yard with tiny flags representing recently sprayed poison. The American flags on the homes and the flags on the lawn were blowing in the same direction and at the same pace.

"I didn't until this very moment—"

Just then, the sound of a vehicle moving fast from behind them accelerated. Nefarious, its driver and passengers without a doubt. The three hustled from the middle of the road to the shoulder as the SUV approached...

"NIGGER!!"

"NIGGER!!"

"NIGGER LOVER!!"

Empty bottles came flying toward them—one hitting Cade in the shoulder and face. The others shattered behind them on the sidewalk. A twelve-pack of empty glass bottles was hurled at once and hit Sammie in her hip, triggering her to scream.

"NIGGER LOVING FAGGOT!!"

"HEY, FUCK YOU, NIGGER!!!" They slammed on their brakes and went in reverse to get a better look at their victims. Lights went on in the houses.

"Fucking nigger cunt!" One stepped out of the car and threw a whiskey bottle which Miles blocked with his hand, yelling out in pain. The assailants sped away up the road just past Sammie's street on the left.

"ARE YOU OK?!" Both Miles and Cade checked on Sammie.

"Yeah, I'm fine. *Fuck*," she said, her hair disheveled. Her emotional state now devoid of fear, a characteristic not of her two helpers.

"Are you all right?!" a man's voice yelled from his driveway.

"Shit," said Sammie quietly as the trepidation of police coming made its way to her brain.

"Are you guys ok?!" said a lady from across the street. Miles embraced his injured right hand with his left.

"Are you ok, Sammie?" he said.

Her pupils filled with terror, emitting infantile helplessness.

She said while her eyes welled, "Dude, I do *not want to deal with police right now.*"

They ran.

They ran in the direction of Sammie's house. The boys found themselves slowing so that Sammie could keep up. They heard her crying and rambling as they ran. Each word she bawled connected to the one that followed it. She raved and raved and ran. They shushed, trying to impede her bellowing, which made it worse. They had six blocks to go. Police sirens were heard and became louder. Sammie fell, scraping her leg. She yelled out. They shushed her and helped her to her feet. She ran faster than before the injury. They saw a car ahead of them, traveling fast. As they and the vehicle got closer, it became visible: a police car with its lights and siren dormant. It had a driver and a passenger. The speed of the car gave all three of them the same hope: that maybe they were going to be passed and they'd head to the scene of broken glass and nosy neighbors. They didn't hear brakes squealing or any sirens turn on. But the car stopped. It stopped with grace in the middle of the road. The two officers gave chase...

"Can I smoke a cigarette, please," she said, amidst the flashing lights. Her trip condensed and erupted.

"How come your eyes are so...fucked up." The flashlight shone upon her face.

"I don't know," said Sammie.

"Where's the third boy."

"I don't know," said Sammie.

"What kind of car did you say it was."

"It wasn't a car," said Sammie, caught between anger and fear. "It was an SUV."

"What color did you say it was."

"I didn't," said Sammie. "It was dark."

"Dark what. Green? Red?" A tear ran down her cheek as she turned away from police in futile hope of *out of sight, out of mind.*

"No," said Sammie. "It was dark. I couldn't see."

"So an SUV came out of nowhere. And threw bottles at you. But you didn't see it."

"*Nowhere?*" She cried. "*What? What are you talking about.*" A cop with latex gloves searched through her bag. Sammie watched him and cried harder. Cade, handcuffed, sat in the back of the squad car with Sammie away from sight.

"Who is the third boy."

"*Third boy? What the hell are you talking about?*" said Sammie.

"There was someone else with you. Where did he go? What is his name." Finding humor in her bewilderment, a cry leaked out as a laugh.

"WHO ELSE WAS WITH YOU. WHAT IS HIS NAME."

On a dime, her crying ceased.

"Can I have a cigarette," said Sammie.

"No. You cannot have a cigarette. You think I wanna smell that shit?!" An older officer, unseen until now, approached Sammie from where Cade was detained.

"The other boy says you know where the one who got away is."

"What?" said Sammie.

"What's his...the guy...we've got."

"Cade."

"Cade says you know who the other boy is. Where is he."

"*Cade* said *what?!*" said Sammie. Her eyes unloaded again as she sobbed. Sitting on the curb amidst bright light, her head in her hands, she peered to her left and saw a man and a woman moving toward them, bathed in her rainbow vision. They were in their fifties, stern-faced, and unafraid. The woman wore slippers and a bathrobe tied tightly with her arms crossed. The man walked, swinging his arms, and wore plaid shorts and a long-sleeved shirt. He had nothing on his feet. The closer they got to Sammie, the slower and deeper her breath became. The confused cops stood in silence, looking at the humans walking toward them.

"Gentlemen," the woman said. "This young lady has been victimized." She changed tones to address Sammie, "Are you ok, honey?"

"*Yeah?*" said Sammie, as if she were asking rather than answering. The woman approached her, arms extended. She put her arms around Sammie and held her while she cried.

"Where are your parents?" the woman said.

"My dad is out of town," said Sammie, her pitch now higher like a child's.

"They threw bottles at her and called her nigger," said the man.

The woman softly shushed Sammie's cries kissing her on the head. "I know...I know," she said.

"Who? Did you get a look at the vehicle, sir?" said an officer with an affable tone.

"No. I only heard it from my backyard."

"Where is the other boy?" another cop said.

"What other boy?" said the man. His question was unanswered.

"Do you have a cigarette?" Sammie said to the woman.

"Phil," the woman said. The man reached into his pocket, pulled out a pack of Marb reds, lit one, and gave it to Sammie.

"Thank you," said Sammie, quivering. Her chin was low. Her hair covered her face. For a moment, to meet the warm gaze of the maternal human consoling her, her timid eyes ventured like a bear cub taking its first steps.

"They were running because they were attacked," said Phil. "There's about a half ton of broken glass outside my house. A car stopped and threw bottles at them, shouting obscenities."

"They look like they're high," said a more aggressive officer who was met with blank stares.

"Oh yeah?" said Phil. The cop shone his light in Sammie's direction. She hid her face in the arms of Phil's wife.

"Their eyes are both dilated."

"Whose eyes?" said Phil.

"Cade and Samantha."

"Officer," said the woman, holding Sammie. "Elevated stress can adversely affect the nervous system and how the sensory organs function, causing the pupils to dilate. These kids were taken by surprise and attacked viciously by a car full of cowardly thugs. Now, I'm sure you have searched them both. Have you found anything incriminating?"

"No."

"Well, I suggest with deference that you let them go so you don't traumatize them further."

One officer made himself scarce and a moment later, Cade came walking toward Sammie. His calm body language wrestled with the anger inside. His legs were scraped and red. His face was flushed from impact. He had been kicked. Brushing gravel from his palms, he wanted to hug Sammie but refrained.

As the caravan dispersed, Sammie, whose home was less than a block away, was led there on foot by her matron. Cade walked to the scene where he volunteered to help clean the glass with some neighbors. Then his protector drove him to Heltons' where, in the car, the two didn't say much.

"Is Samantha your girlfriend?" said Phil.

"No," said Cade.

"Just friends for now," said Phil with a tender smile.

"There was—" said Cade. "Her—"

"What do your parents do?" said Phil.

"They're dead," said Cade. "They died."

"Recently?" said Phil.

"Yeah," said Cade.

"My parents died when I was your age too," said Phil, lighting a smoke. "Help yourself."

"How?" said Cade.

"Car wreck," said Phil. "It was icy. Do you have a comfortable place to stay?"

"Yeah," said Cade, exhaling smoke. He ashed out the window as his giver ashed in a plastic cup labeled *Brewer's Blackbird.* The water-swept *Inn* barely clung to the cup as the final word. "I live with Sammie's boyfriend. And his family. We grew up together."

"That's good," said Phil.

Cade flicked his cig and embers incidentally came back into the car and onto the floor. He scrambled to locate and smother them.

"Not to worry," continued Phil compassionately. "This car's been burned more than you've lit cigarettes. More marks will only add character...and give me something to remember you by."

"Cool," said Cade. "I really appreciate it."

"I know you do."

They pulled into the driveway.

"I'm sure your friend Samantha is doing great. Cheryl has a comforting way about her," said Phil.

"*I'll* say," said Cade. Phil smiled. "Thank you so much for all your help," said Cade as he extended his sore hand which was met tenderly and with confidence. The two made eye contact for a second and Cade walked into Heltons' backyard and sat before heading up to have a drink and a smoke.

Cade would not remember the names of the couple who helped them. He would not remember the make or model of the car that drove him. And soon, he'd forget the face of the man who drove the car. He'd remember the attack but not exactly where. And he'd remember the police and their disdain. He'd remember the kindness, the caring, and the special characteristic that he and his driver shared.

And for reasons unsourced, the vision of the cup with the blackbird, he'd keep.

"Your father is away?" said Cheryl.

"Yeah, he's at his girlfriend's in Fredonia," said Sammie, keying into her home, still crying and mildly struggling to breathe normally. It was just the two of them.

"Thank you," said Sammie, hugging her new friend goodbye. "You don't know how much this means to me."

"Don't think twice. It's all right," said Cheryl.

"Oh, would you like to come in?" said Sammie.

"No, I should get back," said Cheryl. "You're a beautiful young girl."

"Thank you," said Sammie.

"Is your mother black?" said Cheryl.

"No, she was Irish and Dutch or some shit," said Sammie. "My dad's black."

"Oh. Well, biracial people are very beautiful," said Cheryl. "I'd kill for your looks."

"Thank you," said Sammie, smiling and nearly laughing.

They hugged. And with a touch of social inelegance, the neighbors, once unknown to each other, said their goodbyes.

Sammie, from inside, closed the door, locked the deadbolt, leaned with her back upon the wood, and slid slowly to the floor. She cried there, alone. And with each breath, pieced the night together. Her cries turned to whimpers. Her whimpers turned to sighs. She began to breathe efficiently.

There was a knock at the back door. Her breathing ceased. The tapping became quieter and more continuous. She opened the door slowly and peered out.

Cade, at Heltons', was having a drink after a nice shower. He was lucky. No one bothered him. No one wanted answers. The shower made his wounds dry and tight and more painful. The sting of lying on his bed reminded him of when he was handcuffed on his knees and kicked by an officer in his back. Anger had at him.

He finished his drink and had another. Then some food. It was 1 am. Keeping in mind that Sammie's dad was out of town, he picked up Heltons' portable phone and dialed her house. It only rang once.

"Hello?" said Sammie.

"It's Cade."

"Was hoping so. Saw *Helton* on the caller ID."

"How *are* you?" said Cade.

"Good, that chick *saved* me," said Sammie. "Are you ok?"

"Yeah, the dude dropped me off," said Cade.

"Do you know who he was?" said Sammie.

"He lived right by where those assholes threw bottles at us," said Cade. "I helped him clean up the glass."

"Do you remember what house?" said Sammie.

"No, I remember getting the shit kicked out of me by cops," said Cade.

"I'm so sorry, brother," said Sammie. "Cops are the worst. Are you ok?"

"Yeah, just hittin' some vodka," said Cade.

"Ooooh, bring me some," said Sammie. "If you need a ride, just call a cop, I'm sure they'd be happy to swing you over here."

"Uh huh," said Cade. "Is Miles there?"

"Yeah, he ran to my yard and hopped the fence," said Sammie. "He was in my backyard the whole time."

"That sneaky little track star," said Cade.

"Yeah. I nearly shat sideways when I heard him knocking at the door," said Sammie. "I almost forgot he existed."

"What?" said Miles, who could be heard faintly by Cade over the phone.

"I said I love you. You're the one." To Cade, she continued, "Dude, you have *vodka?* I wonder what my dad has here."

"I would've already found out," said Cade.

"Here, Miles wants to talk to you," said Sammie. "Peace, Cade, I love you."

"I love you too, Sam," said Cade. "Peace."

"Dude," said Miles.

"'Sup yo," said Cade.

"You're at our pad?" said Miles.

"Yeah, all is quiet," said Cade.

"Sammie told me an angelical couple came and rescued you guys," said Miles.

"It's...yeah," said Cade. "Do you have any idea who threw shit at us?"

"No, probably from Williamsville North or some shit," said Miles. "Racist bastards."

"Don't get me started," said Cade. "I think I hear someone walking around."

"Try and keep this on the DL, ok?" said Miles.

"No doubt," said Cade. "If it's Major and he says one word to me, I'm going to punch him in the throat until his ass bleeds shit," said Cade.

"Ok, that sounds good," said Miles. "Get him once for me."

"Peace."

"Peace."

8

———————

BLUE GHOSTS

There was a party several blocks away from Heltons'. Cade was nervous so he got drunk by himself before stepping out. He had recently gotten his second tattoo, a Celtic moon, just below his right shoulder and wore a basketball jersey to show off the ink. He drove three and a half blocks to the party which was raging upon his arrival.

"Hey, nice car, Cade," came a woman's voice. "Is that purple?"

"Um, it's more of a *periwinkle*," said another.

"I call it purple haze," said Cade. "It works."

"You left your lights on, purple haze!" said Jake, stumbling with a beer in hand. He placed his hand on Cade's hip in order to guide him to his car to speak more secretively.

"Dude, this party is already out of control," he said. "Cops will probably be here any second."

"Whose party is it?" said Cade.

"Elena Semenov's."

"*You're shitting me,*" said Cade. He turned off his headlights and shut

124

the door.

"Yeah, she's got no back here at all," said Jake. "I really feel bad for her."

"Is there a keg?" said Cade.

"Yeah, two," said Jake. "One inside, one outside."

"That's good."

"Let's go get a drink."

The party was loud with lots of people. The vast majority were from the local high school, including the evening's unprepared host, Elena, an overweight 18-year-old Russian student who thought she'd be taking advantage of her parents being away. There were high school students of every grade there, including Cade and Jake who were experiencing their post senior class summer. It was their group of friends who represented the oldest ones there. And they felt rough.

The party had been loud for hours and police had not been called. The house was huge and sat at the end of a cul-de-sac, allowing for noise to travel, and vehicular traffic was sparse. Just before Cade had arrived, eager to greet his friends, things got out of control for Elena. He walked to the backyard with Jake.

"Cade Caybul!" shouted Kelly.

"What's up," said Cade as he greeted Berk, Ty Jai, and Larry.

"Cade, since your last name rhymes with table, I think you should break this table," said Kelly.

"Um," said Cade. "Nah."

"Ok, then *I* will," said Kelly, jumping on a plastic patio table and snapping its legs. He laughed wildly while his friends watched. A group of younger kids walked by, grinning.

"Any of you faggots wanna get fucked up, I suggest drinking my bottle of Jameson on the counter," said Kelly. "That means don't drink my Jameson. Cade, there's Jameson inside."

Kelly wore shorts to his ankles and a sleeveless shirt revealing his muscles which he visually checked on and flexed from time to time. He looked around and ran his fingers through his hair before staring at Cade's chest and accosting him, "I like your jersey. You a big Kentucky fan? Or do you just like to show off your tattoos?" With that, he snared eye contact from Larry and they sniggered. Cade didn't respond.

"Cade, I'm candy flippin'," said Kelly.

"Oh, yeah?" said Cade. Kelly approached him and looked into his eyes from close-up.

"*Fuck* yeah. Fuck yeah, I'm fuckin' candy flippin'."

"Good," said Cade.

"I'm gonna see what these hos are up to inside," said Larry.

Kelly watched as Larry walked into the house and out of earshot. "Yo, Cade, you seen Sammie recently?" he asked.

"Yeah," said Cade. Kelly paused. His eyes unfocused. He continued speaking loudly and the tempo of his speech stayed twofold while his jaw vibrated. "I'd like to have that bitch suck my dick," said Kelly. "Those big, luscious nigger lips wrapped around my dick."

"Um, ok, she's probably with Miles," said Cade.

"Fuck Miles," said Kelly. "Miles is fuckin' lucky. You think he hits that shit from the back?"

"What?" said Cade.

"DOGGYSTYLE, CADE!" shouted Kelly, moving closer into Cade's space.

"Yeah, I know," said Cade. "What—"

"My bad, you two are like brothers. I forgot," said Kelly. "If Miles was here? I'd fight him."

"Dude, *what?*" said Cade. "Why?"

"Just kidding," said Kelly.

"Kelly, you sure you're only on X and acid?" said Jake.

"Jake-and-Cade-sittin'-in-a-tree," said Kelly. Beat-boxing lethargically, Berk pretended not to notice the tension among his pals.

"How much pussy have you gotten, Cade?" said Kelly.

"How does one even measure pussy?" said Jake.

"I remember all the pussy I've gotten," said Kelly.

"That's great," said Jake. "Nobody gives a shit."

Ty meandered over from a separate conversation. Kelly acknowledged him then was distracted by a fire that came to life in a pit in the yard.

"Holy shit, we can probably burn anything we want," said Kelly, laughing loudly as the destructive thought nestled.

"Dude, Elena is…" said Cade.

"Fuck Elena," said Kelly. "This is my house."

Cade, Ty, and Jake moved toward the keg and got busy.

"I've got some nice sugar cubes," said Jake.

"Now we're talkin'," said Cade.

"Shmell S D?" smiled Ty. "Sounds nice."

They each put one in their mouths and let them dissolve. A group of younger men carried a living room chair out of the house. They struggled getting it through the door. Trying different angles and becoming frustrated, they argued and yelled at each other while people at the party watched them struggle.

"Ok, put your end out! OUT, Will."

"Now spin it! Spin the middle part top-wise!"

"It's not gonna fit!"

"Oh, it'll fit."

"We're gonna make it fit."

"Why are you two moving the chair outside?" said a smiling girl.

"The chair needs a new home."

"Ok, set it down. Just set it down."

"Why does the chair need a new home?"

"It just does. Now you can be a part of the problem or you can be a part of the solution."

"Movin' on up!" said a larger kid from inside the living room who pushed his weight into the chair, cracking the door jamb. The chair wiggled its way out, conjuring a cheer from the patrons. They picked up the recliner, walked it over to the fire, and put it on top where it began to burn. Dousing it with lighter fluid got it going.

Cade peered at Jake and they looked around for Elena whom they barely knew. Ty and Jake sipped their beers while Cade chugged his and refilled. A group staggered from the lawn onto the patio and one dragged his foot and kicked decorative stones onto the walkway. The person behind him picked up a stone and heaved it at the house, nearly hitting a window. Then, several boys did the same. Before any glass could shatter, a girl, shocked by the flying rocks, shrieked as if one had nearly hit her. This aroused a larger senior, Dustin Bennett, who leaped at the opportunity to come to her defense although no one, including he, felt it was necessary.

"WHO JUST THREW A ROCK AT JESSICA?!" he said. The younger, smaller (somewhat) responsible boys froze. They pointed at each other. Jessica had gotten past the initial shock of witnessing an unexpected act of attempted vandalism and she settled into the thought of having a burly protector, despite the knowledge that she was never targeted.

"WHO DID IT?!" said Dustin.

Jessica grinned, entertained by the boys' fear. Dustin took off his shirt. He had his last name tattooed on his upper back in large black ink. Heaving his shoulders back and approaching the group, he shouted, "WAS IT YOU, BERNARD?!" The backyard became quiet. The fire crackled and sang. Cade and Jake looked at Jessica who had begun to sympathize with the quivering boys. They gave her a moment to speak, an initiative that she did not take. Jake walked over to Dustin B.

"Yo, Bennett. Nobody threw rocks at anybody. They were aiming for the house and nothing came close to hitting her. She screamed for no reason. Now put your shirt on before Kelly's hard-on gets any bigger." There was silence. Then Dustin smiled and slapped hands with Jake. The rock throwers scampered away.

"Why don't we all have a drink," said Jake.

Kelly was too confused to speak. They all had swigs of beer as the party reformed.

They did keg stands and mingled with the people whom they knew. Jake, Ty, and their friend with the purple car later began to trip. They laughed, smiley-eyed as their drinking pace slowed, even Cade's who, as his mind transformed, had forgotten about Elena and his misplaced sympathy for her. Still, no one had seen the girl.

The grass, once dark and still, was now fluorescent and in motion. The spider webs by the lights on the house sparkled white and the movement of their inhabitants, transformed into something to hold dear.

The humans and their debauchery turned intimidating. Cade imagined if that was how he looked when he was inebriated. He found solace in the stars.

Later, Sammie and two other girls entered the backyard. Her

patchwork bag slung over one shoulder. Ty noticed her long legs.

"Sammie's here!" he said. "Sammie!"

"Dude, what the hell is this?" she said. "This place is trashed."

"Yeah, Elena Semyonov—" said Jake and Cade, nearly simultaneously. Sammie, taken aback by the volume of their voices, receded a step. Her eyes widened, reflecting the visage of the two who were thrilled to see her yet under a dissonant spell.

"One at a time, weirdos," she said while casually pouring a beer.

Cade said robotically, "This. Is. Elena's. house. ...It's fucked." He accidentally spat a little on Sammie's cheek as he spoke and she pretended not to notice and didn't brush it off. Her beer filled to the top.

"Where is she?" Sammie asked, caressing the foam with her lips, one hand on her hip.

"Nobody knows," said Cade.

"Are these your friends?" said Jake.

"Yes. Milla and Gabs, this is Cade, Jake, and Ty Jai," she said, scuffing Tai Jai's hair. "They're from Buff Sem," she said, rolling her eyes to Cade. "You guys tripping?"

"Yeah," said Jake.

"Fungus?" said Sammie.

"Nope," said Jake. Silent intrigue radiated from Milla and Gabriella who had conversed quietly about whether or not it was a good time and place to light their cigarettes.

"Cool, hook me up," said Sammie, drinking her beer.

"With what?" said Jake.

"Your sister, dipshit," said Sammie. "A dose!"

"You sure you want to get started this late?" said Jake.

"Yes," said Sammie. He reached into his pocket and pulled out a sandwich baggie and one last sugar cube. He put it in her hand.

"Whoa!" said Sammie, inspecting it at eye level from atop the palm of her hand. "Is this a sugar cube?"

"No, it's his sister," said Ty, grinning.

"Shut up, Ty Jai!" said Sammie.

"Her name is Lucy," said Ty, making Sammie smile. She gathered it from her hand via her mouth and swirled her tongue around it.

"Mmmmmm, that is *sweet!* You guys can get a beer if you want," she said to her lady friends.

The noise from the party segued Sammie's loud whisper to the boys, "They have poppers."

"What's a popper?" said Cade.

"It's VCR cleaner or some shit," said Sammie.

"What?" said Cade.

"Yeah," said Sammie. "You huff it." She had a quick look at her friends from Buffalo Seminary who spoke to each other. Her eyes returned to Cade's as she continued talking, disguising uncertainty. "Like, through your nose."

"Did you do it?" said Cade.

"No. Not *yet,*" she said, looking around the yard. "Why does Dustin Bennett have his SHIRT OFF?! HEY, BENNETT! PUT YOUR SHIRT ON!"

"SCREW YOU, HAYES!" he shouted.

"YOU WISH!" said Sammie.

The shouting triggered people to shift their attention, a characteristic to which the three boys already on their psychedelic sojourn were sensitive.

Sammie laughed. "That tattoo is ridiculous; he looks like an idiot!"

"Back to these...poppers," said Ty.

Sammie had her last sip of beer and flung the remaining foam onto the ground. She refilled.

"What? Oh. I don't know, they sell it at porn stores as VCR cleaner," said Sammie. "Apparently gay dudes do it a lot. It's like nitrous."

"Why gay dudes?" said Cade.

"I don't know," said Sammie. "Apparently it makes anal sex super awesome."

All three boys thought the same thought, despite their LSD deterrent. And all three boys spoke not a word of their thoughts.

The party raged.

Kelly and Larry returned to the crew and greeted Sammie and her friends. Kelly, whose presence was more ominous than usual, was stumbling. His eyes were low and vacant. Sammie spoke with Larry who began to direct his attention to the ladies whom he had just met.

Kelly silently stared at Jake. An almost-smile shown on his face. He fiddled with his own hair. People waited for him to speak.

Jake's eyes found Kelly's.

Jake looked away, giving Kelly a chance to do the same.

Jake's eyes met Kelly's gaze again. It hadn't faltered.

Jake tilted his head to his left, holding on.

Kelly broke, walked over to the stones, and picked one up. He threw it at an upstairs window. It missed. He picked up another and missed. He went faster and faster, gathering stones and heaving them. They all missed.

"Dude, Kelly," said Cade. Kelly faked a throw toward Cade and Jake and everyone reacted protectively in unison. At that, Kelly laughed, threw one, and watched it connect with the second floor window, cracking the glass. Before anyone could make sense of it, more and more started throwing decorative rocks onto the siding of the house, cracking windows when victorious.

And the destructive wind made its way through the party like a flying demon.

They cut into the tires of the car in the driveway. They smashed outdoor furniture. Indoors, they threw lamps into windows, cracking them from the inside. A kid had an idea to rummage through the kitchen pantry for canned goods. He passed the heavier artillery around and each can went through a window. They kicked out screens and smashed the TV. A group busied themselves in the refrigerator, taking out bottles of condiments. Mustard and ketchup were squirted all over the kitchen and dining room.

"ELENA SEMEN HOG!" drunken teenagers yelled. Still the hostess, Miss Semyonov, couldn't be found. By anyone.

The group left the party and headed to Sammie's place so as to not be tormented by police whom they deduced were on their way. Her father, like usual, was out. Milla and Gabs went their own way as did Kelly,

Larry, and Berk.

Cade was behind the wheel of his '94 purplish Elantra. It had several Bob Marley stickers on the sides and back along with an Allman Brothers sticker made to resemble a Georgia license plate on the bumper. There was a 12-inch subwoofer in the trunk. Jake and Ty were in back. Sammie rode shotgun and turned the music down to speak.

"Dude, that was FUCKED UP! Oh my GOD, poor Elena! Did anybody see her?!"

"I didn't see her once," said Cade, one hand on the wheel and a smoke between his fingers.

"I saw her," said Jake.

"You did?!" said Sammie, gasping then whipping her head around to look at Jake.

"I saw her too," said Ty. "It was before you guys came."

"How did she look?!" said Sammie.

"*Not* well," said Jake.

"Yeah, that party got out of hand quick," said Ty.

"Cadey-Cade, how ya doin, bro?" said Jake.

Cade was drunk, tripping, and driving comfortably just over the speed limit, enjoying the wind and his Camel. However, the more his friends spoke about their victimized schoolmate, the more his mind yearned to feel as if he were her.

Cade said, "It's ok... ...with the lights.. ...I can see everything."

His slow tempo and breaths between words were alarming to his friends. Silenced, they aimed their focus on him and his driving, an exertion they had overlooked until this moment now that their fast-paced entertaining conversation had stalled.

Behind him, Jake and Ty kept their fear of crashing or being pulled over at bay. Ty was able to keep an eye on Cade's face from his diagonal perspective. Jake, aware that his friend might notice him trying to hook a glimpse of his eyes in the rearview mirror, settled on looking placidly through the window to his left. And Sammie, still processing the odd phrasing of the man behind the wheel, was motionless, her head cocked left, staring directly at Cade.

"Sam, maybe turn the music up just a tad so we can enjoy the ride?" said Jake with grace and sympathy.

Sammie adhered, settled, and looked ahead and to her right. With that, all three passengers calmed and catered to their friend's jangled nerves.

They approached the townhome-style pad, feeling like it was a sanctuary of bliss.

"Should I pull into the driveway?" said Cade.

"Yes," said Sammie.

Cade's car came to a stop in the big empty four-car driveway. He put it in park and exhaled.

"Way to go, Cade," said Jake.

"Yeah, *sweet* driving, man," said Ty. Sammie swiftly kissed him on the cheek and they all exited the car and headed in.

After 2:00 am hit, Jake and Ty were to leave on foot together. Cade and Sammie went out to the backyard with them to say peace. They all lit

smokes on the patio.

"Ready, Ty Jai?" said Jake.

"Uh, yeah," said Ty. "We gonna cut through Delwood?"

"I don't see why not," said Jake. "Hey, you know what I heard the black dudes at work call each other?"

"What?" said Sammie.

"Fam," said Jake.

"Fam?" said Ty.

"Yeah," said Jake. "Like *family.*"

"Yeah, I've heard that before," said Ty. Cade looked up as his thoughts bubbled. His three friends waited for him to speak. They watched him and waited. They wondered if he was even paying attention.

"I like that," said Cade with his eyes on the sky. "I like that a lot."

"Me too," said Jake smiling. They all smiled together.

"Like, what up, fam?" said Cade.

"Yes!" said Jake. "Chillin, fam."

"I really, really like that," said Cade. Ty and Jake reflected joy while Sammie laughed out loud at high pitch, keeping her smiling eyes on Cade.

"Yeah, like, we should start saying it a lot," said Jake.

"Definitely," said Cade.

The four stood silently. And although the sympathy for Elena had not faded and they remained conscious of the destruction of her parents' house, they stood comfortably. They were grateful.

Sammie, in particular, felt strong and thankful. She was comforted by her guys who she knew would never let anything like that happen to her. And as the LSD trip lingered, responsible for amplifying the trauma of witnessing the unabashed heartlessness and feeling remorse for standing idle, it forged and strengthened a new bond among the four friends.

"Peace, fam!" said Jake. They hugged and Jake and Ty headed out into the night. Cade and Sammie went inside and the door closed behind them.

Cade felt the chill from the air-conditioned home. He searched for the words to ask Sammie to turn it down but came up short.

"It's too fucking cold in here," said Sammie, adjusting the thermostat. Then she opened the fridge and took out two beers. Handing one to Cade, she led him to the couch in the living room.

"Whoa," said Cade. "Labatt *Ice?*"

"Yup. I stashed them away," said Sammie, twisting off her cap. Cade followed suit as Sammie quickly took the cap from his hand and put it with hers on a coaster in the middle of the glass coffee table.

"Does your dad—how's—how's he doing?" said Cade.

"He's fine," said Sammie. "In Fredonia with Liz."

"They've been together for a while?" said Cade.

"Yuppers," said Sammie.

"Where's Miles?" said Cade.

"At some lake house with his family or some shit," said Sammie.

They sat on the green faux leather sofa, each of them at either end. Cade sat with one knee in the middle of the couch and on an angle, making conversation easy. She sat cross-legged with her lower back resting against the arm of the couch, facing Cade directly. Her shorts, the color of which reflected her bright unparalleled teeth, receded almost completely from Cade's vision by her chosen style of sitting.

"Maureen gonna be mad that you're out late?" said Sammie.

"Dude, maybe," said Cade. "I don't know."

Sammie sipped elegantly from her bottle. Just then, she realized she wanted details about Cade's discovery of his mother when she died. She suppressed her curious mind.

"Oh, yeah?" said Sammie. Calmly, she observed Cade's face and emotional state. "How's this gonna look?" she said.

"How's what look?" he said as his eyes crawled from her painted toes up to her hair.

"I dunno, bro," said Sammie.

"Are there more Ices?" said Cade, running low after some big swigs.

"Yeah, check by the condiments," said Sammie. "*Jesus*, you drink fast."

"Time is running out," said Cade, making his way to the kitchen. "You need one?"

"Um, *no*," said Sammie. He returned and twisted the lid. Sammie whistled and said, "Give it here." He put it in her hand and she leaned up to put it with the others on the coaster. "I don't want Daddy Hayes to find these."

"Has he?" said Cade.

"Sure," said Sammie. "*Sammie, this house talks to me, you know,*" she continued in mimicry of her father.

"What does that mean?" said Cade.

"He notices little things that are different from when he left. He's told me he's noticed shoe prints in the kitchen, bottle caps, cig butts... one time he found a beer bottle under this couch."

"Who the hell put a beer bottle under the couch?" said Cade. "An empty one?"

"Yes. Who do you think?" said Sammie. "Kelly probably. Or Melvin. One a those fuckin' assholes."

"Why would they leave a beer bottle under there?" said Cade.

"'Cause they're dirtbags and they don't care. It was done on purpose. I found a beer bottle behind my toilet once. I knew it was Melvin's 'cause there was a Marb Red in it."

"Jake smokes Reds," said Cade.

"Um, *yeah*, but Jake wouldn't do that," said Sammie.

"Yeah, I know," said Cade.

"Well? Think about it," said Sammie. "Our friends aren't as nice as you. And Jake and Ty Jai." Cade looked ahead, away from Sammie, and processed what she had just told him. She noticed his hypertension and furrowed brow.

"That sucks ass," said Cade. Sammie wanted to mention the rule that boys weren't allowed in her bedroom. And an impression of her father reciting that law was on the edge of her tongue, along with the fact that she needed to keep sex with Miles secret from her dad. But, keeping her eyes on Cade, she withheld.

"Oh, I have poppers!" said Sammie.

"What?" said Cade.

"Poppers!" said Sammie, getting up and heading to the living room. Grinning, she returned with an unlabeled vial of liquid. "Remember when I gave you your first E pill?'

"Yes," said Cade.

"Are you ready?" said Sammie.

"Sure, what's it do to you?" said Cade.

"Makes you fucked up," said Sammie.

"Oh," said Cade.

"It makes you feel dizzy...and crazy...and like really, really fucked up for only like two minutes," said Sammie.

"And you just inhale it?" said Cade. "Do you put it on a rag?"

"A rag? No. Ok, watch," she said as if she were about to perform a magic trick. "Here we go." She twisted the cap and inhaled deeply through one nostril. Cade watched. Before it hit her, she put the cap back on and placed the vial on the table. Green irises rolled upward and her eyelids flickered like struggling electricity. To Cade, she looked as if she were in pain. She gently wobbled and burst into laughter. Tears formed in her eyes. She took the vial with her right hand and lay back, resting her head on Cade's thigh and handed it to him. She closed her eyes and stopped smiling.

Holding the vial, Cade pulled hard from his Labbatt's.

"Put your beer down," said Sammie, looking up at him. "After you inhale, hand me the poppers."

He hit it hard through his nose like she did and moved the vile over several inches in his left hand. She took it and watched him. His eyes nearly shut as his smile curled up like a Peanuts character in love. Sammie unleashed her trademark high-pitched sound of irrepressible joy. Then Cade inhaled slowly and deeply and the breath burst out of him, like a horse.

Although Sammie's head was resting on his thigh, she seemed startlingly distant. Even upon glancing at her face, he did not see her eyes, nose, and mouth, but instead an obscured countenance without character. He felt her spirit and smile transform to a neutral place of concern as fear took over.

The drug sent him to an unmistakable place: his mother's bedroom where he heard the infomercial and found her body. Her face multiplied over and again at the speed of fire running a course of gasoline. In perfect lines from left to right as if on a computer screen, he saw his mother's lifeless face appear and reappear repeatedly. The vision showed via lineage stacked on lineage as identical microdots followed by the anticipation of one of the snapshots to be different from the others as if her eyes might open. But they were all the same. Motionless. Lifeless. And the sound of angry electricity ran between his ears, working in conjunction with the mirage.

The torment ceased and the high became pleasant like it had started. But the trauma left a mark.

"Dude, are you ok?" Sammie asked.

"Yeah," said Cade. "That was cool. I got really high. Do you have any hard liquor?"

Said Sammie, "Uuuum, yeah. That was intense, man. You did not look—" She was interrupted by Cade's gentle hand moving her hair away from her eyes. She understood the moving of her hair, from his perspective, to be a task that needed to be completed rather than a romantic advance. "Let me see what I have."

Sammie got up and went to the kitchen, returning with a bottle of cognac.

"Hennessy?!" said Cade, laughing.

"What?" said Sammie.

"I don't know," said Cade. "I didn't expect Hennessy!"

"Well, my dad *is* black, ya know," said Sammie. She sat next to Cade, leaning her shoulder on his and he had a nice pull. He passed back to her and she had a sip.

"I'm gonna go get some ice," said Sammie. "Wait, can you drink Hennessy on the rocks?"

"You can drink anything on the rocks," said Cade.

"Ok," said Sammie. She got up and went into the kitchen. Cade heard ice churning and Sammie returned with two glasses. She poured two drinks and became comfortable again. "You drink so fast, dude."

"Yeah," said Cade.

She laid her head on his shoulder. "What do you think of the poppers?" said Sammie.

"Poppers are intense," said Cade. "Why are they called poppers?"

"I dunno," said Sammie. "Gotta call stuff something." She inhaled again from the vial.

Cade followed suit. This time, he hit it softer than before but got nearly as high. Again, despite his proximity to Sammie, he felt far away as if she became inanimate. And instead of hallucinating vividly, the inadequacy that he felt every day came down one hundred fold. He thought of the lack of sex that he had had compared to his friends. And the brief trip revealed to him that not only did he have no place of warmth and peace to feel contentment and solitude, but that was a part of life that he did not deserve and would never feel.

He came down. With a laugh, he felt close to Sammie again. They smiled at each other.

"I gotta piss," said Cade.

"Me too," said Sammie. "I'll wait." She let her vision descend before re-assigning it to his body as he headed through the hallway and into the bathroom across from her bedroom.

The task of overcoming the awareness that he was in the same room as a mirror was tricky. He urinated, flushed the toilet, put the seat down, and splashed water over his face for refreshment. He dried his hands and turned off the light, doing it all without making eye contact with the strange guy in the mirror.

"You pee with the door open?" said Sammie.

"Yeah," said Cade.

"Weirdo," said Sammie. She rose and walked to the bathroom. Upon returning, she found Cade had refreshed their glasses with ice.

"Can I pour some more?" said Cade

Sammie said, exclaiming a rhyme, "For sure! Wanna have a smoke?"

"Yes," said Cade.

"*Yes,*" said Sammie in mimicry.

They sat on the patio steps within the confines of the fenced yard. The night was quiet and calm. Sitting with her legs apart like a boy, Sammie lit two smokes and handed one to Cade.

"Fences are weird," said Cade.

"What do you mean?"

"I didn't notice how different they were from how I knew them before," said Cade.

"How did you know them before?" said Sammie, turning to face him.

"Tonight," said Cade. "I was thinking about them when I saw it."

"When you saw what?" said Sammie.

"That fence," said Cade. "Is it yours or your neighbor's? I can't tell."

Said Sammie patiently and with intrigue, "It doesn't matter. It's the fence. What do you think about it?"

"It's not a fence. It's a barrier," said Cade. "If I were on the other side of it, it would mean my ass." Sammie turned to the fence and pondered how serious his demeanor had become and wondered why. She attributed the look in his eyes, which was both spooky and captivating, to the trauma he suffered when his mother died.

"I understand," she said. "I never thought of it that way."

"Me neither," said Cade. "Wait," he smiled. Their laughter played together.

Sammie leaned her head on Cade's shoulder and closed her eyes. The closeness reminded him of his experience with Jane, urging him to shy away from the embrace. Sammie sensed his tenseness and slowly lifted her head back up.

They sat in silence and smoked. When she was done with her cigarette, she flicked off the ember and pocketed the filter. Cade did the same as Sammie extended her hand to collect his. He took a long cold pull from his glass and dropped his head onto her shoulder.

Now he thought of his mother and leaning upon her in church when he was little. And he recollected her crying upon seeing Sammie, her father, and her sisters walking through the church aisle and selecting their pew where they sat. This was a memory that had been dormant until this moment. Just more than a week had passed before the Hayes family returned to mass after Sammie's mom was killed when they were children.

"Doesn't that hurt your neck?" she said.

"Yes, it...it isn't that comfortable," said Cade, regaining normal posture.

"Well, let's try this once more," said Sammie, again resting her head on his shoulder. He felt stronger. Lifting his glass and finishing the drink, Sammie remarked, "You can have mine if you want." Bittersweet the deal, and he accepted.

A loud car drove by, tearing through the quiet night, triggering an unwanted flashback for both of them. Cade drank from Sammie's glass.

"Your ice is smaller than mine," said Cade.

"You drink *so* fast," said Sammie wearily.

"Somebody's gotta drink something," said Cade.

They heard an animal noisily make its way up and over the fence from the neighbor's side.

"Raccoon!" they both shouted. It looked at them and darted over the smaller chain link fence.

"Oh my God!" said Sammie. "I *love* him!"

"You see? I could never do that," said Cade. "5-0 would get called on me if I was that raccoon."

"Plus you're too drunk to climb a fence!" said Sammie.

"That is also true," said Cade.

They watched the leery raccoon run until it was out of eye's reach.

"What's your spirit animal?" said Sammie, rejuvenated.

"What?" said Cade.

"You know, your spirit animal!" said Sammie.

"I'm not sure," said Cade. "What's yours?"

"Elephant," said Sammie.

"Why?" said Cade.

"Cause they're smart and unique," she said. "And they grieve like super hard. They mourn like we do."

"Yeah," said Cade. "Yeah, elephants are fucking sick."

"Right?!" said Sammie, wide eyed and smiling. "Like what the hell made that?! It doesn't look like anything!"

"Well, it looks like a mammoth tooth tiger," said Cade.

"A WHAT?!" said Sammie.

"A mammoth...a wooly tooth—" said Cade.

"A wooly toothed tiger!?" said Sammie. "That's your spirit animal! A wooly toothed tiger!"

"No, I want elephant," said Cade.

"No," said Sammie, nearly overrun by laughter. "You can't have elephant! I'm elephant! You're mammoth tooth tiger!"

"Oh, fine!" said Cade as he stood, wobbling. "Give me the one with all the special needs and extinct!"

"Gotta pee again?" said Sammie.

"No, would it be all right if I had some more Hennessy?" said Cade.

"Um, how much is left?" said Sammie.

"I dunno," said Cade. "Probably not enough for your dad to not know."

"Well, I can water it down," said Sammie. "Just don't kill it."

"I'll see what I can do," said Cade.

He went inside, sliding the glass door closed behind him. The bottle of cognac, he deduced, was already too devoid of substance to take any more. He looked in the fridge and took out the last bottle of Labatt Ice. After a quick twist of the cap, he tossed it toward the kitchen trash but missed hearing the metal connect with the floor and bounce several times. He sipped the beer then put the bottle down as he knelt to find the cap. Sammie heard him struggling.

"What's goin' on, duder?" said Sammie, poking her head in.

"I lost a cap," said Cade.

"What kind of cap?" said Sammie.

"Beer," said Cade.

She knelt and looked with him for a moment.

"Dude, it's all good," said Sammie, "I'll find it tomorrow. I'm too drunk." Cade raised his hands to his face and grimaced. He began to rock back and forth. "Dude, what's up?" she said tenderly.

"I'm sorry," said Cade. "I'm really sorry."

"It's ok, man, we'll find it tomorrow." She rubbed his back gently. "Everything changes when the sun comes up and my dad won't be back 'til afternoon. We'll find it. I'm gonna smoke then lie down." Cade pried his face from his hands and looked into Sammie's eyes. She saw he was close to tears. "It's *ok*," she said. "Let's go outside."

Again, they sat in the same place, this time a little further from each other. Sammie lit two smokes and handed one to Cade. Looking up, she could almost see the stars.

"My dad beat my sister 'cause he caught her smoking weed," said Sammie.

"When?" said Cade.

"Like right after my mom died," said Sammie.

"Like when?" said Cade.

"I don't know," said Sammie. "Like two months after or some shit."

"Which sister?" said Cade.

"Marissa," said Sammie. "She was in high school. He gave her a black eye. My sister Rachel's boyfriend Oakley went after my dad because of it. And they fought. It was scary, man."

"Just cause he doesn't understand weed?" said Cade.

"Yeah," said Sammie. "Plus he was fucked up from my mom dying."

Cade watched her silently as she read the night's message in the sky.

"I dreamt of blue ghosts," she said.

"When your mom died?" said Cade.

"Yeah, I don't know for how long," said Sammie. "It kept happening."

"Recurring nightmare?" said Cade.

"Yeah," said Sammie speaking softly, her glazed eyes a product of strict recollection. "They were in my room. Always in my room."

"What did they look like?" said Cade.

"They didn't have faces," said Sammie as if under hypnosis. "They were blue."

"Good or bad," said Cade.

"Definitely bad. It was scary. I couldn't move. But they didn't attack me or anything. They were just there. I screamed for my dad. But my sister always came instead. And she held me."

"Which sister?" said Cade.

"My dad never came," said Sammie. "I remember talking about it with my dad. Like, the next day. It felt so real."

"Did they have—what did their bodies look like?" said Cade.

"Blue. They didn't have faces," said Sammie. "Like...they didn't have eyes or noses or mouths. It's hard to describe. They didn't do anything but watch me. They were just...there."

"Blue ghosts seem scary," said Cade.

"Yeah. They were," said Sammie. "Where ya goin', wooly?"

"Gotta piss," said Cade as he walked to the gate leading to the front yard. He unlatched it and, leaving it ajar, went beside the garage, unzipped his pants, and began to urinate. They heard squealing brakes coming to a slow halt. Instantly, he recognized the insidious presence within the vehicle.

"5-0!" he shouted to his left after peering around the garage at the squad car stopped in the street, blocking the driveway.

"What?" yelled Sammie.

"5-0!!!" he shouted louder yet trying to obscure the sound from reaching the police as his confused body struggled. He ran through the open gate and latched it behind him then buttoned his pants.

"5-0!" he said, making eye contact with Sammie who got up and hurried to the door leading to the kitchen. They heard the small section of chain link fence between the house and the wooden fence judder. They were surrounded. Cade glanced and saw the cop with his one foot atop the fence making his way over. They heard the gate unlatch, which made the matter scarier than the respective vision and subtle noises coming from their left.

"Get in. Get in," said Cade.

They made their way as both cops leapt up onto the wooden patio. The one coming from behind, realizing that the frightened twosome were probably not intruders but rightful to the home's furnishings, stomped loudly. His coworker did the same, intending to further unnerve the young man and woman who shut the door and locked the deadbolt.

Sammie closed the blinds that ran down along the door and they slowly walked backward from it as if there were monsters on the other side.

Cade, in this moment, had thoughts that he hadn't before but would come to know well in his future. The fear and tension that followed him and the woman by his side was suddenly purged. With a slow exhalation came a vision, crimson and calming, destined to root and multiply in his brain. He had found a new friend, one that would never leave him, a guide with whom he'd at times find peace. His mind, impregnated with the desire to kill, took a long fresh glimpse of the future, while the flow of blood filled the amatory space as if he were alone, enveloped in a reverie more common. Terror then, evicted. Serenity in its place. Wide eyes still. A sure thing.

"CADE? CADE? HEY, CADEY Cadey Cade. Let's go. My dad will be home soon." From the sofa, his eyelids unglued.

"Ok." Thought brushed against his sighing breath. "Do we have smokes?"

"Yeah, here," said Sammie. "But you can't smoke it here." The digital clock under the TV read 9:48. Then Cade eye's found the bottle of

Hennessy on the glass table. It was almost half full of clear liquid.

"You finished the Hennessy and then poured water into the bottle," said Sammie.

"What," said Cade. "Why?"

"I think you were trying to like...water it down so my dad wouldn't know that we drank it all," said Sammie, giving pause for her friend to try and process things. "But there was nothing to water down. You just poured water into the empty bottle. I think you drank some of the water too."

"Shit," said Cade.

"Gotta stay hydrated," said Sammie. "It's all good. Maybe he won't notice that it's gone."

"Cops didn't get in?" said Cade, preparing to leave.

"Dude, *what?*" said Sammie. "Um, no they didn't get in."

"So they left?" said Cade.

"Uh, yeah, they left," said Sammie. "How did you sleep, duder?"

"Um, fine. I didn't know that I...slept," said Cade.

"Yeah?" said Sammie. "So you remember the cops coming and chasing us inside?" said Sammie.

"Yeah," said Cade. "Why did they come here?"

"My fucking neighbors probably," said Sammie. "Remember the raccoon?"

"Yeah," said Cade.

"They probably called when we shouted," said Sammie.

"Jesus Christ!" said Cade.

Sammie held her breath while looking into Cade's eyes. Then she swiftly moved to his core and put her arms around him. Her eyes closed for the embrace.

"Ok, Daddy Hayes is on the way," said Sammie. "Gotta clean up."

"I'm sorry I drank all the Hennessy," said Cade, leaving.

"It's ok," said Sammie. "I'll just water it down some more."

Cade lit a smoke and drove to the liquor store on the Eastside. Getting there before they opened, he had to kill some time. He went to the gas station and bought a six-pack of Red Dogs. He drank two then bought a bottle of Henny which was more expensive than he anticipated. Driving back to Sammie's, he saw her father's car in the driveway. The delivery was not made.

9

TIRE ROTATION

At Heltons', another day had begun. Cade went to his parents' house and drank some of the cognac as afternoon approached. He figured he could get away with drinking plenty before he'd relay the bottle to Sammie to put back in the liquor cabinet as her dad's bottle had been about half-empty when they started drinking it. Feeling more comfortable downstairs, Cade fell asleep on the couch in his living room.

Several hours later, he woke to his aunt's unfriendly touch.

"Cade! Get up. I don't know what the hell you're doin' here, but ya gotta get up. I've got people coming to appraise this shit so we can sell it, and I can't sell the goddamn house if you're asleep in it, drunk! Now get up."

"Shit, Jesus Christ, all right," said Cade.

"I don't know where the hell you are and neither does Maureen," said Aunt Jackie. "I just got back from Heltons' place, and they say you didn't come home last night, and you're not supposed to be living here-you're supposed to be living at Heltons' house. THAT'S THE DEAL!"

"All right, shit," said Cade.

"I come here and you're squatting," said Aunt Jackie. "Is that what you're doing, Cade?! Are ya squatting?! Ray doesn't even want you over there. He says it's not a good fit. Did you know his father died? What's his name? Miles' grandpa. Grandpa…"

Cade's disposition moved to sympathy. "Ted," said Cade.

"THAT'S right," said Aunt Jackie. "Ted. Did you know that Grandpa Ted died, Cade?"

"No," said Cade. "When?"

"Yesterday morning or something like that. Ray found him at his house on Westfield. But you didn't know that, did ya. Too busy gettin' drunk and squatting. You're gonna end up like your mother, Cade, do ya know that?! You're headed down a bad road, kid, and you're gonna pay for it with your life. Goddamn devil's got a hold of ya. Why don't ya get the hell out of here and go take a shower at Heltons and go be with your friend? His grandfather just died, ya know. What is this?" she said as she picked up the bottle of Hennessy from the floor. "Is this—was this your mother's?! Ya get this out of the liquor cabinet? I thought I put a lock on that Goddamn thing." She turned and headed toward the kitchen with the bottle.

Cade, upon hearing the news of Grandpa Ted's death, listened lethargically to his aunt's ravings. He had known Grandpa Ted and liked him. His thoughts were mainly of Miles, but quickly, he was reminded of the importance of the bottle.

"Give me that," he said sternly.

"What?" said his Aunt. "Give you what? This? This fuckin' bottle? You're crazier than my goddamn dead sister if you think you're gettin' this Goddamn bottle back."

Cade's Aunt Jackie was strong for a woman. She had short hair like a man and walked, dressed, and acted like one. She was tough and suffered from the same ailment as Cade and his mother. And at this moment, she was withdrawing from the drink and nicotine too.

"Give me the bottle," said Cade. "I need that. It isn't yours."

"What did you just say to me? Give *me the bottle?* You're only 18 years old. What the hell do you mean *give me the bottle.* I'm gonna put this back in the liquor cabinet and you're outta here, boy. And I mean outta here!"

She opened the pantry door and took the unlocked padlock off of the cabinet handle and put the Hennessy bottle inside.

"Now the estate sale people should be here any minute to have this shit appraised. Now, I've gotta call a LOCKSMITH TO CHANGE THE LOCKS TO THIS PLACE SO YOU STAY THE HELL ON OUTTA HERE! And I'm also gonna call the Amherst police department and tell them to keep an eye on this place after I describe what you look like, so stay outta here. I've got power of attorney and believe me, I NEVER WANTED IT!"

Cade got up and headed for the side door.

"Where do you think you're going?!" said his aunt.

He got into his car and drove away as another vehicle approached the driveway.

Cade drove to Jake's place on Lamont Drive, ten minutes away. There were no cars in the driveway. He walked to the backyard through the gate. Feeling no need to knock at the door, he sat on a patio chair and, like the peaceful clouds he observed and envied, the boy drifted away.

EVERYONE AT HELTONS' WERE in mourning. Extended family convened there along with Sammie who had begun to feel overcome by anxiety. The long driveway that ran all the way along the huge yard to the rear of the house was packed with cars and the street handled the runoff. Grief-stricken, Miles and Maureen still had room in their hearts to be concerned about Cade and his whereabouts.

After Aunt Jackie completed her tasks at her deceased sister's house down the road, she joined the Heltons at their place to socialize. They ordered pizza and wings. Labatt Blue beer flowed and soon, the home was packed with people whose grieving became garnished with joy.

Besides immediate family, there were neighbors, cousins, and friends of Miles and Mary. Grandpa Ted was an integral part of his sons' lives as well as his sister-in-law's. And his many grandkids, who remembered him fondly, were there as well, making Heltons' place seem much smaller.

Cade mourned too, recalling Ted's involvement teaching Miles and him how to ride bikes together. He and Jake tied one on at a party close by. And for Cade, that party ended early.

"You all right to drive, bro?" said Jake.

"Yeah, I'm straight," said Cade. "Just goin' to the Heltons'. Oh, dude, I need you to help me break into my house soon."

"What?" said Jake. "Why?"

"Cause there's this bottle a Henny in there, and I gotta get it to Sammie's," said Cade.

"Why *break* in?" said Jake.

"Cause my aunt said she'd change the locks," said Cade.

"What?!" said Jake. "Why?"

"Dude, I don't fuckin' know," said Cade. "She's a bitch. And I don't know. I'm not supposed to be there or some shit. She's a bitch." He nearly fell, losing his balance as he leaned against his car.

"And there's Hennessy there?" said Jake.

"Yeah, I drank all Sammie's dad's shit, and I gotta replace it," said Cade. "She said she's gonna change the locks."

"That sucks!" said Jake.

"That's what *I'm* tellin','" said Cade.

"Ok, let's talk tomorrow," said Jake. "Why don't I drive you home?"

"Nah, it's just right up the street," said Cade.

"Make sure your lights are on," said Jake.

"...No doubt," said Cade after burping loudly. Standing in place, he stumbled forward then back, nearly falling.

"You got smokes?" said Jake.

"Yeah, I got smokes. Thank you, brother," said Cade, going in for an embrace. "You're my brother. I love you, fam."

"Love you too, fam," said Jake. "Go straight home."

"Can't, locks are changed," said Cade, entering his vehicle slowly and dropping all of his weight at once as if he were obese and out of breath. He reached for the door in vain.

"Seatbelt, bro," said Jake, shutting it for him. Cade started the car, checked his side-view mirror, and went into the night.

"Cade is drinking too much," said Maureen.

"I'm not surprised!" said Aunt Jackie. "I am *not* surprised. Do you have any more scotch?"

"Sure, Ray?" said Maureen. "Could you freshen Jackie's glass? We're just talkin' about Cade and think he can benefit from a sit-down? Ok?"

"Mo, I've gotta bury my father," said Ray, preparing liquor and bringing it to them. "I don't want to talk about this now."

"I think that's a good idea, Jackie," said Maureen. I don't know where he is, but I'm sure he—"

"I know where he isn't," said Jackie.

"What's that?" said Maureen.

"I'd like to keep him here so you and Ray can keep an eye on him," said Jackie.

"Easier said than done, ya know!" said Maureen, smiling and laughing.

Cade had made it past the busy intersection of six corners and had half the distance of Hendricks to go.

His stomach rumbled. Deciding to head out past the limits of the suburb for pizza, he turned left onto Olney Drive to get a glimpse of his house along the way. He thought about parking and trying his key, but hunger diffused that idea. ...Main Street approached.

"Sammie, honey, have you heard from Cade?" said Maureen.

"No, no, I haven't seen him in a few days," said Sammie, getting her third beer out of the fridge.

"How many beers is that for you, Sammie?" said Jackie.

"What?" said Sammie. "Um, my second."

"My?" said Maureen, addressing her son. "Do you know where Cade is?"

"No," said Miles. "He's probably at Jake Armao's place."

Cade rolled through the red light from Eggert Road onto Main heading toward Sal's Pizza in the University Heights district of Buffalo. It was just after 10 pm.

"That kid is in for a rude awakening if he keeps pulling this shit," said Jackie, finishing her glass.

"Well, Jackie, I understand where you're coming from," said Maureen. "But Cade...Cade is a great guy, ok? And I think he's just going through a difficult time without his mom, ok? And I think he's gonna get through this and show some improvement soon, ya know? Ok?"

"He'd better," said Jackie.

People filtered out as the gathering started to dissipate.

"I think he will, ya know," said Maureen, calm and sympathetic. "I'm committed, ok, to helping Cade. And...ya know...he and I just need a little bit of old-fashioned communication and—"

"Communication?!" said Jackie. "Good luck!" Maureen mentally acknowledged the difference between herself and Cade's aunt regarding being in touch with the boy but held her tongue. She knew the candidacy lied heavily in her favor as the rapport between herself and Cade was strong. She continued to try and ease Jackie's mind as she recognized how similar she looked to Cade's mother, her departed best friend.

He approached the hard bend of Main Street nearly devoid of cars with loud music going and all four windows down. Visually, he processed the police car gaining on him via his rearview mirror but continued driving fearlessly. The lights swallowed up the car which he steered to the side of the road directly in front of the all-girls high school, a desolate grey with massive pillars in front.

"Cade just needs a friend," said Maureen.

"License and registration."

"He's gonna wind up in jail."

"All right, sit tight. I'll be right back."

"Well, I think we can help him."

"Have you had anything to drink tonight?"
"Yeah, just two beers."

"Well, I think he's got a long road ahead of him, but we care about him. I think he'll be all right in the long run."

"Where are ya coming from tonight?"
"A friend's house."

"I know he used to steal from my sister."

"Aup! You...You think so?"

"I *know* so!"

"A friend's house? Where."

"Lamont Drive."

"What's your friend's name, Cade?"

"Um, Tom."

"What did he steal, mon—"

"Money! Out of her purse! She was too damn trusting. And too damn drunk!"

"Tom? And uh, where ya headed tonight?"

"Sal's Pizza."

"Sal's Pizza? What's at Sal's Pizza?"

"Dude. What? I'm goin' ta get my tires rotated."

"I think Cade just needs a little TLC."

"Uh huh. And what have you had to drink tonight?

"Just a forty."

"Well, I appreciate you and Ray taking him in. And I know he and Miles are like brothers. But that kid needs more than TLC."

"Can you say your ABCs for me?"

"He needs a kick in the B-U-T-T."

"A,B,C,D,E,F,G.....and so forth."

"Why don't you step outta the car for me. What did you say your friend's name was?"

"Jeff."

"Step over here behind the vehicle. We're gonna do some sobriety tests, ok?"

"Yeah, ok."

"Stand up straight—keep your hands out of your pockets. Now, without moving your head, keep your eyes on my pen, ok?"

"Ok."

"Keep your hands out of your pockets....With*out* moving your head."

"Ok."

"Keep your hands out of your pockets."

"Ok."

"Just relax your arms and keep them at your sides. Ok, just follow my pen....ok, with*OUT* moving your head."

"All right."

"Cade. Don't move your head, ok?"

"Gotcha."

"Just follow the pen *with your eyes*, ok? Do not move your head."

"I *am* moving my head. Just hold the pen still, and I'll move my head."

Another squad car arrived soundlessly with its lights flashing. Cade peered around the officer in front of him. He saw another cop walking toward him with a kid around his age dressed in plain clothes. The two approached. Cade was puzzled and transfixed on the boy his age. He spoke to him: "Did you get busted too?" The two officers communicated quietly to each other while the plain clothes boy stared at Cade.

"Ok, Cade, we're gonna give you a breath test. Is that ok?"

"Uh, yeah, that's fine." The second cop put the breathalyzer into his mouth.

"Ok, blow. ...Keep blowing, keep blowing, keep blowing, keep blowing, keep blowing, keep blowing, keep blowing..."

Cade's eyes widened with the unexpected intensity. He released his lips in order to inhale. After breathing in, his wet mouth returned to the device after using his tongue like a lizard's to find it.

"...keep blowing, keep blowing, keep blowing, keep blowing." The device was pulled from his mouth.

To the kid, Cade said, "What the fuck are you staring at?"

"You sure you guys can handle him being here with your three kids and everything you've got going on already, Maureen?"

"You're under arrest for driving while intoxicated."

They cuffed Cade, read his rights, and placed him in the rear of a police car. The two coworkers spoke outside the car as Cade watched in pain from the handcuffs. The original cop walked over to the car, opened the door, and spoke to him: "Are your parents at the address on your license?"

"No, they're dead," said Cade.

"They're dead?" said the cop, chuckling. "Where do you live?"

"I live down the street. On Hendricks. With my neighbors," said Cade.

"With your neighbors?"

"Yep," said Cade. "With my neighbors. I live with them now. My parents are dead." As requested, he recited Heltons' home number without a flaw. "Hey, what level did I blow to?" The cop closed the car door.

Cade waited alone in the back of the squad car, somewhere between sleep and consciousness. He became comfortable. He felt safe. His vision defended the flashing colorful lights and the yellow streetlamp's emissions by stretching and obscuring it. Cars passed slowly to his right to catch a glimpse of the arrest which didn't bother him. Cade had reached contentment in his predicament. A complete surrender washed over him.

Maureen arrived and she and Ray got out as a confused Cade watched them converse with the officers. He closed his eyes and as the weight of his head dropped before his chest, he fell asleep.

The car door opened. "Let's go, Cade," said the arresting officer. He helped the prisoner to his feet. "You're gonna go home with...Maureen, is it?"

"Yes, officer, thank you," said Maureen.

He unlocked the cuffs. Maureen guided Cade to the passenger side of her van. He sat alone as Ray climbed into the periwinkle Elantra. Maureen said goodbye to the officers who gave her a couple of papers. She entered the van. "What about my car?" said Cade. "What's Ray doing inside my car today?" said Cade.

Suppressing her anger, Maureen said, "Ray is taking your car to my house, ok?"

"How come I'm not in the cop car anymore?" said Cade, hiccupping.

"I talked to them, Cade," said Maureen. "You're going home. And tomorrow, we're gonna talk."

THE SUN RAN THROUGH the bedroom like a shakedown at a rave, waking the man of the hour from a slumber reminiscent of before he was born. His tongue was thick and dry. His pulse, tormented, gained pace. Shellshocked again, sick and pale, he wondered if he had any pizza left. Or was it all in his stomach? *Grandpa Ted,* he thought.

He looked over at Miles' vacant bed. Pain darted to his knuckles. It was quiet. A head rush, his penalty for standing, led his posterior back to the mattress. He waited there for an answer.

Amidst bright light, he was born again into a void, hopelessly obsidian, that carried him over to the third story window by which he thought might be apt to leave. Putting his head out after lifting the screen, a languid wasp communicated with the air around his face. There was a boy questionably too young to be by himself peering up at him from the sidewalk. And among the hot calm afternoon, the two in negligence of the gift that sang from around and above looked into each other's eyes. To Cade, the child spoke.

He lowered the screen and headed back to the bed. There was no water. He needed out.

After a shower and change of clothes, the message that ran between his hand and brain cried louder. Stepping out of the bathroom, Maureen was there, shaken. Oddly, her eye contact with Cade faltered. Her voice like a bow in a storm befell. "I suggest you have some breakfast. There's leftover pizza and stuff in the fridge you can heat up. I'll be down to talk with you."

"Ok," said Cade. "Thanks, Maureen." The sound of her name and humility in his voice conjured tenderness.

"Hi, Major," he said, making his way to the kitchen.

"Hi," said Major, who kept moving.

Taking Maureen's advice, Cade filled his belly.

"This family has been through a lot, ok?" said Maureen. "And with the death of Grandpa Ted, what happened last night is very problematic for this family, ok? Do you know?"

"Yes," said Cade.

"What happened last night...I'm glad to have helped you...and your aunt doesn't seem to have as much sympathy for your situation as I do and that is...hard for me to understand, Cade. But nonetheless, I think you're a great guy and you have so much potential....and I'm willing to work with you...and Ray...Ray is willing to work with you too. Or at least, he's gonna allow, for lack of a better word, me to work with you, ok?"

"Ok," said Cade.

"SO...there's the matter of these tickets," said Maureen, fiddling about her purse and putting on her glasses. "Crossing the yellow line... sounds so elementary, don't ya think? And speeding. Fifty in a thirty-five. Well, that doesn't sound so bad, does it. I think you and I can handle these if we get a good lawyer and I think I know who to get, ok?"

"Ok," said Cade. "Whose tickets are those?"

Maureen's mouth opened in disbelief. She looked at him.

"Those are...mine?"

"Augh, YES, CADE! MISTER CAYBUL! THESE ARE YOUR TICKETS FROM THE GODDAMN AMHERST POLICE DEPARTMENT! You mean you don't remember?"

"Um, kinda, I…" said Cade.

"Oh, wow, I never thought of that," said Maureen.

"Um, I remember some—um, a little...I remember…"

"Cade, honey...ok. Ok, let's just regroup here a minute," said

Maureen. Embracing the urge to both omit and express details, she decided that Cade blacking out was too good a gift to destroy. This unspoken conclusion was easily sensed by the guilty party in front of her. "You know, we're gonna take care a ya, ok?" Maureen was calm and smiled. "You got these tickets last night and they were gonna give you a DWI, but I showed up and spoke with them...ok? ...The police...and they let ya go with only these two fuckin' tickets, ok?" she said as she slapped his face gently with the papers.

"Ok," said Cade. "I have to stop drinking so much."

"YA THINK?!!" said Maureen. "HOLY SHIT, CADE CAYBUL, YA THINK SO?!! WOW, STOP THE PRESSES; THAT'S THE MOST INTELLIGENT THING I THINK YOU'VE EVER SAID!!" She smacked each side of his face with papers and laughed. "WOW! COLLEGE GRADUATE, CADEWELL CAYBUL IN *MY* KITCHEN! WHEN'S YOUR NEXT DISSERTATION?! YA GONNA RECITE THE PERIODIC TABLE?! PERIODIC CAYBUL! PERIODIC CADE CAYBUL!—"

"All right!" said Cade.

"Yeah, all right is right!" said Maureen. Cade did not want to ask for information. Not then. He thought he might go and talk with Miles. He remembered driving out to Main Street after leaving Jake's and the issue with police was not entirely gone from his memory now that Maureen had filled him in. He retreated upstairs after being released by the stern yet comforting grip of his dead mother's best friend.

Now that he had seen a glimpse of the truth and it was met with sympathy, his mind rested upon the mission of seeking more. But last night's turning point, to the humans at Heltons' household, was anything but a mystery...

"Cade, you're going to have to calm down if you're going to go into my home," said Maureen from her driver's seat, anticipating the drunken teenager's entrance among her mourning guests and family.

"What the fuck is everybody here for anyways?" said Cade.

"Grandpa Ted died, Cade," said Maureen.

"Aw, fuck, oh no. Aw fuck," said Cade. "What the hell is my Aunt doing here, shit."

"She was down at your house doing some work and—" said Maureen.

"Yeah, she changed the locks," said Cade. "That's the work she did. Fucking bitch."

"Cade," said Maureen.

"What?" said Cade.

"I don't know what to do now," said Maureen. "I understand you're feeling bad, but we've got to...oh, look, there's Ray." Ray had parked Cade's vehicle in the street and walked past the car in the driveway where his wife tried to pacify the pariah. He ignored her and his long term houseguest and walked into the house via the back door.

"He hates me," said Cade.

"He doesn't hate you," said Maureen. "He's just a little...frustrated."

"Can you get my keys?" said Cade.

"Cade," said Maureen. "Shit, duder. I can get you a lot of things. Your keys ain't one of them."

"I gotta use the bathroom." Cade walked toward the rear of the house and Maureen, in conceding, followed. He entered. His Aunt Jackie was sitting at the table.

"Hello, Cade," she said. "You are a piece of work, you know that? I don't know how the hell you think—"

"Shut your goddamn mouth," he said, opening a box of pizza and helping himself to a slice. He stumbled to the fridge, took out a beer, and popped it open. "GRANDPA TEDDY REST IN PEACE!" Out of the kitchen, he headed toward the bathroom where Sammie was just exiting.

"Cade, hey," she said.

"Gotta piss," said Cade, entering the bathroom with pizza in one hand and a beer in the other. "Sometimes I wonder if women shit." He left the door ajar and urinated.

"Any a you goddamn motherfuckers comes near me?" he said. "I'm gonna kick yer ass. I hate cops." The toilet seat came down loudly against the porcelain before he walked into the living room where his presence gained the attention of Ray's brother, sister-in-law, and nieces.

"Oh, hey everybody," said Cade.

"Cade, hello," said Ray's brother.

"Yes, hello, you girls used to wipe my ass, didn't you?" said Cade, addressing Ray's nieces, who used to babysit him. "Well, I bet this is weird, pretty weird, right now. Don't even think about it," he said, turning and heading for the stairs. "I wash my own fuckin' ass right now." He doubled back, went into the kitchen, and retrieved two more slices of pizza, two beers, and headed for his and Miles' room.

"YOU BETTER NOT BE FUCKIN'!" he shouted, ascending the attic stairs to the room illuminated by every lightbulb within it. Among the eleven people looking directly at him, Cade noticed Sammie's eyes the most. Casually he said, "'Sup everybody. I got pulled over by the cops. What the hell is goin' on in here with it?"

"'Sup, dude," said Miles, walking apprehensively toward his inebriated friend with a brooding look.

Maureen entered the room, following Cade.

"Chillin'," said Cade, chewing pizza and tossing the other two slices on the edge of the pool table. Sammie tended to the misplaced food swiftly to prevent a stain on the felt. "Those are mine, beautiful ass," said Cade. "You people gotta go or else I'm gonna start jerkin' off here with the lights on. So turn the lights on, it's time to go."

"Why don't you guys go hang out downstairs, ok?" said Maureen to the mortified humans in the room, some relatives and some Miles' friends. Cade fell onto his bed.

With guests filing out of the bedroom and down the stairs, Maureen kept her eyes on Cade's motionless face. When everyone was gone, she turned out all the lights and went downstairs to face the music.

10

_____

WITHOUT EYES

After the chat with Maureen and some sleep, Cade went to his old home and tried keying in. It was true, his key no longer worked. He easily got in through a window from the backyard.

Along with some of his clothes and an old bottle of gin that was almost full, he returned to his car with the Hennessy and a buzz. He drove to Sammie's and noticed that the only car in the driveway was Ray's, signifying that Miles was there. Sammie was happy to accept the token of restitution.

The three of them went to Grandpa Ted's wake. At the signature book at the funeral home, Cade's hand was shaking so much that he couldn't sign. Sammie became aware of his fear but, following Miles' lead, the couple pretended not to notice. And for most of the time spent at the wake, Sammie and Cade grouped together.

They stayed for slightly over an hour as Ray had encouraged them to leave early to protect the house from thieves as calling hours were made public. Miles dropped his friend at Heltons' and he and Sammie went back to her place.

Cade was alone. He put on music and cleaned the kitchen and both bathrooms. While mowing the lawn, he waved at the neighbors then swept the driveway. He bagged trash from inside and brought it to the curb beyond bee balm flowers and black-eyed susans.

Enjoying the hot summer air and the scent of cut grass, he strolled up the driveway when his work was complete. He was greeted by a man coming from the house next door, a man he had never seen before. He was in his early fifties wearing blue jeans, a banal shirt, winter hat, and sunglasses.

"Hey!" said the man. Cade slowed to a stop and turned to him as he approached. "Hey, I wanna talk to you! Who the hell do you think you are?!"

"What?" said Cade.

"*What?*" said the man. "My mother lives next door. She says you've been shouting at her from the attic window. She says you've been calling her a cunt and whore and all sorts of crap!"

"What?!" said Cade. "No! I have no idea what you're talking about!"

"I just want it to stop. And it *better* stop."

"It isn't me!" said Cade. "I would never say things like that to an old la—"

"*Look*, you son of a bitch, I want it to stop and it better stop 'cause you do not want to piss me off."

"Listen, your mother is wrong," said Cade. "I don't know what the hell you're—"

The man grabbed Cade's shirt by the chest, clenched his fist, cocked his arm back, and began shouting. "*LISTEN* TO ME, YOU DEGENERATE PIECE OF SHIT, IF YOU EVER DO IT AGAIN,

YOU'LL REGRET IT! IT STOPS NOW!"

Cade had planted one foot behind him to brace down and his left hand against the man's shoulder and held tight. He readied his right fist. What, in an instance, had become a fearful moment that came on like an oceanic wave gaining unseen momentum transformed as quickly as Cade's eyes changed from wide open to narrow and concentrated. The man's eyes, on the contrary, were unseen as his sunglasses were mirrored from the outside, reflecting Cade's face to himself. Looking into his own eyes and gripping his accuser as hard as he could, Cade remarked, "*Do not fuck with me. I do not care if you live or if you die.*" The man let go, turned his back, and walked away.

Cade waited without blinking until he was out of sight. He went to his and Miles' room and embraced his solitude although confusion had flourished.

The Heltons returned to their home after retrieving Major from his sitter's. Amidst a mild argument over who would take out the garbage, all were surprised to see that it had already been done. Ray and Maureen were pleased that their place had been tended to and cleaned. They let Cade alone, but in a rare moment, he craved consolation, particularly from Maureen.

Night wrapped its somber arms around the earth, darkening the attic bedroom. After watching a movie on which he could hardly concentrate, followed by carnal self-preservation, Cade laid upon his bed in need of rest. Although he replayed the attack in his mind over and again, he made room for a common thought that typically flourished at bedtime. He thought of the massive amount of people in the world, some in darkness, some in light. He thought of the maltreated and dwelled upon the ugliness of the intention of humans. He thought of dogs and cats in cages with excrement. He thought of women mass raped. He thought of starvation and disease. In futility, his young mind pondered how many were suffering at that very moment all over the planet. And he thought of his mother and visualized her calling out to her son who wasn't there before she died.

The mind's hunger for a reset triumphed although the goal was far from attained. Cade heard the mechanism of the door at the foot of the stairs click as if shut. Then the steps creaked impossibly louder than usual as if the stairs were made of wood without carpet. From his back on the mattress and without choice, he waited for the stranger to arrive.

A creature entered swiftly. Resembling a man, it glided instead of walked. As if on an assembly line that hit an L, the apparition came forward to the bed then cut parallel toward Cade, making itself more visible. Conjoined with the sudden realization that the intention of the intruder was to attack, Cade's fear grew as he anticipated not only the dwindling space between them but the thought that he would soon see its visage from up close.

It came to Cade's side, crouched down as if to eat his face but instead, only hovered. The beast had no features whatsoever. It had no mouth, no eyes, or nose—just blackness. And the more its victim struggled, the less he could move and the more afraid he became. Cade, his eyes several inches from the mass, scoured the levitating head for a human resemblance. He concluded that its garment was seemingly a part of its body rather than a physical form wearing clothing. The thing, without eyes, looked directly at Cade from point blank range and in complete control like a child observing an insect impaled on a stick under a magnifying glass in the torrid sun.

Cade wiggled his toes and his eyes shot round his head until there was nothing in sight but the objects in the room.

He'd lie awake for hours, afraid to return to where he'd been.

11

HEY, TIGER, WAKE UP

"We should take drugs and go to Darien Lake."

"That...does not sound like a bad idea," said Miles as they laid together in her bed. "But I think my heart might explode if I was tripping on a rollercoaster."

"Nah, bruh, X," said Sammie.

"Oh, I don't know," said Miles. "Doesn't that stuff put a pin hole in your brain every time you use it?"

"It's called *rolling*, not tripping. And who cares. Life sucks and then you die," said Sammie. "I'm gonna have Alzheimer's from all the weed I smoked in tin foil."

"Ecstasy at *Darien Lake*?" said Miles. "I don't know. That sounds weird."

"We can make out on a roller coaster," said Sammie, increasing her intensity seductively.

"*That* sounds good," said Miles. "Or a Ferris wheel."

"Ferris wheels are lame," said Sammie.

"Yeah," said Miles. "But they'd be easier to kiss on."

"Yeah, whatever, let's do it soon," said Sammie. "I bet my sister's peeps can score."

"I don't know if I can handle that right now with my family the way we are," said Miles while Sammie realized the error of her overzealous proposal. "I should try and keep it together. Doing X for the first time might be better at another date."

"Ok," said Sammie. "How's your dad?"

"I think he's ok," said Miles. "He's weird. He's been talking to himself and saying weird stuff that doesn't make any sense."

"Has he cried?" said Sammie.

"Yeah, the first night after he found him," said Miles. "I heard him from their bedroom."

"That's healthy," said Sammie.

"I bet Cade would be down to do that," said Miles.

"Do what?" said Sammie.

"Darien," said Miles.

"Oh," said Sammie. "Cade'll do anything."

"Yeah, he would!" said Miles.

As Sammie mounted her lover and put her hands on his chest, she said, "But I wanna go with *you!*" Miles felt her naked breasts silently. "It's ok, I understand," she added.

"I love your tits," said Miles.

"My tits suck," said Sammie.

"I suck your tits, but they certainly don't suck," said Miles.

"They're small!" she said, grinding her body on him.

"Careful, you might trigger round two," said Miles.

"Uh, yeah, and what's wrong with that?" said Sammie. Miles visually focused on her bust squeezing and massaging as Sammie watched too. "I want big ones," she said.

"You gonna get implants?" said Miles.

"What?! Hell no, dude!" said Sammie. "Implants are gross."

"Yes, they are," said Miles.

"I guess I'm just doomed with little ones," said Sammie, putting her hands flat upon Miles' chest.

"They're not so bad," said Miles.

"Um, *thanks*, dude," said Sammie.

"Well, no, I mean—" said Miles.

"You mean nothing," said Sammie, sliding his hands off of her and replacing them with her own. Peering down with her bottom lip protruding, she massaged her nipples with her thumb and middle and forefinger.

"I could get used to this!" said Miles.

Sammie paused, gently bit her lip, made eye contact with Miles, smiled, and squeezed her breasts slowly and adamantly.

"Oh, baby!" said Miles.

"Oh, me!" she said, revolving her hips and grinding her butt. "Augh! Oh me! Oh, God, I'm so fuckin' hot!"

"Holy shit," said Miles. "I'm getting hard again," said Miles.

"Um, yeah, thanks for the news flash," said Sammie.

Miles reasserted his hands before she brought her face to his and they kissed. He ran his fingers all the way down her back and took hold of her bottom.

"Put it in," he said.

"No," said Sammie, retreating to her side where they kissed more.

"Try being on top," he said.

"No," she said, flopping to her back. Her shoulder communicated with his arm to relinquish the center of the bed before his place she took over. Gently easing her knees apart, he made himself between, pushed through, and moaned.

They had only had sex in this position. She was defiant to his requests of unconventionality, a consistent rejection he didn't mind too much. She took a monthly contraceptive and allowed him to frequently ejaculate inside of her. But recently, during sexual union, her mind would wander. That drifting wasn't exactly uncommon, but of late, she had been visiting and revisiting the same new place. And she found that the more removed she became, the closer she embarked to the nether.

"DUDE. Thanks for cleaning when my 'rents were at the wake. That made them happy. Even my dad."

"Um, no problem. It felt good to clean up." Cade wanted to tell his friend about the assault but withheld.

"Do you wanna play pool?" said Miles.

"Sure," said Cade.

The boys meandered about the big red table in the room they shared and talked.

"So how have you been feeling?" said Miles.

"Um, not too bad," said Cade.

"Yeah?" said Miles. "How have you been sleeping?"

"Ok, I guess," said Cade.

"Really?" said Miles.

"Well, I've been having nightmares still," said Cade.

"Like...about your Mom still?" said Miles.

"Well, yeah," said Cade. "That and...other stuff too."

"You want to run it by me, bro?" said Miles.

"Um, I don't know...what to...what's this?" Between turns, Cade had picked up *The Kama Sutra* from Miles' dresser.

"Kama Sutra!" said Miles.

"Whoa," said Cade. "Where did you get this?"

"It's Todd's. He loaned it to me," said Miles. "By the way, I think he's coming over here with Connor and maybe Ked."

"Oh, cool," said Cade, disguising his disappointment. "This chick is hot."

"Yeah she is," said Miles. Cade set the book on the edge of the pool table and continued the game. "Look, I know you and my mom have a rapport, and—"

"A what?" said Cade.

"A rapport," said Miles. "Like a...special bond. A trust."

"Oh, gotcha," said Cade.

"But, like, you know I'm here for you too, right?" said Miles. "'Cause I know she can get overbearing."

Cade's admiration for his friend almost seethed into envy. Miles' ability to balance assertion with kindness was perplexing right down to the way that he walked, spoke, and held eye contact. Cade almost always felt as if he didn't belong in the same room with Miles. And with word of his friends arriving shortly with whom he had significant trust and past experiences of camaraderie, a panic attack had reared its head.

"Yeah, I know, thanks, My," said Cade. "Your mom saved my ass the other night."

"Yeah, I heard about that," said Cade. "How drunk were you when you got pulled over?!"

"Pretty damn drunk," said Cade. "After we talked about it, I started to remember things...such as trying to say my ABCs, which I could not do."

"Ah, brown out," said Miles.

"What?" said Cade.

"Brown out," said Miles. "It's like a black-out but not as severe. Like when little things start coming back to you."

"Whoa," said Cade. "Yeah, if it weren't for your mom, I'd have a DUI."

"Word," said Miles. I just hope that she can save me one day like that."

"Yeah, just don't get pulled over by the same cops as I did," said Cade.

"Yeah!" said Miles.

"Oh, and there was a little ride-along pussy there too!" said Cade.

"What?!" said Miles.

"There was this kid my age there with the cops," said Cade. "Our age. With the cops."

"Like a wanna-be future cop?" said Miles.

"Yeah," said Cade.

"What a bitch!" said Miles.

"Yeah, he sucked," said Cade. "The whole thing sucked ass," said Cade.

"I'll bet," said Miles. "Well, except for not getting a DUI."

"Yeah, that part was good," said Cade.

"YO, YO!" they heard from the foot of the attic stairs.

"YO!" said Miles.

The steps, to Cade, resounded an intimidating amount of noise just before there were three more humans in the room, swallowing up space.

"What up, My. 'Sup, Cade," said Todd, who struggled with the more blue-collar handshake from Cade.

"Hey, Cade, how are ya," said Connor, the most mellow of the three. "'Sup, Miles."

"Yo, yo!" said Ked who hugged both of his hosts, comforting the fearful one.

"Who's stripes?" said Ked.

"I am," said Miles. "But I don't think it matters, 'cause Cade and I both suck at pool."

"You guys live and sleep next to an awesome pool table but you both suck?" said Ked.

"Pretty much," said Miles.

"I'm only good when I'm drunk," said Cade.

"Connor, what happened to your eyes?!" said Miles.

"Oh, nothing," said Connor. "Allergies."

"What's this?" said Ked. "Oh, Kama Sutra! Nice."

"Yeah, it's mine, I loaned it to My," said Todd. "After I mastered it, of course."

"After you masturbated it?" said Miles.

"How's it going with Sammie, My?" said Todd.

"Pretty good," said Miles confidently.

"Oooooh, this one's my favorite," said Todd. "What about you, My?"

"Which one?" said Miles. "Oh, Sammie's not flexible enough for that."

"Dude, is there porn in here?" said Ked, inspecting the VCR.

"Probably," said Miles.

"Yeah, how do you two work that out?" said Todd.

"We don't jack off when each other is here!" said Miles.

"Yeah, it's pretty simple," said Cade.

Ked pressed play on the VCR and turned the volume down.

"Hey, My, Mary's little friends downstairs are gonna be pretty hot soon," said Todd.

"Mary's gonna be pretty hot soon," said Ked.

"Shut it," said Miles.

"Ok, Mary *is* pretty hot *now*," said Ked, play-punching Miles who smiled and played along.

"That reminds me," said Todd. "Cade, can you get any blow?"

"Nah, I don't think so," said Cade. "I can try somebody."

"Damn, this chick is hot," said Ked, engulfed in the book.

"What about X?" said Todd.

"Maybe," said Cade. "Probably."

"Oh!" said Miles, noticing his girlfriend ascending the stairs quietly. "'Sup, baby!"

"Hi," said Sammie. "'Sup, white stains."

Cade approached for a hug unexpectedly. She dodged him and hugged Miles then initiated a hug with Cade, letting go quicker than usual. The other boys greeted her too then Sammie walked to the couch parallel with the windows, knelt on it, and peered out. She accentuated her posterior in a comfortable stretch.

"I like your skirt, said Todd, patronizing. "Are those elephants?"

"Well, they ain't dinosaurs," said Sammie, looking through the glass.

Ked quietly turned off the VCR, which displayed soundless pornography.

"You look beautiful, baby," said Miles who brushed his hand along her hip and buttocks.

"Thank you, baby," said Sammie. "Who's winning?"

"I think Cade was but we weren't keeping track," said Miles.

"Ok, so, I'm playin' Cade?" said Sammie.

"No, I don't feel like playing," said Cade who became ill at the thought of five people watching him closely at once.

"Damn straight," said Sammie, getting up from the couch and straightening her back slowly. "Good porn, Kederick?"

"What?" said Ked. The only one smiling in the room was Miles.

"The porn-you-just-shut-off," said Sammie. "Any good? Did I interrupt the upcoming circle jerk or what?"

"Yeah, I was about to start myself," said Connor.

"Now *that* I'd like to see," said Sammie, triggering undetected jealousy from Miles. "Babe, I wanna go to Darien Lake."

"When?" said Miles.

"I dunno," said Sammie. "ASAP?"

"I, uh—" said Miles.

"What up, Cadey-Cade?" said Sammie.

"What up," said Cade.

"Can you score some X?" said Sammie.

"Maybe, yeah," said Cade. "We were just talkin' about that."

"Cool, so, grab some pills aaaaand let's go to Darien Lake and ride roller coasters," said Sammie, her back to Cade, doing an almost backbend and looking at him upside down. "My sister might be down. And let's ask Ty Jai."

"Wow, that sounds like…" said Cade, taking a long pause of intrigue. Everyone in the room waited curiously for him to finish and oddly, he felt no anxiety amidst the silence. "A really good idea," he concluded. Sammie smiled.

"Cool," she said. "You're all invited too, ya jerks."

"That sounds intense," said Todd.

"Your face sounds intense," said Sammie who had started to rack billiard balls for a game.

Miles, after witnessing Cade's clarity of mind and decision of the proposal, began to think as if he'd be missing out on something. In that moment, he compared his lifestyle to Cade's, along with the lifestyle of his friends who, although they were bound by friendship to Cade as well as himself, were closer to the man of the house and had been connected to him for much longer. And he thought of those who were closer to Cade. The hands of his mind ran their fingers along the jagged ideals of Cade's crew who, until this moment, he thought of as dumb and reckless. The idea of taking drugs at an amusement park was, at its inception, too strange. But observing Sammie's intention, Miles gained a new outlook. And for the first time, he felt frighteningly distant from her.

"Break 'em up," she said.

The force from Connor's body and mind sent the colored orbs wheeling and crackling as Miles put on tunes and packed a bong.

"By the way, can you sell my sister some weed, Con? She'll buy a lot," continued Sammie. "What happened to your eyes?"

"Nah, not at the moment," said Connor like he was on downers. "Nothing. Just allergies."

"Really?!" said Sammie. "Since when do you not have weed to sell?" Sammie's pushiness aggravated Connor, but he continued to chew his gum calmly, waiting for her to hush and play. "Dude, whatever," she said. "Fuck this." She laid her cue onto the table, disrupting the places of the balls. "Let's just smoke."

"Your hair feels silly!" said Sammie, chuckling and stroking Todd's head, to his dismay.

"Yeah," he said, dodging her hands lethargically and grinning.

"You should not gel your hair," said Sammie.

"But I like to," said Todd.

"Ok, fine," said Sammie. "No, gel is weird. You shouldn't."

"Darien Lake, huh?" said Ked.

"Dude," said Cade. "Rolling through the clouds, I mean soaring through the clouds and rolling is a fantastic idea." The sensation of Sammie's smile traveled to their minds as she nodded at Cade, excited.

"Just make sure your hearts don't explode on a roller coaster," said Miles.

"I think we'll be fine," said Sammie.

Connor contradicted the energy of the room with his slow tempo. "I like the Ferris wheel."

"The Ferris wheel blows," said Sammie. "I'm gonna ride the mind eraser like ten times."

Miles passed her the bong then he opened the windows wide to ventilate the room. Sammie had a hit and passed it.

The bong came around to Cade as Maureen started up the stairs to socialize. He sensed her presence then passed without hitting.

"Aup! You guys better have a window open in here!" said Maureen.

"They're two open, Mom," said Miles.

"Wanna hit, Mo?" said Sammie.

"Me? No! I just wanted to see what you guys are up to in here," said Maureen, rubbing Cade's back.

"We're gonna go to Darien Lake, Mo," said Sammie.

"Oh?" said Maureen.

"Yeah, we're gonna go on pot," said Sammie.

"I see," said Maureen. "Well, don't go gettin' busted, ok? You goin', My?"

"I'm not sure I'm into it," said Miles. "But Cade and Sammie are."

"Sounds like fun," said Maureen. "Be careful drivin', you two." She kissed Cade on the forehead and walked away. "Come down and eat if anybody's hungry."

"Thanks, Mo," all said, excluding Miles and Cade.

They finished the bong, packed another, then finished that one.

"Cade, who can you get ecstasy from?" said Sammie.

"I—uh," said Cade.

"You get it from Carlos, don't you?" said Sammie.

"Uh, kind of," said Cade. "I can probably score."

"You should start selling weed, Cade," said Sammie.

"Weed smells," said Cade. "I've got nowhere to put it."

"That's weird," said Sammie. "Connor, let's play pool."

"Cade," said Todd. "If you get extras, I know who can take them off your hands."

"Oh, yeah?" said Cade. "Who?"

"Some kids from Williamsville South," said Todd.

"Are you talking about Roy and his idiot friends?" said Ked.

"Yeah," said Todd.

"Dude, those guys are shady as hell," said Ked.

"Yeah, I know," said Todd. "But they have lots of money and they keep asking Aaron if he can get X and he can't."

Miles watched Cade as he thought about it.

"I'll see what dude has," said Cade.

"Yeah, let me know," said Todd.

"Todd, do you trust them?" said Miles.

"Well, it's Erica's cousin, she knows them," said Todd. "And Aaron knows Roy and the one dude."

"So that's a no," said Miles.

"Well, kinda, I—" said Todd.

"Let's beat 'em and take their money," said Sammie from near the pool table. "Hey, Cade, when do you want to go to Darien Lake?"

"I don't know," said Cade. "After I get the shit sometime?"

"Perfect," she said.

Sleep for Cade came a bit easier that night, but like always, he had a disturbance. This time, his dream was one of lucidity.

He was walking through woods in search of a trash can in which to drop what he was carrying when he felt and saw a white tiger following him. The tiger's intention was to kill. There as well, Sammie and some other friends were drinking at a table among the trees. She was the only one watching him and her focus and thought was of Cade and his safety near the beast. Everyone else was sitting on stools with their backs to him and the tiger who, no matter how fast Cade ran, gained pace.

As the tiger walked to him, Miles, unseen until this point, drew a gun from his body and shot the tiger who transformed from dangerous and powerful to meek, humble, and close to death. Cade, upon approaching the tiger, immediately turned from frightened prey to concerned helper. And as he looked into the tiger's eyes that were no longer cunning but more like that of a scared dog, he saw how helpless it was and his fear gave way for sadness and pity for the dying cat.

Waking, he cried.

12

LOVE BLOOD

ade set out to buy ecstasy. A friend of his, Carlos, knew a guy from his work who said he could get a lot. He met him downtown at Carlos' apartment complex and he purchased fifty pills on the man's word that they were good. Cade trusted Carlos and had a good vibe from the dealer who was short, timid, and effeminate, which gave Cade a sense of superiority and safety. The price made it easy to profit later.

That night, Cade, Jake, and Ty tried the X, which were the best pills any of them had done. During their roll—which they experienced together all night by driving, smoking, talking, and listening to music—they had conversed about selling some to the guys that Todd had mentioned.

The next day, Cade reached out to Todd who devised the trade by giving him the number to a person known as Roy. The deal was to go down in the woods at Winston School which served as a suitable halfway point that both sides of town used as a hang-out spot. Cade convinced Jake to go with him to get rid of twenty-five pills of ecstasy at twenty dollars each, which Roy agreed to immediately.

Sammie was having dinner with Miles and his family when they started to discuss future plans, both near and distant.

"Miles is gonna go to Loyola for college, Sammie," said Ray. "What do you think about that?"

"I *might* go to Loyola, Dad," said Miles. "I might take a year off."

"I don't think that's a good idea," said Ray.

"Ray, whichever thing Miles wants to do is the right thing," said Maureen, winking at Sammie.

"He's gonna be a history teacher," said Ray, staring at Sammie and chewing his food too fast.

"I like history," said Sammie.

"I *might* be a history teacher, Dad," said Miles, taking a big bite of steak.

"What do you like about history, Sammie?" said Ray.

"Dad," said Miles, laughing. "What the hell are you talking about?"

"I just wanna know what she—" said Ray.

"She likes the history part," said Miles. "That's enough."

"What's Cade gonna do when he gets older?" said Major. "Besides live with us."

"That's a good question, Maje," said Ray, his mouth full of food.

"No, it isn't," said Maureen as Miles, Mary, and Sammie sniggered.

"He's probably out driving drunk right now," said Major, basking in the attention he was receiving.

"No, he isn't!" said Maureen. "He's with Jake."

"Well, maybe Jake's driving drunk with Cade!" said Major, looking at Sammie, who was laughing with her head down.

"May*be,* Mo," said Ray.

"I don't think so!" said Maureen.

"Did he pay those tickets, mom?" said Mary.

"Yes, he did," said Maureen, becoming frustrated.

"You sure he didn't drink the tickets?" said Ray, chewing food.

"Now that's enough!" said Maureen as nearly everyone at the table laughed. "The kid could come walking in here any damn minute, Ray!"

"Ok, Mo, ok," said Ray, enjoying his audience, not unlike his youngest son.

"How would you feel if you were alienated like that in your own home?!" said Maureen.

"It's not his home; it's *my* home," said Ray.

"IT'S EVERYBODY'S HOME!" said Maureen. "He's 18 years old, Ray! And his mother's dead! I'd be drinkin' too!"

"Ok, Mo, we're eating," said Ray.

"What the hell does that have to do with anything?!" said Maureen.

"Come on," said Ray.

"Come on what, Ray?!" said Maureen.

"Easy, mom," said Miles as Sammie laughed.

"I'm changing the subject," said Maureen. "Miles, Sammie, I—well, I don't know what the hell to say."

"So anyways, I might become a history teacher!" said Miles.

"Yeah, what do you think of that, Sammie?" said Ray. "He might be going away to Loyola."

"Where's that?" said Sammie.

"Chicago," said Ray.

"He doesn't know where he's going yet," said Maureen nearly speaking through her teeth at her husband. "Would ya knock it off, Ray?"

"Knock what off?" said Ray.

"You know what you're doing," said Maureen.

"We're gonna be excused," said Miles and he and Sammie went outside.

Miles lit his last and was about to toss his empty pack into the canister.

"Camel Cash," said Sammie.

Miles handed her the bill from his pack. "How many of those do you have?" he asked.

"A whole bunch," said Sammie. Miles sat, put each hand on her hips, and pulled her into his lap where they sat together.

"I have to pee," said Sammie.

"Me too," said Miles, thrusting.

"Stop!" she said, smiling. He kissed the back of her neck as they smoked.

"Loyola, huh?" said Sammie. Miles took a slow drag from his cigarette, exhaled, and held his pause.

"It's a thought," said Miles.

"Cool, bra," said Sammie. "Your dad's a trip."

"He just gets nervous around lots of people," said Miles.

"Lots of people?" said Sammie. "You mean his family and me?"

"Yeah, well, uh—" said Miles.

"That's dumb," said Sammie before initiating a kiss.

The couple, minds fluttering in and out of sync, sat together in silence.

"How much Camel Cash do you really have?" said Miles.

"Enough to buy and sell your sorry ass," said Sammie.

The sun shone brightly at the parking lot of the private and costly Winston School. Cade and Jake were nervous and hungover. Especially Cade. They were early. To faculty and students, they looked suspicious but the woods around the school provided plenty of space to blend in.

The meeting place was at the "docks" with the graffiti. Cade and Jake knew the spot. For them and their friends, Winston school was frequented just enough to have enough confidence to know their way around. There were wooden walkways throughout swamp-like water with tall grass and plants. The environment embodied characteristics of Florida or Louisiana rather than the Northeast. Cade and Jake looked about the parking lot, making incidental eye contact with a few uniformed students as they headed into the marshy place.

Their feet hit the wooden planks, which creaked and moaned as they walked. Jake lit a smoke and handed it to Cade, then he lit one for himself. No dialogue between them triggered the tobacco exchange.

They saw two boys a couple years their junior who were smoking. Jake turned behind and connected eyes with his friend. Cade, who was given a brief description of the humans he was expecting, looked at the two, then with subtlety shook his head left to right.

They continued. Black birds flew up in front of them. A pair of dragonflies gave chase to each other. The loud sound of a creature splashing in the water made its unexpected way to their ears as the boys turned their heads in unison, seeing only the short life of ripples crashing against thick green grass.

A red bird landed in a tree to Cade's right and he watched its head move rapidly and mysteriously. A woodpecker from somewhere played his tune. The creaky wooden path over the dark water opened to a resting area with a bench. It was the inaptly named "docks." They had reached the spot.

"Where would you live in Chicago?" said Sammie. The two lay in Miles' bed after sex. "A dorm?"

"Probably an apartment," said Miles. "If my dad can fit the bill." Silence then between the lovers.

"Why Chicago?" said Sammie.

"Because Loyola has a great program that fits my needs," said Miles. "And it's only an hour plane ride. I hope you—"

"It sounds—" said Sammie.

"What?" said Miles.

"Nothing," said Sammie

"It's Catholic," said Miles.

"What?!" said Sammie.

"It's a Catholic college," said Miles.

"You're shitting me," said Sammie, laughing. "You gonna be an altar boy too? You get fitted for your gown? Gonna fuck the priest?"

"You'd like that, wouldn't you?" said Miles grinning. "If you'd like, you can—"

"Watch?" said Sammie. "No thanks, chief. Not my cup a' sauce."

He kissed her forehead. "I'll miss you when we're away, but it won't be for a while," said Miles.

"Yeah," said Sammie, turning to her other side. "Just wish I didn't find out like that."

"I know," said Miles. "I wasn't sure how or even when to tell ya."

"Whatever," she said.

He put his hand on her hip and slid his other arm around her neck and held her.

They waited together in silence, but what each boy was waiting for had changed. Of Jake's view, there were ripples and bubbles coming up from the pond. He remained focused on the surface of the water in anticipation as Cade and he sat upon the long wooden seat. Jake almost turned to look at his friend but didn't amid his hope to not miss what was going to be surfacing. Quickly, in his periphery, Jake had a peak at Cade on his left. Cade's toes were bouncing on the floor, causing his leg and arm to vibrate. Processing his friend's obliviousness, Jake got back to the bubbles.

Both boys waited: Cade who could hear his own pulse, his eyes watching from where they came in, and Jake's vision steadfast to the water, breathing comfortably, waiting for a change.

"Shit," said Cade.

Jake's mind was pulled out of its lull as if he had awakened suddenly from a dream. There were five boys their age walking toward them. No mistake, it was them. Cade felt his forehead soften with sweat. Jake had the urge to ask but withheld due to the energy his friend radiated.

The boys approached, walking almost in congruity. The biggest one in front was easily six inches taller than Cade and eight inches taller than Jake. And he was thick as hell. Both friends put out their smokes.

"You bring enough guys or what?" said Jake shortly before he looked right again to check on the water. He saw that the ripples were faster and there were more bubbles, but there was no time to keep watching.

"You Cade?" said the front runner.

"Yeah, you Roy?"

"Heard you got some nice pills for me?" he said with a grin. The rest of the boys stayed behind him. Some filled the space up front to his sides out of obligation.

"Yeah," said Cade.

"Well?" said Roy.

"Where's the cheddar?" said Jake.

"Oh, I'll show you the cheddar," said Roy. "Let's see the bag." Cade reached into his pocket and pulled out a sandwich bag with every ecstasy pill he had agreed upon selling inside.

"Show me."

"Money," demanded Cade, disguising fear.

"Ok, I'm gonna level with you boys, you're gonna give up those pills or we're gonna beat you and throw you in the river and take them."

"River?" said Jake. "What river?! This is Winston School not Niagara Falls, you dumb fuck."

Before Jake had let out that little number, Cade felt like running. Now, Cade felt like screaming the word *help*.

He put the pills back into his pocket. Roy walked over to the two, eradicating the ten-foot safety net as the posse followed. With laser eyes, he stood in front of Cade, then came an uppercut to the body. Jake had at Roy with both fists one after the other. He was swinging so hard and fast, he screamed from adrenaline. Cade, winded, was surprised at his freedom that a second blow didn't follow the body punch. With his attacker vulnerable from Jake's pummeling, Cade started in on Roy's face and head with his right. Hitting him was unexpectedly addictive. That's when one of the boys on the buyer's side pulled out pepper spray and shot at his opponents but the main stream only hit Roy who had turned round in desperation. He ran into the wooden railing and flipped over and into the water. In the wake of being hit by the rebound of the pepper spray, Cade took off his hat and covered his face. The stream then hit Cade's hat dead on. Jake, screaming as loudly as he possibly could, went after the one with the weapon and managed to finagle it out of his hand with his left as he swung frantically with rights to his face. Still screaming and now in control of the pepper spray, Jake, unfamiliar with the device and still clinging by his left hand to his prey, pushed the control to shoot as it was inches from the target. But the mace was backwards in his hand and he sprayed himself in the face from point blank range. Bewildered and in pain and still screaming, he turned it around and sprayed just before the stream ran out. He let it fall then kicked and punched one of the boys and screamed as Cade came to his defense.

"YOU FAGGOTS!!!" screamed Jake. "I LOVE BLOOD!!! I LOVE IT!!! THE BLOOD!!! I LOVE PAIN!!! YOU FAGGOTS!!! DO YOU KNOW?!!! THE BLOOD!!! IT COMES!!! I LOVE IT!!! YOU FAGGOTS!!!

The boys ran away. All four of them ran as one swam and waded.

"FUCK!!!" screamed Jake as he jumped over the edge and into the water and dunked his head. Cade planned the same, but took his time remembering the pills which he removed from his pocket and placed on the bench before taking a refreshing dip.

The two drove to the hood for beer and then to Armao's where they drank most of it until Jake's dad showed up and yelled at them. Cade was used to this except it was the first time that the angry man called him an asshole.

At Heltons' as the sun was setting, Cade didn't see anyone face to face but Ray in the upstairs hallway on his way to the bathroom.

"Cade Caybul, how are ya," said Ray.

"Hello, Ray," said Cade. "Kind of a rough day."

"Why is your face red?" said Ray. "Like, redder than usual."

"I um, I—" said Cade.

"Never mind," said Ray. "I don't wanna know. Why don't you head up and see Miles? He's waitin' for ya up there."

Cade opened the door and walked quietly upstairs to his and Miles' room. He turned the corner and headed toward the beds when he heard a sound that he processed as a woman in pain. He lifted his gaze from the floor to Miles' bed where he saw Miles thrusting from on top of Sammie. Both boys stopped their respective paths of motion at the same time and Miles and Sammie locked eyes with Cade.

"I—what's up," said Cade, looking with an ample view of things. Sammie looked from Cade to Miles.

"Nada much," said Miles.

"I—I'm gonna go," said Cade, without moving.

"Yeah, ok," said Miles.

Sammie looked at Cade who finally turned around and left.

Sammie and Miles looked at each other.

She said, "Is it me...or does his face seem really red to you?"

1 3

____

THE PARKING LOT ACCORDING
TO SAMMIE

A spritz of summer rain made its way from the heavens that morning to cool the earth. A Barred Owl warning its partner sounded like an engine turning in the distance. Heavyset adults existing on the Western New York flatland planned to emerge from their chambers and gathered the black and white folded faces from their patios. And the friends wishing to divert from woe woke and prepared to meet and discuss the big day forthcoming.

"Why did you invite Kelly?" said Cade.

"I don't know," said Sammie. "He was there with my sister when I like, talked about it." Cade and Sammie looked into each other's eyes while they spoke. Almost a week had gone by since the big interruption.

"How much did you get the pills for again?" said Sammie.

"Like seven or eight a piece," said Cade.

"Wow, dude," said Sammie.

"Yeah," said Cade.

"Are you selling the rest?" said Sammie.

"I'll sell some, and I'll do some," said Cade.

"Can I sell some to Lil and Esham?" said Sammie.

"Who are Lil and Esham?" said Cade.

"Lil Brunski and Esham," said Sammie. "They're a couple. If you went to Amherst for four years instead of transferring from Cardinal, whatever his name is, you'd know them."

"Oh yeah?" said Cade. "Are they older?"

"Esham is," said Sammie. "Lil is our age. She dropped out when we were sophomores and he's like 22. They're great. We should roll with them sometime."

"Cool," said Cade. "Rolling with Kelly is gonna be stupid."

"No, it won't," said Sammie. "Trust me."

Ty and Kelly arrived at Sammie's and the four of them got into Kelly's dad's jeep bound for Darien Lake amusement park. They had been traveling together for about twenty minutes when Sammie said, "Did you remember the pills?"

"Yeah," said Cade.

"How much do you want for the roll, Cade?" said Kelly, hands at ten and two.

"Fifteen," said Cade.

"Fifteen?!" said Sammie. "I thought you got them for seven bucks."

"I, uh, I," said Cade.

"Fucking Jew bag," said Kelly.

"Fifteen is the going rate for a pill," said Ty. "Fifteen is a solid price. Can we smoke back here, Kelly?"

"Yeah, try not to burn my seats," said Kelly.

"This is gonna be so much fun," said Sammie.

"Make sure you get the ash out of my jeep and throw the butt outside when you're done," said Kelly.

"What roller coaster is your favorite, Kelly?" said Sammie.

"Predator," said Kelly.

"Lame," said Sammie.

"What's yours?" said Kelly.

"I don't know," said Sammie. "Something that goes upside down. Like the Mind Eraser. Predator is weird. Feels like I'm gonna die on it."

"Hell, yes," said Kelly. "If you die, I won't tell anyone that you took X."

"Gee, thanks," said Sammie.

"When should we take it?" said Ty, smiling and rubbing his palms together. "The ecstasy that is."

"Probably right when we pull into the parking lot," said Sammie, poking her head in back. "Is there water here?"

"Yeah, and beer," said Kelly. "I've got a case of Blue behind you, Cade. You can have some of it if you give me a pill."

"Let's just have a good time," said Cade.

They pulled into the gigantic parking lot. Sammie and Ty split one pill while Cade and Kelly each had a whole. They finished their cigarettes, paid admission, and headed into the park on a hot sunny day with a clear blue sky.

"My ass feels wet," said Sammie.

"I can feel it for you if you want me to find out," said Kelly.

"I'm good," said Sammie.

"What should we do first?" said Ty, rubbing his palms together.

"Here's a map," said Sammie. "We are here. The Predator's here. The Viper is here. Mind Eraser is right...here. I say we start big and do the Mind Eraser first. The line is probably so long, we should be rolling by the time we get on."

"Sounds good," said Cade.

The crew began their journey.

There were people of all ages strewn about the hot asphalt as far as their eyes could see. Everyone, despite the commonality of the pursuit of games and fun, Cade noticed, had an unwelcoming look to them. Lacking intrigue, the cold visual discernment of each patron didn't venture too much for the company of strangers. Fear would pull it back. The collision of apprehension and eye contact with humans unknown was all around them.

With the flow of the crowd, the four gravitated toward a beat cop who was standing in the middle of a path. As they walked, Sammie, Ty, and Kelly were in front of Cade. They looked away from the man in uniform as they strolled.

"Hello," Cade said with bold venturing eyes. The officer smiled and nodded back to him. All three of his friends, startled, whipped their heads around and processed the unexpected comfort of their friend. No one spoke about him greeting the man in uniform.

"It's gonna be a good day," said Cade. Sammie became excited and made a noise high pitched before scampering to Cade and locking arms.

They made their way over to the Mind Eraser. As foreseen, the line was humongous. Most of the people were under a ceiling but the line leaked past it and the foursome began waiting with squinted eyes under the angry sun.

"Mad people," said Ty.

"Yeah," said Cade and Sammie.

"Ya think, Ty Jai?" said Kelly.

"I do," said Ty laughing.

The line moved slowly. After twenty minutes, they were barely inside and under the ceiling where it was cooler and darker.

"I'm starting to roll," said Cade quietly. Again, his friends turned their heads around. Sammie's eyes, expelling intrigue to Cade, shone brighter than they did earlier.

"Really?" said Ty. Cade nodded several times with certainty.

"Do we have gum?" said Cade.

Sammie gasped, "Yes," she said. "I brought two packs." She waited for Cade to direct her.

He continued to nod, "*Fucking* awesome."

"Do you want a piece?" said Sammie.

"No," said Cade sternly. "Not yet."

"I think I'm starting to feel it too," said Ty happily.

"You're darker, Ty Jai!" said Sammie, which triggered Cade to shush her delicately as people turned to see who was making noise.

"Then I'm definitely feeling it," said Ty.

"I wanna feel it!" said Sammie.

"You will," said Cade. "Oh, you took a half, didn't you?"

"Yeah," said Sammie, making way for Cade's response.

"Dude, I have a feeling you're gonna be just fine."

Time rolled by and they were more than halfway to the front. Now, all four were feeling effects of the X.

"Dude, it's too bad we can't smoke right here," said Cade.

"Oh my God," said Sammie. I know." She brushed his chest with her hand.

"Dude, I'm like, kinda *mad* nervous about getting on this roller coaster," said Cade.

"You don't look nervous," said Sammie.

"Ok," said Cade.

"I think it's—" said Ty.

"I think it's just like...the typical nervousness that, ya know, I'd get if I wasn't, ya know, about to be straight rolling," said Cade.

"Yeah, like, it's like, amplified," said Sammie, nodding.

"Exactly," said Cade. "It'll be nice afterwards. Just walking and puffing a smoke with you guys."

"Yeah, definitely," said Sammie.

Ty put his elbow and forearm on Cade's shoulder and rested some on him. As the line progressed, he took it down.

"Imagine if we smoked on the roller coaster," said Kelly, laughing before they all laughed together.

"We're getting close!" said Sammie.

"Ok, who's riding next to me?" said Cade. The group looked about, unsure. "It doesn't matter who does."

"Let's just let things happen naturally when they happen," said Sammie.

"Deal," said Cade.

"Can I have some gum, Sam?" said Ty.

"Sure," said Sammie. "Wait. Are you sure you want some now?"

"Hmmmm," said Ty. "I am not."

"Cause what if we like…" said Sammie.

"*Choke?*" said Cade and Kelly.

"Yeah," said Sammie.

"Might as well wait," said Ty, putting his arm on Cade's shoulder again. Cade matched the affection by rubbing Ty's lower back. Soon, the crew made it to the portion of the line where smaller lines started, one for each car of the ride.

"Where should we get on?!" said Sammie. "You wanna do very back?!"

"Doesn't matter," said Cade. "Let's just get on."

They chose the path of least people which led them to the middle. Cade and Sammie went to one slot as Ty and Kelly went to the adjacent one. Sammie smiled and squeaked and flailed her hands with glee. The three boys tried to keep it together.

Ladies and gentlemen, welcome to the Mind Eraser. Have all personal items securely fastened to your person. Please keep your hands and feet to yourself. After you are seated, please fasten your seat belts. Your…body harness…should…fit tight and snugly to your body. If you need a hand, let Rudy or Misty know and one of us will be sure to help.

Thank you for riding with us here at Darien Lake and enjoy the Mind Eraser.

Cade's heart rate doubled and his sweat glands went to work.

Sammie's jubilance made him feel a little better. Kelly bit his nails. Ty hyperventilated.

The riders before them shot into the station, traveling fast as hell before the coaster jerked and slowed dramatically. The demeanor of the passengers now versus when they climbed aboard intimidated Cade. Their skin was flushed and hair tousled while they panted and spoke loudly. If he were by himself, he would've bailed.

Finally, it was time.

"Here we go, dude!" she said.

"Yeah," said Cade.

"Are you all right?" said Sammie.

Cade sat motionless with his eyes straight ahead.

"Yeah," said Cade. "Let's just.... yeah."

"This is gonna be fun," she said, looking at him. She watched him swallow and take a breath. Then she looked ahead and did the same.

The ride shot away on its course, climbing. It climbed slowly, higher and higher. Cade kept his sweating hands on his harness.

"Oh my God!" said Sammie. "We are so fucking high right now!"

"I know!" shouted Ty from ahead.

Sammie heard Cade murmuring something that she couldn't understand before it hit the apex and started down.

All it took was the initial descent. They didn't stand a chance. As the ride reached its low point after the drop and began to turn and thrust, Sammie's happy screaming silenced. All four went completely silent. And they stayed silent as every single stranger on board made plenty of joyful noise. Each of the four's pulse reached a complete pandemonium. Cade and Sammie looked at each other. Cade was too sick to be scared. Sammie was terrified. Cade tried to speak and tell her it was all right. Nobody could talk.

After what seemed like an eternal trip through hell, the ride shot into the station. Their bodies above their waists went numb. Their hearing distorted and gave way to the sound of their own heartbeats which made each of them think that they'd be dying soon.

The sick foursome very slowly got up and out. They walked down the ramp, passed by the happy crowd who rode with them, ignorant to their situation. Sammie began to cry. They reached the bottom and Kelly looked at Cade and spoke:

"WE JUST GOTTA CHILL."

They found a clear area and sat by some bushes, gasping for air. Sammie murmured incoherently. Cade put his hand on her back but that made his arm go even more numb. Ty tried vomiting in a panic but only dry heaved.

"This was...a *really* bad idea!" said Ty. He stuck his fingers down his throat.

"No, Ty!" said Cade. "You'll blow the pill!"

People stopped and stared.

"Dude, bail," said Cade and they walked.

Sammie shot out in the lead. People she passed thought for a moment that she was running from someone. They looked at who was trailing her to see the guys just as sick as she was, which made them confused.

The group, in idleness, relaxed in the shade for nearly an hour. They began to speak after nearly 20 minutes. They talked about their nightmare. After they became comfortable, they settled into their roll and their roll settled into them.

Along their pleasant strolling, they happened by the Ferris wheel.

"Ferris wheel?" said Sammie.

"Definitely," said Cade.

They waited in the long line.

"There are a lot more young kids here," said Kelly.

"Yeah," said Cade. "Nice and chill ride."

"I feel that I'm ready for another big roller coaster after this," said Sammie.

"Definitely," said Ty and the group conquered.

"Yeah, I think that we just shouldn't have gotten on during the come-up," said Cade.

"DEFINITELY," said Ty.

They approached the front. The line moved quicker than expected as the wheel held many more patrons than met the eye. Each cart held a maximum of four people, so they were ecstatic to be able to ride together. There were two bench-like sides that sat across from one another. Kelly and Cade sat next to each other across from their other friends. Sammie sat like one of the guys with her long legs open. The ride began.

As they got higher, the feeling of isolation increased. And they became happier. Soon enough, the ride reached its maximum speed and they were cruising.

"Oh my God!" said Ty. "Oh, man! Oh, wow! This is really something, man, WOW!"

"I don't know if this is..." said Cade. "This may be the best thing that's ever happened in my life!"

"We're so high right now," said Kelly. "Look how high we are! WHOA! We're higher than all the other rides, look!"

"I never thought that the Ferris wheel could be this amazing," said Sammie. "I just never would have thought this, ever! I am definitely smoking." She struggled with lighting a cigarette in the wind. Cade tried shielding it with his hand. She flicked her Bic over and over. Pretty soon, all three of the guys were helping her block the wind with their hands.

After it was lit, she took out another and lit it with the ember of her cigarette. She passed it to Ty. She did the same for Kelly and Cade. They relaxed and smoked, enjoying the breeze.

The group had done two full circles before their third ascent. Riding their high, they didn't bother gracing the crowd on the ground with their eyes as they passed.

Breaths were deep and slow. The winds affably competed, applying their caress to each of their skin, inviting the hairs of their bodies to rise. Ty had his arm behind Sammie's head as if they were on a date. Kelly had his arm behind Cade's head as if they were on a date. Not having learned the meaning of *presence of mind,* they were *in* it. All four of them became the moment of peace. Of the world, looking out, their cart again reached its peak and began its descent. Sammie spoke, breaking their silence. She spoke slower and lower than before with her eyes on the horizon: "Thank you. All of you. Thank you for being a part of this."

"Dude, you said it, Sam," conceded Ty.

"This is the greatest moment of my life," said Kelly.

"I wish—I just wish that this would never end," said Cade.

"Well, afterward, we can just do it again, man," said Kelly.

"Oh, *YEA!*" said Sammie.

"Dude, I'm so down!" said Ty.

"Me too," said Cade.

"Me too!" said Sammie.

"Me six!" said Kelly.

"Look, we're near the ground again," said Cade.

Confused, Sammie said, "Are we...are we slowing...are we stopping?!" The ride came to a stern, unexpected halt as they heard a rumble from the crowd.

"Ride's over!" said a worker.

"Dude, *what?*" said Sammie.

"What the hell?" said Ty.

"No smoking! Get off now!"

"God damn it," said Cade.

"Let's go!" yelled an older employee. "On your feet! Let's go!"

Sammie looked at Cade in disbelief. "Dude, what."

"Looks like we gotta bounce," said Cade.

"YOU FOUR, OFF THE RIDE!"

They stood and were escorted away. The crowd yelled and jeered. They were truly upset. Everyone was looking at them. Even the children were mad as they reflected the energy of their parents.

"Can none of yous idiots hear?!!" a man's voice yelled from the crowd. "NO SMOKING!"

"We were hollerin' atcha," said a more civil employee who was their age. "We didn't want to stop the ride just for ya'll. Ya'll didn't hear us?"

"No," said Cade.

"Don't come back!" said another with genuine anger.

Workers tended to the ashes and butts as if it were anthrax. They walked away together while the people snarled and glowered as if the gang had committed an atrocity.

"*Soooo*, that was...*fucking terrible*," said Sammie.

Their minds processed the barrage in mania.

"Jesus, they must have been yelling at us when we were...looping down," said Kelly.

"Yeah," said Cade.

"I thought we were gonna get kicked out of the whole park," said Ty.

"We're still here," said Cade.

Their breath caught up with them and their heart rate settled.

They wandered to a pond where children paddled in small boats built to resemble ducks and chicks and fish. Sitting on the grass in silence, they did not speak of the visual hallucination that accompanied the euphoria as they looked out over the water which shimmered especially for them.

"Oh my God, baby ducks!" said Sammie.

"Wow!" said Ty as Cade smiled and Kelly's jaw dropped. A mother duck led her babies for a swim.

"I wish I had a camera," said Sammie. "Oh my God, I *love* them!"

"When I was little, my mom and me pulled up to a stop—uh, a red light," said Cade. "No, it wasn't a red light or a stop sign. It was just a point in the road." His three friends stopped watching the ducks on the water, turned to him, and listened as his tone was commanding yet delicate. Sammie turned to check on the ducks but her vision returned to Cade who spoke as he looked out on the water. "She stopped for ducks crossing. And the people behind us...cooperated...too."

"How old were you?" said Sammie.

"Ten, I think?"

"So we were in Saint Ben's together," Sammie said softly. "That's how old I was when my mom died."

"Yeah," said Cade. "I didn't tell anybody…ever...I don't think."

"Go on," said Sammie.

"So, she, well...*we* were in front and another car had pulled up from the opposite direction. And there was no one behind him. They were teenagers. All dudes. Four of them. At first, he stopped with like...fear or...obligation in his eyes. I was watching him. Then the car started rolling like...a stick shift roll. And they started...communicating. And then he smiled. And he gunned it and ran over the baby ducks."

Sammie covered her open mouth with her hand as her eyes started to water.

"They took off and then beeped the horn, smiling and laughing. The mother duck came back to the...she turned and walked back to the street and started making noise. She was confused. Her...the babies who lived were squeaking and scared as hell. And she waddled out to the road and didn't know what to do. My mom and me didn't know what to do either.

People started honking behind us. The living chicks gathered around the mother and she...she just...watched and quaked. It was as if she was still doing her job as the leader but she didn't know what happened or what to do."

"So finally, we just drove away. They were out of the street...the living ones were. And I don't know. I think I wanted to see her just...move on. Like for...closure. Like I wanted her to just leave the dead ones and go with the living ones. But we drove away. And I didn't get to see it. The last thing I saw was her and her chicks, mad confused and standing there. And I wish that I would've gotten out of the car when I saw their car rolling back and forth. And stood in front of it. Preventing them from doing it. 'Cause I could feel that was about to happen. But I stayed in the car."

"You were just a kid," said Sammie. "Don't—"

"I know," said Cade. "But I was smart enough to see what was about to happen. And I was big enough to prevent them from doing it."

"Was the father duck there?" said Kelly.

"No," said Cade.

"He was probably up in some duck pussy two towns over," said Kelly.

Sammie laughed, quiet then becoming louder, triggering everyone to smile and laugh.

They unwound and it was back to the rides. They went on the bigger ones that were the staples of the park over and over as if they were kids again.

Nightfall came and the famed laser light show drew interest. They thought it would be a psychedelic adventure. They were wrong. The music was popular and slowly turned into a visual and auditory Backstreet Boys theme. Sammie booed the loudest until *YMCA* played and she danced with a group of unknown guys who were having a great time. Cade, Ty, and Kelly watched enviously.

Night was a different scene at Darien Lake. The foursome strolled about the park, still tickled by the drug and taken by innumerable colored shining lights. They noticed others, some holding stuffed animals they had won, stumbling about drunk, but no friend on their voyage suggested they drink anything but water as the idea of using alcohol felt superfluous, even to Cade.

Sammie sat on a bench to smoke by herself as the boys checked out games for prizes. There were still lots of people out, but there were far fewer children.

As Sammie puffed her smoke, she took in the scenery. Across the way, she noticed a group of guys several years older than her, one of whom she found attractive. Her eyes followed him as he sat on a bench close to his friends and reached into his pocket. At first, Sammie thought he began to roll a joint, but as she stared, she deduced that he was rolling a tobacco cigarette. She looked over at her friends who were shooting hoops, trying to win a prize. Her attention stayed on them long enough to realize that they were occupied and not interested in what she was doing.

She looked back at the man. Never having seen someone rolling his own cigarette, her gaze transfixed. Casually, she looked left to right then back at the man. She placed her purse on her lap. Taking the last hit from her Camel, she dropped it and stepped on the butt.

With her left relaxed and on her knee, she slid her four fingers of her right hand past the button of her shorts and underneath her delicates, finding her clit. Watching the man, she grazed and pawed as he finished rolling, picking up speed while he put it entirely into his mouth and pulled it out slowly, sealing the paper. Her legs opened some. People walked by in between the girl and her subject while she struggled to keep a face of banality. Every time a man, woman, or family walked in front of her, obstructing her vision, she became tense. And when they passed enough for her to be able to see him enjoying his roll-your-own, her hand moved more confidently.

She perspired. Losing control, the metal button on her small grey shorts came undone. The big ample corduroy bag did its job concealing her hand, but her poker face started to fail. As far as she could tell, no one, including the attractive older boy she watched, knew that she was getting closer and closer.

"Can you put one through the hole, Cade?" said Kelly.

"I think so," he said. "I bet it's smaller than it seems. The circumference." The kid working the hoop toss game was their age. He could tell his three peers were high by the size of their pupils.

"Eight bucks for two shots," said the worker spinning a ball on his finger.

"I'll throw down," said Kelly. "I want that Zeppelin poster. Score me that Zeppelin poster, Cade."

Cade took one shot and missed. He took another and made it. Kelly and Ty cheered. Cade proudly waited for his prize.

"Uuuh, you've gotta sink both to win a poster," said the worker.

"Oh, really?" said Cade.

"Yeah," said the worker. "You've got to sink two to win anything."

"Can you sink two, Cade?!" said Kelly.

"What's up, jizz rockets," said Sammie who had moseyed over.

"Cade, can you do it?" said Kelly.

Sammie looked at both of them with intrigue.

"I don't know," said Cade.

"What are we doing?" said Sammie.

"Cade's gonna win me that poster," said Kelly.

Sammie, still confused, cheered, "Hell, yeah, do it, Cade!"

But it was too much for him with everybody watching and someone else's money at stake. "Nah, I don't think so," he said.

"Can he try for free?" said Sammie.

"Um no, I don't—" said the worker.

"Just to see if he'd make them," said Sammie. "No money. No prizes. Just you. Him. The ball. The net. The fucking cosmosis."

"I don't know," said the smiling worker. "He doesn't seem too into it."

"Well, then, I'll take it." Her body language called for the ball and he tossed it to her. She shot an ugly shot that hit the front of the rim.

"Once more!" she said, calling for the ball again. "This one's in there like swimwear." She missed by a few feet, knocking over some prizes. "Thanks, chief," she said. "Gotta run!" She playfully ran, devoid of fear. The three boys turned to greet the demeanor of the worker who didn't mind too much before catching up to her.

She lit a smoke.

Cade walked the slowest, feeling somewhat defeated. He fantasized about how this moment would be if he had taken the challenge and sunk two. It was now when the first temptation to drink had at him.

The foursome walked through the colorful amusement park together in a kind of diamond pattern. Sammie up front, Ty and Kelly in the middle, and Cade, lagging behind, his eyes on Sammie. She looked left to right and all around, repeatedly taking in what the night had to offer. Her legs moved swiftly, taking big confident strides, almost too long, for which she was known. Cade's sight traveled past his male counterparts and fixated on her. She reminded him of a cat the way she surveyed the world around her. A proud leader, she commanded the pack without aim.

Cade saw men digging into her with their eyes and wondered if she knew as she didn't seem to care or even notice. Her tie-dyed shirt cut through the darkness around her like a star. Cade's eyes followed it, her favorite shirt, and began to see it like he never had, without knowledge of where they were headed or, really, where they had been. Ty and Kelly laughed loudly together. Cade saw Sammie's neck and head emit the slightest reaction to the sound and he wanted to know her in that moment so he gained pace.

"It's pretty out here," said Cade.

"Hell yeah," said Sammie before a short silent look at Cade. "The Ferris wheel was so awesome."

"Yes, I don't think I'll be forgetting that anytime soon," said Cade.

"There's bumper cars," said Sammie.

"That sounds like hell," said Cade.

"What?!" said Sammie.

"Dude, no way," said Cade.

"Why?!" said Sammie grinning.

"Because," said Cade. "They all like....bump me and shit."

Sammie, for a sliver of a second, tried to hold back laughter before she unloaded until she was nearly in tears.

"THEY ALL LIKE BUMP YOU AND SHIT?!!" she said.

"Yes!" said Cade, reflecting the fun she transmitted.

"Holy shit!" said Sammie.

"Yes," said Cade.

Sammie released a left-over burst of jovial sound, familiar to everyone who knew her.

"They fuckin' bump me too much," he continued.

"Do they?" she said.

"Yes," said Cade.

"How hard?" said Sammie.

"It's not so much the hardness of the bumps," said Cade.

"Oh yeah?" said Sammie.

"It's the *amount* of bumps," said Cade.

"How many bumps?" said Sammie.

"There's too many bumps in bumper cars," said Cade.

"16?" said Sammie. "Is it 17? How many bumps, Cade?" Smiling, and for the first time during their conversation, his head shied away, drooping downward. "Dude, I get it," said Sammie calmly. "It's not a chill ride or even a rush. Bumper cars suck donkey balls."

"Dude, it fucking sucks," said Cade. "I just hate everybody around me during bumper cars."

Sammie let out her one-note gleeful sound. "When were you on bumper cars?" she asked. "I mean *in*. It sounds like a drug now. How long have you been addicted to bumper cars? You ever suck some dick for some bumper cars?"

"I think it was, I don't know, I went with Jake, I think it was here," said Cade. "It was like, really frustrating. That's when I learned that I don't like them."

Sammie noticed a change in him then. And some confusion. She subsided.

"Word, fam," said Sammie.

A group of women walked closely past the group and two of them spoke to each other: "I mean, he's got a drug problem and he just won't fix himself."

"Uh, huh. Yep. That's exactly right."

Sammie and Cade slowed to let them pass as they listened to the strangers' words until they became inaudible.

They walked silently and invitingly, allowing Ty and Kelly to gain ground.

"So what are we up to?" said Ty who placed his forearm on Cade's shoulder.

"We were just about to hit up the bumper cars," said Sammie, peering at Cade, drawing out his smile.

"Bumper cars?" said Ty. "Really?"

"Yeah, Cade's really into it," said Sammie.

"Really?" said Ty. "Bumper cars seem kinda...not smooth right now."

"I'll fuck some shit up in some bumper cars," said Kelly.

"Not today, boys," said Cade, living in that moment solely for the light of Sammie's smile. "Not today."

Up ahead, there were a couple of cops meandering. They noticed a woman on a bench with her dog and they approached. The bevy of rolling misfits kept an eye and an ear on them as their pace slowed to take it in.

"May I?" said the lady cop to the woman with the dog.

"Oh, he's a service dog," she said as she began moving items around in her purse, looking for papers.

"No," said the lady cop as her male counterpart stood and watched. "May I?"

"Oh, sure," said the woman with the dog.

The girl cop squatted to pet the canine. Sensing his owner's anxiety, the dog bit the cop's hand and growled. The male officer moved his hand to his pistol as the owner pulled all twenty-five pounds of her best friend away from the woman's barely bleeding hand.

In disbelief, the four stood and watched as others began to notice the spectacle too.

"I'm so sorry," said the woman, crying.

The lady in uniform moved swiftly to a cotton candy stand to grab some napkins for her hand. Her partner yelled at the dog's owner, demanding to see papers. Sammie also began to cry.

The sight from Cade's unblinking eyes focused on the dog, taking in his demeanor. There was no doubt. It was fear. Cade's mind enveloped itself empathetically in compulsion. The ambivalence of whether to attack or cower shone brightly from the pup through his eyes and quivering jowls.

The female cop returned and she too yelled at the woman: "ID! License and registration of the dog! NOW!"

The confused animal's restless eyes darted about in terror before jumping onto the bench where he barked, snapping his jaws at the cops like a turtle lurching at a school of fish. Cade looked over at the cotton candy stand. He saw bags of the stuff, pink and yellow, hanging from a metal line.

"Where's the entrance to this place?" he said to his friends.

"What?" said Sammie.

"The entrance," said Cade. "Where is the entrance? Which direction? The parking lot!"

"Um, back there," said Sammie, pointing. Cade deduced the

probability that the officers had not gotten a clean look at him and his crew.

"Go to the car," said Cade.

"What?!" said Sammie.

"The parking lot," said Cade. "Go to the car. I'll meet you there."

Cade hurried over to the cotton candy stand and grabbed a bag of the yellow and yelled: "HEY YOU MOTHERFUCKIN' COCKSUCKIN' PIGS!!!" The two uniformed humans turned quickly as did everyone in earshot, including the dog. "CAN YOU FUCKIN' PIGS BREAK A HUNDRED?!!!"

He ran. He ran in the opposite direction of the parking lot according to Sammie with a bag of cotton candy in his hand. The candy slipped out of the bag and onto the ground almost immediately.

Both cops gave chase.

Before hustling in the other direction, Sammie made eye contact with the woman who had the dog. Their bewilderment, a sheer reflection of each other's eyes:

"Uuuuuuuh….you're free now!" shouted Sammie before she and the guys headed swiftly toward the exit. "Oh my God, what the hell just happened," she continued.

"We just gotta get to the car and be ready for him when he gets there," said Kelly.

"What if he doesn't make it?" said Sammie.

"Then he doesn't make it," said Kelly.

The group, now a trio, moved through the park, emotionally castrated. They all lit cigarettes. Being careful not to move too quickly and draw attention, they traveled at a fast walking pace, looking behind them every so often. Weaving in surrealistic thought, they walked in unison as Sammie's nature to take long strides was dormant.

They made it to the exit.

"Thank you for coming to Darien Lake! We hope you come visit us again!"

"Um, bye!" said Sammie.

The parking lot had become mostly vacant. Groups of people in their teens drinking beer huddled around cars emitting loud rap music. Boys stood aggressively, on the lookout for passing strangers, as if they were protecting something. It was almost 11 pm. And the moon was full. They had reached the jeep.

"I'm having a beer right now," said Kelly.

"Me too," said Sammie. "I don't care that they're warm."

"I hope Cade gets back," said Kelly. "You want a beer, Ty Jai?"

"Yeah, I'll take a beer," said Ty. "Thanks."

"I mean…WHAT?!" said Sammie pacing. "Was he…what the hell was…why did he—"

"I do believe our friend Cade jumped on the grenade," said Ty.

"So to like…help her?" said Sammie. "To help the dog chick?"

"I think so," said Ty.

"Maybe he just flipped," said Kelly, taking his second last gulp of beer. "Maybe he just flipped and wanted to toy with the cops and have an adventure. Cade fuckin' hates cops. Make sure you toss the caps on the ground. I don't want paraphernalia in my jeep."

Kelly walked over to a light post and discarded his empty. During the short time he was away, Sammie and Ty looked into each other's eyes and, without speaking, they conveyed both concern for Cade and the realization that Kelly really didn't care about him.

"How long do you think we should wait for him?" said Kelly upon his return. He burped.

"Um, as long as it *takes*," said Sammie with a touch of attitude.

"I'm smokin' a bowl in my jeep," said Kelly who made himself scarce. Sammie and Ty nursed their beers outside.

"I wish I brought my hoodie," said Ty, admiring Sammie's.

"Do you want to wear mine for a minute?" said Sammie. "We could trade on and off for the night."

"Nah," said Ty. "No thanks. I'll be all right."

"Dude. Here," said Sammie, removing her zip-up sweatshirt with ease and handing it over.

"You sure?" said Ty.

"Dude, yea," said Sammie. "Look, it even fits you."

"Sweet, that feels better," said Ty. "I'll give it back after I warm up. Actually, Kelly might have an extra in the car, I can see if—"

"Dude, I don't wanna wear his clothes," said Sammie lowly.

They smiled together.

"I *would* like a hit of weed, though," said Sammie. She approached the driver's window and took a puff. Returning to the rear of the vehicle, she exhaled and coughed.

"Oh Cade, where are you?!" she said.

The two friends looked about the lot and waited.

An hour and a half slithered by. The three had drained about six beers while they waited. Kelly had become restless.

"We can't wait for him anymore," he said.

"I can't just leave him!" said Sammie.

"He's with 5-0," said Kelly. "He got arrested. We can't roll up asking questions."

"Jesus," said Sammie. "What do you think they'd charge him with, I mean—"

"Shoplifting," said Ty. "Resisting arrest, obstruction of justice... um—"

"Jesus!" said Sammie.

They sat in silence in Kelly's blue two-door jeep. Ty was in the back looking around behind him for his friend and Sammie sat shotgun. She felt too guilty to put on music. The windshield had completely fogged over, so Kelly put on the defrost. They waited.

Sammie positioned herself slightly so that Kelly was just out of her field of vision and softly, she cried. They lit cigarettes. Ty scooched toward the middle of the back seat and leaned forward. They waited.

"Why the hell isn't the fog going away?" said Kelly.

"Maybe, turn it up?" said Sammie.

"It *is* up," said Kelly.

"Maybe make it hotter?" said Sammie. Kelly turned the dial to red. They waited.

"Maybe it's a sign," said Sammie.

"Maybe what's a sign?" said Kelly. "That I can't see out of my jeep?"

"No, that we're supposed to wait longer for Cade," said Sammie. She faced Kelly and waited for a response, but he just bit his nails.

"Try the wipers," said Ty. Kelly did. And in one back-and-forth, the fog was gone.

"Well, shit," said Sammie.

"How was I supposed to know that that would work?!" said Kelly as if he had been accused.

"I don't think anybody did," said Sammie.

He put it in drive as Sammie repositioned and looked away again. They drove in the dark in search of the exit as humans their age staggered about. They passed groups of people huddled around their cars, laughing and drinking. A couple kissed with vigor beside a van.

"Where is the—which way is the exit?" said Kelly.

"I don't know," said Sammie. "It's different in the dark. I think we came from…dude, I don't know." Kelly bit his nails as he drove. A drunk boy stared at the jeep as they passed.

Kelly's response, "Fuckin' faggot," was heard only by the others in his vehicle.

"We were here before," said Ty, pointing. "That's where we came in. I remember the flag."

"It's closed off," said Kelly. "There's no way out here."

"Really?" said Ty, leaning forward more. "I think you can just drive through."

"No, we can't," said Kelly, doubling back and becoming more agitated. The silence as they drove about the lot ate at them.

"Why are you awkward?!" she said to the boy with a V-neck undershirt.

"What?" he said.

"Why are you crazy? I mean, we love you. You can stay. But why are you crazy and awkward?" she said, spilling her drink.

"Hey, new guy," another girl said. "Come take my turn. I'm too drunk."

"I'm not sure if I should leave this engaging conversation with your friend," he said.

"He has nice eyes. Emma, look at his eyes!"

"I can't! I'm getting my ass kicked," said Emma, playing flip cup.

"Dude, your shirt has pit stains," said a guy with the group.

"Sweet."

"They're not so bad. I have pit stains too, see?!" she said. "He's just jealous and feels threatened by outsiders. Where are the poppers, Kim? You want a popper, new guy?"

"Sure."

"Fill up my cups! Fill up all of our cups!" A young man poured beer into everyone's container in their waiting hands.

"Turn yours over, new guy! He's spilling it!" she said, laughing. "Your cup's upside down! See! You're so awkward, new guy! Hey, what's your name again?"

"Cade!"

"Cade!" she said. "That's right! I thought it was that. Emma, come look at Cade's eyes."

"Whoa! Iridescent!"

A blue jeep approached the after-partying group in the Darien Lake parking lot.

"Is that...is that fucking Cade?!" said Sammie. "Is that Cade with a different shirt on?!"

"NO WAY!" said Ty.

"Holy shit, it *is* Cade," said Kelly.

"*CADE!!!*" yelled Sammie.

Kelly stopped the car and Sammie ran out for him. Everyone at the little gathering stopped and stared. She ran and leapt up onto him and they held each other.

Cade no longer felt crazy or awkward.

AFTER THE JUBILANT RIDE back to the suburb, the group stopped at Sammie's to drink. While funneling beer and having shots of vodka, Kelly surmised that since he could only see straight when he closed one eye, it was time to go. He dropped Cade, Sammie, and Ty at the Heltons' and drove away.

There, everyone was home. Ray and Maureen were asleep in their bed as were Major and Mary. And Miles was winding down in his and Cade's room. It was almost 2 am and the three staggered in, trying to keep quiet.

"Where should I crash?" said Ty.

"Basement, Ty Jai," said Sammie, opening the fridge on their way past. She grabbed three of Ray's beers and they headed down the soft carpeted stairs to the most isolated room in the house.

"I don't know if I can drink another," said Ty. He laid upon the L-shaped couch with his head close to one of the two polar arms, leaving plenty of space for another body to lay feet-to-feet.

"Here's a pillow, Ty Jai," said Sammie, softly whacking him in the face, covering his eyes with a headrest that Major had left on the floor.

"Why, thank you," said Ty.

"I'll get you a blanket," said Cade, going upstairs and feeling unusual comfort in the home that wasn't quite his own.

The coast was clear on the main floor. He grabbed some pillows and blankets from the couch and brought them down to see that Ty had his eyes closed. He delicately laid an afghan over him and joined Sammie who was sitting cross-legged on the floor. She had been waiting for him. They sipped their beers and spoke.

"I cannot believe today," said Sammie.

"Yeah, shit was intense," said Cade.

"So you just jetted into a bathroom and took off your shirt and ran back out?" said Sammie.

"Yeah, I stuffed it in the garbage and walked out calmly, cause like, by then, I lost them."

"I'm still, like...computing this," said Sammie.

"Me too," said Cade. "It was the biggest rush of the day!"

Cade was able to visually hold onto her eyes. Her wonder slow danced with his peace of mind.

"I should probably head up," said Sammie.

"Wanna chug a beer?" said Cade.

"Sure," said Sammie. They finished theirs and Cade cracked the sweaty third.

"Ty Jai," said Sammie. Ty murmured on the brink of sleep. "He's out. Oh my God, the Ferris wheel was so awesome!"

"Yeah, until we got kicked off," said Cade.

"That was so weird," said Sammie.

"Yeah, those people are terrible," said Cade. His tone intensified while his sight ventured. "They ruined that moment for us. That perfect moment. I had never felt so good before. I never felt that in, I don't think, ever."

Sammie began, "Yeah—"

"And they robbed it from us. We weren't doing anything wrong. We were smoking tobacco outside. *Outside.* In the air." She took the beer from his hand and sipped as he continued. "They're shallow. They're shallow people with no sense of anything outside of their own needs. Or wants and shit. They're the type of people who call the cops when they see someone who isn't them having a good time. It must be awful being them. Constantly looking around instead of like...looking at the sky or something and just..."

"Breathing?" she said.

"Yes!" he said. "Breathing and living as yourself!"

"And understanding others' subjectivity," she said.

"Exactly," said Cade, taking the shared beer and stammering. "Sub—subjectively." She sensed his excitement and scooted closer which calmed him.

"When my mom died, well, after my mom died, my sister got caught smoking weed and my dad beat her," said Sammie.

"Really?" said Cade.

"Yeah," she said. "I was there when it happened. It was in the kitchen." She smiled, almost laughing. "It was *really* scary."

"At your current place?" said Cade.

"Same exact house," said Sammie. "It's hard to have people over there. You know, when we party. And some of our friends treat it like shit. I feel used a lot."

"Why do you do it?" said Cade.

"Do what?" said Sammie. "Have people over? Because sometimes it's like, where else are we gonna chill. We gotta kick it somewhere. I'm in a position to accommodate, for better or worse."

"Damn, I didn't—"

"It's all good," said Sammie. "I don't mind too much. It's fun."

They conversed as the night grew older, with their weary friend resting quietly. Above, there were faint footsteps to which they paid little mind. Cool air seeped in through the open basement windows. The night had settled blissfully upon its numb inhabitants.

Cade laid on the sofa opposite Ty. He arranged a fleece throw that blanketed his skin. Sammie crawled in his direction but spilled what little beer was left in the one remaining can. She laughed and quickly covered her bright smile with her hand, ceasing the noise. Cade, from his prosperous location, kept his eyes on her. He smiled. His lazy eyes saw nothing but her.

"Should I finish it?" said Sammie, holding back laughter.

"I don't think there's anything left to finish," said Cade.

She moved closer to him and turned round, sliding her back against the sofa. Her hair fell onto the blanket between them. She had the final sip of beer and put the can down.

"Do you think he's asleep?" she said.

"I don't know," said Cade, almost whispering. He gently ran his fingers along her long black hair. She lifted her bottom from the floor and, as he made room for her, placed it on the sofa then laid on her side with her back to his chest.

A message he had no intention of sending, he became hard and repositioned his waist further from her backside. She understood and respected the distance between them.

For a moment, they laid together, still. He brought his face to her hair and inhaled through his nose. She felt for his reach and took hold. Their hands squeezed and tickled each other's, taking turns dominating and subsiding. Palm to palm, theirs slid delicately while their fingers struggled to interlock until they found firm unison.

Biting her lip, she took back the space for which he had asked and there, she enjoyed moving in circles all over his secret, exposed. He gave in as her breaths reached their slowest, longest, and loudest they had been this night. As she allowed his arm to be under her neck, he heard her smile take shape. He wanted to let go of her hand and grab onto the thickness below her back but knew it was too strong an investment. Instead, he leaned in and let his motionless lips graze her shoulder. His mind settled, inducing calmer breaths. He let go of her hand. She *turned around* while their minds each unraveled both hesitation and certainty.

Her face tilted down against his. His lips puckered and pressed against the flesh atop her cheekbone, cautiously and considerately. Her chin elevated. Her mouth captured his bottom lip and all anxiety left his brain.

He had kissed these lips before in haste as a child under torment of pressure. He had kissed other girls between then and now, destined by affectations of fear. The jagged smoldering pieces, unparalleled until now, had made their way home under a dark sea of calm stars.

They kissed harder, wetter, and faster. He held her lower back, guiding her middle to his. Rubbing high and low, and venturing lower with each stroke, his hand at last grabbed a hold and squeezed the flesh of each cheek over and again. Breaking the rhythm of their oral union, she smiled.

They got back to kissing. His relentless hand made her smile again.

Softly to her, he said, "Is this really happening?" They kissed deeper, Sammie dominating and breathing fast and hard through her nose.

And her voice in reply like he had never heard it before,

"You have *no idea.*"

Instantaneously, their hands made way to their waists and unbuttoned each other. She gently tickled below then took hold of the prize above.

"Easy," he whispered. Her hand slowed but she squeezed just as firmly. "Not so hard," he said faintly before receiving an unwanted verbal apology that he quelled with a confident thrust of the tongue.

He wedged his hand under her lingerie as she opened her thighs and skimmed along the surface while she stroked. Just then, someone entered the room from the stairway. Together, they shut their eyes and froze. Cade's still hand rested atop her vulva. It seemed to be Mary who made her way to the office connected to the basement and quickly retraced her steps back out of the room.

The sun would be appearing soon.

"Holy shit," said Sammie. "I'm gonna go." Taking her time, she buttoned up and stood. "Great."

"Where are you gonna go?" said Cade.

"Well, I can't stay here," she said.

"I'll go with you," said Cade.

"What?" said Sammie. "No. Stay here. Bye, Cade."

She ruffled his hair and was gone.

14

———————————

MAGNUM PROPORTIONS

"Dude, what the hell is wrong with you!"

"I know."

"Wow! *Wow.* I just...I just can't believe...wow!"

"Yeah."

"Aw, man. Do you even...do you even know...do you even know what you're doing?!"

"Yeah. I mean, no."

"Dude, it's not happening. Whatever you're thinking is not happening."

"Yeah."

Ty was awake for the fireworks. As Cade drove him home that morning, he had at him. They had hardly slept.

"Did you see Mary come in?" said Cade.

"What?" said Ty. "Yes!"

"Shit," said Cade.

"What are you gonna do?" said Ty.

233

"Are you sure you saw her?" said Cade.

"Yes!" said Ty.

"Ok," said Cade.

"Can you stop at On the Run," said Ty.

"Yeah," said Cade.

They stopped at the corner gas station. There were cop cars outside and cops inside. Cade didn't care. The boys went in and got cigarettes and Gatorade and Cade dropped Ty at his place. They parted ways and slept.

Maureen cleaned the kitchen but paused halfway through. She stepped outside through the back door before stopping in the hallway at the top of the basement stairs and looked at the shoes on the ground.

Outside, in her nightgown, she stood as the sun shone. Its light guided noisy blackbirds in flight. She walked down the long driveway to the sidewalk, approaching Cade's car parked slightly irregularly. Her neighbor disappeared closing the door behind her just as Maureen's wave failed to meet reciprocity.

Her bare feet, finding a different, more comfortable path to return to her kitchen, met with the thick healthy grass. A crow took off from the tire swing, sending it to swing briskly.

She thought of her romance as a girl where she was kissed under a viaduct by an older boy and how she noticed excrement from birds on the pavement as she obliquely accepted his advance. He had enticed her to follow him with offerings of a joint, but it wasn't until this moment that she recollected that they had never smoked anything.

They kissed hard and after getting her shirt and bra off, he felt her breasts and his mouth absorbed her nipples. She remembered the suction being too hard and unpleasant, a nuisance she didn't communicate.

And at that moment, in her yard by the swing, her brain struggled with trying to reveal more of the memory and it failed her. There was nothing else.

Maureen approached the swinging tire and sat.

Cade woke and wanted a shower but it was occupied. Wondering if it was Mary who was in there, he came upon the stairs. As he sensed Ray's presence in the kitchen, he avoided entering, descending the basement steps instead. He peered through the window, spotting the tire swinging on its line, then perched on the couch and feasted on the memory of kissing Sammie. Worry followed the daydream.

He headed back up to the only shower in the house. The bathroom was vacant and steamy. He went up to the attic bedroom for clean clothes and returned to find Mary brushing her teeth.

"One sec," she said casually. Her mouth was muffled by the task.

"Um, that's cool. Take your time. I was just gonna take a quick sh-shower if that's cool if you didn't mind," said Cade. Mary spat then rinsed. She walked out of the bathroom, passing him on her left.

"*Quick* might be a good idea," said Mary. "Not sure how much hot water is left."

"Ok, that's cool," said Cade. She headed for her bedroom.

"Oh, and Cade?" said Mary.

"Yeah?" said Cade.

"There's probably a lot of hair in the drain cause I washed my hair, my bad," said Mary.

"Oh! Nice! I bet that feels good! I always like to wash too!" said Cade.

"Enjoy," said Mary as she closed her bedroom door.

The shower got cold fast but he didn't care. He washed every inch of his body and masturbated. Just after putting on fresh clothes, he reached into the drain, pulled out the hair, and discarded it. Refreshed, he passed Ray on the way out.

"Hi, Ray."

"You didn't use all the hot water, did ya, Cade?" said Ray.

"Yup," he said before heading upstairs to relax.

There, he saw Miles getting ready. After asking how the trip at Darien Lake went, to which Cade replied vaguely, Miles informed him that he had to go to Grandpa Ted's house to take care of some business with his dad. This unexpected news pleased Cade as he desired to be with Sammie.

He waited until they left, then picked up the phone. As usual, her father was out of town. She invited him over.

Bushy-tailed squirrels ran for cover as dark clouds convened over the basketball courts and gazebos at Delwood Park across from Sammie's place. She waited inside for Cade who arrived with a six pack not long after they spoke over the phone.

"Hey."

"Hey."

"How are you?"

"Pretty good."

"Yeah?"

"Yeah."

They hugged.

"I'll take a beer for sure," said Sammie. She popped one for herself and Cade followed suit.

"So?"

"Everything is...seemingly cool," said Cade.

"Yeah?" said Sammie.

"Yeah, I crossed paths with Mary," said Cade.

"Oh, yeah?" said Sammie.

"She seemed...like she didn't know," said Cade.

"Really?" said Sammie. "How was everybody else?"

"Fine," said Cade. "Miles went off with Ray to Grandpa Ted's to do some—"

"Yeah, we talked," said Sammie.

"Oh," said Cade. "Also, Ty Jai knows?"

"What," said Sammie.

"Yeah," said Cade. "He was awake."

"Oh, God," said Sammie.

"Yeah, he gave me quite the verbal thrashing," said Cade.

"Really?" said Sammie. "Will he—"

"No," said Cade. "He won't."

"Ok," she said. "So I think...it looks like...shit is...pretty cool?" Sammie twisted her hips invitingly and smiled. Cade moved in for a hug and they kissed. He was confused but it felt good. They kissed there in her kitchen without fear.

"I can't believe this is happening," she said.

"Me too," said Cade. They kissed again.

"I've had this...thing for you for so long," said Sammie.

"Really?" said Cade. They kissed more and then headed to the living room and sat on the sofa where they were free to be without interruption.

Cade drove home later that evening. He did not stop for more beer.

The summer in Buffalo, unlike its unsophisticated inhabitants on Hendricks Boulevard, was past its half-life. The long days of the neighborhood where the cohabitating boys were raised had taken on a new glow while their uncertain future, together and alone, was taking shape.

The fiery star heating the earth in overdrive made it hard to slink between the cracks unseen and unheard. The recently depraved were now seemingly always out and about as they say in the place known for its coldness and desolation. Out and grazing nearly round the clock these days, civil tups all over, hiding in sight and rinsing their wounds in the waters of banality, waited for it to freeze over yet again. For there is little forgiveness amidst manifold human existence. Lifeless, nothing, but nothing calls to you when you're surrounded by the others amidst the warm deceitful wind of the Northeast USA.

"BRO. My dad is in one of his moods. I think he's gonna want to *clean* our room."

"Shit," said Cade.

"All right, everybody up!" said Ray upon entering the boys' shared attic pad that he owned.

Miles had nudged Cade awake to give him a head start but it was too late.

"Ok, you bums, rise and shine," Ray continued. It was just before 9 am. "Cade Caybul. Are you up?"

"Uh?" said Cade.

"Uh, nothing," said Ray. "You don't know that I turn the other cheek with you, Cade? You don't know how many times I've turned the other way? Countless times, Cade. Countless. I go into my refrigerator for my beer and it's not there. Then I find the empties layin' around my basement floor. Great. Let's see how many of my empties are up here."

"Dad, take it easy!" said Miles. "Everybody drinks your beer, including me."

"Miles Helton, don't start with me, all right?" said Ray. "I'm not in the mood."

"Neither are we," said Miles. "It's the middle of summer, and it's nine in the morning."

"No, it isn't," said Ray.

"You find any beer, Dad?" said Major, walking into the room, dragging his blanket.

"Hello, Major Helton," said Ray. "No, not yet."

"I got your back," said Major.

"Oh my God," said Cade. Miles grinned at Cade as they connected eyes before Cade quickly looked away.

"Oh my God is right," said Ray. "This place is a mess."

"Major, get out of our—what are you even doing here?!" said Miles.

"I'm helpin' Dad!" said Major.

"Heinrich Himmler over here," said Cade, triggering a laugh from his friend.

"What?" said Ray. "Major, come over here and help me with—lift up this loveseat with me."

"Shit," said Cade.

"Ah-ha!" said Ray. "Beer cans and bottles. Olde English. Red Dog. What is this crap in my house?!"

"We can't afford the good stuff, Dad," said Miles as Cade slipped on pants and stood.

"These are yours, Miles Helton?" said Ray.

"Yes," said Miles.

"I need a garbage bag for this," said Ray. "Major Helton, go get me a garbage bag, please."

"*Glad* to, dad," said Major. "Get it? Cause the garbage bag is *Glad* brand!"

"Jesus Christ," said Miles.

They excavated the graveyard of smelly cans and bottles, Miles working and his dad supervising. By the time the room was standardized, Cade was out the door and in his car, headed toward Sammie's.

Her driveway was occupied by Katie's familiar SUV, which surprised and upset Cade. He parked next to it and walked toward the fence barricading the backyard and unlatched the hinge. Closing it behind him and approaching the door, he heard the sound of a man laughing, probably Katie's boyfriend. At that moment, for the first time that day, he saw himself. He thought about what he was doing. As he began to sweat, he made up his mind that coming over unannounced was a bad idea. All that separated him from the inside of the home was the screen door.

"Someone's here," said Katie.

Cade could barely see her due to the bright sun. Sammie's silhouette made its way to the door in half the time he expected and the furrows above her eyes relaxed as the light hit her face.

"Cade man," she said.

"Hello," said Cade. He thought he'd be mocked by her at that moment. Instead, she ran to him.

"Hello yourself!" she said with arms around him.

"Who's here?" said Cade. "Is it Ka—"

"Katie and Leon," said Sammie.

"Oh," said Cade.

"What brings you by?" said Sammie.

"I—uh."

"You just wanted to see me," said Sammie, hugging him again, this time inhaling deeply through her nose against his chest.

"Yeah," said Cade.

"How's it going?" said Sammie.

"Fine," said Cade. "Ray is going apeshit on a cleaning frenzy, so I wanted to bail 'cause it sucked."

"Cool," said Sammie.

"Hi, Cade," said Katie coming out onto the porch. Her boyfriend, Leon, followed her. Katie hugged Cade then Leon did the same, preceded by a hand slap.

"You remember Leon, right, Cade?"

"Uh, yeah, what's up?" said Cade.

"How've you been, Cade?" said Leon.

"I, uh, just chillin'," said Cade.

"Why are you so tall?!" said Sammie.

"Genetics?" said Leon. "Although my mom is 5'1"."

"Oh shit," said Katie. "Sammie, shit. A bird just shat on your head!"

"What?!" said Sammie. "No!" Responding to the drop she had felt but not seen, Sammie touched then ran her fingers across her hair, collecting the matter and inspecting her hand.

"Shit!" she said, heading for the house.

"That's good luck, I hear," said Leon.

"Good luck, my balls!" said Sammie.

The other three followed her, grinning. Katie laughed, holding the door for the guys.

"Do you need help in there?" she asked from one end of the hallway to the other.

"No!" said Sammie. "I'm just gonna shower. Cade, com'ere!"

Silence then.

After Cade made his way down the hallway, he and Sammie spoke face to face.

"Can you believe a bird just shat on my head?!"

"No. I cannot." As she took off her socks, she smiled, inviting. Cade gathered the message that she wanted a kiss. He looked at her mouth and zeroed in. Their lips touched then Sammie impersonated what she had just seen, criticizing his lack of eye contact before the less-than-affectionate peck in sardonic mimicry.

Cade, becoming hyper-aware of the silence among their friends in the living room, imagined they were slyly communicating as to the peculiar closeness of Sammie and him. And he was taken aback by Sammie's apathy of the presence of their friends who, in friendship, to her were much closer.

"You're boring," she said, closing the door gently.

Cade heard the shower turn on. Moseying back to the living room to greet his silent friends, he remarked nervously, "Shit bird."

Katie chuckled.

"Yeah," said Leon. "That shit is crazy."

"Good pun," said Katie.

"Thanks," said Leon.

Katie's phone rang.

"How much does that thing cost?" said Leon.

"I don't know," said Katie. "It goes by the minute."

"I think you're the only one I know with a cell phone," said Leon.

"Oh, yeah?" she said.

"How much does it cost?" said Cade.

"It goes by minutes," said Katie.

"How much per minute?" said Leon.

"Not sure," said Katie.

"Do people look at you weird when you answer it?" said Leon.

"Sometimes, I guess," said Katie. "You're kinda lookin' at me weird right now," said Katie.

"Really?" said Leon.

"No," said Katie. "Everyone will have one soon."

"I don't want one," said Leon. "I can't picture, like, everyone getting a hold of me all the time."

"You can just turn it off," said Katie.

"What happens when someone calls when it's off?" said Leon.

"Does it ring when it's, um, does it go to silent?" said Cade.

"It has a vibrate feature," said Katie.

"Oh, like a pager," said Cade.

"Right," said Katie. "Do you still have a pager?"

"Not anymore," said Cade. "Pretty soon again, though."

"How much does that cost?" said Katie.

"Like twenty," said Cade.

"A minute?" said Katie.

"A month," said Cade.

"A minute?!" said Leon.

"I'm high," said Katie. The three chilled silently for a while.

"What are you talking about?" said Sammie, entering the room with her hair wrapped in a towel.

"You changed dresses," said Cade.

"Yeah," said Sammie, turning and facing Cade. Their eyes locked. She took the garment from her head and manually dried her hair with it as she smiled innocently and invitingly into Cade's eyes. The pleasant scent of warm clean hair filled the room.

"What were you talking about?" said Sammie, turning to her original guests, welcoming them back into her formerly biased vision.

"We were discussing the costs of modern communication," said Leon.

"That's boring," said Sammie.

The phone rang and Sammie stood, walked to the kitchen, and answered.

It was Miles.

Cade decided to make his way to Jake's. He had gotten halfway across Delwood Park on foot before he realized that he had left his car at Sammie's.

During the short drive, it ate at him. He traveled slowly, drinking in the day with his eyes. Every piece of trash along the road, like specks of poison in the bloodstream, spiked any potential for tranquility. He stopped to try his luck at Red Apple for beer.

As he stepped out of his car, he paused and attempted to recall what he had seen on the way from Sammie's to the familiar store and there was little connection of there to here, then and now.

Inside the shop, the clerk in his mid-thirties, had just caught someone stealing. He was standing in front of the thief between two end caps of the center aisle.

"Here's the evidence right here!" said the clerk. "What if I call the police?! Huh?! Would you like that?! Huh?!!"

As the door slowly closed behind Cade, his pace slowed. He grabbed a six pack of tall cans.

"Put those back," said the clerk with authority. "I've got a situation and cannot tend to that matter right now."

"There's a matter?" said Cade.

"I'm dealing with this shoplifter," said the clerk, seemingly oblivious to the air, good and sarcastic. From this angle, Cade could only see the towering man and not the person he was reprimanding. He continued with the beer to the counter, taking good look at the mortified boy with his head slunk over.

Cade deduced this was not a child of epically cool proportions. His clothing suggested that he was dressed by a strict matriarch without much style of her own. His haircut did not match the times. And his blinking was hard with eyes shut phase held five times as long as normal.

"Answer me!" yelled the clerk. The child murmured wordlessly.

"What the hell happened here?" said Cade to the clerk's back. The child's chin raised some. "What did he steal?" said Cade leafing, through his money.

The clerk blasted into a furious 180 with his finger pointing outward: "THIS IS MY STORE AND THIS IS NONE OF YOUR BUSINESS! Are you even old enough to buy beer?!"

"If you wanna come over here and cash me out, you can check for yourself."

"Don't start with me!" said the clerk.

"Whatever he stole, I'll buy," said Cade. "What did you steal?"

"Condoms," said the perp and Cade barely heard it. The boy began to cry as the triangle descended upon him becoming smaller. Cade saw the three-pack in the once angry clerk's grip, slowly reached, and took them out of his hand.

"Magnums? You're not fuckin' around are ya, kid." Cade headed back to the counter. "Let's add a pack a Magnums, chief-o."

Confused, the clerk slowly made his way behind.

"Is there anything else?" he said from his fading position of power.

"No thanks," said Cade.

"You really buying this kid condoms?" said the clerk. "That might be illegal."

"It isn't," said Cade.

15

LIFE HAD BEGUN

"I can't just break up with him. We've been together for so long.

If we were together for like, a few months, then I could maybe see doing it.

It's been almost a year. I can't just leave him."

Sammie had become an exclusive part of Cade's life romantically and sexually which was an energy that remained unreciprocated.

Problem solved, she said happily after their first time that lasted longer than a minute or two of apprehensive thrusts. It took putting a prophylactic between them, a tactic applied specifically to quell the issue. She had worked with him and his inability to stay inside without ejaculating before either of them could completely value each other's bodies and union of trust. Sammie never infantilized her lover even at times when he'd beat his fists against the wall over it.

Among gatherings of friends who only knew Miles through Cade, they'd sneak lustful looks at each other. They'd rendezvous in the kitchen at Sammie's house to kiss deeply and let their hands run over each other while the others were just one room away.

I've never felt happy in my life, he'd say to her at the baseball diamond blocks from her house which was but one of their hidden places in the small town. It was true. The synergy amongst the pair was not one for which he had longed nor was it something that he knew could be. Nonetheless, it was a feeling that kept him needing more. And, tagging along like a starving beast, it was shrouded by the dark perception that it couldn't be real. Not yet. And it wouldn't be until he was no longer shackled by chains of deceit.

So unto her, he'd plead.

"I don't understand why you won't."
"It's not that I won't. I can't."
"Well, who do you love? Me or him?"
"Babe."

"This is so fucked up."
"He's gonna go away to college pretty soon."
"So?"
"He'll break up with me then."
"How do you know?"
"I know."

Soon, Cade's night had a new demon. He would return to Heltons', hopeful to see his old friend in bed as that would mean he wasn't sleeping with Sammie. And he'd lie awake after discovering the bed empty.

In person, to her, he'd communicate his anger and confusion aptly, but he'd draw from a well of sensory remembrance as, when he was with her, those emotions would disappear into a tranquil sea. They'd hide together in darkness and in sight and at the end of the day, there was nothing unusual about them being alone together. It wasn't so far-fetched. They were old friends with years of history and common experiences, which was something that she did not have with her boyfriend, Miles. And unlike her public partner, Cade and she had the same affinity for the hard stuff.

"I'm digging myself into a hole here. I'm digging myself into a serious hole."

Although the statement from her secret love was not one of ambiguity, it was met with silence. They aimlessly walked through the dark streets of their familiar neighborhood on ecstasy.

"This is gonna be so bad," said Cade.

"Babe," said Sammie.

"I'm sure that I love you," he said. "I'm sure that I'm *in love* with you."

"I'm in love with you too," she said. They kissed then looked into each other. "I love your eyes so much."

"I love your eyes so much too," said Cade. The soul windows reflected concern. They reflected concern and comfort.

"Wanna keep walking?" said Cade.

"Yeah," smiled Sammie.

Holding hands atop the quiet suburb streets, they'd let go of each other when they'd see a car or hear one from behind. Rubber and metal passed and they'd grab ahold again.

If there'd be encroachment of a house that belonged to someone Sammie knew on the left, she would go and walk along the shadows, painting the sidewalk on the right.

They'd come across someone that Cade knew and *he* would divert from the path. Then silently, like pooling water, they'd reconvene.

"I feel like shit when you two are together," said Cade.

"Can we just enjoy this night, please?

Can we get menthols?"

"Sure," said Cade.

Being on a busy road posed a threat that the side streets didn't offer. But tonight, despite the despondence of the more gallant of the couple, they became more carefree with every gale that blew against their skin.

They approached Jack Mason's gas station next to the 24-hour laundromat. Sammie stood still and lit a smoke.

"You're not coming in?" said Cade.

"No," she said, exhaling. "Can you just get me a pack of Marb menthols?"

"Yeah, man."

The clerk was familiar to Cade. They made eye contact as he entered. In that moment, he saw Stanley, the gas station attendant, typically brash and impatient, in a state like none other. There was humility in his calm eyes. Cade grabbed a water and Sammie's favorite iced tea. Then gum, gummy candy, and two suckers.

"How's it going tonight, Stanley?"

"Good," he said. "How 'boutcha self."

"It's a wonderful night," said Cade.

"I heard dat," said Stanley. "Anything else tonight?"

"No thank you. Oh wait, Marb Menthols, please. And Camel Lights if you do not mind."

"What are you listening to?" continued Cade.

"Radio. I'm not sure who it is."

"No doubt," said Cade. "Life is easier when there's music."

"There is *no doubt*," said Stanley, smiling.

"Ok, brother," said Cade. "Thank you."

He exited to find Sammie sitting on a parking cinder with her legs apart like a boy. She put out her smoke.

"Oooooh, Arizona," said Sammie. "Spank you very much. Did you get me a straw?"

"No, I forgot," said Cade.

"Cool," said Sammie. She headed in, patting her bottom to make sure her skirt was down.

The fickle moment sometimes eluded Cade. When fear would strike, it wasn't uncommon for him to feel inferior for letting the bastard get away in the first place. As the night continued to sing its song, he remembered his predicament and again let despair wash over.

The gas station parking lot was just eight blocks from Heltons' place and his childhood home. The sidewalk was the very path to it. It was the way to where he slept since he had found his dead mother. They were kind enough to ask him to stay. They called him "family." But he knew he wasn't. He was their guest. And he was having a secret relationship with his oldest friend's partner…his oldest friend who squandered his privacy to let him in. And this night, amidst moments of peace, the curse of *there's got to be more* tightened its hold on the eighteen-year-old man.

Sammie came out, grinning. "Ok, Stanley, we love you!"

"Did you smile—did you say hi to Stanley?" said Cade.

"Yes!" said Sammie. "He is lovely! He told me I look like I hung the moon. I'm not sure what it means, but I love it!"

"Wanna go?" said Cade politely.

"Sure," said Sammie, almost surprised by the proposal of moving on.

The couple turned and waved to their helper who, from behind the window, waved back.

"Bye, Stanley!" they said together and began walking.

"What do you think his life is like?" said Sammie.

"I don't know," said Cade.

"I wonder where he lives," said Sammie.

"I hope he has someone who cares about him," said Cade.

"Me too," said Sammie, taking ahold of his arm as they walked along the sidewalk of the busy street.

"What color do you want?" said Cade, displaying the suckers.

"Uuuum, what color do *you* want?" she said.

"I, uh—"

"Fuck it, we're just gonna share anyway," said Sammie, grabbing and unwrapping one.

Making a right on the familiar side street, they followed it all the way to the alley leading to the park across from what used to be their elementary school where they seemingly had the dark place to themselves.

Cade's mind and legs led them to the area behind the adjacent bank's dumpsters where he used to smoke as a kid on the down low.

"Um, dude," said Sammie. "Let's go to a bench."

"Are you sure?" said Cade.

"Yeah," said Sammie. "We're not doing anything illegal. Besides rolling. But no one knows that. Or they can't prove it."

"Ok," said Cade.

He sat, opened his legs, and Sammie sat between his thighs. She leaned back.

"Trade," she said, handing him her sucker.

"They're at prime sweetness," said Cade.

"Aw!" said Sammie. "You bit yours!"

"Hell yeah," said Cade.

"Aw!" said Sammie.

"You want it?" said Cade.

"Want what?" said Sammie.

"The piece," said Cade, before enjoying the oral trade-off.

They shared a long, strange kiss.

After the suckers and more tobacco, they discussed fate and how it brought them to each other. She encouraged him to live in the moment, easing his worry about their predicament involving Miles.

They sat near the colorful playground, dampened by darkness, and reminisced about how when they were kids, it was different and made of metal—not plastic. The equipment used to be rusty and the ground beneath the swings wasn't padded. And it used to be colored flatly. Now it was stained with vibrant yellows and reds and blues.

Cade, his forearms crisscrossed, held Sammie's breasts gingerly in his hands. He inhaled the scent of her hair and as the wind struck harder, so did their embrace.

Calmly, Sammie got up, turned round, and straddled him. She gently bit her bottom lip and looked into his eyes. She guided his chin upward with her index and middle fingers and licked his neck slowly up to his nose. Giving pause and moving her head back to immerse herself, visualizing his reaction, she did it again, but this time, she put her tongue in his mouth before timidly retreating. Once more, she went in then pulled back. And again. He tried chasing and catching her tongue with his mouth but couldn't.

"You're—" he said before she occupied his tongue silencing him. She did it again. And again. She teased his mouth with hers, licking then receding. He took the flesh of her upper arms into his hands, attempting to hold her still. Quelling his effort by planting her palms on his chest by his shoulders and pushing him away, she continued licking his lips and tongue, dominating, licking, and withdrawing.

After giving in and wiping spittle from her lip, they heard the unmistakable sound of two men laughing. The sound became louder as the sweethearts processed the new addition without releasing each other's gaze.

Walking along the path leading to them came three men, slightly older, drunk and bored with the night's offerings. Sammie's back was to the noise which became louder. Cade was able to see them coming. Their pace slowed.

"Should I get off?" said Sammie quietly.

"Yeah," said Cade.

She dismounted and sat to his left as the three men approached.

"Damn, baby," one said as he noticed Sammie. She fiddled with her tank-top, pulling it a little higher as she watched from over her handy work.

"What's up, you two?" said another. "Sorry to interrupt."

"It's all good," said Cade, just as Sammie's alert eyes darted to him. The group slowed and stopped in front of them.

"Whatchoo guys up to?" he continued.

"Chillin' an' shit," said Cade.

"Dude, I'm sorry, bro, I don't mean to offend you, but your girl is sexy as fuck," said the one who hadn't spoken. "I imagine she's your girl."

"She's a woman," said Cade.

"Like, I don't even know where to begin," continued the most smitten chap.

"You guys jus' chillin'?" said the primary speaker.

"Yeah," said Cade.

"Your eyes look big. You guys trippin'?"

"Maybe," said Cade.

"It's a good night for it," said the leader.

"Dude, her mouth, oh my God," continued Casanova from the background.

"You got a smoke?" said the leader.

"And her skin, Jesus Christ."

"If we give you one, will you leave us alone?" said Sammie sternly.

"Damn. And she got a attitude, damn, baby."

"Well, there are three of us," said the leader. "You got three smokes?"

"Red Apple is right down the street," said Sammie.

"Red Apple? But you got smokes right here."

"Yeah, a fine girl like you and not gorgeous—I mean, generous? A nice young lady like you shouldn't be smoking anyway."

"Whatever," said Sammie, turning to Cade.

Cade Caybul's head moved to meet the shining eyes of the woman he loved. They projected beams of fear and trust at once, illuminating the dark, like moonlight feeding a piece of glass at the bottom of an oily puddle. The strangers' intrusion escalated as fast as his certainty. No connection to any human before this moment could compare to the closeness he felt to Sammie Hayes this night on the wooden bench across from where they had learned to read. And where, in adolescence, they formed their first utopian bond.

LIFE HAD BEGUN.

In the fall of 1990, Cade and Miles, then age seven, were playing not too far from their homes on the quiet street called Olney Drive. Sound sang out of TVs in houses airing hockey in the Western New York village while suburbanites sat storing extra lipids in their cells as they watched and jeered.

Don't play in the street! And stay out of the leaves in the road! A drunk driver could drive right into the pile and crush you to death!

The severity in Cade's mother's voice echoed in their minds. But for fun, one street from their own, they were ringing neighbors' doorbells and running before the occupant came to the door.

On a particularly close call, they hid behind the big air conditioning unit immediately next to their chosen victim's house. Squatting single file, they waited for clearance, but instead of simply shutting the door, the curious human ventured out and approached them.

They heard each step rustle the dry leaves, getting louder before the person stopped at the idle machine that poorly hid them. They never got a look at the merciful man or woman who saw their little crouched bodies, sensing their fear and innocence before peacefully and forgivingly returning inside.

After calling it quits on the game, they moseyed to the common park where they played on the rusty dark-colored playground. Spinning each other on the roundabout, which was noisy and dented from being trounced upon by so many, was no easy task given their size and that it was only the two of them.

"When my dad does this, I go so fast," Cade said, winded.

"Look at that umbrella!" said Miles, grinning at a discarded parasol blowing about in the wind.

"Where do you think it came from, My?!" said Cade.

"I don't know!" said Miles. "Should we give it to one of our moms?!"

"Good idea!"

"Who are these little penises?!" said an adolescent boy and his three friends, approaching the two little ones.

"Hey, aren't you little Cadey and Miles?!" said another.

The mean boys were known by most of the kids in the neighborhood and some parents too. Cade stopped spinning his only friend in the world who stepped off of the ride and stood next to him.

"Look at these two faggots! They've got the same fuckin' haircut!"

"Yeah! Little penises! They look like little fuckin' penises!"

"Which one of you takes it in the ass?" the boy said, ruffling Cade's hair. "This one?!"

"Don't touch him!" said Miles. "We'll tell on you!"

"Oh, no! You gonna tell your big-titted mom, ya little penis?"

"No, this one is the one with the mom with big tits," said the boy with the deepest voice, extending his index finger and poking Cade's forehead.

The boys had lost track of time and the autumn sun had set on them. If they were at the fence overlooking the hill, they'd almost be able to see Cade's house. Back then, Miles' place was right across the street. Wind blew cold against their skin. Confused and helpless, they stood shrouded by the deviant agenda of the older boys.

"Your mom's got big tits, ya little faggot," said another. Too scared to make eye contact with each other, they stood in front of the bullies, trying in futility to process what they were hearing.

Young Cade saw an old man and his little dog appear in the distant parking lot just before the fence at the top of the hill. The strolling man looked over at the six boys, two of them too small for the other four, as he was headed for the cement stairs in the gap of the fence. He looked hard to his left three times and forward again, gaining speed each time before turning his back entirely and descending the hill. Cade wanted to yell out to him but did not. The older boys noticed the old man as well.

"I think we gotta take these two over to the dumpsters."

"Yeah! Let's go!"

And with that, the laughing four guided the young ones by their shoulders and led them forty yards or so to the wall on the other side of the dumpsters. Their small Velcro shoes moved along the blades of grass slowly. The motion found itself propelled by the energy of their assailants whose big skater sneakers had to stop short frequently so as to not trample the yearlings.

Miles and Cade walked side-by-side over to the foot of the dirt hill with broken glass and cigarette butts. The ascension of the gradual incline was more daunting to the little children who slowed and stopped before it. It took yet a solitary boy to hoist each one to the more secluded area along the graffiti tagged wall and then, it started to rain.

"Get his shirt off!" said one, before doing it himself. After removing Miles' shirt, he swiftly ran his hands over his chest, back, and belly, halting his fingers at the naval to fondle the three dimensional piece of flesh that grabbed his interest. He put his face toward the wall and pulled his little pants down around his ankles. "Get that one's shirt off! Face the wall, ya fag!" The leader's friends, confused in that moment, their ambitions dwarfed by their commander's, merely ruffled Cade's clothing, buying time in appeasement.

"Suck it, little boy!" he said, forcing Miles' face to his genitalia.

"Caleb, what the hell are you doing?" said one of the accomplices.

"Shut the fuck up," he said, taking a suspicious look around and behind him. "Get that umbrella and bring it here! Face the wall and take your fuckin' shorts off like your pussy friend here!" A boy came with the apparatus as told. He held Miles by his hair, moving his face over his genitalia. "Open your mouth, faggot! I said open it!" The boy slapped his penis upon Miles' face. "Face the wall, faggot! Both of you!" He took the umbrella in his hand.

"It's time to go," said Cade calmly after abandoning his lover's eyes. Sammie was confused as were the unwanted three. "Why are you still here?"

"Look, we're just trying to be friendly here, man. It's a nice night and we're just trying to get a couple squares."

"I do not want to give you any cigarettes," said Cade in monotone, leaving generous space between words. "These cigarettes are ours. You are being rude, and I am trying to have a good time with my girlfriend." His eyes were steadfast on the leader, they were only on the leader.

"You guys have a good night," the man said before stepping away. His two friends followed. Silently.

"Hold hands! Hold hands, you little faggots!" The hook-like handle of the umbrella, inserted between the buttocks of the tiny victims, posed a problem for their rapist, so without penetrating, he drove it upon the flesh of each boy one by one, moving them closer to the wall. He was careful not to bruise their faces upon the brickwork. The adamance was somewhat reflected by one of his friends; the other two stood looking about in fear with almost no interest in the sexual task.

One hundred eighty degrees went the umbrella and the weapon became more ample. Miles squeezed Cade's hand harder. Cade squeezed back and held tight. Back and forth the deed went as the boy, thirteen-years-old, laughed and shouted, mindful of the consequence of bruising or shedding blood while the henchmen watched. "Stay that way!" he said before his escape. He picked up small rocks and threw them at his victims as the four receded.

That night, before they went into their respective dwellings, young Cade and Miles hugged for the first time.

"Oh my God, I've never heard you talk like that!" said Sammie, excited. They lit smokes and relaxed.

"I hate this place," said Cade.

"I love being anywhere with you," said Sammie.

TEAM

"What's Miles' penis like?" said Lil.

"It's pretty big," said Sammie.

"Cut or not?" said Lil.

"What?" said Sammie.

"Is he circumcised?" said Lil.

"Um, I don't know," said Sammie. "I think so. Yes."

"Does it have freckles all over it?" said Lil.

Sammie was the only one in the room who was entertained by the odd questions during the daytime visit from friends. Lil's partner, Esham, sat with his legs apart on the faux leather couch, shaking his head slowly from left to right.

"Why are you asking so many questions about homeboy's dick?" said Esham.

"It's what we do," said Lil. "So, is it?"

"I don't know," said Sammie, smiling. "A few?"

"Will you stop talking about this?" said Esham.

Wilma had come out of the bathroom. She had dyed purple hair, thin sculpted eyebrows, and chronic back pain due to the size of her breasts.

Lil and her boyfriend, Esham, had dropped out of high school together at ages 16 and 14 respectively, a deed for which they were admired. He, despite appearing Hispanic, was Caucasian like his partner and wore baggy clothes and furry Kangol hats that he coordinated with the rest of his clothes. At 21, he was the oldest in the circle.

Lil dressed like most girls her age and had brown hair and a particularly youthful face. She had a very unique sense of humor and aura to her. The couple smoked Newports and enjoyed the highlife.

Sammie cherished her girlfriends and had enjoyed the company of these two at her place since high school began. And to her, the relationship between Esham and Lil was enviable. They had been living on their own in the cool part of town outside of the suburb for over a year. They had dogs and cats and, despite Esham's hustle, brought in plenty of money on the books.

"Where's Miles, Sam?" said Wilma.

"I don't know," said Sammie. "I think he's out with Cade."

"What's Cade been up to," said Wilma. "Is he feeling less...zombie... ish?"

"Yeah," said Sammie. "I think so."

"He is so weird, but he's so cool too!" said Wilma.

"Is that that guy who lives with Miles, who was your first kiss?" said Lil.

"Yeah," said Sammie. "His mom died."

"And his dad did it or something?" said Lil.

"Damn," said Esham.

"I don't know, dude," said Sammie.

"I always feel so weird when I'm in the same room as him, but his eyes, though," said Wilma.

"He's not so bad," said Sammie.

"Do you think I should fuck him?" said Wilma.

"I, uh-" said Sammie.

"You sure you can squeeze him in to your busy fuck schedule, Wilm?" said Lil.

"Oh, I am *sure* I can squeeze him in," said Wilma.

"I think he might be talking to this chick from South," said Sammie.

"No chick from Williamsville South is hotter than me," said Wilma. "I can get him."

"You know," said Sammie. "He said that he wasn't focusing on chicks right now because...something about how it slowed down his healing from what happened."

"That's understandable," said Lil.

"Shit, when my mom died, I was tryna fuck like mad," said Esham.

"I remember, baby," said Lil.

The afternoon sun was hot. It was a typical day on the quiet street and Sammie's worry slipped undetected by her peers. Not only was Wilma's promiscuity well known but her lack of shame was equally recognized. Although what might transpire was something to acknowledge or even prevent, despite the residence being her own, Sammie never thought of stopping the gathering during its formation.

"I could be just what he needs," said Wilma.

The day before, Cade had played basketball at Jake's with a neighborhood group, giving some space and time for Sammie to withdraw from serotonin on her own accord. This was a task she chose to complete with Miles.

Not that Cade was trying to turn over a new leaf, but the desire to pick up drinks was never fulfilled. He had simply played an intense game of one-on-one with Jake in the street like they did when they were younger. And he had talked to Jake about his relationship with Sammie and how it ate at him.

"It'll all work out," Jake had said.

Cade returned to Heltons' after exercise. He had parked in the street, keeping an eye on the next-door-neighbor's house and walked almost the entire length of the driveway, by and by.

Crows fought over scraps in the distance. Cade heard someone shout his name from a ways behind him. Turning around, then realizing that the sound came from so far they could not be seen from where he stood, he decided to let the mystery sleep.

He entered the house and kicked off his shoes. The stairs creaked as Ray headed down.

"Cade," said Ray who noticed an air of trouble within his long term house guest.

"There's ants everywhere!" said Cade. "Ray, how come there are so many ants?! They're everywhere!"

"What?!" said Ray. "Where?! I don't see any ants! Where?" Both humans looked about the room hurriedly.

"There's no ants here, Cade. How drunk can you be on an afternoon like this? Look at your face! You're red and covered in sweat!"

"I—"

"I, nothing," said Ray. "Looking to get another DUI? Or another almost-DUI? Wow, man. You are a piece of work."

"A piece of work, right, Dad?" said Major, dragging his blanket into the room and standing next to his father, intermittently looking up at him and across at Cade.

"That's right, Major Helton," said Ray. "That's right."

With an empty stomach, Cade's plans to eat had changed as he went up to the room he shared with his friend, Miles. He waited until after sundown. He waited, hoping for his return until he gave up. And the idea that Miles was sleeping in the bed of the woman he loved painted his mind red.

After Miles awoke from Sammie's bed, unaware of the gathering in the living room, he and Sammie, Wilma, Lil and Esham went out to eat and returned with drinks and LSD. Lil and Esham decided that they wanted to buy ecstasy from Cade, for which Miles tried to act as conduit.

"Miles, call Cadey!" said Wilma.

"Ok," said Miles. "You lookin' to score too?"

"Um, you could say that," said Wilma.

"Bro," said Miles.

"Yeah," said Cade.

"We're partying over at Sammie's if you want to stop by," said Miles.

"Great," said Cade.

"How did you sleep?" said Miles.

"Not great," said Cade.

"Major up your ass again?" said Miles.

"Kind of," said Cade.

"Well, we're chillin' over at Sammie's," said Miles. "Lil and Esham wanted to take some of those rolls off your hands."

"Word," said Cade.

"Yeah," said Miles. "Everyone is starting to party."

"I'll be over."

"Peace."

"Wait," said Cade. "How many rolls do they want?"

"Hold on," said Miles.

"Ten," said Miles.

"Contrary to what Sammie might be telling them, they're fifteen a piece," said Cade.

"Ok, I'll tell them."

Cade showered and while his skin became raw, masturbated without finishing. Upon returning half naked to the bedroom, he became even more perturbed when he saw little Major going through his drawers.

"What are you doing up here, Major?" said Cade.

"I can do whatever I want," said Major. "This is my house."

"Let go of my things," said Cade.

"What *is* this?" said Major. "Drug para—drug para—drug things?"

"That is a bottle opener," said Cade.

"I know you and my brother do pot up here," said Major.

"That's nice," said Cade.

"You're only here 'cause my mom wants you here, ya know," said Major.

"Yes," said Cade.

"Pretty soon, you won't be here. Then where are ya gonna go?" said Major.

"Away," said Cade while he gathered clean clothes.

"Mom and Dad fight 'cause you're here," said Major.

"I'll bet," said Cade.

"What?" said Major.

"I'll bet," said Cade.

"You'll bet what?" said Cade.

"I'll bet that—Major I need privacy," said Cade.

"What's privacy?" said Major.

"Jesus Christ," said Cade.

"I'm tellin' dad!" said Major before heading downstairs.

Cade got settled in his attire and took one last peek at all his hiding places, finding only empties. The call for a drink and the opportunity to make some money put some pep in his step as he pocketed the pills and headed out to his car and over to Sammie's. He got halfway there and realized the journey would be better if he had some pre-arrival beer, so he doubled back and hit the reliable store.

After downing three tall Red Dogs in the car, he cruised to the home of his romantic partner where she and her romantic partner were hanging.

"What's up!" said Cade, making his entrance without knocking.

"Brother, how are you?" said Miles. "Red Dog. Nice."

"Yeah," said Cade.

"Hey, man," said Sammie, entering. Cade busied himself in the fridge making room for his beer. "How are you?"

"I'm fine," he said finally. "You want a Dog?"

"Sure," said Sammie.

"Love what you've done with the place," said Cade.

"Yeah, well, you know me," said Sammie. "Always doin' stuff with the place. I'll introduce you to Lil and Esham."

"Cool," said Cade.

"Hi, Cade!" said Wilma, moving toward him for a hug. "I'm tripping!"

"That's awesome," said Cade.

"You want a sugar cube?" said Wilma. "It's *so* clean."

"Sure," said Cade. Lil and Esham joined them in the kitchen.

"I hear you have X," said Wilma.

"Yeah," said Cade.

"Cade, this is Lil and Esham," said Sammie.

"Hi!" smiled Lil.

"Yo, what's up, buddy," said Esham.

"Hello," said Cade. "Good to meet 'cha."

"They want to buy some rolls," said Sammie.

"Ok," said Cade.

"Are they speedy or dopey?" said Lil.

"Um—I—I'm not sure," said Cade.

"Well, we'll buy a lot if you have 'em,'" said Esham.

"Yeah, how are they?" said Lil. "Are they speedy or dopey?"

"I'd say speedy," said Sammie.

"Really? Sweet!" said Lil. "How much?"

"The second time I did them, they weren't as speedy," said Sammie.

"I didn't know you did them twice," said Miles.

"Fifteen," said Cade.

"Sammie said they were—" said Lil.

"Inflation, nigga," said Sammie.

"Can you give us a break if we buy a lot?" said Esham.

"'Cause we can get them for ten apiece from my cousin," said Lil.

"Damn, your cousin seems interesting," said Cade. "What's his name?"

"I, uh—" said Lil.

"Fifteen is fine if they're the shit," said Esham.

"They are the best pills I've ever had," said Sammie.

"Tell ya what," said Cade. "Let's just have a good time, and see what happens. Are you gonna flip, bro?"

"Nah," said Miles. "I'll just pop some sugar and kick with my friends Red and Dog."

"So laaaame," said Sammie.

"I know," said Cade.

"I'll save my first roll for another time," said Miles. This served as a great relief to Cade.

"Wanna shotgun a beer?" said Sammie.

"Sure," said Cade. And they went outside together.

"I wanna come!" said Wilma.

AFTER A NIGHT OF drinking and social oddities that died harder than the life they took from the essence of the group, they all piled into Lil's car and went over the city limit to get pizza. As the guys were inside the pizza shop with Lil, Sammie confided in her friend. She told her that she had been hooking up with Cade secretively and that her feelings for him had become troublesome.

They ate and smoked and, despite Esham's efforts to fight nearly every man who walked past him, a characteristic to which Lil seemed indifferent, his behavior to the rest of them was captivating and, if it weren't for the booze, scary.

The ride back was quieter than the way there. And this time, Wilma sat on Cade's lap to consolidate space, unlike the first trip which found Sammie on Miles. The music was lower this time and Lil didn't drive as fast.

"Did you like your pizza, Cade?" said Wilma.

"Sure," he said. "Always do." She ran the tip of her nose along his beard. He continued out of obligation before turning to face the passing buildings. "I don't think I could live without pizza."

"Dude, me too, bro," said Esham.

Wilma whispered something to Cade which made him smile. Sammie, sitting in the middle of the back seat, turned from the upsetting vision and looked out through the window. This action Miles mistook for the desire to exhibit affection of their own and he kissed her cheek tenderly and took hold of her hand. Wilma's voice turned to laughter, which triggered Cade to forcefully reflect the noise. Only Sammie could detect the dissonance within the sounds he made.

Unscathed, they returned to Sammie's where, for a change, she began to drink faster than anyone, including Cade. The tempo of her walking about her own living quarters was nearly doubled before she became settled. "Your eyes are like...see-through," said Wilma.

"Ok," said Cade.

She pawed at his chest like a small dog trying to get into a room as

Sammie went into her bathroom and cried. After washing her face, she returned to see that the objective in the room had changed to one of a money and pill exchange. Lil haggled with Cade while Wilma headed to the hallway, leading to the bathroom and, passing Sammie, looked down and away from her.

While the embers of the assembly dimmed and sun-up was around the corner, one of the five guests cozied at Sammie's to stay while the others, including Cade who was inebriated mainly from liquor and LSD, left in Lil's car. They cruised past Heltons' and onto Cade's childhood home, still vacant of human life.

"You guys wanna comin' in?" said Cade.

"Nah, we're good, fam," said Esham. "It was nice to finally meet you. We gotta kick it again." Cade hadn't noticed that Wilma had gotten out of the car with him.

"Bye, Cadey!" said Lil. "You're beautiful, baby, it was so nice to meet you!"

"Oh my God," said Cade. "My mama used to call me Cadey. I love it when people call me that! How did you know?"

"You, me, and Eesh are in sync," said Lil. "We're three Libras, remember?!"

"Where the hell did the other one go?" said Cade, looking into the backseat.

"I'm right here!" said Wilma from right next to him.

"JESUS!" jumped Cade.

"No, it's Wilma!" she said.

"Ok," said Cade.

"Peace out, guys," said Esham.

"Have fun, you guys," said Lil.

"Dude, I can't believe you guys are drivin' a car right now," said Cade.

"Believe it, baby, muah!" said Lil, blowing a kiss.

"Peace," said Cade and the loud exhaust cut through the quiet night as Cade and Wilma stumbled to the house.

"Wait here," said Cade.

"Where?" said Wilma.

"Here," said Cade.

"Why?" said Wilma.

"I gotta break in," said Cade.

"What?" she said.

"I gotta break in," said Cade.

"Why?" said Wilma.

"I don't have a key," said Cade.

"Isn't this your house?!" said Wilma.

"Kinda, yes," said Cade.

"Ok?" she said.

"Take in the night air for a second," said Cade. "It's a beautiful night."

"Is anything wrong?" said Miles.

"No," said Sammie. "I just don't feel too well."

"Welcome to my humbly abode," said Cade.

"It's nice," said Wilma.

"Thanks, I found my mother dead on the floor not too long ago. You want a drink?"

"Um—"

"Aw, fuck!" said Cade.

"What?"

"I forgot my beers! God damn it, shit. So you want a drink?"

"Sure!" said Wilma, stroking his arm and chest.

"Cool, I think I know where there's some-A-HA! Bingo! What kind do you want?" said Cade. "We've got all kinds here. It's a...majestic plethora as they say."

"Any kind!" said Wilma, watching him busy about the liquor cabinet.

"Great," said Cade. "This'll do. Good old gin. Rich man's vodka."

"What?" said Wilma.

"Yep," said Cade, swigging from the bottle and offering it to her.

"Do you have glasses?" said Wilma.

"Nah," said Cade.

"Oh my God, it's so bad," she said after a small sip.

They kissed.

Although Cade wasn't attracted to her, he was an 18-year-old man and there was significant intrigue. Making it to the sofa, he pivoted to sit normally, enticing her to straddle him. She sat next to him. Straining his neck to continue kissing in their new position, with his wandering hand locating her bicep, he gently took ahold. Their tongues, bolder now, had at each other.

"This is better," she said, moving his hand to her breast. He squeezed and slid his hands down to her waist where he lifted her shirt. She raised her arms and before Cade began to fiddle with her bra, she spun it around and unhooked. He ran his palms and fingers all over and squeezed.

"Get on top of me," he said.

After straddling him, she moved laterally, and her breasts smacked his face over and over again.

Still processing and unable to get a proper mouthful, he took ahold of her shoulders, stilling their motion, and licked and sucked, giving pause to squeeze and caress with his hands. He withdrew his head leaning back upon the cushion to take it all in visually. Staring for too long, he took a hold again, one hand on each breast. His eyes slowly crept up to find hers.

"Pretty good, huh?" she said.

"Dude," he said. "Your tits are huge."

She smiled.

Wilma had mistaken his being overwhelmed with excitement as he replaced his hands upon her. Now, it was seeming more like a doctoral examination. Cade was frustrated that he could not get his entire hand around each one. Sammie's breasts weren't like this. They could be grasped and shaken easily. They could be dominated. Plus he could locate her nipples.

His eyes widened and his stare intensified trying to escape abstract vision. Then, using his tongue, striving for more of an accomplishment rather than pleasure, he began searching for her centers as he was almost convinced he had found them before.

"What are you doing?" she said.

"What?" he said, before continuing the investigation.

"What are you doing?" she said.

"I'm..." The search went on. "Trying."

"What?" she said.

"I'm trying to—" he said. "Where the hell are your nipples?"

"Here!" she said, squeezing one breast and guiding it to his tongue. He caressed it gently in his mouth.

"*Thank* you!" he said sarcastically. His mouth drew upon it. "Are you sure this is it?"

"What?!" she said.

"Your nipple," he said.

"Am I sure this is my *nipple?!*" she said.

"Yes," he said.

"What?!" she said. "What else would it be?"

I don't know," he said. "Like a mole or something?"

"Asshole!" she said.

"What?" he said.

"What the hell?!" she said.

"Yours doesn't get hard?" he said.

"I'm done," she said and dismounted.

"You want some more gin?" said Cade.

"I can't believe I'm stuck here now," said Wilma.

"Yeah, it's a real pickle," said Cade, taking a swig.

"Do you have ice?" said Wilma, putting on her shirt.

"There's a chance," said Cade. She walked away and into the kitchen. He heard her struggling as his eyes located the curtains finding some peace. Still tripping.

"I can't get it!" said Wilma.

"Get what?" said Cade.

"What?!" said Wilma.

"Get what?!" said Cade.

"The ice!" said Wilma.

"It's in there," said Cade.

"What?!" she said.

"It's in there!" he said.

"It's all stuck together!" she said.

"Yeah," he said.

"What?!

Well, do you have a chisel?"

"No," he said.

"I can't get it," he heard her say softly.

She was closer now. She was calmer. From the curtains, he redirected his vision to her in the kitchen. She looked different in her shirt with no bra. She stood with humility and reminded him of a child. Cade got up and walked toward her.

"I'm here," he said. "You want ice?"

"Yes, please," she said.

He reached his hand into the familiar ice bin from which he used to make drinks for his mom. It was true, it had frozen into one big chunk. He located a hammer and screwdriver and dug out some pieces. They rummaged through the fridge and found some old cola for her that wasn't completely flat. She enjoyed her unorthodox cocktail while he pulled from the bottle. They spoke to each other from on the couch.

"Are you talking to a girl from South?" said Wilma.

"No," said Cade. "Who said that?"

"Sammie," said Wilma.

"Oh," said Cade.

"Or maybe it was Miles," said Wilma.

"I don't know anybody from Williamsville North," said Cade.

"South," said Wilma as she laid her head on his shoulder.

"Oh," said Cade. "There neither."

"Maybe they got it mixed up," said Wilma, while kissing his neck. "Sammie can be quite the gossip."

"I love her," said Cade.

"Yeah, me too," said Wilma. "Sammie is like...the best. I save all my Camel Cash for her. You should see my bag."

"Were you there, or like, around when her mother died?" said Cade.

"No," said Wilma. "I think that was in elementary school? We didn't meet until high school."

"It's hard to sleep," said Cade.

"What?" said Wilma.

"It's hard to sleep after shit like that happens," said Cade, drawing from the bottle.

"I'll bet," said Wilma.

"Do you...are your parents still...are they alive and doing good?" said Cade.

"Um, I think so?" said Wilma.

"That's good," said Cade.

"Yeah, I think so too," said Wilma, gently rolling her eyes.

"The nightmares are strange," said Cade.

"Oh yeah?" said Wilma.

"Yeah, it's...I don't think I had nightmares like this before," said Cade.

"Like what?" said Wilma. "I have nightmares all the time."

"Like, I used to dream about being in different places," said Cade. "And they didn't seem real. Like, I couldn't feel it. Now I can feel it. And the place where it is, is like, wherever I am."

"What?" said Wilma.

"The place where it is," said Cade. "In the dream."

"I have no idea what you're talking about," said Wilma.

"The setting," said Cade.

"Setting of what?" said Wilma.

"The dream," said Cade.

"What dream?" said Wilma.

"The nightmares," said Cade. "The nightmares that always happen."

"This is depressing," said Wilma.

"Yeah," said Cade.

"I can't believe I'm stuck here," said Wilma.

"Ok," said Cade.

"Can I use your phone?" said Wilma.

"If it's still on," said Cade, pointing.

"Why wouldn't it be on?" said Wilma.

"Cause it might be off," said Cade.

"There's no dial tone," said Wilma.

"Then it's off," said Cade.

"Shit," said Wilma.

"We should just do it in the tomorrow," said Cade.

"What?" said Wilma.

"Like, whatever you're trying to do," said Cade.

"I wanna call my brother," said Wilma.

"Ok," said Cade.

"Can I?" said Wilma.

"Not if there's no dial tone," said Cade.

"How come there's no dial tone?" said Wilma.

"The phone's off," said Cade.

"Why would you have a phone then?" said Wilma.

"Oh, boy," said Cade, taking a drink.

"What?" said Wilma.

"So, how about we just chill for now," said Cade. "Then tomorrow, we'll get a hold of your brother from Heltons' place or something. Or I'll just walk you there."

"Now?" said Wilma.

"No," said Cade. "Not now."

Wilma sighed, retreating to her beverage for a few sips. Cade had never seen a woman with breasts so big without a bra on. His mind grappled with both sympathy and shredded lust.

"I'm gonna puke," she said.

"Bathroom," said Cade.

"Where?" said Wilma. He pointed and she stood and moved swiftly to the tiny bathroom to the left of the kitchen just atop the single step leading from the living room. He heard her retching.

After a moment of letting her have her privacy, his eyes found her drink nearly devoid of matter. The instinct to consume what was left deteriorated by the sound of her heaving and crying. The crying turned to sobbing.

Cade noticed her strange shoes near the door. They had high heels and odd straps. He thought of Sammie's sandals and their simplicity. Then he thought of her feet and her legs and her butt... and her bright eyes and smile.

Wilma's expulsion of semi-digested matter became louder. Cade retrieved water and knelt beside her.

"I have water," said Cade.

"Hold my hair!" said Wilma. He helped her and she rinsed her mouth, flushed, and drank some water. "God, that gin is awful!"

"Yeah," said Cade.

"Is it like...past its expiration date or something?"

"Probably," said Cade.

"My God!" she said, before spitting and rinsing again.

"I'm glad you're feeling better," said Cade.

"Fuck!" said Wilma. Cade gently rubbed her back before she used some of his toothpaste and they made their way back to the sofa. "I have a headache."

"That's cause you just puked," said Cade. "It'll settle. You gonna kill this?"

"Get that away from me," she said nuzzling with a pillow.

Finishing what remained of hers, then tidying and using the bathroom, had refreshed Cade. He stepped around her odd shoes and approached the sofa where he saw her sleeping peacefully.

A few more sips of gin enticed Cade to lay next to her and silently they drifted together and alone.

Two hours later, Cade opened his eyes. Fate's misconception still lay asleep next to him. He looked at her face and breasts and face again before standing and walking to the bathroom. Mindful of the potentially hazardous sound, he closed the door until the commode filled and became silent. He thought about drinking more from the bottle which had enough gin for two cocktails. But leaving it where it stood, he concluded he should let *it* rest as well, for in this moment, there was promise.

He walked away from the girl, through the kitchen, stopping at the liquor cabinet to have a peek. Although the lightbulb came on at first pull, the string severed from the device and fell to the floor. Leaving the cabinet within ajar, he closed the pantry door, which smothered most of the insubordinate light, and he headed toward the front of the home and the stairs.

The first step brought a touch different from the soft carpeted steps of the Heltons' stairway. These stairs were hard and cold and had misguided nails. And the emotions related to their ascension were more than enough to overwhelm the boy.

Atop the second floor, Cade took a hard left, passing the room where his mother died. His eyes caught the warped wood on the door where the sign from his childhood used to be: *No Girls Allowed.*

In sixth grade, he had decided he was too old for it to be hanging there when he had some friends over as guests. He and Sammie had escaped the group for some solitude in his room where she had hoped for a kiss, but he was too nervous to make it happen. *You're breaking the rule now,* he remembered her voice.

It was time for a smoke. How many cigarettes he had in his hard pack was usually a mystery. He reached into his pocket where his hand found dilapidated material serving as a sign that there was a slim amount remaining. The wish was that they weren't all broken. From his shorts, the old friend exhumed: three left. None broken.

It was time for a light. The stale scent of the uninhabited house mingled with his brain, and he wondered about the science behind its existence. It was as if the smell that he recalled from the attic had traveled down like a curious invisible plume that had not the courage yet to make it to the first floor.

He traveled back through the hallway to the bedroom on the right. Stepping lightly, mindful of the human sleeping below, he came upon the bed and sat. From his perch near the nightstand, he located matches. *Owl Red* was printed on the box. The first strike on the worn stripe triggered an ample flame that he brought to the Camel's tip. He breathed in and exhaled the grey. This energy gave the needy walls their wayward fix, reminiscent of what they had come to know so well, only to have it unjustly ripped away.

He picked up the phone. She was right, no dial tone. Dragging again and peering at the carpet, he was surprised to see the stain from the deluge that had leaked out of his mother's mouth. Resting the filter of the cig on the nightstand with the ember teetering off the smooth wood, he took to his knees before it. His index finger meddled with darkened fibers of the rug until he pressed three fingers down firmly on its center, almost expecting a kind of wetness and warmth. The delusion subsided and he returned to his cigarette which he gathered along with the match box, and headed back to the room where he used to sleep.

Approaching the windows and kneeling then sitting, he recollected this place where he used to puff his bong every night when he was convinced that nobody cared. And again most mornings when he would wake. The wind blew hard onto the glass outside, enticing Cade back onto his knees, and he opened the window. The loud sound of the gust comforted him. The branches swayed in the breeze. One broke. He looked down upon the driveway and pretended his mother's car was there, serving as a signal that he wasn't alone.

"Hi, Cade!"

"Hi, Daddy!"

"How's my favorite boy?"

"Good, what's that, Daddy?"

"This? This is something for your mom, Cade."

"Oh, nothing for me, Daddy?"

"Not now, Cade, this is for your mother. You see, it's hard being the man of the house when I'm not being treated like the man of the house. And this family, *my* family, would not be what it is without me. *You* are *my* son, Cade, just like mommy is *my* wife. And Daddy makes money for this household and deserves a little respect and reassurance. And I don't feel as if I'm getting that respect, Cade. That's why I got your mother this.

So how about we give it to her, Cade, huh? What do you think? You think that's a good idea?"

"You son of a bitch."

"There. You see, son? Do you see how she is?"

"Leave him alone you goddamn son of a—"

"Maybe we can give it to her together, huh, Cade?"

"He's confused."

"That's why I got it, Cade."

"He doesn't know what you're talking about."

"'Cause I want your mother to see it."

"He's confused—he doesn't know what you're TALKING ABOUT!"

"What do you think, Cadey? Should I—"

"Leave my boy alone!"

"He's my boy, Margaret, just like when you married me, you became mine too. And I'm not gonna have this continue, goddamn it. She is a two-faced demon from hell, you bitch, and you're gonna—"

"Stop it, you creep."

"Carry on this way in this house—"

"Stop it, you creep."

"With *my* son. You lying, manipulating bitch. Sociopathic whore."

"Stop this! Get the hell away from my son! We're gonna leave!"

"Bull*shit!* There's no way out of here!"

"Cadey, come here. Come here, baby." The sound of his father's footsteps to the basement conveyed a kind of calm after the storm even when the door slammed behind him again and again before his feet hit the stairs and he descended and vanished. The sound that, despite his mother's hands muffling his ears and rocking him in her embrace, was still prominent amidst the boy's senses.

"It's ok, Cadey. It's gonna be ok. I love you, baby. I love you, sweet guy. One day, it's gonna be just you and me, ok? One day, it'll be just you and me. I promise. Just you and me. Ok, baby? Ok, Cadey?"

"Yes, Mommy."

"One day, it'll just be you and me. And I'm never gonna leave you, Cadey. I'm never gonna leave you, I promise. It's just you and me. We're a team, ok? You and me are a team. That's why I have the T over there on the wall. Do you see? It's T for team, Cadey. You and me. You and me are a team, you know? Do you know, Cade? What's T stand for, baby?"

"Team, Mommy."

"That's right, Cadey. I love you so much, baby."

The sun was coming up. He finished his smoke as if it were the last he'd ever have and headed back down. Guided by a tug-of-war between fear and reason, nearing the basement door, he listened for his father. To his surprise, Wilma was, again, on her knees in the bathroom vomiting, so he prepared another water before taking a fat swig of liquor.

"Oh my God, I hate gin forever," said Wilma.

"Yeah, me too," said Cade, holding her hair back.

"I need to get out of here," said Wilma.

"There's no way out of here," said Cade.

"What?" said Wilma.

"Ok, we'll get you taken care of," said Cade.

"The phone doesn't even work," said Wilma.

"Yeah," said Cade. "You think you're done?"

"Yeah," said Wilma. "Do you have toothpaste?"

"Yeah, I think we used it last night," said Cade.

"I need some," said Wilma.

"We have some," said Cade. "And I'll walk you home. The sun's up."

"Thank you."

She freshened herself and fastened her strange shoes and they left. The walk was more peaceful than Cade expected.

Upon returning, he knew that he should spend time at Heltons', but he was tired and withdrawing, so he decided to stay put and finish the gin.

After sleeping, he awoke to darkness and opened another old bottle and drank that one. When he was out of tobacco, he decided to walk down to Heltons' place. Leaving the typically empty house on Olney, Neighbors saw him essentially trespassing but he was too drunk to care. He stumbled up Heltons' driveway at the end of the street and in.

Wishing to see his housemate, traveling up the stairs to the shared room, he found himself alone and in the dark. He paced about the room, angrily yanking at his hair and pounding the mattress with his fist. He sat on it and put his face into his hands, hyperventilating.

After laying for a moment, he stood again and paced. Taking Miles' pillow to his face to lessen the sound, he screamed into it.

"Fucking bitch," he said as he sat on his mattress again and rocked forwards and back. He thought he sensed something that wasn't usually there with his foot. Taking his pillow to his face, he screamed again until he was out of breath.

When his pulse calmed, he took off his pants, became more

comfortable, and began to masturbate. He tugged for four times longer than orgasm typically took before he spoke aloud:

"Yeah, baby, God, I missed that perfect pussy, you're so fuckin' hot, aw, yeah, did you miss me? Yeah, I've missed you so much, I love you so much, baby, yeah, God, that ass is so hot." Frustrated, he gave up, only to pace about the room once more as his erection diminished. He laid upon the bed and tried again.

"I missed you so much, I love that big warm ass, my God, you're so perfect, baby, I wanna cum in you so bad, did you shave that pussy for me, yeah? Did you shave that perfect little pussy for me? I fuckin' love it, baby, you're so fuckin' hot."

He pounded and pounded, spitting into his hand until there was no saliva left. He tugged and pulled, murmuring and cursing until he finally gave up and passed out.

The sun like a lightbulb on an old string was as invasive as it had ever been to the young man's mind after its rays came tumbling in. Cade's eyes and tongue were dry. He was desperate for water, a malady of which he wasn't quite sure. Then, the sting from below his waist reminded him of his fruitless sexual intent. Lifting the sheet, he saw pink angry skin along with red lines running perpendicular to his shaft, like dried tree bark. He tested the flesh by taking ahold, only to wince and gasp in pain.

Curling his body in a fetal position and facing Miles' bed, Cade's heartbeat fell victim to his hangover as he tried to piece together the last couple days. As his eyes journeyed over the sunlit room and he thought about Sammie lying in bed with Miles, he realized that he was not alone. Major, from the floor directly next to Cade's mattress, stood in the dead center of his field of vision. He put his thumb into his mouth, stooped low, grabbed his blanket, and walked toward the stairs and out of the room.

In disbelief, Cade stretched his neck to see the floor between his and Miles' bed, finding a makeshift sleeping area. There was a pillow and comforter and even a little glass of water where Major had been the entire night.

He pulled the sheet up over his head and shut his eyes.

17

EFFIGY

Desire is not a truant ghost. The next couple weeks went on as usual for Cade. Some days and nights, he was with Sammie and the other occasions found him trapped between worry and wonder. And the bruised ego of their companion decided it had other plans for their secret romance. Disguising her jealousy with compassion, Wilma informed humans closer to Miles than Cade of what she had known. And the small town was not atypical.

Danny Kederick, with warmth in his heart, contacted his strong, smart friend over the phone conveying vague severity about getting together to have a discussion. It was close to noon as Cade came out of the bathroom, headed downstairs. Miles was seated at the kitchen table and burped before standing as Cade entered.

"'Sup," said Cade.

"Nada much," said Miles.

"Hi, Cade," said Maureen coming in.

"Hi, Mo," said Cade, preparing water.

"My, I'm gonna take Major to his ear appointment, ok?" said Maureen.

"Cool, Ma," said Miles.

"Can you or Cade clean up in here, ok?" said Maureen. "Or maybe you two can do it together."

"Sure," said Miles. "When's the appointment?"

"Now," said Maureen. "He didn't sleep well last night and he's... moving rather slowly. You guys can help out in the kitchen, right, Cade?"

"Sure thing, Mo," said Cade.

"Thanks, Cadey," said Maureen. "You're my third son, ya know." She kissed his forehead and headed toward the belly of the house.

It was rare that Cade saw her real world ready. He was used to her as an unkempt homebody. But today, in her faux leather jacket, make-up, and an agenda to keep, Cade felt more distant to her than usual.

Miles approached him.

"Can you come chat with me outside?" he said.

"Sure," said Cade.

Miles paused in the mudroom to put on his sandals, which confused Cade who was barefoot.

"Should I—" he said.

"Doesn't matter," said Miles who continued out the door as his friend followed. They got several feet down the driveway and Miles turned around. The sun stung their eyes as they squinted into each other's. To Cade, Miles never stood so tall.

"Ked is on his way and we're gonna go have lunch," said Miles. "Is there anything that you want to tell me?"

"No," said Cade. "No, I don't."

"Cool," said Miles. "I'll see you later."

As Cade headed back inside, he peered around Miles while he walked toward the foot of the driveway as if someone there was waiting for him. There was no car and no human as far as his eyes could see as Miles strode slowly toward the street. The door shut behind Cade.

At the sidewalk, the eldest of three siblings lit a smoke and waited. His eyes took in the blue and white from above and the cars and trees and grass all around. He blew at the ember on the edge of the Camel preparing it for its journey to the end.

He sat on the rock by the curb then came a remembrance of when he and Cade were little. Neighborhood boys excitedly lifted the very rock on which he sat, seeking a worm to put in their bottle of household poisons to watch it die. He and Cade were both chastised for their resistance by their slightly older chums who killed the creature joyously before their frightened eyes and idle bodies.

Then he moseyed over to the neighbor's front grass where there was trash ready for pick-up, alongside rows of cinder blocks. The broken ones at bottom level were in support of the healthier, more solid ones. There was a corner piece like that of a puzzle that was trying to break off and fall. Miles blew smoke toward it then pulled it off to inspect its underside. A clover mite ran onto his hand.

He put the piece back neatly, avoiding sugar ants and other mites while the wind blew, arousing the sense within his nose. Foul air triggered curiosity as he peered around the stones, looking for the source.

As he was about to give up, he walked further down the road to the nearest tree where the odor was emitting. There was a nest on the ground with baby birds deadened by malnutrition. Not certain what to expect, he looked up at the branches and leaves where the only life he saw was green.

The foliage before his eyes shook in the wind before he became transfixed again with the carcasses on the ground. He felt as if something should be done, but there was no use. And from death, he walked, bringing his feet to the more familiar patch of grass at the foot of his driveway.

It wasn't too long before Ked arrived.

Cade called Sammie and they spoke with fear in their minds and without much liberty. He wanted to be with her, but felt as if he couldn't. After spending hours disguising his anxiety at Heltons' and pacing the ground in the attic bedroom, he decided to drive to the hood to get some beer.

He bought two six-packs of Red Dog tall cans and drank one in the parking lot where he was bothered by passersby for cigarettes and money. Out of loneliness, there was a moment where he nearly invited one of the beggars into the car to have a drink with him.

A change of scenery several blocks closer to Heltons' brought some solace. At the roadside, he drank five cans of beer and smoked plenty of Turkish blend then drove back to the house and parked in the street, fighting the urge to urinate. He drank one more beer and headed in.

The mudroom door opened and Cade heard the family talking as they ate. He took off his shoes, scanning for Miles' voice, and before he took the first step of three to the kitchen, he heard it. Miles was laughing with his mother.

"Hi, Cade," said Maureen.

"Hello," said Cade. "Um—"

"Hi, Cade," said Mary.

"'Sup, dude," said Miles.

"Sweetie, are you having a good day?" said Maureen.

"Um—yeah," said Cade. "How are you?"

"Pretty good," said Maureen. "There's steaks and potatoes and green beans if you want to join us."

"I helped with the green beans, right, Mom?"

"Yes, you sure did, Major."

Cade opened the fridge aimlessly. With a full bladder, he selected the pitcher of water and retrieved a glass and poured. He stood there in the kitchen.

"You look like you're waitin' on a bus, Cade," said Ray, drawing laughter from Major. Miles kept his eyes low while he chewed.

"Ray, stop," said Maureen. "Honey, you don't have to eat with us if you don't feel up to it, ok?"

"I was just about done if you wanna chat in our room later," said Miles.

"Yeah, ok," said Cade, moving toward the hall then upstairs. He entered the bathroom and urinated. After washing his face, he sat on the lid of the toilet and drank his water.

As he exited the bathroom, Miles had just rounded the banister and the two boys were moving toward one another.

"We need to talk," said Miles, extending his hand to their door inviting his friend to lead him to the attic. On the way up the stairs, with Miles just behind him, Cade shut his eyes in lieu of seeing his reflection in the window.

They reached the top of the steps and Cade walked to the far end of the pool table. Miles stopped at the other end as if they were about to play. Their eyes connected, triggering tears in Cade's.

"How long has this been going on?" said Miles.

"Since Darien Lake," said Cade.

"How could you do this to me?" said Miles.

"I don't know," said Cade. "I haven't been happy in so long. I don't understand. I don't know why she didn't break up with you! I told her to break up with you. She told me she couldn't. I didn't know what to do!"

"I can't believe I had to hear about this from Ked," said Miles. "What were you thinking?"

"I don't know," said Cade. "It just happened after Darien Lake. We were drunk and rolling and we—it just happened. I haven't felt good in so long. It was as if—as if nothing had—as if I didn't—as if I didn't have a choice. I haven't been happy in so long. I knew it was bad. I didn't mean to hurt you."

Cade's pleading with his friend was coupled with the knowledge that the house was shared with other humans and he didn't want anyone else to hear. His suppressed volume worked in conjunction with his emotion. "There is nothing I wouldn't do to make things right. I didn't mean for this to happen. You've been so good to me. I didn't mean for this to happen. I told her—" Miles walked toward his friend, extended his arms, and hugged him. "I'm really sorry," Cade continued as the hug empowered the flow of his tears.

"I know," said Miles. "It's ok. We'll get through.

Let's go talk to Sammie."

The boys' reticence upon exiting the house aroused only minimal suspicion from the rest of the family. They got into the jeep with Miles in the driver's seat and began what would be a short ride.

"You said since Darien Lake this has been going on?"

"Yeah," said Cade.

"If you're considering a relationship with her, I wouldn't. Cause she'll do the same thing to you."

"I—"

"Think about it," said Miles. "Think about it."

The boys approached the busy intersection. *Let's stop at Red Apple for some beer* was on the edge of Cade's tongue, so forthright in his mind that he almost heard himself say it.

"Can we stop at Red A for smokes?" said Cade.

"Sure," said Miles. They pulled to the dumpster in front and as Miles showed no signs of wanting to go inside, Cade hopped to it. "Dude."

"Yo," said Cade.

"No beer, ok?" said Miles.

"Ok," said Cade.

As he heard the chime of the door, Cade nodded his head to the older woman behind the counter who seemed less than vigilant as she chatted on the phone. He went to the refrigerated rear end of the store and opened the door to ice teas and pretended to browse. The door shut gracefully in front of him. He peered over his shoulder to assess his watcher's position to see her without much awareness of his location. Opening the door to the beer and taking a Steel Reserve, he crouched, coughed to muffle the sound of the can opening, and drank it as if it were water.

Discarding the can among some snacks, he proceeded toward the counter and grabbed some gum on the way. He got a pack of Camels, popped in a piece of Winterfresh, and headed out.

After a genuine ebb and flow of communication, the two boys, calmer than before, pulled into Sammie's driveway and exited the vehicle.

"You're taking this very well, Cade," said Miles with his head high.

"Thanks," said his confused yet relieved brethren who did not reflect the same stature. They walked to the back and unhinged the gate. Sammie heard the familiar metal-on-metal *ping* and came to the door.

The whites of her eyes shone like a child's. And what centralized within them were gateways to vulnerability. There they were, before the girl: her two lovers, adorned with emotion. Cade and she, devoid of agenda, like planets in orbit revolving around Miles, their sun, who would fulfill his.

Before the boys left Sammie at her place, there was only one hug exchanged and it was between Miles and her. The trek back to their domicile took place after the discussion which took less than thirty minutes. Miles' energy hadn't changed much and although Cade felt better than before, he didn't let on as such.

"I hope you're not considering a relationship with her," said Miles, who was met with silent discord. "Because she'll do the same thing to you."

"Yeah," said Cade.

"No," said Miles. "She will."

Cade thought of the immediate future as he avoided pondering the existential awakening his friend directed to him. Miles had one hand on the wheel, looking ahead and intermittently to his right at his companion riding shotgun who didn't know whether to celebrate or drop dead.

"And this is how I'm gonna leave for college," said Miles. "With this on my plate." Cade couldn't reassure him as he understood that life would be changing for both of them. This new taste of clarity segued the murky abyss ahead. "Do not trust that human."

NEARLY THREE WEEKS had gone by since the relationship with Sammie was no longer undercover. Cade was in and out of dreams when the disturbing sun made its way to his sleepy eyelids. He wasn't precise if he had imagined his roommate walking out of their room, shirtless and dreary, so he glanced at the other bed and saw only disheveled sheets. Rising, he decided that he wanted to make himself clean and then go see the one he loved. The time in between revelation day and this moment had been busy for the house's other inhabitants and less than confrontational for the men of the hour.

Cade moved quietly down the attic stairs and into the bathroom. After a shower, the retreat to the bedroom where he changed clothes was fruitful, and in his haste, he put on Miles' socks. Cade listened as he prepared. He listened to the house around and beneath him. And he listened to his own sounds so as to not disturb anyone or anything within.

The balls of his feet moved from stair to stair, favoring the edges on the way down to the second floor. He peered into Maureen and Ray's bedroom, barely turning his head as he strolled past to the main stairs where he began his quiet descent.

He listened to the silent kitchen. The only way a human could be in it now would be if they were alone and motionless and that was unlikely.

As the truth bearing tiles neared his misappropriated socks, his hope turned into a wish and he took the obligatory steps into the kitchen.

There was Miles sitting at the table by himself doing absolutely nothing. His cold eyes shot into Cade's from all the way across the big room.

"I'm so depressed," said Miles.

"Yeah," said Cade, remorsefully, after hesitating.

"I can barely eat," said Miles. "I try to sleep, but I keep waking up."

"Yeah, I—" said Cade.

"I'm having nightmares. I feel weak. I can't see how I'm gonna leave town and start a new life after this shit."

"Do you want me to fix you some couscous?" said Cade.

"*NO*, I don't want any fuckin' couscous!" said Miles.

"All right," said Cade.

"And you can just go along with this?" said Miles. "Like it's nothing. Like nothing happened."

"No," said Cade. "I don't—I'm sorry," said Cade.

"You got a smoke?" said Miles.

"Yeah," said Cade. The two calmly walked outside together and Cade propped up the flip top of his Camels toward Miles who fidgeted about in his pocket, pulling out a faded soft pack.

"I've got one," said Miles who lit the last crooked stick that somehow hadn't broken in his shorts. Then he lit Cade's pristine Camel and the boys acclimated to their new environment by sitting upon the wooden chairs on the small patio.

Miles felt meticulously for a hidden cigarette then deemed the pack empty. Before he threw it into the old coffee can with butts and things, he removed the Camel Cash within. Then he lit it on fire, held it up, looked at Cade, and they both watched it burn in silence.

"You're gonna have the room to yourself when I'm gone," said Miles.

"Yeah," said Cade. They nearly spoke at the same time as Miles subsided. "I might have to take down that one Yardbirds poster."

"Really?" said Miles, half-smiling. "Why?"

"'Cause it's weird," said Cade.

"How so?" said Miles, his smile growing more.

"It freaks me out a little," said Cade.

"Why?" said Miles. "How?"

"I don't know," said Cade. "They're so freakin' weird."

After they laughed together, Miles said, "Yeah, they *are* making strange faces."

The tension in Cade's chest and head had unfurled as the conversation transformed. He almost began to enjoy himself, but guilt still had a hold.

Miles too enjoyed the laughter. And the last couple weeks had revealed to him a sharp sliver of revisiting truth amid the onslaught of disillusionment. Of his lucid nightmare, a part of him made peace with the new reality of his friend and his lover sharing the same dream. He knew that the path beneath his guided steps was more recognizable versus the forsaken earth below their tempestuous roving. Perhaps they needed each other more than he needed Sammie. And more than she needed him.

"She'll do the same thing to you," said Miles.

Cade was not entirely immune to each moment that his friend said this to him and Miles' tone meant business. The thought that was planted in the guilty man's mind had not exactly flourished, but when Miles fattened the seed, that portion of Cade's cognizance once dormant grew bigger.

"And if she does, I'll be there for you."

Take care of her," said Miles.

"Thanks, My," said Cade.

"And give me my Goddamn socks."

The boys finished their smokes together and parted.

That night, Cade said goodbye to Sammie earlier than he would typically and headed back to Heltons' to unwind and rest. Both he and Miles slept a little better that night.

AFTER THE SUN had risen and settled into its afternoon state, Cade woke to a room with no one but him. Downstairs, as Maureen and he crossed paths, she beckoned to him to have a seat and talk.

"Now, Cade," she said, scatterbrained. "I—"

"Do you mind if I get some water?" said Cade.

"Sure," said Maureen. "That might be a good idea 'cause I—I don't know just what to—I don't know how long this is gonna—I'm just not sure what...is gonna happen here." Cade was not eagerly looking forward to the forthcoming discussion but he did not feel uncomfortable as the vibe projecting from Maureen was of neutrality. "I am bewildered here, Cade. You're gonna have to bear with me."

"Take your time," said Cade.

"*Take your time,* he says," said Maureen, head low, massaging her temples. "Ok, Cade. That's what I'll do."

"My son...is one of my favorite humans in this world, Cade, ok? My son, Miles. His feelings are very...important to me. And this situation with Sammie, I just...I just don't know what the hell to do, Cade, ok?"

"Yeah," said Cade.

"Pretty soon, My is gonna be going away to college in Chicago, and he is gonna be leaving on terms of life that are...not...ideal...in any sense of the word. And Ray...honey...Ray wanted you to leave. But I explained to him about...the heart wanting what it wants....so, tell me, how is your relationship with my son?"

"Pretty good," said Cade.

"Oh, yeah?" said Maureen.

"I mean," said Cade. "We talked about it."

"Uh huh?" said Maureen.

"Yeah," said Cade.

"Well, ok," said Maureen. "That's what he said too. So tell me, what is your relationship like with Sammie?"

"Pretty good," said Cade.

"Uh *huh*," said Maureen.

"Yeah," said Cade.

"Jesus, this is so fuckin' weird," said Maureen. "So...you two are...*dating* at this moment?"

"I think so," said Cade.

"Jesus," said Maureen. "And for how long have you two...how long were you two *dating* when she was dating my son?"

"Um, I don't—I'm not exactly—"

"Ok, Cade, ok, I'm not quite sure asking for details is not...exactly... the route I want to take," said Maureen, laughing for the first time in the conversation. "I want you to know, Cade, that...Miles is my son, but you are my son too. And as long as we can grow from this, and that we can—shit, I think Ray's home."

Maureen turned away from Cade to confirm that her husband's car had driven up the driveway. Her volume lowered, "So, just don't hurt anybody, and know that I understand, ok? I remember what it was like being young, ok? Life is fucked up and weird, and we gotta live it together, ok, Cade?"

"Yeah, ok, Mo," said Cade.

Ray opened the door and walked in. He glanced at Maureen sitting between the entrance where he stood and Cade at the far end of the table. Ray looked at Cade with anger. He opened his mouth to speak when Maureen stood reflecting his visage and extended her index finger.

"*Ray*," she said.

In silence, his motion altered by his partner's form redirected to the fridge where he took out a beer, discarded his briefcase on the counter, and headed upstairs.

Maureen again sat at the kitchen table and watched and waited as she saw Ray's feet and ankles ascend the steps. Then she turned back to Cade and said: "He can be such a pain in the ass, am I right or what, kid? I'll talk with my husband if you do one thing for me. Start takin' better care of Miles and yourself and treat that girl right."

"Ok," said Cade. "Thanks, Maureen."

Ray didn't exhibit angry or retaliatory energy toward Cade regarding his relationship with Sammie ever again.

18

DEATH OF THE SUN

Miles, before leaving for Illinois, reestablished his blessing and parted amicably with his former housemate and lover who had at last become a publicly recognized couple. Sammie even started hanging over at Heltons' after she and Cade spent their time almost exclusively at her father's place. "I don't want to be known as the slut who moves on from Miles to Cade in the eyes of the Heltons," she said with tears as Cade had become frustrated with her not wanting to stay over.

But after Miles became instituted in his college across state lines, with the lion's share of support coming from Maureen, Sammie was welcomed back as a part of the family as if not much out of the ordinary had happened. She simply slept in Cade's bed in the same room the boys had shared while Miles' mattress laid barren atop the carpet.

Cade had been working at a pizza joint and had learned how to take advantage of opportunities when customers paid cash after ordering a delivery. When he played his cards right, he was able to pocket 100% of the money from those transactions. Between that, Sammie's job at the dry cleaners, and their synergy of selling weed and similar miscellaneous hustles, the two were able to amass enough money to rent an apartment near the famed Elmwood strip area of Buffalo.

Sammie's foundation of knowledge of the area differed from her man's as she had gone to some of the bars with older boys when she was sixteen and seventeen. To Cade, this world was new.

The couple looked at nearly ten places before they found the one they chose unanimously: the third floor apartment at 824 Forest Avenue near Forest Lawn Cemetery on Delaware Avenue.

The streets were busy, noisier, and narrower in this part of the world. The people, much busier than those in the burbs, didn't stare at them here. They kept moving. And both he and Sammie liked not being known and pondered over. Nobody cared if they held hands or kissed. The twosome had become but a swash flowing underground, traveling with the colorful current to the place where they belonged.

Cade eventually gained connections at a nearby bar, Lowell's. He became infatuated with it and worked there as a daytime busser in lieu of risking stealing pizza money out in the burbs. "I made sixty dollars in tips today!" he said, upon returning home after his first busy Saturday. He nearly ran up the steps to inform his partner of the first new implication that the job he sought so much would be a success. In congratulatory response, she leapt onto him, straddling his waist and kissing all over his face and mouth as he held her thighs and backside.

The couple made perpetual love. And each time, Cade gained more self-trust and was able to last longer. But despite his newfound sexual ability, Sammie still had never felt an orgasm, a featurette that after the move-in, she had disclosed to her lover. And although she never upbraided him, they both knew a significant part of the problem was

Cade's endurance struggle. They worked at it, employing advice from her friends and books as the less-than-common internet had not made its way to most.

"I want to do it to you from behind," he'd say. These advances would be consistently denied and as he'd plead, she'd inform him, "No, it wouldn't be like making love, it would be like we were just fucking."

And so it went. While Sammie adamantly took her monthly pill, from Cade penetrating and even amidst using her own hand, the couple were nineteen-years-old, they had jobs, cars, and a new life as adults, they had the freedom to be together however and whenever they desired…and she still had never truly let go.

Cade and Sammie, after becoming settled, were the first ones in their group of friends besides Esham and Lil to maintain an apartment. Now the couples were just ten blocks away from each other and they'd party together frequently. Lil would even imply that she and Esham were interested in experimenting sexually with the two, an endeavor that was all too strange to Cade and Sammie.

Cade discovered a rich connection to ecstasy pills as well as MDMA powder and he and Sammie did plenty of it. Almost every time they hosted friends, it turned into a party. They became close with their downstairs neighbors who shared their proclivity for the high life. And besides the uncommon times when the second floor inhabitants would bang at the ceiling for them to lower the noise, all the folks in the house would get along and drink and laugh together.

And as their involvement with ecstasy became stronger, they became almost reliant on it sexually.

"Do you like *this?*" she said before putting his penis into her mouth while the metal stud through her tongue remained. Cade knew that she would later remove it and that this was a waste of time. He wanted the stud out. Disguising his agitation, he was silent and let her head thrust on a trial basis. "Ok," he said calmly.

She let loose and unscrewed the metal piece from her mouth and placed it on the coffee table that she had moved to better have at him. While Cade lay back on the futon upon its broken frame that lied flush to the carpet, she started again.

The back-rest was permanently tilted due to the damaged furnishing presenting an obtuse angle, making it ideal for their lover's endeavor. He rested with his legs apart as she knelt in front. His feet were comforted by the carpet as her knees embraced the folded fleece blanket that he had placed for her on the same surface.

"What do you—"

"Leave it out," he said.

She patiently absorbed him through her mouth with her eyelids low and adjusted the angle of her head slightly to the left and to the right every so often while thrusting.

"That feels so good, baby," he said as he watched her with his mouth half-open. This positive reinforcement made her tempo increase while the breaths through her nose he heard more prominently. The rhythm was consistent until she ebbed and held just the tip in and sucked so hard that it made a smacking sound as her lips slipped off. She let go to lick the base of the shaft on up where she'd start again faster. This was a feature and break of repetition that Cade found dramatic and unnecessary. Breathing slowly, he saw her eyelids flutter and those green circles he adored rolling up and back some into her head.

"You're so beautiful," he said.

As affection went on, he noticed that both of their naked bodies were abstractly visible from the reflection in the window. Embracing his sudden urge to enfold his favorite portion of her physicality with his hand, he did so, causing his back to become upright which made him slip out of her mouth. So began a moment of confusion within Sammie, soon quelled by the feeling of his hand on her butt and middle finger running up and down her anus, triggering deep inhalation from the girl.

She then raised her chin and pushed out her bottom, widening the gap between her cheeks and closing her eyes. The hair on her arms and neck stood as he drew back his head and hand, running it up the small of her back. His nose skimmed along her hair from which he deeply inhaled, leading to a second of hazy eye contact and a perfectly harmonious long, wet kiss.

Their tongues, fully extended, spiraled around each other's until she pushed his chest with both hands away from her, causing him to fall back upon the futon where she started on him again with her mouth. Moaning softly, he kept his eyes on her face.

In their cozy, quiet, colorful attic apartment with musical accompaniment, Cade felt peace within his body and mind. His breath was slow and reached a depth as if his lungs grew twice their size. "I'm so lucky to have you," he said. In response, she widened her eyes and met his stare with hers in slight pause before returning to her chosen phase of calmly yet sternly imbibing upon him. "Look at me," he said.

Her sight met his eyes. Holding it there, she stayed in control of his girth at its fullest potential. Both partners in submission of each other, she didn't falter until freeing her mouth just long enough to address him, "I love rolling with you in my mouth."

Her expression of enjoyment made the perfect moment better for the boy as she didn't waste time waiting for his response. She broke eye contact and directed her sight to his stomach. "Look at me," he said with affirmation. This was enticing, despite the strain from which she had recently shied away before the unexpected command that made her wetter. He stroked her hair with his fingers, moving it to the side before reaching behind her head and pressing it there.

"I'd like a smoke," she said as she slowed the pace of her sucking. "Would that be ok, baby?" Her mouth let loose in order to show him a pretty grin before having at him more gently. He softened. "I guess," he said, smiling. She stopped and ran her tongue along his parts below. "Well, hey now," he said. She smiled, biting her bottom lip, and grabbed the pack of Camels.

"Dude, I want menthols whenever I roll. We should get some next time," she said.

"That's a good idea," he said. She sat next to him with her knees spread and spine forward and lit her smoke.

He picked up the ashtray from the table and put it to her side. While her eyebrows furrowed, she exhaled the leaden plume. He placed his hand on her sternum and tenderly pushed backwards. She scooted her rear end to the crevice of the futon and laid back. Cade assumed her former position in between her legs.

"While I'm smoking?" she said with glee and a shred of nervousness. In need of more space than her, Cade forgot about the coffee table and kicked it incidentally, making a noise that startled only him. "Oooh, careful boy, don't hurt yourself," she said, causing him to giggle without embarrassment. She laughed, "You want me to do it for ya, big guy? My yoga pants aren't just for show, ya know."

He made his body comfortable and became serious, kissing her inner left thigh, then right, then left, before slowing his pace and kissing then licking each outer boundary.

"Does that feel good?" he asked with a slightly feminized tone before grazing some more. "When I lick the outside?"

"Yes."

He continued kissing and licking her majora tilting his head some to kiss each side as if it was her mouth and easing her legs apart and away, exposing her bottom. Moving his tongue to the middle and discovering wetness, he redirected his focus.

"*Damn*, baby," he said, taking pause.

She said, "Um, yeah, save yer sermon for the choir, K chief?" He started in the middle, feeding the tip of his tongue with spittle. Sensing her coil unwind, empowerment came over him as he ran his tongue up and down and in between her minora, barely grazing her clit at intervals.

"You don't care if I smoke?" she asked gratefully with a bright smile. A splash of guilt garnished her pitch.

"I don't care, just be comfortable. I want you to cum," he said, sparing only enough time to get the message across.

She puffed away at the stick, enjoying each drag yet keeping in mind that it'd be more enjoyable when she could offer complete focus on her man between her legs.

She put out the cigarette.

THE NIGHT HAD FALLEN upon the town slowly for the couple on the corner of Forest and Delaware in the three-unit house across from the cemetery on the top floor. Cade had taken the risky journey to the suburb of North Tonawanda to pick up ecstasy pills from the guy. Maneuvering through the burbs with drugs wasn't exactly pleasant as a young man in an old car with Allman and Marley stickers not to mention the deal in daylight at the nervous dealer's choice of gas stations. But the connection was solid and dude had a reputation of having the right stuff.

The ever present threat of police was real and every young person knew it. He took off during daylight, saying goodbye to Sammie who was worried about his safe return. He chose to travel without her after she insisted on checking the car to make sure the brake lights, turn signals, and headlights worked properly.

After a long kiss and waving goodbye, Sammie relaxed on the front ground level porch rented by older tenants who were accommodating and friendly. She waited for him by herself with a book, basking in the vision of his car approaching the driveway an hour later.

His eyes met hers as he smiled and she bounced out of the loveseat on the porch, dropping her book on the ground and jumping with arms extended high. It was her lover's return, with drugs.

She ran and skipped to the end of the long driveway behind the house where he parked and hopped on wrapping her legs around his waist and kissed him.

"Hi, little monkey," he said proudly.

"HI BIG MONKEY!" she said.

"Have you been waiting for me?" he said.

"Yes!" She kissed his cheek and neck repeatedly. He walked with her clinging to his body, slowing his pace as they neared the rusty side door.

"I missed you," she said.

"I missed *you*." Their downstairs neighbor exited his pad, locked it, and walked down toward them.

"What up, Bobby, we got some E-pills!" she exclaimed.

Cade shushed her.

"What, it's Bob," said Sammie. "He doesn't care."

"I might!" said Bob who was ten years their elder. "'Sup Cade."

"I—uh, I know—" said Cade.

"We got twenty of 'em, pot-nuh!" said Sammie.

"Damn, you guys are doin' it!" said Bob.

"You bet my ass we're doin' it," said Sammie.

Cade recognized the open window above his head leading to Bob's apartment which he shared with two roommates.

"Any good?" said Bob.

"Yeah, should be," said Cade.

"What are they called?" said Sammie.

"White dolphins," said Cade.

"White dolphins?" Bob laughed.

Sammie, casually stretching, grabbed her calf and raised her leg nearly parallel with her body. In doing so, she exposed the gap between her legs to her boyfriend while making typical eye contact with Bob before adjusting her vision playfully to cross-eyed.

As she blew and popped a bubble of gum, Bob's eyes darted to her midsection, taking quick notice of her thighs peering out of her small white shorts. Briefly, he envied Cade's position.

"Nice," said Bob. "I'll catch you two later," he said, grinning as he walked down the driveway to his car parked in the street.

Nobody in the three-apartment house dissented to Cade and Sammie's sole use of the driveway. The landlord's reasoning was that they lived on the highest floor and had the longest distance of stairs to ascend.

"Where ya goin?!" said Sammie.

"To work!" said Bob, turning round and back to forward again. "Somebody's gotta turn those engines!"

"What's he do again?" said Cade.

"I don't know," said Sammie. "Somethin' about turnin' engines."

They headed upstairs together, rounding four flights of dirty dusty stairs. It was not atypical for a neighbor to hear footsteps and then open their door gregariously, but now, it was smooth trampling up to the top.

The blue door opened to another two flights of small stairs covered in wall-to-wall carpet. The sound of their footsteps softened. Sammie opened the door to the smell of Nag Champa and Cade's hand on her butt squeezing each cheek and then running his fingers softly up and between her legs. They reached the top of the stairs after Cade locked the door.

"We gonna roll tonight?" he said.

"Uh *yeah*, I want to." They stood toe to toe with her nearly a foot shorter looking into each other's eyes. "Do you?"

"Yeah," said Cade. They kissed.

"Let's see 'em," she said. Cade unbuttoned his pants and pulled out his pubical sack.

"*Aw*. When do you think they'll drop, in a year or so?"

Amused mainly by her straight face and tilted head, he put them away, zipped-up, pulled out the bag of pills, and handed them over.

"White Dolphins, eh?" said Sammie. "Yep. There they are. White dolphins indeed. These boys are thick and juicy too, yeah!"

She swallowed one with some water, handing the bottle to Cade who followed her lead. "Oooh, we get to see the sunset while rolling!"

The couple were the only ones in the house that did not have a balcony or porch. Instead, they had the very top of a fire escape which provided a small platform where they could stand next to their charcoal grill, rarely used. They liked the fire escape. It was all their own, a little spot where Cade could put his arms around Sammie and hold her while they smoked and, if time and chance provided, see the sunset.

Cade enjoyed doing drugs with his girlfriend. And he too was joyous about watching the sun die with her. It was natural for them to get high without any real objective or purpose, but Cade, with a shade of ulterior motive, took with him the intention of having extraordinary sex when they did ecstasy. Particularly, he found it as an opportunity to receive oral sex from Sammie who did not perform the deed often despite his eagerness to go down on her throughout their ordinary lives. She'd be direct while rejecting the idea:

I don't want to.

Let me just use my hand.

You're already hard.

No, just fuck me.

It had become frustrating for Cade to the point where he'd

sometimes yell at her out of frustration and watch porn more frequently. Sammie found going down on him to be unnecessary and physically uncomfortable. And before him, she had never done it. But now, the relationship was established. They shared an apartment. They had a landlord. A bed. They had jobs and came home to each other. And Cade felt that he was entitled to oral sex.

"We should clean up first," said Sammie.

"Ok, that's a good idea," said Cade. "I'll do the dishes."

"I like that idea," she said.

Sammie put on music and began cleaning. She lit incense, placing the stick in the typical holder and elsewhere creatively as it dawned on her to put burning sticks in places she typically didn't. They cleaned and danced.

Sammie redirected her focus to paint her toes. Cade finished the dishes and tended to the multitude of beer bottles in the kitchen. He then hurried into the bedroom and opened the windows to reflect the fire escape door at the other end of the flat in the kitchen which was ajar. The bedroom was the only place that they wouldn't tidy, an unspoken agreement. The floor was so full of clothes that one couldn't see the carpet, but the other rooms in the house, the kitchen, the bathroom, and living room could be made neat, particularly for this night.

Cade swiftly made his way out of the bedroom and into the living room, peeking at Sammie sitting on the broken futon peering pensively at her nails and painting them. It didn't bother him in the least that she had abandoned her cleaning after lighting candles and selecting music. He liked it when she was concentrating quietly on something personal, finding peace in wordless coexistence. And he liked when her nails looked pretty.

Sammie's feet were yet another part of her body that he adored. Cade visualized his lover as physically flawless, a better-than-perfect vessel and face. The sight of her alone was enough to make him salivate and the chance of there being an exception tonight was nil.

"That breeze feels so good, dude!" she shouted to Cade in the kitchen.

"Hell, yeah," he said. Sammie heard the screen door to the fire escape open and a heavy object hitting the ground.

"Did you just throw the garbage outside?" she asked calmly, painting her toes.

"Yeah," he said as he moved quickly through the living room toward the stairs to exit into the hallway.

"Freak show," said Sammie as she blew gently against her feet.

Cade left through the side door of the house and walked up the driveway to the awaiting sack of trash now with a generous amount of broken glass. He picked up the bag that had busted and left traces of debris on the driveway and put it in the city disposal unit then headed back for the pad. "Nice toss, bro," called a man's voice from the lower apartment through the window. "You too," said Cade, eager to get back to business.

He booked it up the stairs and back in. Sammie was still on the futon, but now she was smoking a cigarette with her legs apart, allowing the air to dry her nails. The thinner, more abundant smoke from the Camel intertwined with the defined strands of incense exhaust and billowed between the low ceilings of the apartment and the floor. Almost motionless, suspended there, was grey smoke as if there were fire.

The music from the small speakers had progressed to a slow piece and the sound of a mellotron caressed gently upon the minds of the inhabitants of the room and everything in it.

Cade continued cleaning the kitchen and added a fresh garbage bag to the receptacle. He tidied the bathroom and showered. After putting on fresh clothes, he got down on his knees and piddled about the coffee table. As he caught his breath there, Sammie inspected his face, waiting to snare his gaze.

She typically sat this way. She typically sat this way and smoked. And in his mind, Cade kept a photograph of her coming down from their most intense mushroom trip together before their current romantic journey had begun:

The setting, her porch, while she donned a blue sweatshirt and beautifully dilated pupils. *Lost* read the hoodie with a colorful image that he could no longer interpret through the memory, but her eyes and her face would never leave him. Thus after a long drag and exhale, via intention, her saliva leaked from her mouth to the ground between her legs. Flawed, a long strand of spittle dangled there as she calmly struggled to get it loose from her lip and once it fell, she looked to see that Cade had been watching her. Their eyes locked as she processed the notion that the mishap of salivary extraction had been seen by her friend. Unabashed, she accepted the comforting visual communique as she sat upon the patio while he stood on the lawn digesting her aura, unlike any boy had ever done in her entire life. With her chin angled toward the watcher and her legs apart with shorts too short for the weather, her eyes shone to him like moons, meeting his unjudging, tranquil eyes in psychological understanding and sexual fascination. He kept this memory with him and it often adorned his reflection.

This memory.

His *Lost* memory.

As she waited in their apartment for his brain to tell his eyes to meet hers yet again, they did.

"Are you rolling?" she said.

"No. Not yet. Are you?"

"Uh huh," she continued with unbroken regard to her lover. She smiled. "It's *so* nice."

"Sometimes it takes longer for me," he said.

"I know. How did your trash throwing go?"

"Good," said Cade. "I threw it out, went down, and got it in the garbage can!" They shared laughter.

"Start. Rolling!" she said.

Cade got onto the floor and rolled about the carpet.

"That's not what I mean, silly."

"I think I feel it," he said as a yawn crept up on him. "I'm dizzy."

"That's 'cause you just rolled around!"

"Oh. Maybe."

"I love our place," said Sammie.

"I love you," said Cade.

"I love you too," said Sammie. "We get to watch the *sunset*."

"I'm gonna head out now," said Cade.

"Head out?!" said Sammie. "There's beer in the fridge!"

"No, to the balcony," said Cade.

"Oh, I'm heading out too!" Sammie got up and clung to Cade and he dragged his left side with her attached through the rear half of the apartment.

"Hi, monkey," he said, smiling.

"HI!!" said Sammie.

"Who's bein' a little monkey?" said Cade.

"I am!" said Sammie.

"Monkey train over," he said as he reached the door.

"Ok! Oh, it's so nice out here!" she said as they planted their bare feet on the metal fire escape.

"I want sunglasses," said Cade.

"When do you think it'll go down," said Sammie.

"What?" he said.

"The *sun,*" she spoke slowly and softly as she turned away from the bright sky and wrapped her arms around his middle, drawing her head to his chest from where she inhaled. Then, the indolent exhalation through her nose and mouth.

"Ah, that fat old sun," he said, welcoming her embrace with his.

They held each other.

She felt safe and he felt strong. Cade would hold Sam for as long as it took for her to initiate the end of their embrace as was his steadfast caveat. She held for longer than expected as it was her desire for them to sync their breathing, a proposal and objective she conveyed without speaking.

Time left the couple there *alone.* Cade motioned his face toward her head, signifying that he wanted a kiss. Sammie gripped him tighter, unresponsive to his wish. He wrapped his arms around her and, without squeezing, held tight as a breeze passed over them.

Then the sound of loud motorcycles convening at the red light footsteps from their driveway were added to their realm. Sammie pushed an exhalation of mild chagrin through her nose, breaking the slow tempo of her breath. She brought her face up to meet Cade's and opened her eyes, exposing their watery essence. Her open mouth darted to his bottom lip not once but twice as the first try was without complete success. Expecting a slower escalation, he was caught off guard by her swift forthright tongue as she made her way to the rear of his mouth. They kissed until the moment thereafter he felt her lips swell. She hugged and squeezed him, speaking slowly:

"You're my everything."

"HEY!" came the familiar voice from below. "What are you two doin' up there?" It was Ryan, Bob's more extroverted roommate. "What are you two up to tonight?" he said.

"We're ROLLIN', bra!" shouted Sammie.

Cade quietly shushed her in her ear.

"Oh my God," she said quietly with her hand muffling her mouth.

"Oh, yeah?" said Ryan.

She began to quiver. "I'm *sorry,*" she whispered.

"It's ok, baby," said Cade, sympathetically rubbing her shoulders.

"Got anymore?" said Ryan in a kind of shout/whisper hybrid.

"We um-um…" struggled Sammie.

"Holler at me tomorrow," said Cade.

"Toss me down a smoke, would ya?!" said Ryan.

She lit one and tossed it.

"Thanks," he said.

"You're welcome, later," said Sammie and Cade simultaneously.

"AW, idn't dat cute!" said Ryan as he walked toward the side of the house and out of sight.

"Oh my God, get inside!" said Sammie. They came in and the door shut behind them. "Are you rolling yet?!"

"Yes. I need a smoke," said Cade as he went back out for her pack.

"Dude, get in here!" She grabbed his shirt with both hands. "He's so weird! That was so weird!"

"It was ok," said Cade. "This come-up is nice." He lit a cig, looked at Sammie and held it toward her.

"No, I just smoked," said Sammie. "Wanna split it?"

"Yeah," he said sternly.

"Are you ok?" she said.

"Dude, yeah," he said. "I'm just...whoa."

"You get so intense when we're on drugs."

"I can't wait to be with you tonight," said Cade.

"You're with me now," said Sammie, smiling.

"I know," said Cade. "But I can't wait."

While the night was still young, Cade, with his mouth, fancied every wish of his thankful paramour. She coached him as per his demand, along with his requirement for both correcting him *and* positive reinforcement. At first shy, she became more comfortable with both speaking and more importantly, being the *only one* speaking, while his diligent tongue answered her call and found the ideal rhythm.

Gentle, she'd say. *Softer. Slower. Just my clit. Yeah. Like that. No, go in circles. Yeah. Like that. Keep doing circles. Yes, baby.*

You have no idea.

Oh my God.

Cade.

Just like that.

Faster.

Yes.

Don't stop.

Fuck, baby.

That night with her legs apart and her eager man's face between, she had finally come to a place that she had only heard of, and about which she had suspected her friends of lying. In that warm soft occasion, anointed continuously amidst breaths lingering, she came to realize that to get what she wanted, she had to say it between fragments of patience and trust. That night, while the more elusive part of her womanhood sang praise before she quivered beyond control and gently pushed him away, there was still an uncharted necessity to embrace.

"...How come you didn't tell me?!"
"Didn't I?!"

"You kind of did."

"You're all wet!" she said, wiping liberation from his lips, kissing his mouth and licking his tender tongue.

They watched the sunlight come that day from their neighbors' front porch where she had waited for him to return with the bag. They drank whiskey and beer. She fell asleep like a child in his arms as morning rush hour piqued.

While he carried her up the long stairway to their place, she awoke but feigned as if she hadn't. He couldn't free his hand to turn the knob with his baby in his arms so he struggled.

"Do I have to do everything?" she said, surprising Cade in his naivete. He gently released his grip and her naked feet fell to the floor. He held her there in the dirty hall.

"We get to go back inside now," she said, nuzzling her nose onto his bicep.

"I know, baby."

"I love you, Cade."

"I hate when you're not with me," he said.

"I know, baby. Let's go."

19

APOLOGIES

Working at Lowell's made Cade feel like even more of an adult after the big move to the city with his partner. The pub was built in the 1930s and was a Buffalo staple. Everyone in town knew about Lowell's and pretty soon, Cade felt as if everyone knew about him. He developed friendships with folks who hadn't known him in his childhood or adolescence. They didn't know that he had been sexually dissolved or to what extent he had been traumatized by his parents and their sordid lives. The upper westside of Buffalo did not know that he betrayed his closest friend who sacrificed for him in his hour of need. This was a new crew. A new life. A brand new start. And it felt wonderful.

"You want a tall one, Cadey?" said the bartender, in his mid-thirties, long hair tied back.

"You and Jerry look like brothers!" said a congenial waitress who was warming to Cade. "Except your hair is short!"

"Thanks," said Cade. "Yeah, we do. How many years did it take to grow out your hair, Jerry?"

"Uh, about five to ten," he said.

"Damn, I don't know if I could wait that long to tie it back," said Cade.

"It took a while but time flies," he said. "I used to wear a baseball cap to keep it out of the way. How about it, tall glass?"

"Yes, please," said Cade. The admirable suds slinger made his rum and 7-UP.

"Cade, you gonna hang out tonight?" said another waitress.

"Yeah, should I come back?"

"Hell yeah, you should," she said. "Sundays are the best!"

"Ok, sweet," said Cade.

Lowell's was at the foot of the Elmwood strip close to Buffalo State College. The neighborhood was diverse with Hispanics, houseless humans, black folks, Deadheads, metal kids, skateboarders, gays, Harley Davidson noise, junkies, and everything else that the town of Amherst he left behind lacked. Cade trusted himself there. He had made his way outdoors to smoke.

"You wanna see some jewelry I made?" said a man of mange, walking by.

"No thanks," said Cade.

"Got a smoke?" said the man.

"Sure," said Cade, handing him a cig. He then presented his lighter.

"No, thanks," said the man who began to struggle with matches. There were three left on the flimsy matchbook and hardly any matter on each tip. Cade could not understand why he didn't simply accept his lighter and use *it*. He contended with the first match after three attempts and just as Cade thought that stick was trashed, it lit. And somehow, clinging to life, it fueled the tip enough to light about half. The man worked as if it was a joint.

"I got these matches from in there, ya know," said the man signaling to the bar.

"Really?" said Cade. "Cool." Cade was familiar with Lowell's matches, and he knew those weren't from inside.

"Cigarette," said another man walking by listlessly. Just as Cade was about to oblige, the first man seemed to know him and said, "You never have any cigarettes!"

"I kill people for fun, ya know," said the emotionless man.

"No you don't, you kill nothing in fun!" said the man, enjoying Cade's handout. His anger seemed genuine.

"Ok, thanks for the smoke, man."

"No doubt," said Cade, watching the one catch up with the other. The odd pair surprised him. They knew each other. The proud new employee's eyes followed them as they strolled lazily along the sidewalk, passing and sharing the cigarette. Cade finished his and went in for another drink.

When he was nice and liquored, he asked his new coworker behind the pine how much he owed. He waited on his stool with cash in hand, organized and ready to disperse.

"Just put your money on the bar, Cadey," he said. "I'll take what I need." And so he did.

After lighting another smoke before his stroll to his and Sammie's place, he had realized that his coworker had only charged for one beverage while he had had six.

Cade walked back to the house, saying hello to his neighbors on the porch on his way up. There was chatter coming from his apartment. As a mild surprise, Sammie was entertaining Lil and Esham and all three of them were having beer.

"'Sup, fam," said Esham. "How was work?"

"Good," said Cade.

"Hi, Cade!" said Lil who came to him, hugged and kissed him on the cheek, a motion that was reciprocated. Kissing women casually other than his girlfriend was something new for Cade, and as Sammie, fresh from the bathroom, observed it, she became jealous.

"Hey, baby," said Sammie, kissing her partner on the mouth without making eye contact. Cade noticed Esham sitting on the couch at the coffee table, weighing and bagging powder.

Esham said, "Bro, you don't mind if I—"

"I said he could use our scale," said Sammie.

"Yeah, mah dude, mines is broken or some shit." Lil snorted a bump then licked her finger to gather residue which she brushed along her gums.

"That's cool," said Cade, heading into the bathroom after noticing that they were using his parent's Buffalo Sabres mirror as their surface.

"Yeah, I think I spilled wine cooler on our scale," said Lil.

"Hundred dollar scale, bro," said Esham.

"Ok, *bro*," said Lil. "We have friends, *bro*, and they let us use their scale."

"Sure, no problemo," said Sammie.

"Thanks, Sam," said Lil. "You want a line?"

"No thanks," said Sammie.

"Have you guys still never…" said Lil.

"No," said Sammie. "We haven't."

"It's fun," said Lil as she apportioned a bump for Esham and put it under his nose. "You get all happy and numb."

"You don't, doesn't it, like make your heart go too fast?" said Sammie.

"Weed makes my heart go too fast," said Esham.

"Yeah," said Sammie with her eyes on the prize. "But, doesn't it like...I heard it, like, makes your, makes people have heart attacks and shit."

"Yeah, for old people," said Lil.

Cade flushed and walked out of the bathroom and into the kitchen.

"Isn't having your own place the best?" continued Lil.

"Dude," said Sammie whose eyes met Cade's. "You have *no* idea."

Esham and Lil each did a line then used their fingers to ingest orally.

"That's how I eat Cheez-It shake," said Cade swigging his beer.

"With your fingers?" said Esham, smiling.

"Yeah," said Cade. "I wet them first. Just like you did."

"Cheez-Its are the best," said Lil.

"Are you bagging grams?" Cade asked.

"Yeah," said Esham. "Why, you want one?"

"They don't do coke, Eesh," said Lil.

"Oh, my fault," said Esham.

An hour went by and the guests graciously left to return as scheduled later that evening along with other friends.

Coke was on the mirror that had broken. But cracked, it still served its purpose.

"I'm sorry I broke your mirror, Cade," said Lil. "If I find a Sabres one, like at a garage sale or something, I'll definitely pick one up for you."

"It's all good," said Cade.

"You guys sure you don't want some?" said Lil.

"Yeah," said Cade.

"You wanna smoke outside on the fire escape, Lil?" said Sammie.

"Sure," said Lil and the girls headed out.

Cade spoke to his guest then, in the opposite direction, went into the bedroom. "Do you make a lot hustlin' that?"

"Yeah, sometimes," said Esham.

The doorbell rang and Cade, bladder full, floated down to answer, expecting it to be familiar faces. But there stood a woman whom he had never seen and a baby who looked uncomfortable. The woman wasn't holding the young human correctly and this was apparent from the get-go.

"Excuse me, we're lost," said the woman.

"Oh, ok," said Cade.

"Do you know where Maddy is? He was right here."

"Um, no," said Cade. More concerned with what was to her right, the woman looked about, barely making eye contact while the child's eyes were glossy, hardly blinking or moving.

"Um, who?" said Cade.

"Do you know where Maddy is?"

"Maybe you want someone from my neighbor's place," said Cade. The woman tightened her grip, barely aware of the task to not drop what seemed to be her offspring. A fly landed on the child's foot. Then another on the ankle.

"Maddy. Have you seen our Maddy? She was right here." The woman looked about, worried. "Do you think this can get away?"

"Do I think, what can—" said Cade.

"Maddy. Is Maddy here? Do you think you can get away from what we made?"

"What?" said Cade. As malaise crept, he turned to look behind him.

The woman's grip on the child loosened and the shirtless being slid down. Then further down. "Your kid, ma'am." He reached slowly to support the child with his hand and she jerked the young one back up again.

"What Maddy made?"

"What?" said Cade. "I don't know who that is? You might have the wrong place, but there are three—"

"Where is Maddy, Cade?"

"What?" said Cade. "Who are—"

She stammered, becoming more aggravated. She kept looking to her right. She had yet to make eye contact. Cade apprehensively looked outside, peering to the left to get a peek at where she was looking. His head came closer to the evening air and the setting sun.

"Do you think you could get away?"

"What?"

"Did you think you could get away, Cade?" He looked at her blackened, dirty hands then her gaze shot directly into his eyes: "Did you think you could get away from Daddy, Cade?"

The sound of many, frantic people trampling down the stairs came from above and behind him. Louder, and without end, the sound of humans descending as if the staircase that his feet were at the very foot of had no end. Frozen, he stood.

"So is Cade's penis big?"

"Dude, *Lil*," said Sammie, hesitant and smiling, turning back toward her apartment to see who was in earshot.

"Eesh's is not," said Lil. "But it's not small."

"Well, that's too bad," said Sammie, laughing.

"Well?" said Lil.

"It's *wonderful*," said Sammie.

"Does he give good head?" said Lil.

"Well," said Sammie. "Funny you should ask cause I just had my first O...you know, while getting eaten out."

"Really?!" said Lil. "Isn't that the best?"

"Yeah," said Sammie. "It was truly amazing. Like...all throughout my body. It was warm and then like, really warm. And it was like...this huge like..."

"Relief?" said Lil.

"Yes!" said Sammie.

"I cum the hardest from behind," said Lil.

"Yeah," said Sammie.

"Don't you love doggy?" said Lil.

"Totally," said Sammie.

"It's great for tit grabbing and playing with my clit," said Lil. "Like at the same time."

"You play with your clit during?" said Sammie.

"Um, hello," said Lil.

"Huh," said Sammie.

"That's how you multi, silly," said Lil.

"That might be weird," said Sammie.

"That might be awesome," said Lil. "Because it is."

"No, I mean, like, masturbating during sex," said Sammie.

"It's not masturbating," said Lil.

"When you're rubbing your clit?" said Sammie.

"Yeah," said Lil. "And getting fucked."

"Why not?" said Sammie.

"'Cause it's sex," said Lil.

"Oh," said Sammie. "Totally."

A typical night of drinking, smoking, and music went on in the attic apartment on Forest Avenue on the upper west side of Buffalo. Of those who would come and go, some were friends and some were simply using the place as it was a safe spot in the city to have a good time.

Cocaine had been finding its way to the hands within the pad more frequently but it was only witnessed by the couple who hosted. And that night, Cade's vibe to Sammie projected fragility while he came out of the bedroom with disheveled hair and a headache. He walked past the small gathering and into the kitchen for beer where he drank one quickly and meandered with another toward the festivity.

"You guys should get a dog," said Lil. "Or a cat! A cat would be perfect up here!"

"I don't like cats," said Sammie.

"A cat would be *so* cool up here," said Lil. "Chillin' in these little windows and on the mantle thing!"

"Litter boxes are lame, though," said Sammie. "And gross."

"You wanna blow?" said Lil. Sammie turned and visually located Cade moving toward them. He sat next to her.

"Hi Cadey!" said Lil.

"Hi," said Cade.

"Your eyes look really red," said Lil. "God, they're *so* blue! God, they—Eesh, look at his eyes!"

"I've seen 'em," said Esham.

"Aren't they blue?!" said Lil.

"Indubitably," said Esham just before a fat line.

"Is this a gram?" said Berk to his younger brother.

"I don't know," he said. "Cade, do you have a scale?"

"It weighs," said Esham. "I used Cade's scale today."

Berk peeped Cade who nodded.

As the shindig continued and conversation became raucous, the only two who weren't doing lines looked at each other and spoke quietly.

"You ok, baby?" said Sammie.

"Yeah," said Cade. "I'm pretty tired." They kissed, then kissed again, slowing their motion. Sammie's mouth offered consolation amidst the chaos. Her eyes and breath slowed his pulse, making him feel safe and proud. She initiated a long, final kiss. "I think we should start doing coke."

"Oh, yeah?" said Cade.

She nodded and smiled.

"Hey, Eesh, I'll take a gram," said Cade.

"Oh, word?" said Esham. "Bet." His hand dipped into his leather coat resting on the chair he sat upon and out came a bag.

"How much?" said Cade

"Sixty, please." The deal went down and Cade and Sammie looked at the bag of tricks as if they were children inspecting their first seashell. They looked at each other. And then, back at the bag.

"Giddy up," said Sammie, who took it from Cade's fingers and walked into the kitchen, taking a CD from the shelf on the way. She poured some onto the case and began moving it about with a playing card. She prepared a five dollar bill while the rest of the humans in the living room respected their space. Cade ventured back into the belly of the pad, intruding upon conversation and laughter.

"Do we just snort it as hard as we can?"

"Well, not too hard," said Lil. "But you want to get the whole line up your nose, yeah."

"Ok, thanks," said Cade, retreating to the kitchen and leaving the living room much quieter than when he had entered.

"Ready?" said Sammie. "I'll go first." She did, then handed the bill to Cade who followed her lead. They strolled calmly to the living room, sat, and sipped their beer.

"I don't feel anything," said Cade, his eyes on Sammie but loud enough so everyone could hear.

"You have to keep doing it," said Berk, who had gained experience with his older brother. "It's not like other drugs. You keep doing it and then you feel it."

"Oh," said Cade. He walked back into the kitchen with Sammie following and they snorted more. Noticing the small lines they were drawing from the much larger source, Cade said, "Wow, we get a lot for sixty bucks!"

"Yeah, totally," said Sammie. They each did two more lines.

"I think we need to…" Sammie wet her finger gathering from the surface and rubbed it along her teeth and gums. Then she dipped her wet finger in again and put it into Cade's mouth, completing the same task. She smiled and kissed him. "Wanna smoke?"

"Hell yeah," he said.

Thirteen hours blew by.

"And that's why I think God and the devil are not things that live above us and below and who influence our direction, but like, they live inside all of us."

"Well, do you believe in Karma?"

"Not really. Doesn't Karma mean that everything happens for a reason?"

"No, it means if you do good things then good things will happen to you."

"Oh, yeah."

"Well, that could be the same as everything happens for a reason."

"Do you believe in heaven?"

"I believe in angels, yeah."

"When my cousin died, before the paramedics got there to revive the other two girls, they said they saw a man in a hat and trench coat who like, didn't belong there, and he guided the medics to the car that had crashed in the snow."

"Oh my God."

That's when they heard someone running up the stairs. Berk, who had left to get more beer after painstakingly watching the clock until it turned 8 am, burst into the apartment. Out of breath, he yelled, "JAKE, SOME FUCKING KIDS JUST STOLE YOUR CAR!! TWO OF THEM!! THEY DROVE OFF!! I CHASED THEM IN MY CAR AND MADE THEM CRASH!! YOUR CAR'S ALL FUCKED UP!! IT'S ON DELAWARE AVENUE, ALL FUCKED UP!!

They ran outside and, under Berk's guidance, came upon the green Sentra that belonged to Jake. The assailants had bailed while it was still moving on the busy street and it hit a tree. Both airbags had deployed and the glass shattered while the two young men ran away.

Everyone's hearts were beating too fast. They decided to wait by the wreckage while Cade and Sammie went back to the nearest phone which was their landline at the apartment.

"I can't believe we're calling the police right now," said Sammie. They looked into each other's eyes while Cade, hesitant, held the portable phone in his hand.

"Dude, oh my God," he said.

"What if they come here?" said Sammie.

"I'll just do it anonymously," said Cade.

"You're calling from our place!" said Sammie.

"Shit," said Cade.

"Well, shit," said Sammie. They both looked about the room then their eyes returned to each other's.

"Shit," they said.

Sammie continued, "Ok, well, just tell them that—"

"I'm not calling from here," said Cade. Sammie stared at him blankly. "I'll call from On the Run."

"The payphone?" said Sammie.

"The payphone," said Cade.

On the Run gas station was a twelve-block journey.

"What about this?" said Sammie, pointing at what had become the communal pile of coke on the coffee table in the living room. Esham had sold everyone including Cade multiple bags before leaving with Lil and no one in the group had behaved tightfistedly. Like the night, the majority of the powder was gone, but the interruption left the rest of the compound right there in the middle of the smoky room, silently calling to the confused fried couple.

"Just leave it here?" said Cade.

"How about we hide it?" said Sammie.

"We can just finish it maybe?" said Cade.

"We should probably get rid of it," said Sammie.

"Yeah," said Cade.

They snorted the rest, handing the makeshift straw back and forth to each other between lines which totaled four rails each plus the dust left behind. Sammie licked the surface until it was almost clean and handed it to Cade who had waited, watching her like a dog. He absorbed the final traces through his tongue before they ran water over the surface. Since the crew had piled in Berk's car to cruise to crime scene number two, his car was still there. Cade grabbed his keys.

"No!" said Sammie.

"What?" said Cade.

"Don't drive," said Sammie. "What if a cop pulls you over?

'Cause like, what if a ton of them are coming to this area?"

"You're right," said Cade. "I'll walk."

"To the gas station?!" said Sammie.

"Yes," said Cade.

"Really?!" said Sammie.

"I'll run?" said Cade.

"Holy shit!" said Sammie.

"I'm gonna do it," said Cade. "I'll run to On the Run, use the payphone, then I'll run back. I'm gonna do it right now!"

"Wait," said Sammie.

"What?" said Cade.

"I don't want you to leave me," said Sammie.

"Well, fuck! What the hell am I supposed to do?!" said Cade. "They're waiting for us. We've got paraphernalia all over the place, and I can't drive!"

"Ok!" said Sammie.

"Ok, what?!" said Cade.

"Just go!" said Sammie.

"Ok!" said Cade. He scurried down the stairs, leaping three then four steps at a time. After nearly running directly into the screen door, he stopped short on his toes, tapping the lever on the door to unlatch the mechanism with his fingers. He got to the sidewalk and stopped hard falling backward on the ground then darted back up the driveway, up the stairs, and back to their apartment. He burst into their place and up the carpeted steps.

"Baby?" he said. "BABY?!!

"I'm in here!" said Sammie from the bathroom.

"WHERE?!"

"THE BATHROOM!" Swiftly, he approached the closed door and opened it.

"Jesus," she said from her position on the toilet.

"Are you ok?!" said Cade.

"Yes, I guess, fuck!" said Sammie, moving her palms from her thighs to her face intermittently. "I'm peeing! Or trying to! What are you doing back—"

Cade kissed her. "I love you," he said.

"I love you too, baby!" said Sammie, her smile quivering.

He ran out of the apartment again. And off he went.

He ran full speed as if he were the one who stole then wrecked the car. He ran as if he were invisible to the people in the passing vehicles of the busy street. Grunting and panting, he ran as sweat poured out and off of his body.

"Run, white boy, run!" said someone from a passing SUV.

His mouth dried so much that his throat nearly closed.

He had reached the busy gas station and the pay phone. People pumping gas stared at him. He reached into his pockets for a quarter. He didn't have one. And the wallet that was typically attached to his body via a chain laid on the table back at the crib.

"Fuck!' he said. He approached a car at the pump.

"Excuse me!" he said, doubled over, trying to catch his breath. The lady there was confused and scared. "No, don't be afraid! I'm sorry! I'm sorry I'm like this! It's just....I ran here! I'm sorry! I'm sorry I'm so out of breath! I just need a quarter! I'm sorry!" His hands rested shakily on his knees while he hunched over panting. Trying to stand straight ineffectually, the woman to whom he yelled fearfully looked around.

"Are you all right, ma'am?" said a man approaching the two of them on the way from the store to his car.

"No, she's fine!" said Cade. "I just need a quarter! I just need a quarter right now!!"

"I'm gonna call the police," said the man.

"No!" said Cade. "That's why I'm here! I'm sorry! I'm sorry I'm like this!" People were stunned and confused.

Everyone ceased their motion and looked at him—patrons at the pumps, people at the sidewalk, humans walking toward the door of the convenience market. Everybody had turned to see the fiasco. All about, they stopped and stared. He began speaking to everybody. He spoke to everyone around him by turning round in multiple circles, one after the other, as he spoke: "I'M SORRY I'M LIKE THIS! I JUST NEED *ONE* QUARTER! FROM SOMEBODY! OR NICKELS AND SHIT! JUST NO PENNIES! FUCK!" He noticed that the clerk picked up the phone as he and every human in the store were now watching him too.

"Shit!" said Cade. He took off running back in the direction of his apartment, this time, faster. He crossed the street to go with traffic. He passed an old man walking his dog and terrified both of them in the process.

"I'm sorry!" he shouted. "I'm sorry! I'm sorry!" Every exhale, he squealed louder and louder. His vision clouded with sweat. "Oh God! Oh God! I'm sorry! I'm sorry!" he yelled to no one and everyone.

Finally, he could see his place. His neighbors and a guest were on the porch. They stopped chatting.

"Hey, Bob, is that your neighbor?"

"I'm sorry!" said Cade, gasping for air. "I just wanted to make a phone call! I'm sorry!" He ran past the front of the house to the side, up the stairs, and into his pad.

"Baby!" he called. "BABY!"

"WHAT?!" she yelled from inside the bathroom. He barged in again. There she was, once more, on the toilet. "You pissing again?!" She was shivering. Her face was in her palms as she sat with her lingerie around her feet. "Baby?! BABY?!"

"WHAT?!" she said.

"Oh my God, I need water!" said Cade as he flipped on the faucet, put his mouth underneath, and drank. His body craved water and air desperately.

"Oh my God, are you ok?!" said Sammie.

"Just……a……just a minute," he said, struggling.

"Oh my God," she said. "Did you call the cops?!"

"No!" said Cade. "Just a second! Have you never….have you…have you never left the toilet?!"

"No!" said Sammie. "I mean, yes! I can't piss, I'm so fucking high! How come you didn't call?!"

"I forgot a quarter!" said Cade, gasping over the sink.

"What! A quarter?! Why didn't you just get change?"

"I didn't have change!" said Cade.

They heard a knock at the door.

"Oh my God, who the fuck is that?" she said.

"I don't know," said Cade.

"You think it's cops?" said Sammie.

"It sounds like fuckin' cops," said Cade.

"Oh my God," she said. "Did we get rid of all the coke?"

"I think so," said Cade.

"The bongs," they said simultaneously.

"Ok, put your pants on," said Cade. "I said PUT YOUR PANTS ON!"

"OK!!" said Sammie. Cade headed out to the living room and grabbed the resinated glassware at eye's reach, hiding it in the kitchen. Quickly moving back to the living room, he passed the bathroom where Sammie stood after opening the door. He looked into her bright eyes as she waited for him to make the move. Following his lead, she stopped at the halfway spot of the carpeted steps and peered around the bend as he opened the door just a crack and looked through.

It was the crew.

All of them.

"Are there any cops here?" said Cade.

"No," said Jake. "They never came. Well, one passed by and we flagged him down. I told him what happened and he just drove away."

Sammie inched closer.

"What?" said Cade.

"He drove over to us, I told him that this was my car which was stolen and wrecked, he looked at the car, then back at me, then he drove away."

"Dude," said Cade. "What?"

"Dude," said Jake. "BPD doesn't give a fuck."

"And no one came back for us," said Berk. "No other cops showed up."

"Did you call the cops?" said Jake.

"No," said Cade. "It was...tricky."

"Can we come in?" said Jake.

"Yeah," said Cade. "Berk, did you score more beer?"

"Yeah," said Berk. "We drank that shit waiting for the cops."

The friends settled around where the coke used to be and asked Sammie and Cade what happened to it. The constraint of the guests conveyed skepticism that it was truly gone, although the couple swore repeatedly that they snorted it with haste to ditch the evidence. Cade told the withdrawing crew about the chaotic experience at the gas station.

"A call to 911 from a payphone is free, dude."

"Shit," said Cade.

Their company lingered for a while. They used the bathroom, smoked some weed and tobacco, and looked about the refrigerator where three beers remained. Everyone wanted one, but not one cap was twisted. No one even asked. They knew that Cade would not be giving up any of the last of the beers, knowing what he had snorted. They could hear his teeth grinding amidst the silence between words. And Cade, out of respect for their presence, waited for them to leave before he and Sammie cracked them open.

"All right," said Jake. "Berk, you tryin' to drive me home?"

"You just gonna leave your car on Delaware Avenue?" said Berk.

"Well, I'll report it stolen from here," said Jake. "I'm too tired to give a fuck about waiting for them. You guys mind if I call 5-0 from here?"

"No," said Cade.

"Go right ahead," said Sammie.

"No problem," said Cade.

"No problem at all," said Sammie.

The call was made and everyone bounced after they hugged and slapped hands in slow motion.

Cade opened a beer and sat on the sofa. Lighting a smoke, Sammie said, "I could drink a gallon of whiskey right now." She stood and walked toward the kitchen.

"Open the cupboard under the microwave," said Cade, looking at his reflection over the cloudy mirror on the table. Connecting with his eyes and seeing his mother within their likeness, death became his thought.

"What?" said Sammie. "Why?"

"Look behind the pots on the right," said Cade. "On the bottom."

"Oh, my God," said Sammie. "It's brandy!"

"Hell, yeah," said Cade. "Let's get crackin'."

"I didn't know you hid this here!" she said.

"If you knew, it wouldn't be hidden," he said. "Do you think they think we were lying?"

"I know they think we were lying," said Sammie.

"Shit," said Cade.

"Oh my God," said Sammie.

"What?" said Cade.

"Dude, come here," said Sammie.

"What?" said Cade.

"Dude, *come* here," said Sammie. With still eyelids, he walked to the kitchen and the mystery surrounding it. They had forgotten the cd case with coke on it. The Jack of Hearts laid over the ample pile in plain sight.

After party time's resurrection, the rainy afternoon found them dreaming peacefully of the past.

"Do you remember that time when we were at my place in the back and we saw the raccoon in the yard?"

"Hennessy?" said Cade.

"Right," said Sammie. "And the cops came when you were pissing?" said Sammie.

"Oh shit, I forgot," said Cade.

"Remember?!" said Sammie.

"Yes," said Cade.

"Do you remember what you said to me?" said Sammie.

"No," said Cade.

"About marriage?" said Sammie.

"No," said Cade.

"You don't remember that?" said Sammie. Her excitement fizzled to the point where Cade knew squeaking was imminent.

"No," said Cade. "In your yard?"

"Oh my God," said Sammie, squeaking. "So we were talking about my relationship with Miles."

"That sucks," said Cade.

"I know," said Sammie. She moved her hair behind her ear and slowed the tempo of her speech. "We were talking about getting married."

"You and me?" said Cade.

"No, me and Miles," said Sammie.

"That sucks," said Cade.

"I know," said Sammie. "But we were talking about it. And you were *hammered* off my dad's fucking cognac—"

"Why were we talking about you and Miles getting—"

"Because we just were!" said Sammie. "Ok, so—"

"God, I was *so* in love with you," said Cade.

"I know!" said Sammie. "I was so in love with you too! But anyways, we were talking about weddings and what would like, you know, happen if I married Miles and—"

"Why the hell were we talking about that?" said Cade, struggling to get his mouth on the nearly empty bottle.

"Shut up!" said Sammie. "We just were! Anyways, we were talking, and I said....I said.…...I said something like 'If My is the one I marry, it's got to be outside and with this and that and he should propose to me by a river' or some shit—"

"That's fuckin' gay," said Cade.

"And you, with one eye closed 'cause you couldn't see straight—"

"This was after the cops came and left?" said Cade.

"Yes, this was after the cops came and fucked with us and left," said Sammie. "You got down on one knee...and do you remember this at all?"

"No," said Cade. She took both of his hands and squared her

shoulders to his, slowing her speech and lowering the pitch. "You got down on one knee, and said 'I wanna be your side cock.'"

"Shut up," said Cade.

"Can't," said Sammie, grinning and squeaking with delight.

"Ok?" said Cade.

"Isn't that funny?!" said Sammie.

"Um, yeah?" said Cade. "So, what did you say?"

"What?" said Sammie.

"Did you say yes?" said Cade as she met his lips with hers.

"No," said Sammie. "I said, 'Cade, get the fuck up off of your knees and lay down on the couch.'"

"Oh," said Cade. "Well, I meant every word. And I'm glad I'm main cock now." They kissed slowly with distilled wine on their breath and all.

"*Only* cock," she said.

They made love amidst the sound of invasive birds and noisy traffic before they'd settle for sleep.

"I love you, Cade," she said as the little spoon with her eyes closed drifting away.

He kissed her head and squeezed her tightly. "I love you, little lady," he said.

Unknown to him, her eyes sprang open as she came back online and her pulse gained pace. "Baby, don't call me that, ok?" she said to her unresponsive lover.

20

STILL LIFELESS

Cade and Sammie had learned to incorporate cocaine into their lives, a habit easily accomplished with his promotion to barback at Lowell's. And they, like never before, had learned to argue.

They'd squabble over chores and which friends to have over and they'd bicker over sex. It was difficult to be harmonious after the thrill of a new life had faded and mundane obligations like arriving at work on time became challenging.

Winter had come in the City of Neighbors and the couple of nearly twenty were living in squalor. There were beer bottles all around and moldy food in the refrigerator and the twosome didn't care. They hadn't had sex without drugs in months and were still kissing each other goodbye when they'd part for the day, but they stopped kissing hello.

When other men looked at Sammie, Cade became more jealous than he ever had been, and he somehow found a way to blame her for it. The confused partners had stopped striving to communicate. Christmas time was rearing and the snow had made its way to the streets to stay in

November. Cade was unable to fall asleep without drinking and could not remember the last time that he had. His work behind the bar in conjunction with bussing made him more money and, like the rest of the staff with whom he worked, he drank and did blow as he earned.

Sammie, through Cade and Lowell's, made connections of her own in the hospitality industry. And given her looks, she developed the notion that she could get hired anywhere she pleased. So she quit the dry cleaner's in the suburb from whence they came and focused on applying at nearby bars.

She gained weight which enhanced her physique and what was once an object of lust and appreciation to Cade became a catalyst for anger and mistrust. He had stopped touching her casually and with tenderness, but rather when he pondered the subject of her body, he'd wonder who'd be intrusively looking or even handling what he felt belonged to him.

At night, he'd come home drunk and it became nothing more than a typical inconvenience for the girl when her inebriated lover would fall upon the bed, pawing at her butt idiotically, attempting to penetrate first with his hands then with his penis. She'd shove him away then, laying on her side, would turn to face him with her legs together, separating him from her rear end. He'd then masturbate beside her, sometimes to completion.

When society changed the way it communicated, Sammie had gotten a cell phone, which triggered Cade to get one too. Pretty soon, there was no need for their land line. Cade would keep tabs on her when they were apart and when she wouldn't answer, he'd get upset. And although he didn't understand the merit of texting, they would routinely do so.

FOR THE HOLIDAY, IT was time to take a break from each other. Sammie went to be with her sisters and father while Cade, in the wake of Miles returning from college for Christmas break, made plans to visit the Heltons for the first time since he had moved out of there.

The snow was falling fast in the city of the Niagara River when he set out for the village of Eggertsville with a healthy buzz going. He took the familiar "S Curves" of Delaware Avenue a little too fast, but fearlessly enjoyed the effect the fresh snow had on his tires. Cade was good at driving upon Buffalo's flatland as one had to be in order to exist as a motorist there.

When the city turned into the suburb and the narrow snowy side streets made way for wider clearer paths, Cade became conscious of the more present danger, the police. He hooked up with Eggert Road, passing where he barely remembered being stopped and almost hauled away for driving drunk if it weren't for Maureen's graces.

Passing Saint Benedict's and the first place he had kissed Sammie, he took the long way down to Hendricks in order to bypass the torment of cruising by the house where his mother had died. He took the turn too hard but the front wheel drive car didn't falter too much in the snow on the frozen ground and he was on the road to Heltons'.

To his right near the corner of Rosedale and Hendricks, there it was. He had never seen such a creature before, the white owl flying so low. It blended with the snow in the air before the mighty wings redirected its energy high above the electric light shining down to the road. Out of sight then, as if it had never been born, never grew stronger, and never learned to fly. Gone as if it had never appeared to the boy with blurred vision, driving his car on the slick roads in the town he despised.

Cade pulled over to his faithful parking spot out front of Heltons', number 342. The slow walk up the driveway, past where flowers might bloom again someday, was nice and desolate as the snow contracted beneath his boots.

There is life in the freezing air blowing from Erie at night. There, innocent of human dissuasion, it whispers to you like the menacing sounds one might hear within the strange place just before the wall of sleep. The hostile wind ricochets against the frozen earth that surrounds and there is something that calls out to you. It tells you that you are there and you know. You know that you belong in the cold and in the dark. The sear on your face is in tune with the sting that invades your throat and lungs. It forces you to be there right now.

You are not abandoned in the cold. You are never alone in its darkness. And when the shrilly wind blows past your ears and there is no one outside to hear or see you, it is there where you can be forgiven.

"Dude," said Miles.

"Hey, man."

"How come you didn't just walk in?" said Miles, smiling.

"I don't know, dude." The two hugged.

"Still snowing?" said Miles.

"Hell yeah, pretty sweet. Where is everybody?"

"Major, Mom, and Dad are upstairs," said Miles. "I think Mary is getting ready to go over to someplace to have dinner. I guess she should go quick if it's still—"

"Any beer here?"

"Um, yeah," said Miles. "But we should probably go get some more."

"Cool."

Just then, Maureen walked into the kitchen. "Hey," she said. "There's my third son."

"Hey, Mo," said Cade. They shared a long embrace that didn't falter amidst conversation.

"How's my Sammie?" said Maureen. "How's my second daughter?"

"She's good," said Cade. "She's with her dad. I think in Fredonia."

"Good," said Maureen as she and Cade still held one another. "Tell her I love her and we miss her and we love her and Merry Christmas."

"I will," said Cade.

"I miss you guys, ok?" said Maureen.

"We miss you too," said Cade.

"Cade Caybul!" said Ray with a friendly grin.

"Hi, Ray," said Cade. Maureen released and Ray stepped in initiating a big hug of their own. He held Cade in his arms unexpectedly tightly. "How's mah boy?!"

"Good, Ray," said Cade, nearly stammering from being squeezed by the big man of the house. "Thank you. I'm good."

"That's great," said Ray. "Merry Christmas. Welcome home."

"Thanks, Ray," said Cade. "It's good to be here."

"Come on, dinner in an hour!" said Ray, letting go of their guest.

"Hi, Cade," said Major who barely made eye contact.

"Hi, Major," said Cade.

"Dad, we're gonna go get some beer and stuff," said Miles. "Which car should we take?"

"We can take mine," said Cade.

"Take the jeep, My," said Ray. "We'll meet back here for Christmas dinner. Get me some cigars, My, ok?"

"Ok, Dad," said Miles.

The group filtered to the living room while Cade used the familiar bathroom. Then, the old friends excitedly headed outside. They heard yelling from the attic window.

"What is that?" said Cade. Peering up, Miles responded, "Major's little friend likes to yell stuff out the window from my—I mean, our room."

"You're kidding me," said Cade.

"Yeah, he's got a little sailor mouth on him," said Miles, grinning. "I think one day, I heard him call me a fag."

"What?!" said Cade.

"Yeah," said Miles, laughing heartily. "He's a little bastard!"

"Ya don't say," said Cade, expressing peace regarding his former plea of innocence to Ray and their angry accusatory neighbor.

In lieu of taking the jeep, which was blocked by the larger of the vehicles, they got into the minivan with Miles behind the wheel and headed out.

The all-wheel-drive van made short work of the snowy world and feeling outgoing, the boys visited some friends on the way to the store. Unknown to Miles, upon using the bathrooms along the way, Cade did bumps of snow of his own.

They visited Ked, Connor, Todd, and Jake too, and had a few beers with them. Everyone was happy to see Miles and Cade together after the dust had settled from the conflict involving their relationships with Sammie. The boys were having fun together. It felt right.

Losing track of time, the two piled into the big red van, this time louder and more joyously. They put on tunes and began the trek home.

"Shit, I almost forgot the beer!" said Miles.

"I wouldn't've let you," said Cade.

"So how's it feel to be back, bro?" said Miles. "Is this your first time back since the move?"

"I think so," said Cade. "I don't know. It's nice to be with you. I probably shouldn't smoke in here, huh?"

"Nah, let's wait," said Miles.

"Cool," said Cade.

"Sammie doing ok?" said Miles.

"Yeah, she's fine," said Cade.

They cruised to the gas station on the outskirts, knowing that they could score beer, cigars, and cigs. Miles parked in front and fiddled with the CD player while Cade headed inside.

"Don't you just love it when it snows around Christmas time?!" said a strange woman to Cade in line at the store.

"Yeah," said Cade, smiling politely yet genuinely. "I do love the snow."

"Merry Christmas if I don't see you," she said extending her arms and chest for a hug which was met trustfully.

"Ok," said Cade. "Merry Christmas."

"God bless you, beautiful child," she said.

"God bless you too!" said Cade.

"Mind if I crack one now," said Cade in the van.

"Go right ahead," said Miles. "I'll pound one too."

The boys luckily caught the rare green light onto Lebrun Road from Bailey Avenue and they were cruising. Miles had at his beer and kept it low so onlookers couldn't see.

"I'm getting mad hungry," said Miles.

"Not me," said Cade. "But I can get it together. What's your mom making?"

"I don't know," said Miles. "Something dank, no doubt."

Cade brought his window down some and inhaled deeply through his nose. His slow breath was met with optimism for a flash there. He gazed at the passing houses, enveloped in comfort that he was no longer trapped in this town and that he could be free. In this moment in the passenger seat, clarity made its way followed by the vision of Sammie. He smiled at the passing houses and thought it would be refreshing to be with and hold her.

They took the turn onto Hendricks too fast and slid outward bound for the hydrant just over the curb. Miles, who had been driving for nearly four years, let go of the brake until he felt in control again and right quick, got back on track. Neither boy mentioned the slip. And no one was afraid.

The van came closer to the house. The driveway neared revealing its secret. It was no longer vacant.

"What the—" said Miles. "Is that—"

"Uuuuuuh," said Cade. "Is that—"

"Is that *my* driveway?!" said Miles.

"No," said Cade. "Can't be."

"Yes," said Miles as they approached. "What the hell?"

There were Town of Amherst police squad cars in the driveway. Their lights were off and there was nobody inside the vehicles. Cade thought of the small bag of coke in his wallet then looked at Miles, whom he had almost always seen as a leader, for an answer, perplexed and scared.

The boys parked in the street and headed in. As Miles picked up speed, so did Cade. They opened the door to see officers talking calmly to Ray and Maureen who were in tears holding each other. They entered. Maureen let go of Ray and grabbed a hold of her confused son.

"Mary, Miles!" she said. "Mary was in an accident!"

"Is she ok?" said Miles.

"She was killed in the accident, My!" said Maureen. "She was killed in the accident!"

Ray, shivering, wiped his tears, blew his nose, sipped his beer, and bawled out. The cops squawked on their radios. Mary had been driving in the jeep and lost control. A truck hit it which sent her into shock of which she died. Maureen moaned and wailed, dehydrated from crying and hyperventilating.

"She's gone, My!" she cried and held Miles. They held each other. She screamed and cried as one word chaotically bled into the next. "She's gone! My daughter is gone. I don't know! I'm not sure if she would try it could be too late—it's too much—my God—Mary, please, no! I don't know! I don't know! I don't know!"

Cade, again the outsider, watched the family mourn and cry, his mouth wide open, a reflection of his stunned bewildered mind.

Then Ray looked at him. Ray looked at him. And he had at him.

"Cade, why didn't you boys take the Goddamn jeep like I told you? You had to take the van, didn't you? The tires on the jeep are bad, Cade! She barely knows how to drive! She just got her license! Why didn't you take your fucking car or the jeep?!" Cade's desperate, confused eyes found Maureen and Miles. In ignorance of him, they held each other and cried. The police looked at Cade, waiting for him to respond. "You are a black cloud, Cade, you are nothing but trouble and a goddamn piece of shit to this family."

Cade's eyes shot all around like a machine that short-circuited. Miles cried louder while his mother held him sobbing and screaming. Ray finished, "I want you to get the fuck out and never come back."

Cade left. He ran to his car and drove aimlessly. From his cell, he called Sammie five times but she didn't answer. Making his way to Niagara Falls Boulevard, he found a cheap motel and caught his breath.

The snow was falling too hard. He knew he would be stuck if he tried to drive all the way back to the city. He drove to the nearby liquor store and picked up a handle of whiskey then back to the motel where he checked in.

"SIR, do you have a room here? You need to go to your room and leave the lobby before we call the police." The clerk had some sympathy for the kid despite his making his night unexpectedly strenuous.

"I just wanted a vending machine and my room key," said Cade, stumbling and falling backward.

"If the room is in your name, you'll have to show me ID then I can give you a room key if you lost one. Another room key that is."

"Do you know where my phone is?" said Cade.

"Why would I know where your phone is?" said the clerk who had just come on for graveyard shift. "Did you check your pockets? What room are you in?"

"223," said Cade. "I just need my phone and my room card."

"What is your name?"

"Cade Caybul."

"Mister Caybul, yes," he said, looking at his computer. "You are in room 223. Now, do you have your ID?"

"Can't find it," said Cade, who had managed to sit up and onto a chair.

The lobby of the motel just after 4 am was quiet besides the voice of the night clerk in his mid-fifties, eloquent and effeminate, and Cade, who could barely move or speak.

Upon venturing to the lobby in accordance with searching for the phone, Cade had set out staggering and the door to his room closed behind him. After approaching the vacant desk as the clerk was in the bathroom, he stumbled back to the room, surprised to not be able to key into his door. He flipped through his wallet, dropping a couple of credit cards and his driver's license by the door in the hallway and only retrieved one credit card from the ground. He then returned to the lobby to inquire about his phone and, now, his room key as well.

"I can't find my ID," said Cade, reclining some on the chair. He wore a stained V-neck undershirt and jeans with just socks on his feet.

"I need you to prove who you are so I can issue a new key," said the clerk.

"Cade Caybul. Room 223."

"Yes, you've told me that. What type of ID did you use to check in to the motel?"

"My driver's license," said Cade after a long pause.

"Ok, can you show me anything else? Maybe your credit card?"

"Yes, sir, I do have my credit card right here and right now in this present moment, yes, I do," said Cade as he tried to stand. He fell backwards into the chair, which toppled, causing him to spill out onto the floor with a thud.

"Don't call the police!" said Cade. "I'm nonviolent! I'm nonviolent!"

The clerk nearly laughed, staying calm. "Ok, how about I come to you," said the clerk. "Here," he continued, walking to Cade who had managed to get to his knees. "How about this?" he said, helping Cade to the chair. "Now just try and sit still. Now, you said you had a credit card or something with your name on it?" Cade struggled to sit upright. His head moved to the right of his body as he eyed his wallet suspended by its chain. The clerk realized that Cade had lost balance due to his head moving about and that he struggled to gain control of it as it swirled. "Ok, let me." The man picked up Cade's wallet, took out a card, and read it. It was an obvious fake. "No, that's not it. Let's see what else."

"That's thing is, isn't, that's not real," said Cade.

"I hope not," said the clerk. "Let's put that back and see what else there is in here."

"That was a gift, it was a present, something stupid," said Cade, hiccupping.

"Yes, what are friends for? But here's this, Cade Caybul, bingo. Ok, you sit here, and I'll be back with a new room key for you, Cade. Don't go running any marathons now. I'll be back."

"Ok, I won't run away, I promise."

The man strolled down the hallway and opened Cade's room. He took a brief look inside before propping the door open and headed back to the lobby.

"I'll be right with you, folks," said the clerk to a befuddled couple who had stopped in for a room and seen Cade in the chair with his head rolling about. "Ok, Cade, it's bedtime."

He helped him to his feet and they walked together. They approached the room and he guided Cade in and sat him on the bed. "You did great. I thought that would've been much harder."

"I know, I did it," said Cade. "I just needed to not fall."

"Ok, check-out is at eleven," said his helper who roamed out toward the hallway. A moment later, he came back and approached Cade's body on the bed.

"It's payday," he said. "Here is your credit card and ID on the nightstand. Nice eyes, Cade Caybul."

Less than an hour passed and Cade opened those eyes to the hum of the motel fan built into the air conditioner. He stared motionlessly into the corner of the room. His ambiance consisted of the walls and where they met in the corner, illuminated by soft lamplight and a cobweb that ran from one wall to the adjacent one. He focused as best as he could while it swayed in the tender breeze unfelt by the only human in the room as the sound from the fan cradled the vision.

Calmly, he lived here in this moment as the strands of the web never seemed to move the same exact way or in precisely the same direction more than once.

The dust on the web, the more he glared, transformed its shape to that of an old key with a heart-shaped tail end. The key swayed and wiggled and twisted in front of his eyes, still lifeless, as the quiet night outside shone the moon's glow that never made its way through the glass behind thick banal drapery.

And before his vision darkened, like the last moribund embers of what had been a wildfire beneath a saddened sky, his heart rate dwindled to a pace slower and slower, slower than it had ever been. Yet he did not recollect a scary musing of the past nor from any imaginable future came a worrisome morsel. There was only the benign sound from the fan and his rare discovery, the swaying whirling key.

As he lay thoughtlessly, without intrusion, an unfathomable distance from any conceivable home, he didn't reevaluate the night that had leaked into this short sweet while.

Cade had checked in to the motel and drank a pint of brown liquor and did half the blow he had on him before walking, bound for one of the bars on the boulevard. He had entered a dive that had southern rock playing.

"ID," said the bouncer.

"Sure, man," said Cade. "How are ya?!"

"No cover?" said Cade.

"No," said the bouncer.

"How much?" said Cade.

"*No* cover," said the bouncer.

"All right, thanks," said Cade.

There were two female bartenders who said hi to Cade and smiled. Men and women sat at chairs and stools smoking cigarettes. An amorous couple played darts and kissed. There was plenty of space inside.

Cade took a stool at the bar and was visited by one of the smiling bartenders.

"Hi, what can I getcha?"

"Hi!" said Cade.

"You want a beer?"

"No, uh, double ginger and Captain," said Cade.

"Captain and ginger?" she said. "Want a big boy glass?"

"Yes, please," said Cade. "What's your name?"

She walked away. He saw in his periphery, a man smiling, entertained by the rejection. Cade had at his drink.

Despite contempt for the shackled revelry from the unknown drinker near him, Cade kept it together. He had a few more drinks and plenty of shots. He was generous, buying for the pretty girls behind the bar who put each and every shot and drink on his tab, including the ones he bought for them.

Cade's need for human affection led him to the embrace of two women. They were regulars at the joint and Cade was impressed by their appearance, noting specifically their style of dress and jewelry. He felt honored that they were talking and listening to him.

The vibe amidst the three had maintained its friendly and fun spirit with neither party communicating any carnal desire. The girls, Jesse and Sally, smoked tobacco with Cade, introducing him to other regulars until he felt like he was a commoner too. And his observing of Sally's posterior, as the night went on, became less and less stealthy.

"I am telling you!" said a young man on the patio with his woman smiling and leaning on him. "If you have a baby, it will make you want to change your life!"

"Oh yeah?" said Sally.

"It's all true," he said. "The stories are true! Once you look into your son's eyes, everything changes! It's that easy! I stopped drinking! I patched up things with my brother 'cause, you know, I want him to have a part of his nephew's life. It will change your life!"

"Well, dear, you didn't exactly stop drinking," said his other half.

"Well, yeah," he said, swigging from his pint. "Tonight is an exception. I mean, you know that, baby."

"I know, baby," she said. They kissed.

"I just love him," he said. "You got a smoke, babe?"

"Sure, we only have three left," she said, giving him one and taking one for herself. She lit hers and put the lighter back in her purse. Sally handed the man her Zippo.

"A lady with a Zippo," said Cade. "I like that!"

"Thanks, it was my dad's," said Sally.

"Did he—is he dead?" said Cade.

"No, he just gave it to me when he quit smoking," said Sally.

"Oh, that's great!" said Cade. "Can I see it?"

"Sure!" said Sally.

"Aw, cool, Camel!" said Cade, noticing the emblem.

"Yep," said Sally. "Camel was his brand." She watched Cade familiarize himself with the lighter. Playing a bit, he popped the top with his middle and forefinger, lit the flame, and with a quick shuck, closed and smothered it. Sally enjoyed watching him.

"Man, that's a good Zippo," said Cade. "Nice and loose but tight and strong. It's perfect." He lit a Camel of his own and returned her father's lighter.

"Thanks, he loved it," said Sally.

"I bet he wants you to quit," said Cade.

"Yeah," she said. "It's like...hard."

"What was his brand?" said Cade.

"Camels!" said Jesse.

"No, what kind?" said Cade.

"He smoked Filters," said Sally.

"Non-filters?" said the man with the new son.

"No, full flavors," said Sally. "I think he started with lights."

"Me too," said Cade. "I'm ready for a shot. Can I buy you ladies something too?"

"Absolutely!" they said.

"You two want some drugs?" said Cade.

"No thanks," they said.

"I'll be right back."

Cade walked into the bathroom and entered one of the stalls. Opening his wallet, he located his bag and bumped coke up his nose with a credit card. Turning the nearly empty bag inside out, he swirled it around his tongue and gums, dropped it into the toilet, urinated, and flushed.

With that came the presence of a human outside the stall. It came closer. Someone was waiting for him. He opened the door on the stall. It was the bouncer.

"If I ever catch you snorting drugs in my bar again, I'm gonna throw you outta here."

"Absolutely. Won't happen again."

Cade was relieved that he could stay, but he wondered if he meant *throw* in the literal sense. He walked out to the bar behind his authoritarian figure and met the ladies.

"How'd it go in there?" said Jesse.

"Awesome," said Cade. "What's it gonna be."

"Crown," they said.

"Crown!" said Cade. "No girly stuff for you two, I see."

"We're renegades!" said Jesse.

"Yeah, we're breaking down barriers!" said Sally.

The three drank, danced, and played a game of darts. As they interacted, Cade's lechery increased exponentially in the wake of seeing Sally's backside with tunnel vision. He approached her.

"Do you mind if I put my hand all over your ass?"

"What?"

"Your ass," he said. "Do you mind if I put my hand all over it?"

"I...uh," murmured Sally, gaining the attention of her friend.

"It's incredible," said Cade. "You might have the hottest ass I've ever seen. I'd like to touch it. Do you mind?"

"I um, Jess? I," said Sally.

Jesse began to yell, "Hey, Steve! Steve!"

Cade's calm unwavering eyes stayed locked on Sally's. Although he could sense something was off, all he saw was her face. He drank it in, waiting for a change. He waited for a response. There was supposed to be a change. There was supposed to be a response. A no? A yes? Sally, with darting eyes, struggled. She waited.

"Let's go, guy," said the bouncer who grabbed Cade by his shirt with both hands.

"I've got to pay my tab," said Cade. The man's grip softened. Cade walked to the bar as every human there stared. He didn't know how loudly he had been talking. And he didn't understand how intensely his energy projected. "Hi, I'd like to pay. Caybul, please. Cash, if you don't mind." The stunned bartender brought his credit card and tab.

"$108." Cade put the card in his wallet and paid her $140 in cash.

"Thank you for enriching my experience," he said to her and her coworker behind the bar who could hardly blink. They didn't respond.

Cade calmly went for a sip of the drink in his hand. The bouncer read that intention and grabbed his shirt by the back again. Cade planted his foot behind as he turned around to greet the bouncer's eyes. "This is *my* drink, and I am going to finish it. And if you try and stop me, I will fucking kill you." The guard's grip loosened again. Cade pulled out the straw and dropped it on the bar. He put both hands around the glass like a child, brought it to his lips, and downed the icy cocktail. He put the glass devoid of liquid on the bar gently.

"NOW LET'S GO!" yelled Cade, clapping his hands twice.

The bouncer used Cade's body to open the door and pushed him out onto a cold lamp post. The entrance to the bar closed before his eyes.

He walked calmly, destined for his motel and the bottle of whiskey of dangerous proportion.

Moving ghostlike past other bars and staggering humans, Cade greeted people, smiling and trying to obtain connection from their eyes. He was looking for something or someone to show him a different way.

He paused when he heard a loud sound coming from the intersection behind which he attributed to violence or a car crash. As Cade turned back to the perpendicular avenue, he saw a garbage truck headed his way and men jumping on and off retrieving waste. The acceleration, like a beast's breath, led to squealing and squeaking brakes while metal collided with metal over and again.

The light turned green for the truck as Cade crossed the street without taking his eyes off of it. A driver coming from the right had sped in anticipation of the forthcoming green projection but slowed, yielding to the sight of the young man whose mind lacked presence. The garbage truck was getting closer to Cade as the sound cut into his brain.

He walked past the disposal units with heaping bags of trash, some torn open from critters. He thought of rats then one appeared, running along the ground where it met the wall to his right.

The truck stopped beside garbage just ahead of the lonely wanderer, and men worked to the left of the huge motor without speaking. After dumping, one jogged back to collect a truant bag which he threw into the loud massive vehicle. While the men transitioned to the right curb, Cade looked into each worker's unresponsive eyes. They discarded empty bins near his snowy footprints while the truck kept moving.

Ahead, there was another intersection. When he reached it, Cade turned right a moment before the truck went left. The sound began to fade as his cold hand reached into his pocket and pulled out a worn pack of Camels bearing but one broken cigarette.

There was a streetlamp ahead with a small trash receptacle fastened to it. Walking past, the look inside unveiled more than its contents. The container was devoid of matter except for one *Brewer's Blackbird Inn* plastic cup. A warm ushering feeling then came over him.

As he journeyed closer to his motel, sliding and slipping on the fresh snow and ice, Cade Caybul had a thought that made him smile: he imagined himself with the cup in one hand and the empty pack of Camels in the other, running after the garbage truck, screaming for them to stop.

Russa Jari was born in Western New York State and at times can be spotted staggering along the Blue Ridge Mountains.